BACON MASTER OF THE APOCALYPSE

Book ONE of
Bacon Master

BACON MASTER OF THE APOCALYPSE

Book ONE of
Bacon Master

FRANK MORIN

Whipsaw Press

ebook ISBN: 978-1-946910-26-4

Paperback ISBN: 978-1-946910-27-1

Hardcover ISBN: 978-1-946910-28-8

Editor: Joshua Essoe

Book Cover by Luciano Fleitas

1st edition 2023

ACKNOWLEDGMENTS

No bacon was harmed in the making of this novel.

It was enjoyed immensely!

I want to thank all of you for your amazing enthusiasm for this project. I guess I shouldn't be surprised that so many of us love great humor and great cuisine.

In particular, I want to thank everyone who has shared so many mouth-watering recipes with me. You have enriched my life, and forced me to work out so much more dilligently to keep my midsection from becoming too enhanced as a result.

Thanks as always to my super enthusiastic kids, whose brilliant ideas and brutal critiques keep me on track. A special thanks to my amazing wife, Jenny. Her love of food has inspired me for so many years and helped me develop my own food fascination.

Joshua Essoe, as always, applied his deft editing touch to help me unearth the piping-fresh heart of the story, and Luciano Fleitas absolutely nailed the cover art and the character artwork.

So grab a snack or twelve, and enjoy this feast of humor and culinary magic!

Frank

Contents

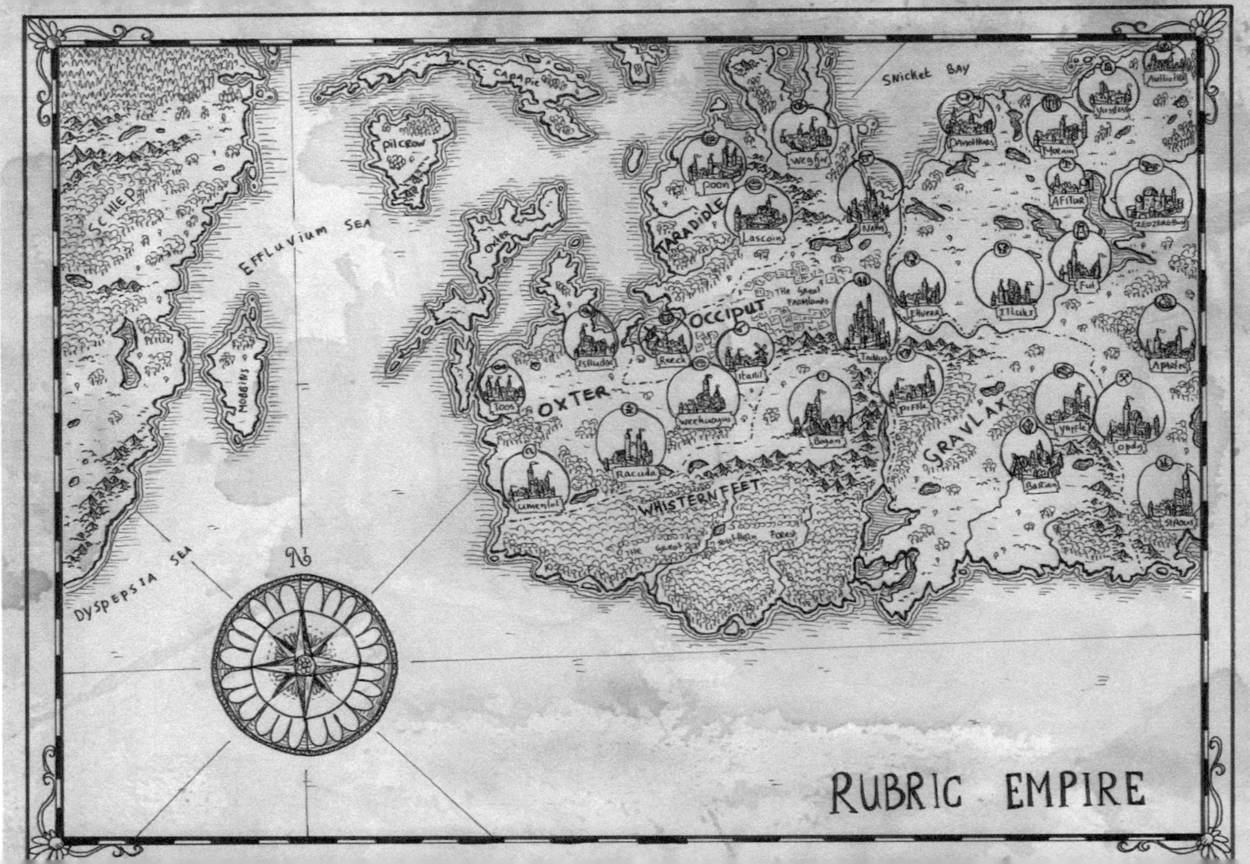

RUBRIC EMPIRE
SCHLEP
EFFLUVIUM SEA
DYSPEPSIA SEA
Snicket Bay
Capri Pie
Pilcrow
Mobbins
OXTER
OCCIPUT
TARADIDLE
GRAVLAX
WHISTERNFEET
The Great Farmlands
The Great Southern Forest
Wegfing
Poon
Lascoin
Nam
Anothians
Moram
Afitur
Zeozergbug
Fui
Ehvera
Illuks
Aphrui
Reech
Itanil
Tackus
Isludde
Taos
Warehousing
Bagan
Piffla
Racuda
Lumentol
Yaffle
Opds
Barian
Sirous

AFITUR
parsley way
Cheddar way
CABAL
Black Pepper Boulevard
Broccoli Boulevard
Boulevard
Castle Flour Way
Garlic Boulevard
THE White River

1

THE BUBBLE & SQUEAK

R asher Dilskin shoved an entire cream-filled pastry into his mouth and savored the explosion of sugary sweetness. No enhancements by confectioners or muffin mages. Just pure, uncomplicated pleasure.

"I can't believe you can eat so much," said the captain sitting across the game table, a look of awe on her face, which was shaded by her wide-brimmed hat.

Rasher glanced down at the stacks of empty plates scattered around him and shrugged. "Some days I need the boost."

"I'd be comatose by now," admitted a fresh-faced legionnaire whose hat barely counted as a cap, and who had watched Rasher eating with growing amazement.

"I can keep this up all night," Rasher replied with a grin, eliciting chuckles from the other players who were doing well, and scowls from those who weren't.

He glanced at his hand of brightly colored playing cards. That last draw had filled it in perfectly. The only thing better than a winning streak playing Thirteen Courses was a long winning streak at the Bubble and Squeak. The popular gaming tavern was packed, and his opponents had enough money and skill to bet with confidence and lose with grace. Mostly.

As he glanced around the table, he adjusted his golden frying-pan-shaped hat and released a partial slice of crispy bacon into his smile, adding that hint of charisma unique to bacon masters. The men and women sitting around him couldn't miss it, not when he laid it on as thick as fresh butter on warm toast.

Most of them glanced at their hands, suddenly nervous. If he was so confident, should they be worried?

More than a few people clustered around his table, dressed from soup to sandwiches to impress. Some wanted to watch the game, hoping to sip off the energy of gambling without making their own bets, like a date who refused to order dessert but liked to sample everyone else's. Others came looking for a chair, eager to join the game, or came to spread the latest rumors about him. A few even looked ready to fry up enough courage to take up the open challenge, share a new recipe, and pose the latest theory.

He already knew most of the public-level recipes, and most of the theories were thankfully way off the mark, but the intrigue kept them coming and kept the plates in front of him full. Rasher applied a bit more of the bacon power stored inside of him onto his pleasantly full stomach, and the food began dissolving into pure energy.

As far as he knew, he was the only bacon master to have discovered the trick. He doubted anyone else needed it so badly. He called that energy his extra sizzle, and that sizzle played a vital role in his success.

Tonight was turning into a delicious evening. The sweet cream on it all was the fact that he got to play with legionnaires of the Reaper legions, stationed together in the Acropolis, the walled mini-city that was their home on the edge of the great capital city of Afitur.

Across from the young private, who played with far more enthusiasm than skill, sat a grizzled sergeant who wore his cap placed precisely, the short front brim polished to a shine. He placed every card with exactness. Next to the sergeant sat the captain of a hundred-man archery Platter.

"I've got one," the private said with a hopeful grin, eliciting a groan from the sergeant.

"He knows all your recipes," the sergeant complained.

"I bet he doesn't know this one," the younger man insisted. "Got it from my mom. If I'm wrong, I'll buy all of you a round of drinks."

That lightened the mood, and the sergeant shrugged and said, "I hope you haven't lost all your coins, son."

Rasher snagged the last bacon-wrapped cheese ball off a plate, again lacking any enhancement but the bacon, and gestured to the private. "Hit me with it."

"Okay." The young man glanced up at the crowd encircling the table, many of whom looked as eager as he did. No one had shared a recipe Rasher hadn't known all evening. "I've got a recipe for maple-glazed, bacon-wrapped broccoli. Should enhance your powers and also grant low-level strength boost."

"That sounds gross," the captain said with a grimace.

"Well, I never liked it much," the private admitted, eliciting a round of laughter. "But I figured a bacon master might."

"Nice try," Rasher told him. "The enhancements sound good, but the flavor combination doesn't entice me much." The young man seemed to wilt, and the watching crowd groaned.

They wanted to hear a theory, and squashing their hope would curdle their curiosity. So he spread his hands wide and added, "But the deal was, share a recipe I didn't know. I've never heard that one, so ask."

"Really?" the young man's face brightened and the crowds drew closer, whispering excitedly.

Few people besides Rasher wore their uniforms. Men wore fashionable suits in conservative pastel colors, while the women's outfits ranged from bright sun dresses to elegant gowns in vibrant colors. Hats of all shapes and sizes adorned their heads, ranging from simple legionnaire caps to vast, multi-leveled creations popular in the highest levels of society.

The sergeant scowled and asked, "So if I invent some stupid recipe that doesn't make sense, I can pose another theory?"

"When skill is lacking, enthusiasm sometimes saves the day," Rasher said.

"And which of Rasher's Rules of Engagement is that?" asked the captain, an amused smile on her lips.

"Number forty-nine."

The young legionnaire blurted out, "Do you have a terminal illness?"

"Not the first time I've heard that one," Rasher said with a shake of his head. Of the dozens of increasingly wild rumors about why a bacon master would be stuck as a paint battle trainer, that one came closest to one version of the truth.

The young man cursed softly to himself, glancing at his tiny stack of remaining coins. "I needed the money."

"So play your card already," grumbled the stocky legionnaire corporal to Rasher's left. He hunched over his cards as if to protect them from another loss, his dirt-smudged cap slightly askew.

Thirteen Courses was part cuisine planning and part strategy, a delicious blend of challenge and skill as each player worked to design the most powerful hands to deal damage to their opponents while enhancing their own abilities and boosting defense. Playing it not only required nimbleness of mind and a solid grasp of culinary magic crafting, but also the ability to read one's opponents, a skill that Rasher excelled at.

He played an oatmeal cookie card onto the table near his other face-up cards. "Power up to my mixing and baking skills. I can now produce one extra incendiary muffin per turn."

The others groaned. The confectioner enhancement magnified his already-strong hand to a tipping point.

The corporal next to him tossed his cards to the table with a scowl. "I'm out. How do you always manage to find the one card you need?"

"It's all about the planning," Rasher told him as he scanned the rest of the table, reading defeat in their eyes. All quickly folded, not wanting to waste time drawing out the inevitable and losing more money in the process.

As he swept coins into the growing stack in front of him, Rasher's attention was drawn to the front door, where a crowd was gathering. The Bubble and Squeak always bustled with activity. The expansive front room served drinks and meals prepared by a talented staff, led by a full tournant chef. The man often left the kitchens to tour the dining area, proudly wearing his tall toque hat topped with three colored bands of black, red, and blue.

A low wall separated the dining area from the huge gaming hall where Rasher sat. The hall offered one of the best selections of entertainment in the sector. Round tables for card games and tabletop games were interspersed with rectangular food challenge counters surrounded by narrow tables, packed with patrons. The chefs running each station cooked recipes using ingredients prepared in advance by the various guilds of magic.

The sound of sizzling meat and the staccato chopping of vegetables by fast-moving knives blended with the constant low rumbling of hundreds of conversations. Dozens of scents melded into a warm, mouth-watering aroma that blanketed the high-ceilinged hall. The juicy scent of grilled steak mixed with the sharp scent of cut spices and the warmth of fresh-baked pastries that wrapped Rasher's nose like a tantalizing blanket. Other scents piled on top, creating a unique blend that stirred the blood and made him grin when he breathed deeply.

Betting was growing heated at the nearest chef station as the patrons tried identifying the mystery recipe. In a moment, they would have to put their mouths where their money was and try the recipe. The results were often hilarious, sometimes painful, and occasionally spectacular. Three Milk Mages and their healing staff remained on hand to deal with any culinary emergencies.

The most interesting areas were at the back of the hall, where the guilds often demonstrated new recipes they'd devised with the chefs, and unleashed samples of devastating new battle cuisine within the protected confines of the food fight arena. An upstairs balcony offered excellent viewing of new recipes and food fights. He was planning to go up there to witness an exhibit of a new gingersnap wheel scheduled for later. Supposedly it reduced friction to nearly zero.

It was not unusual for famous people to drop by the Bubble and Squeak, and that's what seemed to be the cause of the crowds around the door.

"Is that Sumwinkle?" asked the enthusiastic young legionnaire, who had just risen from his chair, having lost most of that week's pay.

"Don't disappear," the sergeant warned. "You still owe us that round."

The young man sank back into his seat, looking worriedly at his coins again as Rasher peered at the distant door.

Sumwinkle Flink was indeed weaving through the tables, heading toward the gaming area. There was no mistaking that distinctive green tricorne Reaper hat. Sumwinkle's bore the Reaper butcher knife emblem on the right side, and the noodle emblem on the left. The tall man cut a heroic figure in that hat, his black uniform also bearing the Reaper emblem on the chest.

The sight of the white butcher knife on a red field filled Rasher with pride, as always. Everyone in the legions dedicated their lives to serving and aiding the Reapers in their gods-proclaimed duty to defend the Rubric Empire from the threat of apocalypse.

"Hey, that's Otamot too," said the archery captain, her face flushing as she jumped to her feet, literally hopping on her toes for a better view.

The rest of the players rose from the table. Even though the entire purpose of the legions was to support and fight alongside the Reapers, most of the troops rarely got to see the famous Reapers up close.

Sumwinkle was a renowned noodle warrior and one of the most popular of the Reapers, a hero who embodied all their best attributes. He waved and smiled as he moved through the room, greeting many people by name. Otamot Lyterian was tall, with famous good looks and an athlete's physique. His black hair and bright blue eyes framed a ruggedly handsome face.

He was also a bacon master, at least ten years older than Rasher's twenty-one. Rasher had wanted to meet him for a long time. Looked like he'd finally get his chance. He shoved his coins into his pouch, then flipped a silver spoon to the young private, who stared at the heavy coin in shock. The lad had started the night with barely three silver spoon's worth of coins.

"What's this for?"

"You have good posture. Don't move for a second."

Rasher sprang to the table, then launched off the lad's head, leaping ten feet up into the air to catch a horizontal pole hanging from the high ceiling.

"There he goes again," the sergeant grunted as Rasher swung from the pole, flinging himself across a wide gap to a vertical pole, which he used to slingshot himself farther.

He released bacon to fuel his reflexes and quickly crossed the hall, swinging and flipping and jumping between fixed poles and free-swinging rings on chains.

The fixtures were usually only used by acrobatic performers who entertained the crowd from above some nights, but Rasher loved borrowing them. Many looked up to watch him, some laughing, some scowling, and no doubt a few generating a new rumor or two. Rasher simply enjoyed the thrill of flinging himself across the room, trusting his skill and his bacon to avoid a painful crash.

In seconds, he intercepted Sumwinkle's party, and with a triple backflip dismount, he landed lightly on his feet between two tables. A scattered ripple of applause greeted the move, and he bowed, sweeping his hat wide in thanks.

When he rose, he found a big, burly fellow, half a head taller than his own six feet, standing in his way. He possessed the golden eyes of a tiger-enhanced warrior. Indeed, he wore a black leather bowler-style hat with a stylized tiger on the crown. That was the hat of the Gleaners, the most elite of the legion forces, who worked as close support to the Reapers. He also wore a lieutenant's emblem, meaning he led a full Fist of twenty-five soldiers from five separate squads.

Rasher smiled, trying to slip around the big fellow, but the soldier held out a thick arm to block his way. "Where do you think you're going?"

His voice wasn't friendly, and he'd failed to note Rasher's captain insignia. Rasher decided to ignore the slight and did not let his smile slip. "Excuse me. I just need to say hello."

The big soldier grunted, a scowl turning his square face menacing. "You've got a lot of nerve, little man."

"Excuse me, but have I defeated you before?" Rasher asked, surprised by the hostility in the man's cat-like eyes. He had an excellent memory for people and names, but couldn't remember interacting with the grumpy lieutenant.

"If you tried, you wouldn't still have all those shiny teeth."

That kind of aggression was as familiar to him as the weight of his favorite hat. He released half a slice of crispy bacon, fixed the big fellow with a steady gaze, and said, "Was it a paint battle tournament, or did I simply best you walking in a straight line?"

The big fellow growled and lashed out with one huge fist, moving with supernatural speed.

Rasher smoothly leaned back, his movement speed enhanced by bacon, just avoiding the fist. He'd expected the reaction and guessed the fellow's reach. He adjusted his stance and smiled, savoring the thrill that raced through him at the thought of impending conflict.

Half a slice of bacon would double his speed and agility for about thirty seconds. He had plenty more already absorbed into his body, pooled like a low-stoked fire in his joints, ready to be released.

"Balter, what's going on?" Sumwinkle asked, moving up beside the big fellow.

"Just a fool who needs to be taught a lesson," Balter growled.

"At least you're self-aware enough to realize you need help. That's promising," Rasher said.

"I'll rip off your ears," Balter growled, taking an angry step forward until Sumwinkle ordered, "Stand down."

His voice stayed calm but carried absolute authority. Balter stopped instantly, and Sumwinkle added, "What started this?"

"Nothing," Balter growled.

Otamot joined them, and the eager crowd pressed in around. Otamot's easy smile faltered as his gaze flicked over Rasher. Before Balter could stop him, Rasher stepped forward and extended a hand in greeting, eager to finally meet the famous bacon master.

"It's a sincere honor to meet you, Reaper Otamot." Even though they were the only two bacon masters in the city that Rasher was aware of, he'd never gained a one-on-one meeting.

Otamot hesitated, his eyes flicking toward the watching crowds. Then he took the proffered hand and spoke in a slightly nasal voice. "Rasher, isn't it? I heard you've got a standing bet of fifty golden spatulas no one can guess why your career has stalled."

Well, that was not the reception he'd expected.

"No one's guessed it yet. If you want to give it a go, you have to tell me a recipe I haven't heard before."

"Tempting, but why ruin everyone's fun so fast?"

The look in his eye suggested he knew. Fish sticks. Rasher flashed his trademark grin again, while inwardly he seethed. That liver-licking turkey chewer must have talked with the guild leadership in Weghiv.

All he said was, "That's the spirit. In fact, how about I give you a free training lesson? I'd be happy to raise your skills a notch."

The comment triggered a round of laughter, and Otamot tried to look amused. The Reaper's unfriendly eyes never left Rasher's. "I heard you're reckless."

Otamot might know his secret, but Rasher had taken control of the conversation. He hadn't planned to push the Reaper, but like he taught his students, when hostility could not be avoided, stomp it like a grape.

"If training with me intimidates you, why don't you sign up for the paint battle championship, and we can meet in friendly competition?"

That generated a round of surprised mutterings, and a few people even encouraged Otamot to pick up the challenge. He never would, but the pressure irritated him, and that was a beautiful thing.

Otamot leaned a bit closer and said softly, "I don't play at war. When I fight, people get hurt."

That triggered a round of whistles and cheers from the crowd. It was disappointing to realize he'd never had a hope of a positive meeting with the man, but he'd long ago learned to adopt flexibility of mind like a well-cooked noodle.

Sumwinkle smoothly interjected before Rasher could respond. "Excuse us. We've got a private function to attend."

Rasher turned to him, hoping to rescue something out of the rare opportunity. "Reaper Sumwinkle, I apologize for interrupting your evening. Balter, I have no idea what I did to offend you, but I apologize for that too."

"Figures. You're clueless as well as useless," Balter muttered.

His hopes fell like a cake pulled too early from the oven. If he backed away now, he'd only make them think he was cowardly.

So he said, "Balter, you've repeatedly insulted me without provocation. Your mouth is bigger than those giant elephant ears plastered to the side of your head. I'm afraid I'm going to have to teach you a lesson in manners."

Balter swelled with menace, and the people pressing in on every side recoiled with audible gasps. Expectant silence blanketed the crowd like a top crust dropped over a freshly prepared pie. Balter's corded muscles bulged as he clenched his huge fists and growled, "I think the two of us need to step outside."

Rasher grinned, a plan forming. Brawling in an alleyway would not serve any useful purpose, but he had Sumwinkle's attention and was not about to waste the opportunity.

"All those muscles have squeezed your brain space. Here at the Bubble and Squeak, we don't step outside." He lifted his hands high, glancing around at the crowd.

As one, they all shouted enthusiastically, "Food fight!"

2

FOOD FIGHT!

As Rasher took his place on the packed sands of the food fight arena, he felt the same thrill that always bubbled through him when he entered the regular training arena. He'd never participated in a food fight, although he'd witnessed some. Few wanted to face a bacon master one-on-one, but Balter was smiling confidently.

Thousands of elite soldiers lived, worked, and trained together in the Acropolis, so arguments were common. Officers tended to get upset when soldiers killed each other, so food fights were a popular outlet to settle disagreements. On the walk over, one of the other soldiers had said that Balter had competed in a dozen food fights and always won.

Not surprising, given his advanced meat enhancements. Balter was stronger, faster, and far more nimble than almost anyone else. To develop those kinds of enhancements, Balter must have eaten tiger meat prepared by skilled meat mages for years. Access to such specialty predator meats was strictly controlled and very expensive.

Either Balter was related to one of the highest primi or secondi ruling families, or he had won patronage from one of them. He'd won a position as lieutenant of one of the Gleaner fists, so he could fight. He'd probably take the direct approach in the food fight. Luckily food fights were chock full of options to modify the contest.

Rasher scanned the rectangular food fight area as the staff finished the setup. The previous battle cuisine demonstrations were gone. Scores of spectators crowded the long galleys surrounding the arena's wooden walls and pressed close to the edge of the upstairs viewing platforms. A hint of smoke hung in the air from a recent exploding cake demonstration, and scents from a dozen other military-grade foods lingered, melding together to form an exciting scent with a hint of danger.

People were making loud bets, and Balter was the clear favorite. "I wager twenty silver spoons on myself," Rasher declared loudly to both cheering and laughter. One of the betting officials waved to him and noted the bet. If Rasher won, he was about to make a lot of money.

He decided not to think about losing. Bacon only sizzled when dropped into the fire.

Balter called, "I shouldn't be surprised you can't see the writing on the wall."

"Can you even read the writing on the wall?"

"This is going to be fun," Balter grinned.

"A personal wager, then," Rasher said loudly.

"What kind of wager?" Balter asked suspiciously.

"If you win, I will publicly apologize for whatever offense it was that you have against me."

"That's a start," Balter said.

How had he developed such a grudge without Rasher even knowing him?

Sumwinkle, who stood with Otamot among the front ranks of the onlookers behind the protective low wall surrounding the arena called out, "And what if you win, Rasher?"

Rasher met his gaze and said, "If I win, then you and Balter join me tomorrow for a private training lesson."

That generated a round of laughter from the onlookers. Balter scowled, and Otamot rolled his eyes at Rasher's audacity. Sumwinkle grinned and shrugged. "Why not? If you can defeat Balter, maybe you've got something to teach."

"Don't encourage the fool," Balter growled. "He's got sugar for brains already."

Rasher grinned at him. "If you're getting nervous, Balter, why don't you bring a couple more of your fist tomorrow for emotional support? That way a little nonlethal combat won't worry you so much."

"You just can't keep that mouth shut, can you?" Balter said as he slammed one meaty fist into his other palm. "I'm going to thoroughly enjoy closing it for you."

Mission accomplished, and in perhaps the most unique way, he might win a private lesson with one of the Reapers. His luck was about to change. All he had to do was defeat the Gleaner champion. As easy as trying to eat a piece of exploding cake without losing teeth.

The staff had set up the food fight with small shelves that locked into grooves set into the wooden walls, spaced widely apart, ranging from about knee height to almost twelve feet up. On each shelf sat a magical food item, ranging from the more common ones, like a trio of already burning muffins sitting on a pedestal in the center of the room, to rarer and potentially more decisive items placed on the harder-to-reach shelves.

He spotted two different varieties of confectioner cookies. On a high shelf was a chocolate chip cookie that would offer a temporary sugar boost to strength and speed. Not very useful to Rasher, who couldn't use it while also releasing bacon. The other one was a fan-shaped sugar cookie that offered more potential, but it sat on the highest shelf halfway down the wall.

Other shelves included a head of broccoli prepared by a vegetable shaman, a rare cup of seafood shaman lobster bisque, and a couple different shelves with little paper bags packed with spice wizard air-manipulating mixtures.

One official with a wide-brimmed felt hat stepped to the edge of the arena and raised his hand for quiet. As the crowds hushed, he called, "Are the contestants ready?"

As soon as they both nodded, the man rang a bell fastened to the wall three times and shouted, "Go!"

As Rasher expected, Balter charged straight at the central pedestal with its burning muffins. Rasher didn't try to beat the big man to the center. Getting that close that fast and losing the initial dash would leave him with burning muffin smashed into his face and probably end the duel in the first seconds.

So instead he scurried to the side to one of the shelves at about knee height along the left wall, closer to his end. The crowd cheered loudly as Balter reached the pedestal, scooped up the first muffin, and instantly hurled it.

The muffin rocketed across the arena, exploding against the shelf Rasher had been reaching for. Burning muffin disintegrated the small block of sharp yellow cheddar cheese he'd been hoping to grab. The crowds cheered even louder, calling new bets.

Rasher stumbled back with a low curse, wiping burning muffin off his hands. The sharp scent of scorched sugar made him want to sneeze. Balter was even faster than he'd feared. Smearing that cheese on Balter's face would have burned like fire. That would have been fun.

As he back-pedaled, Balter threw the second muffin. Rasher released crispy bacon into his body and somersaulted sideways, easily dodging and generating a fresh wave of cheering. The feel of the bacon radiating out through his muscles was like wisps of warm vapor curling up from sizzling bacon on a hot griddle.

Balter scooped up the last muffin, but instead of throwing it, he started slowly advancing, muffin held at the ready.

"Griddle cakes," Rasher cursed softly.

Balter wasn't supposed to be clever as well as insanely overpowered. If he managed to close the distance, he could smash Rasher with that muffin, then beat the stuffing out of him while he was distracted.

Time to show what a bacon master who'd just eaten sixteen desserts could do. Rasher always taught his students when an enemy wants you to hold your ground, charge.

So he released the power of three full pieces of crispy bacon all at once from his internal bacon stores and combined it with the sizzle built up from eating all night.

A single piece of bacon could double his physical abilities for up to a full minute. Three pieces at once could increase his skills by an additional fifty percent. All that sizzle added even more.

With the unrivaled power of bacon erupting through his system, those curling wisps of warmth sharpened into sizzling bolts of crispy lightning. Rasher dashed across the arena, moving even faster than Balter had a moment earlier. The move caught the big man by surprise for a second, and that was all the time Rasher needed.

When he reached the wall, he didn't slow, but jumped, turning in the air and using his speed and momentum to run right up onto the wall. In a flash, he raced down the length of the wall, scooping up items from three separate shelves.

Balter reacted quickly, sprinting to cut him off and throwing the final muffin.

Rasher jumped away from the wall with a forward flip as he soared out over the arena. He caught the muffin as he spun, using a feather-soft touch to redirect its path and send it back toward Balter.

Balter couldn't dodge fast enough and ended up swatting the muffin aside with a forearm, splashing burning muffin all over himself. He ignored the flaming pastry, pursuing Rasher, murder in his eyes.

Rasher threw the head of broccoli he'd just snatched from one of the shelves to the ground right in front of Balter.

A deep pit appeared in the floor under Balter's foot and he fell, shouting angry curses. The crowd gasped as Rasher rushed toward the hole. He doubted it had dropped Balter more than ten or twelve feet. Too bad cats weren't known for landing on their heads.

Sure enough, Balter erupted up out of the hole, golden eyes blazing with anger.

Rasher slugged him in the face with the bowl of lobster bisque.

The bowl shattered, splattering the creamy soup all over Balter's eyes and nose. Instantly a torrent of water exploded out of thin air, blasting the furious soldier back down into the hole.

That was even more impressive than Rasher had hoped for. The waterfall lasted only a second, but it still half-filled the hole. The crowd cheered louder than ever. The air suddenly smelled humid and heavy, carrying a hint of clean, salty ocean breeze.

Rasher dropped to one knee next to the pit. A second later, Balter surged to the surface, grasping for the edge, still wiping bisque out of his eyes.

Rasher hit him in the face with the sugar cookie, mashing it against his skin. Balter gasped, swiping at Rasher with a hand. All of his fingernails had grown into long claws that could have opened his face to the bone.

With bacon-enhanced reflexes, Rasher ducked and retreated a few steps as Balter lunged out of the hole, dripping wet and boiling mad. He pawed at the cookie clinging to his sodden face and growled, "I'll tear your arms off for that."

He charged.

Rasher watched, a smile on his lips, as Balter ran just past him, tackling an empty patch of air. He hit the ground hard, sliding all the way to the wall. Those cookie-fueled hallucinations kicked in fast.

As Balter grunted and fought an imaginary foe, the crowds laughed. Rasher trotted across to the shelf with the bags of spices. One could trigger explosive vomiting, and another unleash a mini tornado in a restricted space. Either could ruin Balter's day. He headed back toward his distracted opponent and hefted the first one, then looked over at the official near the bell.

"Do I have to finish this?"

Balter was still scrabbling in the sand, trying to choke an invisible opponent. He had no idea where Rasher was and could do nothing to avoid the spice attack. Rasher didn't want to totally humiliate the big man, even if he might deserve it. Balter was still one of the Gleaners, after all.

The official looked to the crowds and asked loudly, "What say you?"

Some people, no doubt angered by the loss of their bets, called for Rasher to keep punishing Balter. Most agreed the food fight was over.

Rasher raised his hands in victory to thunderous applause. He'd given them a good show, and the crowds roared their appreciation. He headed toward where Sumwinkle stood, but couldn't see Otamot anywhere. Had the bacon master left early?

Lame.

Sumwinkle smiled, his gaze thoughtful. "We'll see you at the practice field tomorrow morning."

"You won't regret it, sir," Rasher promised.

When he glanced back at Balter, he was startled to see Otamot helping the big man to his feet. He spoke softly to him, and Balter's head snapped up suddenly in surprise. He smiled a predatory grin.

That couldn't be good news.

3

The Icing on the Cake of Fallen Dreams

Rasher arrived at the practice arena early the next day, bubbling with excitement and literally quivering with energy. He'd used a hefty portion of his winnings the previous night to purchase a mountain of food and had gorged himself since just after dawn.

With so much sizzle on top of his full bacon reserves, he was ready for anything. He grinned, feeling as eager as a child about to eat his first sugar cookie. Not that he'd eat a sugar cookie today. Confectioner enhancements sometimes reacted strangely to his bacon food absorption process.

He was about to train one of the Reapers! If he could impress Sumwinkle, doors long closed might finally open.

"Are you ready?" asked Kitan as she jogged up to join him.

He grinned to see her. She was the garnish in his life. Her smile was like the flash of a confectioner sugar burst in his heart, and he could stare at her lovely face all day. Her long hair was the color of crispy bacon, but as thick and silky as angel hair pasta coated with butter.

She stood only half a head shorter than he, her slender frame concealing a strength and vitality he rarely saw in girls of high station. Kitan kissed him, surprising him yet again with her heartfelt affection.

"I am," he told her confidently.

As a daughter of a secondi high house, Kitan van Ihlget yur Lascoin was a member of the elite nobility, but yet somehow managed to avoid getting locked into the stuffy life of intrigue and political sabotage like most girls of her age and station. She joined him several times a week at the practice arena, eager to learn fighting skills. He'd even worked her special talents into some of his teaching plans.

The rest of his training Fist arrived, led by their sergeants. Usually he'd hold the rank of lieutenant, but he was a bacon master. He couldn't imagine what kind of rumors he'd generate as a bacon master leading a training team with such a lowly rank.

As it was, things had worked out as well as he could have hoped.

The stocky senior sergeant, Bungey, grinned, saluted, and spoke with a bit of a whistle between the gap in his front teeth. "Reaper Sumwinkle, eh?"

"Indeed," Rasher grinned as he returned the salute.

"Training plan?" Bungey asked as the rest of his squad drew close to listen.

Rasher scanned the hard-packed sands of the practice arena with a critical eye. The arena formed an oval about a hundred yards long and half that wide, with randomly placed walls, barricades, and short towers scattered throughout. His team regularly adjusted the configurations, depending on the groups and objectives for any training day.

"I think we'll leave things as-is," he decided. "I'm only expecting two trainees."

"Happy to relax and watch the fun," Bungey said. They wished him luck and trotted toward the empty stands to watch.

Rasher caught Kitan's hand and nodded toward a nearby tower, fifteen feet tall with an excellent field of vision of the middle of the arena. "Willing to play shining light for me?"

She flashed a happy smile. "Absolutely." Then trotted to the tower and scampered up the ladder.

Beyond the arena wall to the north loomed the enormous Afitur outer city wall, while the slightly smaller Acropolis wall rose to the west. The Acropolis mini-city fit snugly on the northwest outskirts of Afitur, just within the wide loop of the capital's outer wall.

Only one other nearby building peeked up over the arena wall, making the area feel strangely isolated. That single building rose from within the Acropolis, a slender tower half again as high as the outer city wall. Painted dazzling white like all garlic towers, it was the communications hub for the Reaper legions.

The empty stands surrounding the arena would be packed with enthusiastic fans during the paint battle tournament games. Rasher's team trained using paint battle gear and also ran the official paint battle league with semi-professional sponsored teams fighting for the glory of the Silver Chalice.

Those games were wildly popular. Rasher's team, the Bacon Bits, was made up entirely of trainers. They had won the championship every season since he'd arrived in Afitur three years ago, a naive but determined nineteen-year-old. He was still the undefeated individual champion.

His thoughts were interrupted by the arrival of Sumwinkle and Balter. Sumwinkle wore his shining Reaper breastplate, his noodle whip-swords coiled on either side of his hips, and his Reaper tricorne hat perched slightly forward. Balter wore heavy links of chainmail with thick, leather bracers on his arms and a dueler's sword on his hip. He was already scowling under his bowler hat.

Rasher ignored him and saluted. "Reaper Sumwinkle, thank you for coming."

Sumwinkle glanced around the arena. "I've watched several paint battle matches from the stands, but never participated. It looks bigger from down here."

"It feels small enough when the paint starts flying," Rasher assured him.

Sumwinkle fixed him with his powerful gaze. "No offense, Captain, but I have a very busy day today. I'd appreciate it if we can begin immediately."

"And get this farce over with," Balter growled.

Rasher wouldn't let the big man rattle him, not when he had a Reaper's attention. "I figured you would. Balter likes losing quickly."

"You have no food to protect you today," Balter promised.

Some people simply loved learning the hard lessons.

In moments, he got them outfitted with leather paint battle armor and explained the rules. They would duel with practice weapons coated in paint. Hits to the torso counted as a kill. They each received a box of half a dozen wax-coated balls of paint they could throw. Solid hits would make the balls explode, scoring a kill.

"Let's make it more challenging, shall we?" Sumwinkle asked. "Any touch of paint anywhere on an opponent counts as a kill."

He really was in a hurry. Rasher agreed, and Balter selected a long wooden practice sword and dipped the blade in a basin of red paint. Sumwinkle chose to use his whip-swords, coating their last foot of length in paint too.

Rasher decided not to object, even though those whip-swords could easily kill him if Sumwinkle misjudged a strike. One did not become a Reaper without mastering their weapons.

For the bout, Rasher chose his trusty battle staff. The bottom half of the five-foot length of wood, banded with steel, was hollow, filled with pressurized paint that he could spray at the touch of a button. He paid a spice wizard weekly to refresh the pressure with a custom parsley blend.

They returned to the field, saluted each other at twenty paces, and Rasher said simply, "Begin."

Sumwinkle advanced, his braided whip-swords moving like pale death snakes as they whirled around him. He moved with the confidence of one of the best noodle warriors in the realm.

The unique weapons were difficult to master, but extremely deadly. Curls of smoke drifted from the whips, forming a slight haze around Sumwinkle's leather helm. Occasional flashes of crimson fire danced down their lengths, confirming they were imbued with a subtle fire baking from a muffin mage.

Balter flanked Sumwinkle to his left, an eager look on his rugged face. He wanted payback, and Rasher had no doubt he would hit hard enough to injure.

Sumwinkle grinned. "So you think you can best us both?"

"Do your other trainers beat you?" Rasher asked as he circled, using one of the barriers to reduce Balter's ability to rush him from the side.

"Very rarely," he admitted as Balter easily vaulted over the eight foot barrier.

"Sometimes students won't listen until I pound a lesson into their ribs," Rasher admitted as he adjusted his golden frying-pan hat. "I apologize in advance for any discomfort that may cause."

He embraced the thrill of competition. They were on his turf, and he lived for the contest. As he slowly circled, Rasher studied them. He rated everyone he trained with a simple system to help quickly place combatants in appropriate teams. Most people ended up as common, proficient, or advanced, like the proficient swordsmen and advanced archers he'd trained the day before.

Both of his opponents fit into the rare legendary category. Sumwinkle was more clever, but Balter more savage, wielding more raw power.

Balter flexed his hand on the hilt of his sword, while the fingernails of his free hand extended into claws, a clear reminder of the exceptional danger his tiger enhancements represented.

Sumwinkle said, "If we defeat you, I expect you to tell us the truth of the rumors about you."

"You have to beat me first."

Sumwinkle advanced fast, with Balter hanging back in support. As if he'd let the fight go the way they planned. This was a training moment, after all.

So instead of backing away from those flicking whips, Rasher charged.

Sumwinkle didn't hesitate. The whip-swords flicked out, the flames licking their lengths glowing brighter, as if in anticipation of blackening his face.

Rasher dove forward in a feet-first slide, dropping under the first whip-sword and deflecting the second with a tap of his staff. It snapped the air right next to his face, spraying bits of flame and red paint behind him.

He hit the ground on his right side, leg slightly bent, and slid forward, barely slowed. If they had noticed the thin steel plates fastened to the outside of his pant legs, they probably just assumed they were laughable attempts at leg armor. The slide plates were one of his secret weapons. Coated with a gingersnap mixture from a restricted recipe, they gave Rasher far longer slides than anyone else across the hard-packed sand, and that made for wonderful openings.

Sumwinkle tried to backpedal, flicking the whip-swords in expert arcs to spear down at the ground, but Rasher moved too fast, leaving them to gouge dirt right behind him.

To his credit, Sumwinkle simply released the whip-swords, his hands flashing for the container of paint balls on his hip.

Rasher sprayed him across his leather chest plate, then slapped his hand away from the pouch with a quick tap of his staff for good measure. Sumwinkle stared in shock from his paint-stained armor to his dropped whip-swords, to Rasher, who rose to his feet within arm's reach.

With an angry roar, Balter vaulted right over Sumwinkle in a fantastic leap, slashing down at Rasher with his wooden sword.

Only reflexes honed from hundreds of fights saved him. Rasher instinctively drew deep from the power of crispy bacon and threw himself into a sideways dive. He somersaulted in the air, landing on his feet at the same time Balter did.

The huge man landed as light as a kitten and lunged, blade flashing with the speed of a cat's paw.

Rasher barely deflected the first blow, backpedaling as Balter pursued. The big man rained heavy strikes down at Rasher, arm moving so fast it blurred.

Parrying and dodging, Rasher opened his bacon powers wide, committing ten whole slices of crispy bacon at once. That much bacon could grant him maybe another twenty percent improvement over what three pieces of bacon could do. The sharply diminished return usually wasn't worth the heavy cost.

It was when he also had a cyclone of sizzle also boiling through him. His bacon power ignited that energy, pouring it into his limbs like pure bacon grease, and every muscle quivered like he'd swallowed a bolt of lightning.

Balter attacked with brutal, predatory fury that might have bested Rasher on a normal day.

Not today.

Rasher also released three pieces of chewy bacon to enhance his mind to keep up with his body. He read the big man's forms, recognizing the patterns. Rasher knew all the forms used by all the high houses, and he easily picked up the aggressive power-strike forms from house Beter.

So he knew each blow before Balter did.

Rasher grinned as his world condensed to nothing but the duel, his every muscle, every sense, every breath tuned to perfect harmony as he matched Balter stroke for stroke.

As one second became ten, then twenty, the two of them battled down the length of the practice field. They fought so hard, Balter's hat went flying. He didn't even notice. Sumwinkle trailed them, not hiding his surprise. The trainers sitting in the stands started to cheer Rasher's name.

It was nice to be appreciated.

Rasher reveled in the thrill of the contest. He never felt more alive than when committing all his bacon, all his sizzle, and all his focus on a truly worthy opponent. He wanted to laugh with life, wishing he could walk that knife's edge along the brink of losing control all day.

So he led Balter on, letting the big man think that at any second he'd get that one precious opening. The two of them flowed around each other, their weapons cracking like the staccato boiling of water dropped into hot oil.

Rasher couldn't help pushing a bit more. "You're faster than anyone I've ever dueled."

"I ought to be after twenty years of building these meat enhancements," Balter growled.

Twenty years? Either he was older than Rasher thought, or he'd started dangerously young.

"There's something you should know," Rasher continued, dodging around another barrier as if looking for respite. Balter shouldered into it, sending the barrier crashing to the ground.

"Tell me," Balter sneered. "I already know you're a fraud."

The conversation was not noticeably slowing the big man. Impressive that he refused to be distracted. "Did you realize how badly you stink when you're angry?"

"I'll take your head," Balter roared.

They closed again, weapons crashing so fast, the sounds blended into a constant roar. With every second, Balter's anger grew. He growled, bright yellow eyes glowing. His lips curled into a snarl, and Rasher noted that his canines were sharp, like a cat's.

Did that make kissing a girl awkward?

The idle thought nearly ended the bout for Rasher. He missed a parry and had to throw himself to the ground in a wild, rolling dive.

Rasher sprayed blue paint up into the air. It missed Balter by inches.

Balter pursued, closing the distance with unerring finality, sword poised for the killing blow.

A bright blue beam of light shot between them, leaving dazzling after-images dancing in Rasher's mind, even though he'd been ready for it.

Balter was not. The big man flinched, then pounced, sword ripping the air as it slashed down so hard it would break ribs.

The tiny distraction was all Rasher needed. He sprang off the ground in a bacon-induced spring, twisting as he rose so that the descending sword slashed just past his torso, barely a hair's breadth away from staining the fabric.

The sword struck the ground so hard it snapped, and Balter stumbled.

Rasher landed on his feet and sprayed the big man in the face, then smacked him across the temple with the end of his staff for good measure.

The blow would have dropped most men. It only made Balter grunt. He spun toward Rasher, the jagged end of his broken sword raised to strike again.

Not good. Balter had drawn too deep and drifted into meat euphoria.

"Enough!"

The command cracked like one of Sumwinkle's whip-swords, shaking Balter from his crazed state. The big man shook himself, glanced down at the broken sword, and tossed it away with a look of disgust.

Rasher backed slowly away, staff at the ready, filled with his own kind of euphoria. His poor weapon was battered and covered in paint, but it had held up to the beating.

"That was one of the most impressive duels I've ever seen," Sumwinkle laughed, clapping Balter on the shoulder and taking a moment to stare into his yellow eyes. After a few seconds, Balter's shoulders relaxed and he nodded slightly. He was back in control. Maybe.

Rasher breathed deep, savoring the scents of paint and sand and honest sweat. He wiped his face with a white cloth Kitan had gifted to him a week ago, then glanced up at the tower and saluted. She waved happily.

Balter followed his glance and growled, "You wouldn't have won without that distraction."

Kitan was his secret weapon. She was a seafood shaman. Few could produce much of a light, a glow developed through a complex recipe involving bioluminescent fish. Kitan's special talent was a training tool he'd used many times to teach the importance of not getting distracted.

"Perhaps," Rasher said with an easy smile, drawing from his reduced stores of bacon again. He'd burned through most of his sizzle too. He'd never drained so much so fast. He could store the equivalent of about sixty slices of bacon in his body, and he usually divided that about two-thirds crispy bacon, one-third chewy. He rarely built up so much sizzle before burning it off again.

He wasn't sure he could absorb much more without having to jump out a window or randomly run twenty miles, but the possibilities were intriguing

The power of crispy bacon that he consumed pooled in his joints, which was why no bacon master ever had issues with their knees, hips, elbows, or shoulders. The power of chewy bacon pooled in his sinuses, which was why so many bacon masters had that nasal-sounding voice like Otamot's.

"How did you keep up?" Sumwinkle asked.

"Balter moved so fast he lost his ability to be creative." He wasn't about to reveal his other secrets.

"I used all the forms I know," Balter insisted.

"Exactly. You're faster than you are smart."

Balter growled, hands curling into fists.

"That's not an insult," Rasher explained. "Or at least, not just an insult. You had to rely on habit to keep the flow going and maintain the rhythm. I also know the forms you use, so I was able to anticipate them."

Balter stared in obvious disbelief, so Rasher added, "You train to face legendary enemies, the one in ten thousand who might kill you in a real war, so you cannot assume your speed alone will win the day."

"Brilliant," Sumwinkle grinned, pumping Rasher's hand. "I have to admit, I thought today would be a waste. Otamot thought me a fool to honor the deal, but you proved us wrong."

"It's what I do," Rasher said, flashing his famous smile.

"Why aren't you part of the Reaper trainers?" Sumwinkle asked.

"I want to be," Rasher admitted. He'd applied six times.

Balter grunted, "Don't waste your time. They won't take this one."

"Why not?" Sumwinkle asked.

"Because he can't handle it."

Rasher's smile faded. There was no way Balter could know.

The big man removed his left bracer and rolled back the sleeve over the corded muscles of his left forearm. "Captain Dilskin's got skill, but he's got a fatal flaw."

Rasher opened his mouth to protest, but Balter drew a small knife and deliberately sliced it across the back of his forearm. Dark blood immediately oozed from the wound, and the blood seemed to seize Rasher's gaze.

Inside he screamed as he tried to wrench his gaze away, but he'd been caught by surprise and his usual defenses failed. He'd used up too much sizzle, leaving his reserves too low.

Rasher gasped as the sight of the blood seared his vision. His blood seemed to pound in his ears as his limbs shook and his breathing fell into shallow panting. He staggered, trying to focus, trying to think, trying to release bacon.

The ground hit him hard. He hadn't even realized he'd fallen. His gaze darkened and his ears were filled with a weird rushing hiss. All he could smell was sand and blood. The taste of charred meat clung to the back of his throat.

Some time later, his mind cleared and he found himself lying face-up on the ground. He groaned. His throat felt dry, and his eyes ached.

"Rasher," Kitan called to him, and he looked up to see her kneeling beside him, her lovely face worried as she helped him sit. He still felt woozy, a headache pounding between his eyes, but he looked around wildly.

Sumwinkle and Balter were just exiting the changing rooms, dressed in their regular clothes and weapons. They stopped in front of him, and Sumwinkle asked, "Are you all right?"

"I'll be fine," Rasher assured him as he struggled to his feet. He still felt weak, his limbs wobbly, and he cursed himself for it. He hadn't suffered such an episode in months, and timing could not have been worse. Kitan stood close, ready to offer support.

"I told you," Balter said simply to Sumwinkle. "All the hype, all the rumors, and he's just a fool with a fatal flaw. They'll never take him, and he never should have gotten this job when better men applied."

Rasher blinked at him, trying to get his sluggish thoughts working again. "Is that why you hate me? Did I beat out a friend of yours for this post?"

"My brother, Lagan!" Balter stormed. "You destroyed his career."

Now it made sense. Lagan Fopoon was a very popular semi-pro paint battle team captain who had applied for Rasher's job. His team, the Boiled Tomatoes, usually came in second place to the Bacon Bits, and he had placed second behind Rasher as the individual champion three times in a row.

"Lagan is a good man," Rasher said.

"A better man than you, but his sponsors might drop him if he loses again."

Paint battle games brought in a lot of prestige, especially for the sponsors, which were usually the lower high houses that lacked access to the Food Court and the highest levels of power. The Boiled Tomatoes were sponsored by the van Wewanta mon Opoly house, one of the third-tier contorni houses. Rasher wasn't surprised they were applying so much pressure.

"I'm sorry your brother's having a hard time," Rasher said. "But you realize that if I joined the Reaper training team, I might not have time to lead the Bacon Bits."

Balter blinked and turned to Sumwinkle. "I take it back. You should recommend Rasher as a trainer."

Sumwinkle raised an eyebrow. "Really? After making such a point to discredit him?"

If Rasher didn't want the job so badly, he'd laugh in Balter's face. The big man had effectively iced his own goals.

Sumwinkle asked Rasher. "Have you had a milk mage treat that condition?"

Rasher forced calm on his features even though inside he wanted to howl with frustration. He'd had it! Sumwinkle's good word would have cut through all the bureaucracy like hot bacon grease through whipped cream. Now he could see the truth in Sumwinkle's eyes. He'd lost.

Even worse than losing the training position, what if Balter spread the truth? He'd always known it was only a matter of time before the truth came out. When it did, he'd lose everything. No one would respect a bacon master who couldn't fight in real battles.

"My blood phobia does not seem to have an easy cure," he admitted.

"Pity," Sumwinkle said, and he did look apologetic.

Balter growled, "Useless." Then he took a deep breath, produced a small wooden box from a thigh pocket, and held it out to Rasher. "You may be a waste of talent, but I admit defeat when it happens."

"Thanks," Rasher said as he cautiously accepted the box.

It was about as long and wide as his hand, but thin. Was it a gift or a final insult? Rasher hadn't imagined Balter might have a single ounce of grace in that brutish heart. When he glanced inside the box, he grinned in surprise and reiterated, "Thanks!"

"Chocolate-coated bacon," Balter confirmed as Rasher stared at the little dark-colored bars filling the box. "Enhanced with confectioner buffs to vitality and concentration."

Sumwinkle laughed. "Did you steal that from Otamot's private stores?"

"Borrowed," Balter said with a shrug.

Rasher was stunned, but his mind raced. There was no way Balter would have prepared so well for a potential defeat. Nor would he risk offending Otamot by stealing from him. Not for Rasher.

The memory of Otamot speaking with Balter after the food fight flashed into his mind, and he understood. Otamot, that turkey-sniffing anchovy lover, had told Balter his weakness.

Which meant the gift was a hoax. Chocolate-coated bacon with those enhancements could give him the edge to guarantee he won the next paint battle championship.

Or if the enhancements were really curses, if it was made with turkey bacon, it could guarantee he lost.

How stupid did Balter think he was?

They were interrupted by a courier in a distinctive close-fitting, rounded hat. The man rushed through the outer gate with sugar-enhanced speed and sprinted up to Sumwinkle.

He saluted and spoke quickly. "Sir, you are summoned to the Heart with all speed for a matter of urgency."

Sumwinkle returned the salute, then cast a final glance at Rasher. "Thank you for the training today, Captain. I may not be able to offer you a job, but I'll probably wager a few silver spoons on you in the next paint battle tournament."

"Thank you, sir," Rasher said, saluting. It was a gracious way to spread the last icing on the cake of his fallen dreams.

4

WHEN THE GOING GETS TOUGH, EAT EVERYTHING

"Are you sure you're doing okay?" Kitan asked as they sat together at a little table in the outside courtyard of their favorite café, not far from the training arena.

"Better than if you weren't with me," he admitted.

They sat facing each other, with two other tables pulled up to either side. He wanted to take her hand, but the servers were busy laying out the feast he'd ordered.

They might need another table. As trays and platters and bowls filled the tabletops, he drew in a deep breath, inhaling the wonderful aromas.

Even though they sat outside in a courtyard surrounded by a low wall of cheery, red bricks, overhung with vines that had not yet begun to bud with spring flowers, mouthwatering scents clung to the air in nearly tangible waves. He savored the scents of fresh-baked pie, chocolate-and-cream-filled pastries, the café's famous pancakes, stacks of spicy sausages, and omelets filled with cheese, vegetables, and ham. Those were just the dishes in easy reach.

The place was popular with high society clientele, employing a full tournant chef. The woman possessed an incredible mastery of cooking and a flair for combining magically enhanced foods into unique dishes.

Too bad the café could not offer bacon. Few restaurants outside of the Acropolis or Nutmeg Hill were authorized to serve it. There were too few bacon masters in the capital to justify it. Dueling Balter had consumed far too much of his stores of both bacon and sizzle.

The bout of blood phobia had wrecked his energy levels even worse. He'd replenish his bacon later, but needed to reverse the still-lingering drain on his energy. That meant eating. A lot.

As the servers left, several glanced around at the otherwise empty courtyard with its dozen small tables and ornate, wrought-iron chairs, as if expecting to see the rest of their party show up. He'd never seen the place so empty, but he didn't need more people to eat that much food.

Kitan reached across the table to place her warm hand over his. Her presence was a balm, like whipped cream rubbed on an open wound. Only near her could he handle feeling so drained with calm. "You look tired."

"I'll be fine once I eat everything."

She knew the full truth about his blood phobia, things not even his parents knew, like how every episode added to the slow drain on his bacon powers. Only by constantly binge-eating and fast-absorbing several extra meals worth of food every day and burning through all that sizzle did he manage to keep his energy levels from falling permanently.

Knowing that she knew everything, but did not despise him for his condition, helped more than she could ever know.

"Then let's eat," she said eagerly, tucking in her napkin to protect the bright yellow dress she'd changed into before leaving the arena.

The dress, with its fitted bodice and flowing skirt, flattered her great figure. Her fine linen jacket was taupe colored, one of the colors of her house, but Rasher's eyes were drawn up to her new hat, perched jauntily on her head.

"I can't believe you bought one of those," he teased as he served an omelet onto her plate.

The most powerful effects of cheese were poisons and curses, but the cafe's chef was adept at incorporating the more subtle cheeses that encouraged the opposite, immune-boosting effects. They couldn't heal like a good cream but added a nice counterpoint to the subtle strength effect of the vegetables.

"This?" Kitan asked with a twinkle in her eye. "This was the most sensible hat I could find."

Hats played a vital role in Rubric life, and the higher levels of society pushed the fashion to its limits. That year, high fashion demanded the wearing of enormous hats, many with brims stretching over four feet across. Kitan's was not nearly as bad as most. She always managed to look fashionable, but not ridiculous.

The core of her hat was simple, with a moderate brim all around, fashioned out of a lightweight fabric, the color of a perfectly browned muffin. A layer of white, gauzy cloth encircled the brim in great, billowing waves, extending its width several inches without making the hat seem overbearing. A huge, yellow fabric flower adorned the right side of the crown, lending the hat an airy, elegant feel.

"You do make it look good."

Kitan's father, Lord Niffum van Ihlget yur Lascoin, was one of the most successful of the secondi high lords. He'd raised their house to one the most powerful second-tier families in the realm, only exceeded in might and wealth by the primi families. Those ruling houses made up the First Course Assembly, the governing body controlling the empire that met in the Food Court.

Most women of Kitan's station spent the majority of their time either embroiled in political intrigue, attending lavish parties, engaged in learning culinary arts from the best chefs, or enjoying the glamorous world of the wardrobe wizards. Kitan did participate in those things, but managed to slip out of that world more than any girl of her station Rasher had ever known.

Kitan smiled at the compliment. "Keep talking like that, and I might convince my father to let me come visit again."

It was a miracle she managed to see him at all. Rasher had no idea how she continued to defy her father, who had made it clear he did not approve of Rasher as a suitor. Some days he wondered if she stuck with him just to annoy him.

She was beautiful, vivacious, and very popular. Many eligible bachelors from the highest houses sought her attention. It must drive them crazy to know she had chosen Rasher.

"You wouldn't miss out on knife-throwing training," he countered, and her eyes lit up with eagerness. She loved all kinds of armed and unarmed training when she wasn't practicing in the seafood shaman palace.

Rasher served himself a steaming stack of pancakes, smothered in melting butter, and dripping with sugary syrup. The syrup could easily be imbued with a confectioner enhancement to energy and speed of mind, or the butter to help ease his aching muscles. Instead, the chef had crafted the meal with a focus on the pancakes, enchanted by a muffin mage. The incredible dish would melt on his tongue, spreading a slow, energizing warmth throughout his body.

As he scanned the table, he mentally reviewed the recipe for every dish. He hadn't gotten anything new from this chef in weeks.

"I might have found a higher-level recipe book," Kitan said, as if reading his mind.

"Have I told you yet today that I love you?" he responded as together they removed their hats, took the first forkfuls of their breakfasts, and placed the food inside their upturned crowns.

Rasher shook his frying pan-shaped hat side to side slightly as if frying the piece of pancake while he turned his thoughts to his patron god, Domuz. After a few seconds, the food disappeared in a little flash of light, leaving behind the faintest scent of fresh bacon, while a feeling of strength radiated into him. He smiled, returning his hat to his head.

They ate in silence for a moment. Kitan took her time, savoring the delicious food, while Rasher wolfed down the pancakes, a plate of spicy potatoes, and a platter of scrambled eggs.

Eventually Kitan asked, "What happened? You've been doing so well for months."

"Balter caught me by surprise," Rasher admitted.

"What else can you do?"

"Maybe wear eye patches over both eyes," he suggested with a wry grin.

She laughed again, the sound as dear to him as sizzling bacon. "You think going blind would be an improvement?"

"Maybe. I've heard blind people develop their other senses, and with bacon I bet I could get there faster."

"I've never heard of a blind bacon master."

The thought did have a certain appeal until he realized he wouldn't get to see her either. That opened the door for darker thoughts to slip in. "The word is starting to get out. I'm running out of time, and the recipes I've tried haven't worked."

"You'll find the right mix," she assured him.

Her confidence bolstered his optimism. He would find a way. As a bacon master, usually his career options would be limitless, and he could easily win a position as the commander of the house guard of almost any of the high houses, especially among the secondi or contorni tiers. Some of the primi houses might not trust a bacon master, since they were sponsored by the Takmor house, who were their political rivals in the complex, high-stakes intrigue of the Food Court.

Other bacon masters held high civic positions in key cities across the realm, particularly the border fortresses closest to Whisternfeet and their deadly hordes of glowan monsters, but none of those options were viable for Rasher yet.

Knowledge of his blood phobia was not widespread, but it was known among the leadership of the Takmor house. They would not want to risk embarrassing the good name of bacon masters by recommending him anywhere.

Winning his position in the Acropolis never would have happened if not for his father pulling a lot of strings. Rasher's large family, recently raised to a sixth-tier mini high house, boasted an extremely lucrative meat trade. Now known as the van Notda lam Estone house, they were one of the largest distributors of bacon and other specialty meats.

The Takmor family was one of their biggest clients. His family had cornered so much of the bacon market, the Takmor house could not afford to lose the contract or risk bacon supply shortages.

So they had reluctantly supported Rasher's appointment, but Rasher feared his father might have overplayed his hand. Once Rasher arrived in the Acropolis, he'd fought to build his reputation to ensure his father never regretted taking such a risk for him. He was popular, but he was running a tightrope. Once people knew the truth, everything he'd worked for could easily come crashing down.

Good thing he rather liked tightropes.

Kitan fixed him with a worried gaze. "Rasher, really. How are you? I know you had pinned a lot of your hopes on Sumwinkle."

He sighed and met her gaze, dropping his confident mask for once. "As I said, I'm running out of time. If I don't figure out how to deal with this . . ."

Rasher refused to finish the sentence. Even saying that much drew too close to a line he could not cross. If he admitted even to himself that he couldn't beat his blood phobia, he'd hesitate, and that would doom all of his goals and hope for happiness with Kitan.

"That last recipe I copied from the Seafood Palace had seemed so promising," Kitan said, moving on. She knew the truth, but wouldn't say her deeper fears out loud. If she did, she'd have to admit Rasher would never be able to show to the world he was worthy of her.

Rasher gratefully buried his fears again and forced a chuckle, shaking his head. "That one nearly killed me."

"What?" she exclaimed. "Oh, Rasher, I'm so sorry!"

He patted her hand, smearing a bit of butter on her smooth skin in the process. "I survived, so don't worry about it."

"What happened?" she asked, wiping away the butter on the tablecloth in exactly the way a fine lady shouldn't.

"Made me swell up like a puffer fish. The internal pressure nearly made me pop."

Kitan wasn't supposed to take higher recipes from the palace. The broiled deep-sea cod dish was used by sea divers to protect from the pressures of deep water. He'd hoped the extra internal pressure would counteract the weakness he felt in his veins when seeing blood.

He shrugged and added, "Might have worked if I'd tried it a hundred feet under the surface of Cockalorum Lake."

"Maybe the new recipe book I convinced our family chef to acquire will hold the key we need," Kitan said with her usual determination.

"Maybe," he agreed. He loved trying new recipes, especially the dangerous ones. There had to be a recipe to counteract his blood phobia, and he would find it.

A rumble of distant thunder drew his gaze up to the morning sky. The previously clear, blue expanse was now marred to the north with dark, lowering clouds. Kitan followed his gaze and said, "No one wants to talk about how late the storms are coming, even though they're threatening spring planting."

"Have the drupe wizards forgotten to work this winter?"

She rolled her eyes. "My father won't talk about it, which means something is most definitely wrong."

Rasher did not know exactly how the drupe wizards imbued the seeds with their protective magic, working through the winter to prepare the next year's crop for planting, but they'd always succeeded in the past. One of the great benefits the Rubric Empire offered to all of the vassal kingdoms it conquered was the promise of plentiful harvests, grown in near perfect conditions.

Everyone was required to use the seeds prepared by the drupe wizards, which was both an incredible benefit and a not-so-subtle threat. If any kingdom ever rebelled, like his home nation of Taradiddle had once tried, they would not receive the enchanted seeds and would therefore face a very real potential for famine and starvation.

Despite how vital the seed crop was, he wasn't really worried. The drupe wizards had managed the harvest for generations, and he hadn't heard any recent rumblings of dissent. He needed to stop getting distracted by imaginary problems and focus on the real ones.

Kitan's expression turned nervous and she said, "Um, Rasher, this might not be the best time to bring this up . . ."

He could guess what she was going to say. "Your father found you a suitor?"

Kitan nodded, her eyes huge and lovely, but tinged with worry. She whispered, "We're almost out of time."

Crumpets, that seemed to be the recurring theme of his life at the moment. His fears bubbled up again, but he ruthlessly beat them back down, refusing to acknowledge them.

Lord Niffum had granted Kitan an exceptional level of leeway only because her older sister was the focus of the old man's intrigue. She'd married extremely well just a few weeks ago to a younger son of the van Toffer dan Itluks primi house. That union cemented the alliance between the two houses, who had already been close, and gave old Niffum an even better position for his ultimate goal, which was nothing less than raising his house from the ranks of the secondi to the tier of primi.

Few lower houses had managed that last monumental jump in position and power. To do so, they had to supplant one of the existing primi houses, who plotted, schemed, and fought tenaciously to hold onto power.

A good marriage for Kitan offered another potential benefit to her house that her father could not ignore. Rasher needed to prove he was more than a trainer with no future from a laughably low house.

If only he'd won Sumwinkle's endorsement. If only one of the dozen failed recipes had worked.

If only wishes were bacon, he'd be set for life.

"I'll think of something," he whispered, but it sounded weak even to him. Even with the sizzle of the new feast replenishing him, he still felt drained.

"I rather doubt that," said a deep voice behind him.

Rasher spun in surprise. He usually did a better job maintaining awareness of his surroundings.

Terrible time to get distracted. The newcomer was none other than Niffum van Ihlget yur Lascoin, Kitan's father.

5

AN INSANE PROPOSAL

Where Kitan was willowy and lovely, her father was stocky with a florid complexion, graying-brown hair, and black eyes. He was dressed in a fashionable doublet of pastel green and trousers the same shade of taupe as Kitan's jacket. Over it all he wore a long, fur-lined jacket of bright yellow. It was currently unbuttoned, revealing the ornately carved handle of his long dagger, his only visible weapon.

Niffum was a respected noodle warrior, and although he rarely carried a whip-sword like Sumwinkle, Rasher knew he usually had an eight-inch hollow-tube rigatoni dart gun secreted in one of his deep coat pockets. Those noodle dart guns could be devastating in the hands of one who knew how to use them. Kitan had once told him that her father preferred darts dipped in sleep-enhanced coffee that could knock out a grown man in seconds. He also had a few cheese-cursed darts for more lethal encounters.

Luckily he hadn't arrived with weapons in hand.

Rasher jumped to his feet and bowed to Niffum, who nodded his head in turn, his wide-brimmed purple hat bobbing with the motion. Its design was simpler than Kitan's, lacking the flower and billowing layers of filmy cloth, but the brims extended a full twelve inches all around his graying hair.

"Father!" Kitan exclaimed, rushing over to embrace him.

He smiled warmly and hugged her back. "Hello, my dear. I hear the omelet is delicious here."

"It is," Rasher said. "Shall we draw up a chair for you?"

"Thank you, but no. I will not be staying long."

"What are you doing here at all?" Kitan asked as she stepped back from him.

"I wished to speak with you both in private, away from the manor house."

Rasher's heart began to race. He'd feared this day would come, but now that the moment was upon them, he couldn't imagine hearing the words. If Niffum denied their courtship and refused to allow Kitan to see him again, what would he do?

Probably something foolish. Why wait?

Kitan beat him to it. Her spine stiffened and she said, "Father, I will not hear of you banning Rasher from seeing me."

Niffum raised an eyebrow in surprise and Kitan took half a step back before catching herself, then raised her chin in defiance. "I won't."

"That's my girl," Rasher thought to himself. He loved her strong will, but they couldn't win by directly opposing her father. Kitan loved her father, and he usually doted on her, but in a rage he might do something regrettable.

Niffum made a calming gesture. "I arranged this private meeting, but please do not raise your voice, my dear. It would not do for everyone in half a block around us to overhear our discussion."

Rasher glanced around at the empty courtyard, chiding himself for not thinking more about the unusually empty cafe. Why would Niffum bother? Why not summon Rasher to his manor house, the center of his power?

Despite Niffum's suggestion they speak softly, Rasher bet he'd brought along a spice wizard to place an air shield around the courtyard to prevent eavesdropping anyway.

Kitan took a deep breath and stepped to Rasher's side, grasping his hand in hers. Rasher said, "I'm assuming that by your choice of venue for this meeting, you're here to bless our courtship and encourage us to marry immediately."

Kitan looked shocked and started subtly gesturing him to stop. Niffum's expression became stern. "Not exactly."

"Ah, I see," Rasher said. A tiny part of his mind cringed at Kitan's father's expression, but he couldn't let the man destroy their hopes without making him work for it. "Then I suppose you wish us to elope today and move to the country to oversee your family's noodle estates."

Kitan gave him the look she usually reserved for sparring practice when she was planning to punch him in the face, but she kept her voice light as she said, "Oh, no, Rasher. I couldn't bear to move to the country permanently. We should take up residence in the family mansion in Lascoin."

"Of course, my dear," Rasher told her with a warm smile, but did not look away from her father, who was clearly losing his patience. "We must do what is best for the house."

"Indeed," Niffum interjected. "Are you quite finished with this foolishness?"

At least he hadn't started shouting or swore Rasher would never marry his daughter. If his intentions for setting up the surprise meeting had been to break up their relationship, he would not have hesitated.

Kitan made an exaggerated motion of looking at the empty courtyard. "Foolishness, father?"

He smiled and gestured at the table. "Perhaps we should sit down, after all."

Rasher snatched a chair from a nearby table, and they sat, Kitan scooting her chair close to his as they faced her father over the tables piled high with the remains of their breakfast.

"I had not expected you to grow so attached so quickly," Niffum said after a moment.

"I love your daughter," Rasher assured him. "And I will do whatever it takes to prove to you that I am worthy of her."

Under the table, Kitan squeezed his hand hard. "And I love Rasher," she added in a clear, strong voice. The words filled Rasher with joy more profound than any amount of bacon.

Niffum inclined his head slightly to his daughter, then sighed. "Unfortunately, love is not the only consideration I have to deal with. You realize that I could leverage any one of several high houses to arrange a very favorable marriage for you that would substantially improve our chances of raising our house to primi level."

Sometimes calm logic could be harsher than shouted words.

"I don't care about that," Kitan insisted.

"But I must," her father responded kindly. "And in quiet moments, you recognize it too. Don't pretend you don't."

"Have you forgotten all I'm already doing?" she demanded hotly. "I'm the one who—"

Niffum interrupted. "Enough. This is not the time or place to review that."

What was she about to say? Rasher knew her well, but couldn't imagine what leverage she thought she had to bargain with.

"Then why are you here, Father?" she pleaded.

Niffum leaned back, considering them again. "I like you, Rasher, but it seems you are determined to place obstacles in the path of winning my approval.

Had he learned of Rasher's blood phobia, or was he just referring to the fact that Rasher was a nobody, stuck in a position that seemed on the surface far beneath his potential?

"Maybe we should change paths," Rasher suggested.

Niffum huffed an almost chuckle. "Hopefully news of how easily you bested Sumwinkle won't get out, but these things tend to."

"How did you . . . ?" Kitan asked.

"I have contacts in lots of places," Niffum said simply, but Rasher doubted there was anything simple about it. Had he assigned someone to follow Kitan, or did he have someone watching Rasher? Probably both.

The import of Niffum's words finally sank in and Rasher wanted to slap himself a couple times for being a fool. He hadn't even considered the fact that the Ihlget house sponsored the noodle warriors. By defeating the beloved champion of the noodle warriors, Rasher might have tainted the shining reputation of the entire group, thus damaging the reputation of the Ihlget house in the process.

Crumpets and fish sticks!

Niffum was watching him carefully, and nodded slowly, as if reading his thoughts. "My position is tricky, Rasher, and I am afraid I will need more from you before I can even consider formally approving your courtship to my Kitan."

"Like what?" Rasher asked cautiously. Niffum was a notoriously devious plotter. "I have nothing but myself to give. My family barely won their mini rank."

"Indeed, your family resides far too low on the social ladder to entice me by their position alone, but it is not their social position that interests me."

"What then?" Kitan asked as Rasher released a quarter slice of chewy bacon to his thoughts and abruptly realized what the crafty old man must be after.

Oh, that son of a brisket.

"Bacon," Niffum said with a smile, confirming his fears.

Kitan gasped and Rasher said, "You want my family to abandon the Takmor house and shift our bacon contract to yours?" The idea was ludicrous, but also inspired even within that devious intrigue common to high house maneuvering.

Niffum smiled, but the gesture lacked any warmth. He looked like a predator, regarding an impending kill. "Not just your bacon contract, but all specialty meat contracts currently active with Takmor."

"I still think eloping and moving to Lascoin is a better option," Rasher said, drawing an annoyed frown from Niffum.

Kitan said, "What will those contracts give you, father? Surely Rasher's family is but one supplier of bacon."

"Actually, my family has pretty much cornered the market on bacon, along with several other specialty meats," Rasher admitted. "My father has been quietly expanding our business far beyond what it used to be. If he suddenly shifted all contracts to your house, it could cripple the Takmor family, at least for a short period."

"Long enough to do what must be done," Niffum said. He leaned forward slightly, holding Rasher's gaze. "But if one word of this conversation is ever shared with anyone but your father, I will not only refuse to allow Kitan to see you ever again, but I will use every bit of influence I possess to destroy your house completely."

"Father, this is madness," Kitan exclaimed. "The Takmor house is one of our best allies."

He cast her a warning look, and Rasher wondered what she was alluding to. The various houses shifted alliances so frequently, he never bothered trying to keep up. Until that moment, none of their intrigue directly affected him. His fast-whirling thoughts chewed on the old man's words like a chunk of gristly steak, considering likely motivations and possible outcomes should his family indeed risk the bold move Niffum suggested.

"My family would face severe consequences built into the existing contract language," he pointed out. "Not to mention social and economic repercussions from the Takmor house and other high houses. Such a move could destroy our house."

"Indeed, there is risk," Niffum said calmly. "Should we attempt such a move in the current political landscape, I suspect your house would be crushed and the Takmors would recover with little long-term effect."

"Then why ask such a thing?" Kitan demanded angrily. "Just to push Rasher into a position where he's forced to walk away?"

"Not at all," he assured her. "My dear, there is much going on in the Food Court and among the high houses that even you do not know." He fixed Rasher with a firm stare. "Consider my terms. Should events transpire that create conditions favorable to the move, I will require your agreement to secure your family's cooperation."

"And should favorable conditions not materialize?" Rasher asked, working to keep his tone calm and hide his growing anger at the insane proposal. He'd already created terrible risk for his family. He couldn't imagine approaching his father with this insanity too. The Takmors had not treated him well, but he could not allow his father to destroy their own house in such a reckless move.

Niffum sat back and spread his hands, a smile on his lips. "Should my expectations prove incorrect and conditions not shift within the next six months, I will release you and your family from any obligation, and I will formally support your courtship to Kitan and indeed appoint you to oversee our estates in Lascoin with no additional requirements from you."

Kitan looked to Rasher, hope mixed with concern. He squeezed her hand and gave her a reassuring smile. He couldn't imagine a situation where his family might betray the Takmor house and their contracts favorably. Not within the next six months.

Was this just a theatrical way for Niffum to approve their match, despite Rasher's lack of benefit to the house?

No. As he studied the old man, he sensed that Niffum was in earnest. He honestly believed a moment would come when conditions would align to allow the bold plan. That meant he must be targeting the Takmors as the primi house that he wished to supplant to raise his own house from secondi to primi level.

Intrigue among the high houses who ruled the Rubric Empire from the Food Court was complex and often brutal. He didn't want anything to do with a plot to unseat a high house. The last time that happened, things got ugly and a lot of people's lives were ruined. The guilds tied to those houses would be affected, and there was a slim chance seats within the Pantryon of the gods itself could be upset.

When he glanced at Kitan, her cheeks flushed slightly, her beautiful eyes fixed upon him, seeming to swallow his vision. He would take the risk for her, and Niffum had to know it.

Niffum abruptly stood and adjusted his hat. "Consider my proposal, Rasher. Kitan, my dear, I will see you tonight for dinner."

"Of course, Father," she told him as they rose to bid him farewell.

Her father kissed her cheek, then turned and strode out of the cafe. Rasher watched him go, thunderstruck by the conversation. He'd originally approached Kitan on a dare while trying to make contacts with high houses, seeking sponsors for his paint battle team. Now she owned his heart.

And now another tightrope stretched before him. Could he walk it somehow to win her father's blessing, without destroying his own family?

"I thought I knew all of his plots," Kitan whispered.

"Do you think he could pull it off? Really unseat the Takmor house?" Even whispering the words made Rasher uneasy. If anyone overheard such a plot, the Takmors would send the full might of their bacon master fist against the conspirators. They would die in blood, their houses burned. He shivered and forced aside images of Kitan being cut down by ruthless assassins.

"I don't know. I have to do some digging. Promise me you won't agree to anything yet."

"That's an easy promise," he said with a smile. "But Kitan, what if there's no other way?"

He would approach his father if there was even a shred of hope that the plan might work. He wouldn't be able to help it.

Would that be enough? It had to be.

She kissed him suddenly, passionately, and he could feel her body quivering as she pressed against him. When she broke the kiss, she grinned at him, cheeks flushing, eyes shining bright. "We'll figure it out, my love. We're really going to get a chance to wed!"

He returned her smile, flush with joy. He'd never actually proposed, could not do so without her father's blessing, but now he knew without a doubt that she truly did love him. Kitan van Ihlget yur Lascoin loved him and wanted to marry him. The sun seemed to shine brighter, and his heart sang.

"Now that he's given us a chance, I won't let him back out," Rasher promised.

"We must tread carefully," she warned. "I have to go. I have a lunch party with Mother, but first I need to visit the Creamery."

"Say hello to your cousin for me," Rasher said.

He loved how Kitan always remembered to visit the foolish young man in the Harmful Sugars Addiction Recovery wing of the Creamery every week. The road to recovery could be long, but with family support, his chances were much improved. She volunteered even more time with the milk mages who ran the Creamery, visiting other patients dealing with deeper food maladies, those recovering from culinary accidents, or the poor souls afflicted by terrible ailments from Lahanasi, the evil god of disgusting foods.

He bet she'd have more fun visiting the hospital than the lunch event. He'd attended a few of the less formal social events with Kitan and didn't envy her. Everyone dressed with exquisite fashion, smiling and laughing together while plotting to stab each other in the back.

They left together. She turned right, while he turned left toward the Acropolis. As he strode down the cobbled street, he considered the crazy proposal Niffum had made. He didn't want to do it, which meant he had to come up with some kind of counter offer that might convince Kitan's father to approve their match, even without betraying the Takmor house.

In the meantime, he had a train to catch.

6

DEATH BY PANCAKE

Rasher dashed across the street, dodging between a couple of fine carriages taking high ladies to shopping or brunch parties. Releasing some of his much-diminished stores of bacon, he scampered up the side of the tallest building on the street. The stonework of the exterior of the four-story building gave his bacon-enhanced fingers easy purchase and he quickly reached the flat roof.

There he pulled a long length of stretchy rope from a box and shook out the lasso already set in the end.

Just in time. The distant whooshing of the air-powered train approached rapidly from the right, and within seconds the Reaper line express came into view around a distant manor house, sliding smoothly along its elevated track.

Every few minutes the train passed. A long line of sleek carriages, including both glass-enclosed passenger carriages as well as boxlike supply carriages, all painted various pastel hues. As the passenger cars whooshed past, some of the passengers stared at him, while others waved excitedly. This wasn't the first time he'd hitched a ride on the train. Rasher waved back but focused on the access ladder sticking above the top of the first supply carriage.

As it sped past, Rasher tossed the rope. The open lasso seemed to hang in the air as it gracefully arched across the gap and settled over the top of the ladder.

Rasher charged to the edge of the roof and jumped as high and far as he could toward the train as the loop of rope tightened around the ladder and the train yanked the rope forward. The abrupt pull would have still torn the rope from his hands if he hadn't wrapped it around them several times. He shouted with the thrill as he clung on with all his strength, reinforced by his recent feast and a couple slices of crispy bacon.

The pressure would have still been too much, but the rope was specially crafted by a vegetable shaman to increase its strength and elasticity so it didn't snap or rip his arms off. For a delicious heartbeat, the force yanked his arms to the cusp of dislocating his shoulders as the rope stretched to its uttermost length, then snapped forward again, catapulting him forward.

Rasher whooped as he soared up onto the last car, muscles quivering with that intangible thrill he could only feel in moments of great danger. He landed lightly on the smooth roof and enjoyed the rush of air as the thrill seeped deep into his bones, reversing the weakening effect of his last blood phobia episode and restoring the full might of his bacon powers.

Feeling revitalized, Rasher laughed aloud, again confident he would find a way to win Kitan and his place as a respected bacon master. If he could find the recipe that could impart that same thrill, he wouldn't need to constantly risk death or serious injury.

Everyone had to make sacrifices.

As the train sped across the wide plaza before East Gate of the Acropolis, he decided he needed to add a variant of that to Rasher's Rules of Engagement. His Rules had grown to nearly fifty and were becoming a staple of his training wisdom. As he considered the new rule, he glanced out over the distant majesty of the great city of Afitur and spotted a courier gracefully banking around a palace. Tiny in the distance, the man looked like a great bird.

Rasher needed to get his hands on one of those man-sized kites the couriers used. Traversing the network of powerful winds maintained by the spice wizards, the corps of fast-delivery couriers kept all the high houses informed far faster than even sugar-enhanced couriers on the ground. The only faster methods for communicating were the shout towers or direct spice wizard to spice wizard air tunnels, but those were far more expensive, and in the case of the shout towers, easily overheard.

The train whisked over the wide plaza in front of East Gate of the Acropolis. The plaza was busy with early morning traffic, lorded over by a twenty-foot-tall statue of the drupe god, Tohum. Made of pale granite with a swirl pattern that always reminded Rasher of fresh autumn wild rice soup, it looked like a giant man, dressed in a fashionable suit, carrying a large basket of seeds.

Rasher waved to the guards positioned at East Gate, far below, checking incoming visitors. The Acropolis wall stretched away in either direction, tall and wide, made of huge blocks of dark granite. A token force of guards patrolled in pairs along the wall, or stood watch atop the high towers that flanked the gate.

The train whisked just over the top of the wall, its track leading across the flat rooftops of the four-story buildings marching down the main thoroughfare beyond. Known as the God's Banquet, the wide street was lined with statues of the various gods of the Pantryon. Rasher saluted Domuz, patron god of bacon masters, portrayed as a jolly, chubby fellow seated with a tankard in one hand. He also saluted Karides, patron goddess of seafood shamans for Kitan. Fashioned into a beautiful woman rising from an ocean wave, she somehow portrayed both the grandeur and threat of the sea.

The Acropolis was built in an orderly grid pattern of streets, each one flanked by long rows of functional military buildings. The train would continue to its terminus near the center of the Acropolis, the great square facing the Heart of the Reapers. Rasher didn't need to go that far, so he jogged forward, pulled his rope from the ladder, and watched for his stop.

There.

Rasher jumped, aiming for a long, sloping awning that ran down the side of one of the buildings at the corner of the God's Banquet with Guild Way. He'd made the jump several times and knew he could slide down the heavy canvas awning without injury.

This time he missed.

"Fish sticks," Rasher cursed as he jumped, immediately realizing he'd launched half a second too soon. Instead of a thrilling ride down the awning, he was about to crash at high speed into the brick side of the building.

Rasher released twenty slices of crispy bacon, nearly all of his remaining bacon stores, and poured in some extra sizzle from breakfast. Bacon exploded through his system like savory lightning, and he shouted with the pure joy of it as bacon rippled through him, hardening his muscles, joints, and bones, making him momentarily impervious to just about everything.

Then he slammed into the side of the building with an impact that felt like it must have rocked the entire world. He hung for a second against the stone, a Rasher-sized outline marked in the pale face of the building, then slid down the wall.

Rasher pushed off so he didn't have to scrape his face all the way down, and landed hard in the street next to a pair of arguing sergeants. The two men cursed and jumped back in surprise as Rasher staggered, leaning on the building for support as he oriented himself and made sure he hadn't managed to break every bone in his body after all.

A young woman in a private's cap rushed up, grinning. "Captain Dilskin, that was amazing! What do you call that move?"

"Death by pancake," he muttered.

"Ooh," she gushed, suitably impressed as she held out a piece of parchment and a quill pen, dripping with ink. "Can I have your autograph?"

One of the sergeants he'd nearly landed on barked a laugh. "You'll run out of paper, kid if you ask for autographs from every fool who tries to kill himself."

Rasher took the quill and parchment and signed his name in grand, flowing strokes. "I doubt anyone else tries to kill themself with as much flair."

"Fair point," the other sergeant said, and the two departed, talking about fools and their death wishes. The young private took the paper, careful not to smudge the ink, and said, "Thank you! I watch all your paint battle games. The Bacon Bits are my favorite team."

"I like meeting smart fans," Rasher said, tipping his hat, before excusing himself.

He turned north up Guild Way, thanking Domuz for higher bacon powers. Most bacon masters would need a few days to recharge that impervious ability, but practice made the process more efficient. Rasher had used it so often, he'd be ready to go by mid-afternoon.

Guild Way led north through the Acropolis toward the distant sector housing the various guild palaces. The streets were all paved with stone, perfectly flat and straight, flanked on both sides by identical somber stone buildings that housed warehouses, supply depots, and craftsmen shops. The air inside the Acropolis was clean, but as he turned into a smaller street in the auxiliary forces sector, the hot-metal scent of nearby forges hung heavy in the air.

As Rasher crossed one of the small plazas marking the intersection of smaller streets, he passed a long line of men and women queued up to buy energy bites from a cart vendor. The scent of the fresh-baked peanut butter cookies wafted to him, gently enticing him to join the line.

He did not slow. The cookies were enhanced by confectioners to boost energy for several hours. They were extremely popular, but Rasher only had to glance toward the small fountain in the center of the square to remind himself why he wasn't interested. A young private stood there, rocking slowly from side to side. His eyes looked glazed, and he was muttering to himself as he sniffed something from a tiny pouch.

Sugar addict. They were rare in the Acropolis, but common in many parts of the greater city. Did the long lines of people eager for their daily cookie fix not recognize how easily they too could fall to a debilitating sugar addiction?

They probably told themselves it would never happen to them, or that the benefit outweighed the risks. Of course, he had bacon to fuel his speed, strength, and agility of mind and body. He couldn't imagine living a stale life without the glory of bacon infusing his every waking moment.

Other vendor carts lined the edges of that plaza. One sold creativity crullers, delicious fried pastries imbued by the muffin mages to heat up creativity for a full hour. Another sold fried potato bites imbued by vegetable shamans to improve balance, while a third peddled fortune cookies supposedly blessed by the hand of Arkadas, goddess of prophecy.

A pretty young woman was handing out sample fortune cookies, and she pressed one into Rasher's hand, despite his objections. She flashed a bright smile and said, "Enjoy it, Captain. What harm can getting a peek at your future do?"

It wasn't worth the effort to argue, so he thanked her and cracked open the cookie as he walked. It was soft and warm, fresh from the oven, but he didn't know what sugars might have been used in the baking, so resisted the urge to eat it.

The little note wrapped inside the cookie said, "Expect big changes."

He chuckled as he headed into his training team headquarters. What a useless fortune.

The paint battle training team headquarters was located on the third floor of one of the long stone buildings. His five squads were already there, making plans for upcoming training sessions and the next round of paint battle games. Most of their generous space was split into five large rooms where each squad worked on their various training agendas. Rasher called for a meeting with his sergeants in his office.

As captain of the fist, his office was far larger than the others, situated against the front wall, with a wide window overlooking the narrow street. Beside his desk, cluttered with papers and scrolls, the room included a conference table with six comfortable wooden chairs and a chalk board, covered with a drawing of the latest arena configuration.

His sergeants quickly assembled. Next to Bungey's thick-chested bulk, Volaille looked downright skinny. The tall, slender woman wore her shoulder-length, sandy-colored hair in a simple braid that hung to her shoulders. Originally from Occiput, she had the black eyes of her people and led the unarmed combat training squad.

Stolon sat next to her. He was the oldest of the trainers, heavily muscled, black hair cropped short under his legion-issue cap. He was from Oxter and led the sword training squad. The other two sergeants, natives of Rubric, were both very tall. Jocose was their archer, a good-natured man who was the team's practical joker. Kaets was wide-shouldered, more serious, and he led the axes and hammers squad.

"Captain, that was a brilliant bout this morning," Bungey grinned.

Volaille added, "Ran that cat from hocks to withers."

"Still can't understand half of your Occiput slang," Kaets grumbled.

"You could if you tried listening," Stolon said softly.

"I think she meant captain should have hit him harder," Jocose grinned, trying to diffuse the tension, as usual.

Volaille shook her head, glaring briefly at Kaets. "You barbarians don't understand anything."

"We understand that Captain nearly won his transfer to the Reaper team," Bungey interjected.

Rasher forced a smile. "Didn't work out. Looks like you won't get my post yet, Bungey."

They laughed, but the laughter trailed off too soon, replaced by an awkward silence. Bungey cleared his throat and asked, "Captain, what happened? I thought that last recipe looked promising."

Only the sergeants knew his secret and had eagerly helped him search for recipes and experiment with them. They'd witnessed most of the failures, some of which had been pretty remarkable.

The last one they'd tried was a promising vegetable shaman recipe that altered gravity slightly. It hadn't helped him avoid fainting but had momentarily boosted his jumping to unbelievable levels. He planned to use that one instead of the rope next time he tried to catch the train.

The sound of running feet thundered on the outer stairs, and a thin teen, dressed as a courier, barged into the common room and rushed to his office. The lad wore a full courier wig and wide-brimmed hat. The wig was a long, dark brown affair secured at the ends to snaps on the shoulders of his jacket. Message tubes ran down both sides of the wig in close-packed stacks, like hard-sided curlers.

The courier snapped a salute and pulled a message scroll from one of the tubes in his wig. "Legion-wide alert, sir."

As soon as Rasher took the scroll, the courier bounded away.

"Haven't seen a legion-wide alert in five years," Stolon muttered as everyone leaned close. Rasher never had. He broke the seal, the official legion emblem of a black butcher knife crossed with a red sword on a field of white.

The message was so surprising, it shattered his good mood like a cookie dropped from the roof of the train.

7

ENTER THE APOCALYPSE

The message was brief, and Rasher whistled softly as he read it. "This must have just arrived via garlic tower."

"Ehverr's been attacked?" Volaille gasped.

Bungey leaned closer, frowning. "Can those numbers be right?"

"I've never heard of a horde that big," Kaets agreed.

"But how could they get all the way to Ehverr?" Jocose exclaimed, his smile missing for once. "Tookus should have been the first target."

Rasher read the note again. "Legion-wide alert. The city of Ehverr is under siege from a Gloaming horde numbering in the tens of thousands. The city is standing, but heavy battle is joined. No other cities in the area report sightings of glowan monsters or horde activity. All legions stand at ready reserve."

Rasher said, "It seems they circumvented Tookus completely." His mind raced as he considered the map of the empire. Ehverr was a huge metropolis, well fortified, but should not have been a primary target from the glowan. The much smaller Tookus was a heavily fortified outpost, specifically designed to take the brunt of a Gloaming invasion.

"Think they commandeered the Sugar and Spice?" Volaille asked.

"They've never done that before," Bungey protested.

That was true, but it sounded like they were facing a horde intent on doing new things. That was a scary thought. If they had indeed gained access to the Sugar and Spice Express and managed to run it, they could transport a sizable horde across the empire in a matter of days.

Rasher said, "They won't stay at ready reserve for long. The legions will begin an immediate mobilization. I bet they'll commandeer every express car and try to mobilize by tomorrow at first light."

He bet the courier who had summoned Sumwinkle from the training arena in such haste had carried the same news. The Reapers were no doubt already forming battle plans with General Sigha Nide and her command staff. This kind of emergency was exactly why they existed, after all.

Bungey grimaced. "Looks like our schedule is about to free up."

Indeed, they were legion trainers, not legion regulars. They were not needed during an active campaign. When the legions mobilized and marched forth to succor Ehverr, Rasher and his team would remain in the Acropolis.

Their training schedule would grind to a halt, the upcoming paint battle tournament would have to be postponed, and they'd have to spend their days making up busy work.

How the deviled egg was he going to accomplish anything important? With the legions gone, he'd get no chance to win another paint battle tournament and maybe win a lucrative new sponsorship that might sway Kitan's father to consider an alternative to his plot.

He would figure out something. So he said, "Let's focus on work, people. Send runners to each of the units scheduled for training today and tomorrow."

"They're all going to cancel," Stolon guessed.

"Perhaps, but until they do, they haven't. If the mobilization is delayed for any reason, we have useful training options."

"Glowan battle plans," Bungey guessed.

Rasher nodded. "I doubt there's more than a handful of soldiers in the entire Acropolis who have actually faced a living glowan monster. They'll know the theory, but we haven't run any glowan drills in months. Dust off the plans and work up a schedule."

They all saluted and rushed back to their teams.

Rasher stepped to the window and noted the abrupt increase in traffic. People rushed past with purpose. The entire feel of the Acropolis became charged as word spread, and units raced to prepare for the expected mobilization.

The Reapers of the Apocalypse and their four elite legions formed the backbone of the Rubric fast-response forces. Their primary duty was to remain always vigilant, ready to respond to apocalyptic threats at the drop of a frying pan. A Gloaming invasion from the dark forests of Whisternfeet was exactly the type of threat they stood ready and eager to fight.

Rasher spent the rest of the afternoon keeping his team focused on developing drills they could use to simulate small group battles against various glowan forces. As expected, all of the scheduled trainings canceled. He hoped that once clear orders were issued they'd find ways to squeeze in a few anyway.

Strangely, no new orders came before their workday ended. Rasher walked the streets of the Acropolis, listening. Everyone was talking about the expected mobilization and what forces they might face when they reached Ehverr. No new specifics about the hordes had gotten through the garlic towers as far as Rasher had heard.

Huge wagons trundled past, heavy-loaded with gear, gingersnap wheels whispering, while entire platters of heavily armored legionaries quick-marched in tight formations, fully kitted out with sword, shield, and spear. No doubt all of the guild palaces were scrambling to finish new batches of battle-ready foodstuffs to supplement the legion's magical arsenal.

Entire warehouses of battle cuisine were always packed to bursting, ready to go. The legions could march forth on any given day with a full complement of their most powerful battle cuisine.

Everyone looked determined, and an undertone of excitement rippled through the air in invisible waves. The Reapers and their legions had not sallied forth in their full might since the most recent Reaper team was chosen, nearly a dozen years ago. They were ready and eager to once again cast the looming apocalypse from the realm.

They hadn't faced the Gloaming hordes for two generations. The glowan monsters who made up the hordes were deadly and mysterious but rarely ventured out of the endless dark forests of Whisternfeet in large numbers.

Eventually, Rasher ended up at the Bubble and Squeak, sitting at a small table in the front tavern, surrounded by buzzing conversation. The atmosphere was completely different than the previous night. The gaming tables were subdued, while crowds packed around the bar, excitedly discussing the dangers of the hordes.

"So what kind of glowan do you think we'll be facing?" asked one eager young soldier who was so fresh-faced, Rasher had to wonder if he might be drinking milk. The young soldier's question triggered a new round of the same endless debate that had been raging all day, and again all the darkest legends of the deadliest, mysterious monsters were trotted out as fact.

"Hellhounds, no doubt," muttered a stocky sergeant at the bar, taking a long draught from his ale.

"Lots of goblins," another soldier piped in.

While the conversation heated up, Rasher wondered for the hundredth time how the Gloaming hordes avoided the border fortresses. Luckily Ehverr housed the headquarters of the Fathar family, which fielded one of Rubric's strongest armies. They should be able to hold until support arrived.

"But what kind of goblins?" Asked another soldier. "There's dozens of them."

Valid point, but in a way it didn't matter. There were many types of glowan, and many of the nightmarish creatures were lumped under the generic term of goblins. They tended to be the most human-like, with the least amount of dark magic, and tended to make up the bulk of the ground troops of any horde.

The Reaper legions knew how to deal with them. Killing them was not much different than killing other men. They were not the worst threat the legions would face.

A burly, ruddy-jowled lieutenant muttered, "I just hope they don't have rock trolls."

That triggered another round of raised glasses and tankards, and Rasher joined in. Rock trolls were massive beasts, slow and rather dim-witted. Kind of like a slow-motion avalanche. A mountainside didn't have to be smart to crush you.

Some people claimed that they were actual piles of animated rock, given life by dark Gloaming magic. Others claimed they were merely thick-skinned elemental creatures that could still be banished if smashed apart enough. Rasher had seen enough records to suggest there might be multiple types, and he just hoped they never had to face any.

"It's the changelings and the Bitter Court we need to worry about," said the first sergeant at the bar to more nods.

Problem was, every legend featured different powerful glowan. There was no way to know ahead of time which types they might be facing. Changelings were a common occurrence in many tales, and Rasher mouthed a silent prayer the legions would not have to face them.

The only good thing about changelings was that they usually could only take one human form and not appear as anyone's random comrade. But they could look like a cat one second, a lion the next, and a giant bear a second later.

Identifying changelings was often the hardest part. They were spies and infiltrators and assassins. One interesting fact he'd picked up that day was that apparently most glowan hated wearing hats. Ruzgar, their mysterious god of the evening winds, was a jealous god and hated his creatures donning the symbols of human connection with the Pantryon.

So far no orders had arrived mandating the changing of hats, but it might happen. Rasher patted his own golden frying pan hat, hating the thought of having to swap it for something lesser.

Talk turned to other glowan, including wraiths, slaughter hags, and even possessed souls. As important as the topic might be, Rasher found it kind of pointless. They could talk about glowan all day, but none of that mattered until they received hard facts.

The debate looked like it would last for another hour, but the packed room was starting to feel claustrophobic. Rasher downed the rest of his drink and stared at his empty glass, feeling unusually gloomy.

He'd have to go jump off a building or something to brighten his mood.

Despite his personal problems, the legions had to march. When the orders came, the legions would face the glowan and liberate Ehverr. They would triumph.

They always did.

Rasher had always been proud of his position as a trainer, helping to prepare the legions for the battles that would determine the fate of the empire as they fought to push back yet another apocalypse. He'd never really thought about the fact that he would not take part in their campaigns and would never taste their victories. His team would get to do nothing but cheer the victorious legions when they returned.

For the first time, he wanted more, even though he could not fight in real battles with his condition. He had thought he was reconciled with his life.

Only if that life included Kitan.

So he rose, left some coins on the table, and headed outside.

That was when he heard the shouting.

8

CHICKENS AND SHOVELS

R asher ran toward the sound of shouting, using just a bit of crispy bacon. Maybe he'd get to enjoy a fight. That would be better than jumping across rooftops. He'd eaten a glorious bacon quiche for lunch and ordered in twenty slices of bacon to munch while working with his team that afternoon, replenishing much of his bacon reserves.

Big fights were rare in the Acropolis, but everyone was so keyed up with news of impending battle, frayed tempers were to be expected. A riot was not.

Half a block away, the street emptied into one of the larger squares that dotted the area, with streets emptying in from all four sides. The plaza was about fifty yards across, linking two southern quadrants. To the east lay blocks full of barracks, while to the west reared larger officers' quarters. Statues and fountains marked the borders of each of the streets entering the plaza.

A large group of angry men and women had gathered in the center, clustered around a tall, three-tiered central fountain. There was an enticing feeling of impending violence in the air.

As he rushed closer, he was surprised to see a woman in the center of the crowd scurry right up the tall fountain with the nimbleness of a bacon master. As he drew closer, he recognized her hat. Brown leather with a pointy front and upswept sides that flared into the wings of some kind of raptor bird, it clearly identified her as a meat mage.

She was shouting down at the soldiers surrounding her temporary perch and even flipped one man the chicken leg. Maybe it was a trick of the light, but for that instant when she flashed the obscene gesture, her fingers really looked like chicken toes. She seemed to be trying awfully hard to get someone to stick a knife in her ribs.

As Rasher reached the edges of the crowd, he realized she was quite young, probably not even twenty years old. He pushed through the crowd, shouting for someone to tell him what was going on.

One breathless woman exclaimed, "That woman was fighting with those soldiers, and I heard one of them say she's a traitor! We're going to bring her in."

That kind of vigilante spirit was usually lacking among soldiers, who preferred letting someone higher up make decisions.

Rasher tried to shout above the din, but his voice was lost in the tumult. He spotted one soldier near the front of the crowd holding a bloody hand, and another one rubbing at his eyes.

Another soldier brandishing a drawn sword shouted, "Get down here, traitor!"

"You're the traitor, and I bet your mother weeps every night for having birthed such a moron," the girl shot back. She pulled something out of a leather pouch at her hip and threw it.

It wasn't meat. It was an egg.

The egg caught the sword-wielding fellow in the face and splattered gooey yolk all over his eyes. The man cursed and stumbled back, pawing at his eyes in the same way that other soldier had been.

The gathering was proving more and more interesting.

Rasher had almost reached the front of the crowd when someone threw a rock. It just missed the girl's head, but that unleashed a flood. Other people started throwing everything they had at hand, from rocks to knives to a couple helmets, and even one boot.

"Stop!" Rasher shouted, fearing to see the girl impaled, cut to ribbons, or bludgeoned off her perch, then stomped to death by the angry crowd. She'd really worked them into a spectacular fury.

She jumped.

Vaulting off the top tier of the fountain, more than ten feet above their heads, she leaped remarkably high, clearing the flurry of missiles. The move seemed reckless, doomed to drop her so hard onto the angry crowd that she'd be guaranteed to break bones or injure herself badly.

She didn't fall.

She soared.

Rasher whistled softly as others gaped, watching the girl's jump turn into a glide. She wasn't exactly flying, but she wasn't falling either. It was more like an extremely graceful float as she passed over the heads of the stunned crowd and settled to the pavement on the far side.

She hadn't found wisdom up in the air, so instead of running, she drew a pair of daggers and made a beckoning motion. "Anyone who wants to insult me or my grandmother, issue your challenge now or admit you're cowards."

Rasher decided he liked this girl. Trying to commit suicide by angry mob was the kind of big thinking he appreciated.

So as the crowd gathered their courage to attack, Rasher released a quarter slice of bacon, using it to imbue his voice with that imperceptible extra tone of authority that only bacon could convey, and shouted in his loudest, commanding voice, "Stand down!"

Silence swatted the crowd hard as Rasher pushed through to face the young woman. Even she looked mollified, her daggers lowered to her sides, but she did not sheath them.

By her coloring, she looked like a compatriot of Taradiddle. Her tanned skin was almost as bronzed as his own, despite his additional bacon darkening. Her hair was a shade lighter brown than his, and unlike his blue eyes, her green ones seemed to blaze with anger.

"You trying to die tonight?" Rasher asked, using his gruff drill-sergeant voice.

The soldier with the bloody hand pushed to the front of the crowd and said, "She's a traitor, Captain. Arrest her."

Careful to avoid looking at the blood on the man's hand, Rasher raised one eyebrow and the man quickly amended, "I mean, I think we should. I recommend you, ah, consider arresting her."

Other, wiser soldiers, who remained hidden within the crowd shouted agreement that she was a traitor.

Rasher held up a hand for quiet and turned to the woman, who was scowling, her knives again raised. "I take it you disagree with their assessment."

She spat on the ground with a practiced flair and pointed one of her daggers at the bloody soldier. "Of course I'm not a traitor. This idiot can't think deeply enough to solve his way out of an empty room."

The soldier growled and took a threatening step toward her, but Rasher stopped him with a single look. "Can someone please tell me why you consider this meat mage, an accredited member of one of the guilds, a traitor?"

Silence greeted him so he turned back to the bloody soldier and added, "Well?"

The man shuffled, suddenly less sure of himself, then gestured with his bloody hand, making Rasher's head swim dangerously. "Ah, she turned her nose into a beak."

"Because you were punching it, fool," the girl interjected.

That should teach him to think before punching a meat mage. It was rare for one so young to have mastered the technique of partial transformation. She must have a powerful talent. Rasher would ask her what recipes she used, and what raptor meat worked best when he had the chance.

The soldier added loudly, "And her name is Kucheesa!"

Rasher blinked. That was not a common name and for good reason. Someone had famously tarnished it a couple generations ago. Still, a stupid name wasn't enough to convict someone of treason.

"And?" he prodded.

"And her grandmother's name was Kucheesa too," the soldier added, seeming more sure of himself. "Kucheesa the Reaper traitor."

That riled up the crowd again. Rasher sighed and glanced back at the girl, who stood tall, her chin high and shoulders back, as if daring him to also comment on her name.

He waited, and finally she huffed out a breath and said, "Yes, my grandmother was named Kucheesa. She was a famous cheese wizard and a Reaper."

"A traitor," growled the bloody soldier.

Kucheesa raised her knives, her face a mask of rage.

Rasher held up a hand for her to stand down, and amazingly she obeyed. He turned to the soldier and said, "Really? You blame someone for the misdeeds of a grandparent? Every family's got someone they don't like to talk about."

"True, but my idiot uncle never betrayed his Reaper team and fought for Hilekar," the man retorted.

He had a point, and the mention of the god of the apocalypse riled up the crowd even more. Angry mutterings resumed, and the feeling turned ugly again.

Thankfully, a patrol of Acropolis Watch trotted into the square and immediately moved toward the angry crowd. That was enough for most of the assembled soldiers to disperse.

For her part, Kucheesa reluctantly sheathed her daggers and feigned an innocent look that totally failed.

With an angry grunt, the bloody soldier turned and stomped away, followed by the two men with egged faces. Kucheesa started to leave, but Rasher said, "Hold on a minute."

She turned to face him, again stiff and ready to fight. "What do you want?"

He raised that single eyebrow again and she was wise enough to amend, "Captain, sir."

He stepped a bit closer, waved the sergeant in charge of the Watch away, and asked softly, "Have you never been challenged about your grandmother before?"

She glared, which seemed to be her default expression, and said between clenched teeth, "All my life."

"I would've thought after so much experience you would've realized it doesn't help to antagonize people who are going to hate you for your grandmother's name, regardless of what you say."

He almost said it was a bad idea to egg people on, but since she seemed partial to throwing eggs, it didn't seem like the right word choice.

"What would a bacon master know about dealing with people hating you?" she demanded, glaring at his hat. "Everyone loves you."

True. Bacon imbued its practitioners with extra charisma and an intangible likableness that made them natural leaders. He was surprised she projected such hostility. Most people from their home country loved bacon masters. They'd won the country tons of respect. Other countries absorbed by the Rubric Empire often struggled more to win general acceptance.

Still, it was not uncommon for folks from any of the vassal nations to face discrimination in the capital. He could understand that frustration, and hoped to help her calm down.

"I usually don't start conversations by throwing eggs in people's faces and baiting them to punch me in the beak."

She snorted, not appreciating the attempt at levity. "I'm tired of people judging me, and judging my grandmother."

"That may be true, but do you think it's wise to try fighting that battle right now with everyone tense for deployment?"

He could tell she didn't want to admit it, but she finally sighed and at least pretended to look contrite. For about four seconds.

"I promise to try to be more careful," she said as if she had recited the same empty promise ten thousand times before. He could imagine her saying it to her father over and over and over again. He wondered if she'd ever fooled him.

He doubted it.

"Please try."

A whooping shout from across the square drew them around. An old man with spindly limbs, wearing a tunic that was far too short for him, sandals with straps that wound halfway up his legs, and no hat was sitting astride a statue of a rearing stallion.

How had the old fellow climbed up that far? He looked ancient and should have been walking with a cane, not performing stunts like a really old, wrinkled version of Kucheesa.

The old man waved his hand above his head, as if wielding an invisible sword or a hat and whooped again.

The soldiers of the Watch headed toward him, and the sergeant growled, "How did you get through the gate, you old fool? You've been banned from the Acropolis."

Rasher should just let it go, but couldn't help following the Watch. He was surprised that Kucheesa followed along with them.

"He's crazy," she commented.

"Says the girl who just tried to instigate a riot."

She scowled. "I'm not a girl."

He nearly said, "Then try acting like an adult."

Kucheesa's expression turned curious and she added, "I didn't know the Watch issued shovels."

Rasher followed her gaze and noticed another officer of the Watch entering the square. He wore a centurion's helm, as well as the shiny steel breastplate of a knight rather than the standard chainmail of the Watch. Although he wore a short sword on his belt, he did indeed have a shovel strapped to his back.

"I doubt it's standard issue," Rasher said, really intrigued. He'd never heard of anyone carrying a shovel as a weapon.

The knight was huge, a full head taller than Rasher, with shoulders that strained the limits of his oversized armor. His helm covered his hair, but he glanced at Kucheesa and Rasher with classic Rubric dark brown eyes. As they drew closer, he said in a pleasant, deep voice, "I witnessed your skill with the egg."

"Oh, um, thanks," she replied, more flustered by him than she had been by the angry mob.

"Your father was never very good at math, was he?" the knight asked.

"What?" Kucheesa asked, blinking in surprise.

"Nimble fingers leave the mind free to wander, but it's good to keep it tethered close to home sometimes," the knight commented. Then he gave her a polite nod and strode to where the other Watch guards were trying to coax the old man down.

"What was he talking about?" Kucheesa demanded, scowling after the strange soldier.

Rasher shrugged, suppressing a laugh. That exchange was so weird, he wasn't sure what to make of it. The Acropolis Watch were supposed to be chosen from among the best soldiers in the Afitur city guard, and a centurion knight would usually rank among their highest officers.

The old man on the stallion statue whooped again and shouted, "The apocalypse is coming! As foretold, doom is at the door. You can feel it. You know it, and this time you'll all admit I was right."

"Who is this guy?" Rasher demanded.

"I am the voice of the future," the old man shouted, then leaped off the back of the horse. It looked like he was trying to duplicate Kucheesa's graceful glide.

He failed, and ended up flopping loudly onto his face.

Luckily, he landed on grass and not the pavement. The guards pulled the groaning old fellow to his feet, where he wobbled, spitting a mouthful of blood and wiping grass and dust from his face.

"I warned you that you'd get arrested if you started spouting this foolishness again," the sergeant growled at the old man.

"You'll be singing a different tune when you realize I'm right," the old man shot back, cackling with insane laughter.

The sergeant looked to Rasher and shrugged as if to say, "See what I have to deal with every day?"

The shovel-wielding knight interjected. "Sergeant, just escort him outside of the Acropolis. We have too much to deal with to babysit him."

As a guard started pulling him away, the old man suddenly stiffened and look from the shovel knight to Rasher, and then Kucheesa. He studied them with a wild intensity that made Rasher suddenly uneasy.

The man cackled again and said, "Oh, sometimes it's even more fun being right than I imagined."

The guard dragged him away and Rasher glanced at Kucheesa, who shrugged and said, "You know, most of my life I thought I had the worst grandparents ever."

9

The Mixing Bowl of Divine Intervention

Early the next morning, Rasher had just sent a courier with a message to Kitan, asking if she could meet him for lunch when he received another legion-wide scroll. He expected it to contain the much-anticipated orders for the legion to mobilize, and his sergeants crowded around as he broke the seal.

Instead, it contained orders for a general assembly in the plaza facing the Heart of the Acropolis at eight bells. Attendance was mandatory, and everyone was to wear their parade uniforms.

"Why order a general assembly?" Bungey asked. "That'll just delay the mobilization."

"Maybe the Reapers want to explain about the hordes," Volaille guessed.

Maybe, but it was still unusual. There were a full fourteen Reapers in Reaper Team Twelve, which was widely regarded as one of the most well-balanced and powerful of any Reaper team. Led by the famous spice wizard, Absquatch Youlate, the team included senior wizards and warriors from every guild, all proven through years of training and practice and heroic feats.

They were each famous in their own right. United together as the Reapers of the Apocalypse, they were the best of the best. They would lead the Reaper legions forth to battle and glory. Apparently they wanted to really mark the occasion before launching a new campaign.

It would be a rare treat to see the full might of the legions assembled, so Rasher said, "Get your squads into parade uniforms on the double. We'll meet back here in half an hour and head to the Heart together."

Less than an hour later, Rasher stood at the front of his Fist, ordered in five columns, each led by their sergeant. They stood in formation in the great square facing the Heart, the grand headquarters of the Reapers. The square was packed with the full force of the four Reaper legions. Eight thousand soldiers stood in tight-packed ranks, all facing north toward the Heart.

Rasher's team stood with the other auxiliary units in the southwest corner of the square, farthest from the Heart, but the sight of it still inspired him. The huge, unique building rose four stories above the plaza, shaped like a giant feasting table fit for the gods themselves. The massive wooden pillars that formed the legs stood on each corner, carved with flowing images of the gods of the Pantryon.

The roof was formed by an enormous wooden tabletop that extended several feet beyond the walls all around, while the space under the giant table was filled entirely by a solid, stone building, its front face broken by regular windows, with dozens of banners flapping in the gentle breeze seeming to wave at everyone.

Rasher stood taller at the thought, infused with pride and purpose. The Heart was the beacon of hope for every person living in the Acropolis, from the mighty Reapers who lived there, to the lowliest private or support staff. Their entire purpose was to stand between the empire and the threat of apocalypse, with the Reapers at the fore. Their very lives were intertwined inseparably with their duty and focus, all centered upon the Heart and the mission of the heroes who made it their home.

Just standing in the square facing the Heart reinforced Rasher's optimism. How could they fear any threat while united together at the Heart? His problems seemed to shrink in the presence of the legions all standing united in that square. He only wished he could approach closer to the Heart.

Unfortunately, the square was packed so full, even if he were allowed to approach, moving through the amassed legions would be difficult. Beyond the legions, standing closest to the Heart were the full might of the guilds. Standing at the right-most edge were the spice wizards, their many-pocketed hats flapping slightly in a steady breeze that flowed constantly around them.

Beside them, the ranks of the muffin mages glowed faintly crimson, and flickers of fire danced about their muffin-shaped hats. The nearby confectioners in their floppy, multi-tiered cake hats had come prepared and were already extending long, slender poles with fresh marshmallows over the ranks of the muffin mages. Several were already browning nicely, although one burst into open flame as it dipped too low, and the confectioner pulled it back to blow it out. Rasher imagined his look of chagrin.

The seafood shaman ranks glowed faintly blue-green, and glittering splashes of water danced between the tall crowns of their hats, catching the bright morning light. If only Kitan was a member of the Acropolis branch, she could have joined the assembly and he could have seen her afterward.

Apparently the vegetable shamans had prepared a special anti-gravity recipe for the morning because they each bobbed several inches into the air before settling back down as the next in line levitated up in turn. The effect was like a living wave moving back and forth down their ranks.

The meat mages and milk mages stood next, but displayed no active recipes, while wisps of steam floated up above the coffee-pot-shaped hats of the small but extremely popular guild of coffee wizards. Rasher even spied some of the enormous, gaudy hats of the wardrobe wizards.

And standing in front of them all were the chefs, their tall toque hats worn proudly. The sight of the full might of the guilds on display lent the assembly a more festive air, and the mood in the square was eager and full of anticipation.

The square was ringed with other command and administrative buildings, all towering, four-story edifices designed to look like other furniture in the world's biggest kitchen. One was built to look like a pantry cupboard, complete with great wooden doors fastened to the front facade. Another looked like an oven, its front covered in cast iron. Others included a giant chopping block, food preparation counters, and even one hung with giant copper-bottomed pots all down the front face.

Standing in the Heart, glancing at the unique architecture, with the full might of the legions and guilds on display, Rasher could imagine the gods themselves descending to join them for a feast. Each of the grand buildings proudly flew the banners of every previous Reaper team, celebrating their unbroken successes for the past eleven generations.

Each team of Reapers was chosen to lead the legions for a single generation, their numbers slowly shifting as Reapers died or grew too old and were replaced by new ones. Grand statues of the captains of previous Reaper teams ringed the perimeter. Rasher scanned them, drawing renewed inspiration from his favorite stories of their heroic deeds. They had stood tall against every danger that threatened apocalyptic end to the Rubric Empire.

On the northwest corner of the plaza, flanking the Heart, stood the statue of Kaszanka Kumquat, the famous muffin mage who had called down the very fires of the gods upon the great rebel uprising in Taradiddle. On the east side of the Heart stood the statue of Orgulous Skiff, the confectioner who led his Reapers in a famously daring assault against raiders from the Effluvium Sea, addicting their leadership to his enhanced truffles.

Then there was the mysterious legend of William the Wet, the rare seafood shaman Reaper captain. He had led his team to victory against the Schlep Confederacy in their first major confrontation with that sinister empire, somehow crossing the Effluvium Sea without using a boat.

Of course, Rasher's favorite story was that of Smoot Blatherskite, the bacon master who had single-handedly defeated a Bitter-Court glowan queen and her entire entourage. A master of the highest levels of bacon powers, he'd led his team on the only incursion into Whisternfeet where they'd battled the largest Gloaming horde ever seen.

Every generation claimed their team was the best ever assembled, but Rasher firmly believed like everyone else in the plaza that Reaper Team Twelve exceeded them all.

"Here they come," Volaille hissed, drawing everyone's attention to the front.

A wide, wooden porch floated into view, lifting off the tabletop roof of the Heart. As long as the entire front face of the building, it slowly descended in a whirlwind of air and fire. The classified recipe was a new one, mixing spices and rocket muffins in a revolutionary way to produce steady thrust.

The assembled legions began clapping and cheering, and Rasher and his fist joined in. The sight of that porch descending in stately majesty was truly inspiring. What had they to fear from a horde of monsters when the Reapers had such mighty recipes to draw from?

The long porch settled into position in front of the Heart with a soft thud, landing perfectly on the support beams. At the same time, a great inverted wave of water erupted off the roof of the pot rack admin building and flowed over the square, hovering above the porch and forming a huge, round sphere.

The outer surface of the water smoothed to a glassy sheen, and then it began reflecting the view of the crowd of officers and officials standing on the porch. That view magnified down to the central group until they looked ten times as large, making it easy for everyone to see the proceedings. Rasher spotted General Sigha Nide and her entire command staff. She looked grim, as always, her helm freshly polished, armor gleaming.

Strangely, the entire hero finder team stood among them. They were responsible for nominating candidates for Reaper selection, easily identifiable by their tall black hats with extra-wide brims and no adornment. Usually they only participated in assemblies where new Reaper teams were nominated.

"Where are the Reapers?" Stolon asked.

Rasher hadn't even noticed that the Reapers were not standing among the other officers.

"Maybe they've already mobilized," Kaets suggested.

That seemed odd. Why call for a full assembly if the Reapers weren't going to lead it?

Rasher expected the general or one of her legion commanders to address the assembled legions, but instead a rather timid-looking fellow in the uniform of the hero finders stepped forward. His huge hat made his neck look pencil thin, and the front brim kept dipping down over his eyes, despite how often he pushed it up and away.

The fellow held up his hands and silence broke over the assembly like an invisible wave. His voice boomed like thunder across the plaza, enhanced by spice wizards.

"Ah, hello everyone. I'm Lugubrious Klops, and I bear the sacred duty of officiating in today's assembly."

Bungey couldn't quite stifle a snort. "His name is as uninspiring as he is."

"Steady," Rasher urged.

Lugubrious hesitated and wrung his hands together, looking strangely nervous. Whoever picked him to lead the assembly must be realizing they'd made a horrible mistake.

"Um, you've all heard about the attack on Ehverr," Lugubrious said, squaring his shoulders and speaking fast, as if trying to rush through the words. "The legions must mobilize to help drive the Gloaming hordes from our lands. It's just, well, we can't. Not yet."

Rasher exchanged a confused look with his sergeants, the move mimicked thousands of times across the square. The tight-packed ranks of soldiers shuffled uneasily, the sound building into a low rumble.

General Nide strode forward to stand beside the nervous Lugubrious and he cringed back from her angry stare. She addressed the legions. "We face an unexpected situation that must be resolved before we can mobilize. We are the Reaper legions, but we find ourselves without any Reapers."

"What?" Stolon and Jocose exclaimed together, along with hundreds of other voices. The exclamation echoed between the high buildings hemming them in, and Rasher suddenly felt a growing feeling of dread.

Another hero finder, wearing the even taller hat of an officer, pushed Lugubrious forward, making a sharp gesture, urging him on. Lugubrious said, "General, I can do it. It's my duty, after all."

"Then get on with it," she snapped. "We don't have all day, and you're insulting the memory of the best team of Reapers we've ever had.

"Are they dead?" Kaets muttered in shock. "Did they try to take on the horde alone?"

"Impossible," Rasher objected. "I saw Sumwinkle yesterday."

"Shhh," Volaille hissed as Lugubrious started talking again.

"Yesterday, Reaper Team Twelve was removed."

As shouts of dismay and questions boiled through the disciplined ranks of legionaries, despite angry shouts from their centurions, Lugubrious continued quickly. "For the first time in our long history, a Reaper team has been entirely sidelined by nefarious contract addendums."

Stunned silence slapped its hand down over the square as everyone stared, trying to process the incredible news.

Lugubrious' voice seemed exceptionally loud in the restored quiet. "Contracts are addended regularly, but somehow the latest addendums included language that forbids the Reapers from performing any and all Reaper activities, including legion leadership, inspiring motivational speeches, heroic deeds, the wearing of clean uniforms, eating more than a single helping at any meal, or any act that could be interpreted as impressive in any way."

New ripples of low speech rumbled across the plaza, like angry waves crashing on rocky beaches. Rasher could barely believe what he was hearing. Reaper teams had lost members to battle and to age, but never to contract manipulations.

"An inquiry is being made with the Cheese Palace, but given the dire nature of the threats against the empire, and the inability of other forces to render timely aid to Ehverr, it again falls to the Reaper legions to face unprecedented danger. We need Reapers to lead us, and cannot wait to act," Lugubrious added. "So we are assembled here today to choose a new Reaper Team Twelve to lead the legions until the legal entanglements are resolved."

Again his words were met with shocked silence. New Reapers? Team Twelve was the best. It seemed insulting to replace them so quickly, discard them like cold leftovers.

The assembled legions looked on in silent wonder as everyone tried to process the shocking turn of events. Rasher couldn't imagine the timing of such a nefarious contract addendum could be a coincidence. Did that mean wizards within the Cheese Palace were in league with the glowan?

Such a thought seemed ridiculous, but as he scanned the assembly, he realized he saw no cheese wizards. Not good. The cheese wizards were responsible for lawyers and contracts, and an entire team of wizards and senior lawyers oversaw all Reaper contracts. It was a prestigious post. How could they have turned against the Reapers? He couldn't imagine someone might simply slip in unexpected language without anyone realizing it.

"If it's a mistake, can't they just nullify the addendum?" Stolon asked.

"Good question," Rasher said.

As if reading their thoughts, Lugubrious added, "It will take time to resolve the legal issues. Apparently the cream cheese clause was included."

A universal gasp rippled through the crowd. Rasher paled at the thought. The cream cheese clause was one of the deadliest of the cheese wizard curses, and he'd never heard of it actually being included in a final document. Its inclusion changed everything. The Reaper team might never come back.

Lugubrious continued. "Given the urgency of the situation, we must turn to Arkadas and implore the blessings of prophecy on our efforts."

That was a little unusual, but not extremely so. Their entire purpose was to serve Arkadas, fulfill her prophecies, and block the apocalypse driven by her twin, the plotting god Hilekar. Periodic reminders of that purpose were useful but rarely intoned in public.

"Therefore, today we will dispense with tedious forms of nomination, rounds of testing, and endless contract revisions to produce the team we need to lead us. Today we will draw the names from the Mixing Bowl of Divine Intervention and prove to the world who Arkadas has chosen to fill this vital role!"

Lugubrious' voice grew in volume so the last sentence rang out like the shouts of a true believer.

"Oh, please don't screw this up," Bungey muttered.

"Shhh," Rasher whispered back.

He glanced at the leaders of the various guilds, who stood at the heads of their wizards, shamans, and mages. They seemed calm and unsurprised. So they at least had been warned of the insanity ahead of time. They drew upon the powers of their patron gods every day, but no team had ever been chosen this way. Rasher was an enthusiastic follower of Domuz, but he didn't usually request direct intervention from him beyond his magically powered bacon.

One large, portly fellow stepped forward from the crowd of officials on the porch, and the magnified view in the water sphere focused on him. He was dressed grandly in a bright orange tunic and a long cape in an eye-watering shade of green. His brilliant yellow hat spread so wide, the sides of the brim hung almost down to his shoulders. He looked middle-aged, with a well-trimmed beard and dark brown hair.

"Who's that supposed to be?" one of Rasher's team muttered.

"I hope that's not the prophet," he replied.

Lugubrious motioned the newcomer to the front of the porch. "I am honored to present Borborygmus Squanch, a leading expert on Arkadas' will."

"So, if he's not the prophet, is he the spokesman or something?" Bungey asked.

"Dressed like that, he'll get noticed, that's for sure," Rasher said.

The prophet of Arkadas was famous, having prophesied the success of every Reaper team, but Rasher realized he knew little about the man. Or woman. He'd never realized he had no idea who the prophet might be.

Borborygmus waved grandly, and two extremely tall women stepped from the crowd, carrying a huge, gilded bowl with handles on both sides. It looked just like the huge mixing bowls the chefs used in the dining halls, only gold instead of steel.

Bungey whistled softly through his teeth as the two women stepped to the front of the patio. "They should be the spokeswomen. I'd listen to anything they said."

Several of his squad mates muttered agreement. The two women were gorgeous, with long brown hair worked into intricate braids, wearing form-fitting orange dresses the same shade as Borborygmus, except they made the color look good. Their huge hats were made of a wispy material that floated over them like yellow halos.

"They have to be wearing really tall heels," Volaille said, not nearly as impressed.

However they did it, the height proved useful. As they held the bowl out, its lip remained above Borborygmus' eyes, although his enormous hat still towered over them all.

"That's one way to show us he's not cheating by peeking at the names," Bungey commented.

The entire production seemed a bit overdone, but maybe Arkadas liked taking the spotlight sometimes too. Hopefully that meant they'd produce a great new team of Reapers.

Who would be chosen? His mind raced, and he released a quarter slice of chewy bacon to accelerate his thoughts. Selection of new Reapers usually took a long time and included many steps, but they didn't have time for that. No doubt they'd get a team from the folks who worked most closely with the Reapers, like the Gleaners.

He glanced toward the front ranks of the legions. He couldn't see them clearly through the thousands of legionnaires packed in the square, but he imagined Balter stood proudly in the front ranks. The huge warrior would make an excellent Reaper, but Rasher hoped dearly the man wouldn't be chosen as captain. He lacked the intelligence to lead.

An expectant hush settled over the square, silencing the hundreds of whispered conversations. Borborygmus reached one meaty hand into the bowl, made an exaggerated mixing motion, then withdrew a slip of parchment that sparkled like silver in the bright morning light.

He looked at it, and his confident expression faltered for a second. He looked surprised, as if the parchment wasn't a name, but a note that told him the back of his robe was open for everyone to see his undershorts.

Again the hero finder with the officer's hat stepped forward, and Borborygmus showed him the paper. He too looked surprised but motioned the big man to continue.

All they needed to do was give everyone a name. Rasher prayed nothing went wrong.

Borborygmus spoke, his voice rich and full, like a trained orator. "The first chosen Reaper has been revealed!"

He paused for effect, then shouted the name.

"Rasher Dilskin!"

10

REAPER TEAM TWELVE

The ground seemed to drop from under Rasher's feet, and he only barely maintained his balance. Sounds seemed far away, and he felt woozy, almost as if someone had opened an artery right in front of him.

The five squads of his fist howled with glee, pummeling his back and pumping his hands, laughing with joy and shouting questions, but their voices were like the thunder of a distant waterfall. He couldn't understand anything.

His mind whirled. He couldn't have heard his name. Even as he tried to protest, Bungey pushed him forward and all eyes turned toward him. He couldn't seem to focus on anyone but Borborygmus, who was beaming and beckoning grandly from across the square.

The viewsphere hanging above the square somehow rotated its view to focus on him, and he appeared in the air, ten times larger than life.

Wow, he looked like an idiot with that stunned expression on his face.

It couldn't be happening, but he wasn't about to miss a chance for a fantastic thrill rush. So Rasher squashed his shock, his disbelief, and his confusion, plastered a grin on his face, and waved. His huge double in the sky mimicked the move, and the square erupted with wild cheers.

The sound shook him, and he embraced the thrill that pounded through his veins, replenishing his strength and fighting back the ever-present drain of his blood phobia. Rasher marched toward the porch, and the close-packed ranks of the legions parted, creating a path for him across the sea of soldiers to the Heart.

Many had heard of him, and they all seemed thrilled with the call of a rare bacon master to the new Reaper team. Rasher drank in the energy pouring off the crowd, even as his mind whirled with the impossibility of what was happening.

He kept focus using Rule of Engagement number thirty-four. Survive the moment. Make sense out of it later.

The air felt heavy, as if the cheering exhausted it, and Rasher couldn't seem to get enough breath. All he could smell was steel and leather from the close-packed legionaries, and his ears were overwhelmed by the tremendous din.

One thing became clear on the long walk across the plaza. Arkadas had given the legions a bacon master, but their joy was false. How would they react when they realized he could not lead them into battle without fainting at the first sight of blood?

That thought sliced through the clamor in his mind with a splash of cold reality. How could he be a Reaper?

Then again, maybe this was his big chance. This might give him the leverage to win Kitan's hand without sacrificing his house. Arkadas had to be smoking confectioner sugar to call him, but he needed to find a way to make this work before the legions rejected him as a fraud.

As he neared the Heart, his gaze fell upon Balter Fopoon. Unlike everyone else, Balter was scowling, thick arms crossed over his muscular chest.

Rasher waved again, triggering another tremendous cheer from the crowds. He might not last long as a Reaper, but by the gods, he loved forcing Balter to witness his moment of victory.

Balter's lips curled into a snarl, but no one else seemed to notice, and Rasher ascended the porch with a light step. His life had just totally changed, but if Arkadas believed in him, how could he doubt?

Borborygmus pumped his hand, congratulating him warmly. The man's initial hesitation was gone, replaced by wide smiles.

"Please stand here next to the girls," he whispered to Rasher, guiding him to a place next to the bowl-wielding women.

They made him look short. For some reason, the idea struck him as immensely funny, and he couldn't help laughing. That again triggered a fresh round of cheering from the enthusiastic legions spread out below the porch like a green sea in their dress uniforms.

Without hesitation, Borborygmus continued with the next name. Again, he paused when he saw the parchment, but he recovered more quickly the second time and shouted the name.

"Kucheesa Beeshee!"

Rasher blinked as the name slapped him out of his spinning thoughts. There had to be more than one girl with that name in the Acropolis. There had to be.

Nope.

She whooped, suffering none of Rasher's initial shock. The girl trotted from the very back of the ranks of the meat mages, waving to the wildly cheering crowds, her face flushed with joy, her raptor-shaped hat set at a jaunty angle. In the viewsphere, she looked impressive at forty feet tall, and the legions loved it, cheering and clapping.

She rushed up to the porch and greeted Borborygmus with overflowing enthusiasm. "Thank you! I've dreamed of this moment my entire life!"

"Very good. Please take your place next to your captain," he replied softly.

Another jolt, like hot grease splattering across his face. He'd forgotten that since he was chosen first, that meant he was now the Reaper captain.

When in over one's head, what was a little more depth?

Kucheesa trotted over to stand beside him and waved to the crowd. Without looking at him, saluting, shaking his hand, or making any other attempt at acknowledgment, she whispered, "Hello again, bacon man."

"Really? That's how you start?" he demanded.

She looked at him then, her gaze intense. "You intervened last night before I had to hurt any of those fools in the square, so you probably consider yourself a hero. Maybe you're not as bad as other bacon masters, but that doesn't mean I'm going to worship the ground you walk on like everyone else."

"I expect you to do your job," he said, immensely annoyed, but intensely aware of the cheering crowds watching them.

"And you do yours. I hope you prove me wrong, Captain."

His retort was cut off by Borborygmus, who had already pulled another name. The man was starting to sweat and kept looking back at the hero finder team. For the first time, Rasher noticed that most of them did not look pleased. They tried to hide it, but one didn't have to be a trainer to pick up on the signs of growing anger.

What was going on? They'd orchestrated the entire show. Why would the results displease them?

Borborygmus might be growing nervous, but he concealed it as he shouted, "Quarce Sjambok!"

Rasher frowned. Sjambok was a Gravlax surname, home of the dwarf nation and the hearty men who lived among them. No dwarf or man of Gravlax had ever been appointed a Reaper.

The initial explosion of cheering at the new announcement faltered as the name registered. Rasher looked around. He hadn't even remembered seeing any dwarven companies in the assembly. A deep, bellowing shout drew his gaze to the rear of the small coffee wizard contingent.

The shouting voice grew louder as a short figure pushed through the ranks of his fellows. It really was a dwarf. The viewsphere made him look immense and burly, but in real life he stood barely four feet tall.

He was still far thicker in the chest and shoulders than Rasher, and he charged the porch with enthusiasm. He wore all leather, from his brown trousers to his legion-colored green tunic, to his black cap with a coffee pot crown attached to the top. Even the weathered satchel slung over his shoulder was made out of heavy black leather. His bearded face glowed with excitement, and he laughed as he rushed up the stairs to join them.

Many of the hero finders no longer concealed their frustration. One of their officers hissed, "What games are you playing, Borborygmus? You're making a mockery of everything!"

"Hold your peace," the hero finder leader snapped. Of all their company, he alone remained calm. He looked young to be a commander, which meant he was probably of high birth and won the position because of his family connections.

He didn't look exceptional. Barely average height and build, his dark brown hair was styled well, and he wore his tall, black hero finder hat at a slight angle. He held himself calmly, and the other hero finders quieted at his words.

Quarce never noticed, but bounded onto the porch and rushed to Borborygmus, pumped his hands eagerly, then ran to Rasher and Kucheesa.

"I am so honored to be part of this team," he shouted loud enough for half the plaza to hear as he seized their hands in turn. His were big and calloused and strong. He hadn't even noticed that the cheering for him was much more subdued than it had been for the others.

Borborygmus seemed to realize the best way out of the uncomfortable situation was through, so he quickly pulled the next name.

"Bibble Widdershins!"

Bibble turned out to be a middle-aged, rather portly spice wizard. He raised a hand when his name was called and moved to the front ranks of the spice wizards. They were fewer in number than some of the guilds, but respected, and the cheering redoubled in volume, as if to make up for faltering when Quarce was called.

No doubt folks standing farther back figured the roundness of his midsection was just distortion from the viewsphere.

Rasher knew enough of the man's reputation to know Bibble was a senior spice wizard, a master of his craft. He might be a bit older and heavier than an ideal Reaper, but he would make a solid member of the team. The tension he'd started feeling at the odd intrigue playing out on the porch behind them eased some.

Bibble moved quickly toward the porch, smiling and waving, but still clearly in shock. He dressed in a finely tailored green suit and long coat with many pockets. The long, stacked pockets hanging down the side tails of his hat bulged with spices. He quickly shook everyone's hands. He seemed particularly eager to meet Quarce. Coffee wizards had served with distinction on Reaper teams in the past, although no team had ever appointed a dwarf.

Within seconds, another parchment was pulled from the gilded mixing bowl and another name shouted.

"Noops Finsterwallies!"

Cheering started, but faltered as everyone craned for a sight or sound or any sign of who and where Noops might be. Rasher couldn't see anything, and he hoped whoever Noops turned out to be that he hadn't skipped the assembly. There was enough potential trouble already, they didn't need a black mark like that to deal with.

After several long seconds where Borborygmus started looking decidedly nervous and the cheering faded, a new shout arose from the far side of the square.

Beyond the last ranks of soldiers, even farther than where Rasher's team stood, a figure trotted up the road from around the far side of the admin building that formed the outer boundary of the plaza.

The viewsphere zoomed in on the fellow as Kucheesa muttered, "Who would be standing back there?"

"I'm assuming he is our missing team member," Bibble guessed.

"Well, that's unexpected," Rasher muttered as the armored figure became clear.

"It can't be," Kucheesa groaned as she recognized the man, complete with the handle of his shovel sticking up over his shoulder.

It was the Acropolis watch shovel knight.

Noops' expression was calm, and he mostly ignored the people cheering him on, his gaze fixed on his destination. Tall and imposing, the knight generated wildly enthusiastic cheers until he passed and folks noticed the shovel sheathed on his back.

That was why he had to come all the way from around the admin building. He must have been stationed out there as part of the perimeter guard. Good thing he hadn't been posted on the outer wall.

"Can they appoint someone from the Watch?" Bibble asked.

"Apparently," Rasher said, long past making any assumptions about anything concerning the nomination process.

Noops trotted up the stairs, saluted Borborygmus, then joined them and saluted Rasher. "Noops Finsterwallies reporting for duty, sir!"

"Welcome aboard," Rasher said, saluting out of habit, then extending his hand in greeting.

That seemed to surprise the shovel knight more than getting appointed a member of the Reaper team. He hesitated only a second, then smiled warmly and took Rasher's hand. "An officer who greets his people with kindness sleeps with undisturbed dreams."

"I like to think so," Rasher said.

"What's that supposed to mean?" Kucheesa demanded, scowling again. "And what did you mean about my father the other day?" She looked ready to go for her daggers right there in front of everyone.

Rasher felt another stirring of wild laughter at the horrible thought. What was wrong with him? He had to get it together.

Noops looked unfazed. "Officers who do not abuse their troops are less likely to face the risk of violent insubordination."

"Oh," she said.

"Makes sense to me," Quarce piped in, grinning up at Noops. "Welcome."

"Thank you," Noops said, then turned back to Kucheesa. "My comment on your father's math prowess was a simple deduction based on the fact that you must have practiced much to develop the skill and sensitivity of touch to not only transport eggs without breaking them, but to wield them as weapons."

"I don't understand how they're related."

"If your mother was responsible for reviewing the fruits of your egg gathering, I assume she would not have overlooked the loss of so many eggs and would have likely chastised you to stop wasting them, which would have resulted in you acquiring less skill. Your father then was the responsible one, but he never culled your practice, which meant he never noticed. Either he had much on his mind, or he just wasn't that good at math."

She blinked a couple of times, processing the logic, which made an odd sort of sense.

Noops added, "I bet the pigs got annoyed with you a lot, though."

"Wait, what?"

Rasher hushed them. Borborygmus was reaching back into the gilded Mixing Bowl of Divine Intervention. The big man felt around for a moment, frowning, then pulled the bowl down to look inside.

"I thought he wasn't supposed to do that," Bibble said.

Borborygmus looked to the leader of the hero finders, who stepped closer, one raised eyebrow the only indication he wasn't sure what was going on.

"That's it," Borborygmus said, sounding shocked.

The hero finder also looked surprised but recovered almost immediately. He glanced at Rasher and the others and smiled.

Why then were all the other hero finders looking so angry?

"The will of Arkadas is done," the hero finder said, gesturing Borborygmus forward again.

"As always," the big man agreed quickly, then turned back to the packed ranks of soldiers. The cheering had already been replaced by murmurs, like the rumbling of distant thunder.

"The will of Arkadas is manifest. I give you the new Reaper Team Twelve!"

11

THAT COULD HAVE GONE BETTER

R asher Dilskin, Reaper of the Apocalypse. The title echoed through his mind over and over as he stood smiling and waving with his new team members.

The applause seemed to go on forever. Whatever reservations any of the assembly might have regarding any of them, they ignored it for the moment and joined together cheering for their new Reaper team.

Rasher did not want to let any of them down, but for once, he had no idea what to do. So he simply played the part and drank in the energy pouring from the crowd. It buoyed his spirits, and he decided he had to make this work. Being a Reaper was a total rush.

He thought back to that moment in the Bubble and Squeak when he wished he could do more, and glanced up at the sky. Had Domuz heard him?

He should have been more specific.

"One step at a time," he whispered to himself.

Rule number twelve, one he drilled into his students. Gather information until he understood the path forward. Luckily, there was a literal army assigned to help him. That thought triggered another smile.

All he had to do was lead his team of Reapers and their legions into battle against the biggest Gloaming horde of all time.

A thought struck like a lightning bolt and he nearly gasped. What would Kitan think? He'd sent the note asking her to meet him for lunch, but he doubted he'd be able to make it. What would her father think? Would he drop his requirement that Rasher's family betray the Takmor house?

Somehow he doubted it would be that easy, but maybe it would open a path for him to break free of the man's manipulations. He chewed on that idea over the next couple minutes spent waving while the legions shook the plaza with their cheering. Finally, the leader of the hero finders beckoned them toward the door into the Heart. Most of the hero finders crowded in behind them, along with Borborygmus and his lovely assistants. A grumpy-looking General Nide hung back, speaking with her command staff.

"We're going in," Quarce said in a booming whisper, looking so excited he might jump right out of those heavy boots. Rasher shared his excitement. He'd never gotten to enter the Heart, and despite the insanity of the moment, he couldn't help but feel eager for the chance.

Inside, they entered the wide entrance hall with its three-story vaulted ceiling, covered with bright paintings of Reaper victories through the ages. A huge chandelier hung high above, blazing with soft white light like custard set aflame.

"This is the best day of my life," Kucheesa laughed, turning slowly, head tilted back so far it was a wonder her hat didn't fall off.

Most of the hero finder team encircled Borborygmus and his two assistants as soon as they entered. "How dare you breach the contract and change the names?" Lugubrious shouted, showing more spine than Rasher had expected from the timid fellow.

"We changed nothing," Borborygmus said, his smooth voice easily carrying over the angry hero finders as he made calming gestures with his meaty hands. "We processed the names you provided, with all of the usual safeguards. If there's a problem with the names, it happened before we received them."

"We gave you dozens of candidates," another hero finder snapped, so angry he yanked off his hat and waved it at Borborygmus like a really floppy sword.

"How can we end up with only five Reapers?" another cried, red-faced with rage. "Five! No Reaper team has dropped so low in numbers since the Whisternfeet invasion."

"I was wondering about that," Bibble said quietly as his new team clustered close to Rasher, watching the shouting match.

Rasher had been too. The previous Reaper Team Twelve had been one of the most fully staffed, with a full complement of wizards and mages from all the guilds. With only five Reapers, they faced critical shortfalls in vital areas of culinary battle magic. Figuring out how to compensate for the lack was definitely near the top of the thousand items already packing his to-do list.

"If you gave them to us, they would have been in there," Borborygmus was saying. "We did not break the seal until this morning, done by our blind steward to ensure no glimpses of the names. The mixing bowl was kept covered until we stepped onto the porch. There is simply no way we tampered with the names."

The hero finders turned to their leader, who stood slightly apart, looking far calmer than the rest of them. He spread his hands and said, "You all witnessed the sealing of the nomination package. It remained in my office safe until we removed it to deliver it to Prophecy, Incorporated under heavy guard. No one could have tampered with it."

"Prophecy what?" Kucheesa whispered.

Rasher shrugged. "I have no idea. Must be where Borborygmus works."

"I thought he represented Arkadas somehow," Quarce said, shifting from one foot to the other, as if impatient to get on with becoming Reapers.

He was so short, the coffee pot mounted to the crown of his hat sat just below Rasher's face. The subtle aroma of fresh-brewed coffee that slipped past the plug in the spout lent a calming influence on the turbulent scene.

"We'll find out soon enough," Rasher assured them.

If there was some kind of foul play during the nomination process, their appointments as Reapers might be deemed invalid. As much as he had never aspired to become a Reaper, he did not want to go down in the history books as the shortest-serving Reaper captain of all time.

Unfortunately, Borborygmus headed for the exit on the east side of the huge entryway, with the ladies in tow, and most of the still-arguing hero finders pressing in close behind. Only the hero finder leader detached from the crowd and joined Rasher and his team. He beckoned them deeper into the room.

"I am Gubbins van Moore dan Weekudyus," he introduced himself. "Welcome, Team Twelve to day one."

Rasher had guessed right about the man. The Moore family was one of the ruling primi high houses with a representative in the First

Course Assembly in the Food Court. It felt weird to receive the same team designation as Absquatch's team, almost like the original team Twelve were being scrubbed from existence. That seemed very wrong.

He'd deal with that later. "Thank you, sir. I'll admit, the assignments caught us all by surprise."

"That's an understatement," Bibble muttered.

"But not an unpleasant surprise," Quarce piped in quickly, and Kucheesa nodded in agreement. Noops just followed along, silently watching. Strangely, the handle of his shovel looked somehow right sticking up over his shoulder.

"It sounds like there are some questions about procedure," Rasher said.

"The situation is definitely not standard," Gubbins started, but he was interrupted by the arrival of General Sigha Nide, trailed by her entire command staff.

"Gubbins, this is unacceptable," she snapped by way of greeting. "What by all the gods is the meaning of this farce? What happened to the candidates we submitted?"

Rasher might have backed away from the raging general, but his entire team sidled close behind him, using him like a human shield.

Gubbins remained remarkably calm in the face of the general's wrath. "You were there, General. The will of Arkadas was done."

"Don't give me that blather," she snapped. "Who changed the names? We don't have time for screw-ups."

Gubbins nodded toward the knot of hero finders still clustered around Borborygmus as he tried to retreat down a distant hallway. "As you can see, none of us expected this turn of events."

"So make it null and void," she demanded, crossing her arms, clearly expecting him to fold.

As much as Rasher revered the general, he was starting to feel deeply insulted. Didn't she realize they were standing right there as she badmouthed the nomination process?

"I will not," Gubbins said, remaining remarkably calm. "You do not control the choosing, General. You submit recommendations, but the choosing happens according to the will of Arkadas."

She dropped her arms, her hands clenched, and leaned a bit closer. "Don't test my patience, Gubbins. I shouldn't have to remind you how much a Reaper team that can inspire confidence means right now. I don't have time to train up a team of unknowns."

She finally glanced at them, her hard-eyed gaze sweeping over them, stopping at Rasher. Either she saw his growing anger or realized she was acting unprofessional, because she amended, "No offense, Captain. You've built a reputation most have heard of. Your team appears, ah, uniquely qualified, but we are preparing for war, and I need a team ready to get to work immediately."

Before Rasher could speak, Gubbins said, "Thank you, but I'll hand that 'no offense' back to you, General, and remind you that it's not all about you."

That yanked her attention back to him, and he added, "The Reapers are the heart and mind of everything we do here. You are the sword that strikes at their will. If I tried to undo what has just been witnessed by every member of the legions, it would shatter everything the Reapers and the legions stand for."

"We can work through that."

"No, General, we cannot. If I attempted to undermine the authority of this new team, it would drive a stake through the heart of the faith, the commitment, and the trust of every member of the legion. I will not do it."

Rasher stood taller, inspired by the noble sentiment, even though he was so abundantly aware of how unworthy he was of such trust.

The general leaned close, jabbing a finger into Gubbins' chest. "Figure out a way. This is a disgrace, and I will not turn my command over to a bunch of nobodies."

Rasher again felt his anger rising, and he could feel his team shifting behind him. Kucheesa was edging out, hand drifting toward her knives, her face reddening with anger. She looked ready to transform her nose into a beak again and jump on the general and peck out her eyes.

Few people could stand up to the general, especially when she was so enraged, but amazingly Gubbins stood his ground. "I'm sorry, general. I didn't realize that you are now the lead hero finder, the spokesman for Arkadas herself, and the new military dictator of the Acropolis. The last I checked, you were the leader of the legions tasked with supporting whatever team my office chose."

The general reared back as if struck, her face flushing deeper. Her officers were all glaring, fists clenched, and Rasher could easily read their temptation to draw steel.

Amazingly she did not lash out. With an extreme effort she forced a modicum of control and added tersely, "My responsibility is to ensure success by working with a competent Reaper team."

She glanced again at Rasher and his companions, her glare so powerful Rasher had to wonder if she was utilizing some confectioner enhancements. "If this rabble can be turned into a cohesive unit that we can work with, fine. We will be happy to do so. However, I will make it clear right now that I will refuse to obey commands that I know will hurt or kill my soldiers."

"In war, soldiers are hurt and killed. There is no way around that," Rasher told her. He didn't want to confront her, but he could not allow her to disrespect his new team.

"You know what I mean," she hissed.

"Your concerns have been noted, General," Rasher said.

Gubbins added, "I suggest you see to your troops. Our new Reaper team will need them soon."

The dismissal was spoken calmly, but might as well have been screamed in her face and accompanied by a slap. The general recoiled, composed herself, and leaned forward to hiss, "You created this mess, Gubbins. See that you set it right."

Then she spun sharply on her heel and marched away, trailed by her entourage. Several of the officers glanced back, scowls dark. Rasher hoped Gubbins watched his back.

"Well, that could have gone better," Noops commented.

Gubbins laughed, his voice shaking a little as he released his bottled tension. "That's the understatement of the day."

Rasher was surprised to see the man looking pleased. Did he know something they didn't? He wanted to ask Gubbins about that last comment General Nide had made, but someone screamed, and someone else shouted, "Look out!"

Heart racing, he released bacon from his internal stores and spun, searching for a threat. The rest of the team reacted a bit slower. No one expected to be attacked in the Heart.

Several people were looking up and pointing. Others were running. He followed their gaze up and gasped. The giant chandelier was falling.

General Nide and her officers had just finished passing beneath it and were sprinting away, all pretense at dignity gone.

"Go!" Rasher shouted, shoving his team toward one of the exits.

Together they raced away as the chandelier fell. It remained perfectly upright, lights still blazing until it smashed into the hard floor and exploded in a thunderous detonation. Shards of crystal and gobbets of creamy fire splashed outward in a spectacular display. They cascaded to the hard-tiled floor in a tinkling wave that sounded strangely musical.

Rasher and his team slowed just inside an exit hallway. The devastation had missed them by only a few feet. Rasher did not see anyone caught by the fall. If it hadn't been spotted so quickly, it could have killed a lot of people.

As dozens of voices shouted questions or called for a muffin mage to put out the fires, Gubbins stared at the disaster, face white. He looked far more rattled by it than by the unexpected Reaper names drawn from the Mixing Bowl of Divine Intervention.

Quarce lifted a fist into the air and shouted, "That was amazing!"

He turned to them and noticed them all staring at him. Lowering his fist, he asked, "What?"

"That could have killed us," Kucheesa exclaimed.

"Or the general," Bibble added.

"So, that wasn't part of the new Reaper welcoming show?" Quarce asked, looking disappointed.

Noops chuckled. "Made for a great intro."

"Right?" Quarce laughed heartily. "I wonder what's next."

"Hopefully something less dramatic," Rasher suggested, impressed by Quarce's determined enthusiasm. It gave him something to focus on beside the horrible blasphemy of defacing the entryway of the Heart.

Bibble chuckled. "I've always heard that explosive finishes are better than explosive beginnings."

Noops and Quarce both laughed, while Kucheesa groaned and said, "That's the kind of joke my dad would make."

Bibble shrugged. "Once men become fathers, it seems to happen to all of us."

Kucheesa took a step into the huge room, her face anguished. "Who would do such a thing to the Heart? It's not right."

Gubbins waved a guard over and ordered curtly, "Seal the Heart. Send for the Acropolis Inquisitors. Triple the guards at every exit. Inspect everyone trying to leave to confirm identities and record the reason for their presence here."

The guard slammed a fist to his heart in a legion salute and rushed away. Gubbins forced calm on his expression and turned to Rasher. He took a deep breath and said, "I can't imagine that was an accident, not timed as it was." He scanned the team and added with a chuckle, "You would have broken the record for the shortest-lived Reapers. Not the epitaph any of us want, eh?"

Rasher chuckled too. At least they were taking the unprecedented events of the past half hour in stride. Might be a slightly crazed stride, but at least they were still walking.

He had no idea what the protocols were for a possible attack within the Heart. As far as he knew, no one had ever tried such a thing. Before that moment, he would have thought it impossible. "Do we need to do something about this?"

Gubbins shook his head. "No. The inquisitors will flood the Heart with agents and soldiers within moments. We're facing a time of impending apocalypse, but I hadn't expected it to reach into our home like this." He squared his shoulders and added, "But we have a lot to do today. Let's not get distracted."

He extended a hand and said, "I've heard of you, Captain. Welcome, all of you, to the Reapers of the Apocalypse."

His handshake was firm and he added, "Our schedule is very tight. We need to compress weeks of work into the tightest timeframe possible. Changing the Reaper team will delay the mobilization, but we must shorten that delay as much as possible.

"Wait, the legions aren't mobilizing immediately?" Kucheesa asked.

"How can they?" Gubbins asked. "An army without intact leadership will fail. Why do you think the general is so angry?"

Rasher nodded to himself. He'd always respected General Nide, and understanding her position a bit better helped lessen his resentment at how she'd treated him and his team.

"I hope you're better at names than I am, Captain," Noops commented.

"What?" Rasher asked.

"Why do you think that?" Kucheesa also asked, frowning at Noops. "Because he's got a big head or something?"

Noops gave her a confused look. "Captain's head isn't big. Are you feeling all right?"

"You make weird assumptions about people," she insisted.

Rasher interjected before they could start squabbling. Definitely not the image they needed to present to the world. He raised a calming hand to Kucheesa, whose frown deepened, but she didn't argue. Then Rasher glanced at Noops, one eyebrow raised in question.

The huge shovel knight shrugged. "Best way to build a foundation of trust with people is to learn their names. Sounds like we lack time for more time-consuming relationship building activities like cook-offs and binge-eating challenges."

"Or ax throwing," Quarce added with a grin.

"Or trench digging," Noops responded. The dwarf laughed, his voice booming in the vaulted chamber. "Yes!"

"I wouldn't have thought of the last two," Bibble said with a frown. "But your point about using names is valid."

It was, although Rasher wished Noops would have just said as much to start. The thought of forging this little group into a functioning Reaper team in a matter of days to not delay the mobilization so long that Ehverr fell was immensely daunting. And what if they had even less time than they assumed? Rasher glanced back at the shattered, still-burning mess littering the center of the grand entryway. If it wasn't an accident, who was the target? The general, or the new Reaper team?

Who might have the ability to set up such a sabotage right there in the center of their security? Who would dare desecrate the Heart? If they were discovered, the legions would tear them limb from limb in vengeful anger.

How would they know to attack there at that time anyway? It was a stark reminder that as Reapers they had just stepped front and center into the attention of every enemy of the empire. Those enemies didn't care about anything more than killing them simply because they were Reapers.

Traitors might be standing nearby, pretending shock. He glanced at the shouting officers and stunned officials. Some cast glances toward him and his team, maybe expecting some fantastic feats of magic or leadership, but he'd only been a Reaper for moments.

"So we have work to do," Rasher summed up.

Noops shrugged and asked, "Any chance we could get an early lunch?"

Gubbins laughed. "Good to see your heart's in the right place. Actually, the plan is to begin with a feast to give the chefs a chance to study your preferences and begin planning the best menu to accelerate your additional enhancements. Then we'll tour the Heart, see to your quarters, and begin settling you into your duties and responsibilities."

The nervous little hero finder, Lugubrious Klops, jogged back into the room and skirted the shattered remnants of the fallen chandelier, casting nervous glances at the wreckage. He saluted when he reached them and said, "A full inquiry will be launched to identify potential security breaches of the nomination protocols."

"Keep me posted," Gubbins said. "In the meantime, we proceed." To the rest of them, he added, "Lugubrious will act as your direct liaison and will be heading up the transition process to your new roles."

That must have been why he was given the honor of welcoming the assembly. He still seemed like an odd choice, but at least he wasn't screaming that they were all frauds.

Yet.

12

A Second of Painful Reflection

Gubbins led them on a brief tour of the Heart, sticking to the wide, bustling corridors on the lower levels. So many questions bubbled in Rasher's mind, but he hesitated. He just wanted to enjoy the moment, and savor the experience of exploring the famous Heart for the first time. His team seemed equally awed by the moment, so they followed Gubbins in unusual silence for most of the brief tour.

When they reached the fourth floor, he led them to a quiet hallway with a thick, carpeted runner on the floor. Fourteen ornately carved wooden doorways marched down either side of the long hall.

"These are your quarters," Gubbins said.

"We'll get to live here," Kucheesa breathed, a little smile playing across her lips before she caught Rasher looking and scowled.

"Your name plaques will be affixed shortly, and your personal effects will be moved from your old quarters shortly. Take a moment to inspect your quarters and let Lugubrious know if you require anything else."

He showed each of them to their rooms. Quarce bounded through his door with a whoop of joy. Kucheesa looked just as excited, while Noops looked intrigued. Bibble paused at his door. "What about my family?"

"These Reaper quarters are not really designed to house entire families. We will arrange to move yours to one of the larger apartments on the top floor of one of the other nearby admin buildings," Gubbins assured him.

While they talked, Rasher headed to the end of the hall where Gubbins had indicated his quarters were located. As captain of the

Reapers, he had the corner suite. With a sense of wonder, he pushed open the door that was already slightly ajar and entered.

The entryway was as large as his entire previous apartment and served as a spacious sitting room, complete with a fireplace set in the right-hand wall, with a couch and three overstuffed chairs facing it. A breakfast nook with a small table and four wooden chairs sat in an alcove on the far wall, under a large window.

The room's high ceiling was covered in a breathtaking painting depicting the heroic battle of Smoot Blatherskite and his Reaper team against the Gloaming hordes during their daring invasion of Whisternfeet.

So enthralled was Rasher with the painting as he wandered deeper into the room, he barely noticed the door on the left side of the room open and a figure step through. He assumed it was one of the cleaning staff clearing out the belongings of Absquatch Youlate, and turned to tell them not to hurry.

He was not prepared to see a tall figure in a small, black cap, dressed in the livery of servants of the Heart, but with a white mask covering their face. Definitely was not expecting to see that person swinging a heavy, brass curtain rod at his head.

Instincts honed in thousands of fights and paint battle matches kicked in even as he blinked in surprise, and Rasher dove to the side.

When one needs another half second, a full second feels like an hour.

Instead of braining him in the forehead, the end of the brass rod clipped Rasher on the side of the head, turning his controlled dive into a sprawling slide into the chairs in the breakfast nook. He plowed into them in a crash of falling seats and wasted a couple precious seconds extricating himself.

By then, the intruder was gone.

Rasher leaped to his feet, his head throbbing, his surprise quickly turning to anger. He rushed out into the hall in time to see Gubbins and Bibble poke their heads out of Bibble's door.

"What's going on?" Bibble asked.

"Someone was in my room," Rasher called as he sprinted down the hall. None of the other doors were open, and the intruder would not have had time to slip into one and close it softly. That meant they had simply fled. "Attacked me."

The rest of the team poured into the hall at his words and raced after him, but Rasher didn't slow. He pounded down the hall, back to the stairs, and caught a glimpse of movement as someone made the turn down to a lower level. Releasing a bit of crispy bacon, Rasher dove over the rail, somersaulting in the air over the long drop, and stuck the landing on the lower section.

He spotted no one, even when he leaned over the rail and scanned the lower lengths of winding stairs stretching down to the second level. So he rushed down to the door to the third level and burst through. This level held offices and administrative areas. The hallway was packed with bustling personnel, who turned in surprise at his abrupt entrance. As one they began to clap and cheer, rushing forward to congratulate him on his new role.

"Did anyone else come this way?" Rasher demanded as the crowd pressed in around him. "Someone wearing a white mask over their face?"

All he received in answer were blank looks. One large woman, blushing as she met his gaze said, "People come and go all the time on this hall, Captain, but no one wears masks."

"Thank you," he managed, then extricated himself from the enthusiastic crowd, returning to the central staircase just as the rest of the team caught up. He briefly recounted what had happened.

"Maybe they continued down after all," he said with a frown. "I wouldn't have thought anyone could outrun me with so small a head start."

"Unless they had a confectioner speed enhancement," Gubbins said, his expression grave. "Come on. I'll raise the alarm. We already have guards watching every exit. Maybe they spotted something suspicious."

"I'll see you at the bottom," Rasher said. As the others began racing down the stairs, quickly leaving poor Bibble behind, Rasher again drew upon the power of bacon and descended in a series of acrobatic leaps from one section to the next.

It was a lot of fun, and he decided he needed to always take stairs that way in the future. He was forced to slow as he neared the ground floor due to an increase in traffic, but no one reported seeing anyone fleeing, especially no one wearing a mask.

Rasher realized the huge flaw in his pursuit. The intruder only had to remove the mask, and no one would ever recognize them. They were dressed in the same uniforms as everyone else. Only the strange little black hat made them stand out, but he bet they would swap that too.

Still, he informed the guard on the ground floor to watch out for anyone matching that description, then returned to the entry hall to meet the others. The cleanup of the fallen chandelier was mostly finished, and a pair of muffin mages were meeting with a confectioner and several workmen who were preparing to lift a temporary replacement light.

"This is disturbing," Gubbins said with a frown as the others finally caught up with him.

Rasher's reply was interrupted by the arrival of a milk mage, rushing toward them, her braid flying out behind her. She was young, but the double milk bottles on her hat declared her high rank. Her brown eyes seemed to glow with enthusiasm, and her skin was so pale, he wondered if she rubbed anti-aging yogurt on it every night.

She slowed in front of him, panting slightly, and flashed a warm smile. "Hello," she said with far too much good cheer. "I'm Colly Wobbles, the personal milk mage for the Reapers."

"Hello," Rasher said as Colly lifted a hand to touch his throbbing head. She handed him a clay mug full of cool milk and said, "I heard about your injury. It does not look too bad. I'll have you fixed up in a jiffy."

Rasher sipped the milk, enjoying the rush of wholesomeness that filled him. The air suddenly smelled cleaner, as if an invisible washer woman had just swept through the room.

"Thank you."

She beamed at him. "It is my great pleasure. I was hoping to meet with all of you later today to discuss personalized health plans."

Rasher tried not to tense. Something in her eyes suggested she knew about his blood phobia. He was grateful she hadn't mentioned it aloud. "Again, thank you. I'm sure we'll all be happy to meet with you."

"Very good," she said.

Gubbins interjected. "Unfortunately, Miss Wobbles, we are due in the dining hall."

"Of course. I will see you later," she promised, before turning and hurrying off.

As Gubbins led the way toward the dining hall, Kucheesa asked, "Why would someone be in your rooms? None of your belongings are there yet."

"And why attack you?" Bibble added.

Rasher shrugged and looked to Gubbins, whose expression had turned thoughtful. "That was Captain Youlate's room. I doubt he had any intelligence worth stealing, but someone might have been searching for something else. I will request a full inventory of the room before your belongings are moved in. Perhaps we will get a clue. Nothing like this has ever happened in the Heart before, and I plan to make sure it never happens again."

His tone and expression suggested he was suppressing a towering rage at the desecration of their home. Rasher heartily agreed with him.

"Falling chandeliers, assassins in our rooms, this is going to be even more exciting than I thought," Quarce said cheerfully.

The Reaper private dining hall, located on the second floor of the Heart, was grand enough to host a primi lord and his entire retinue. Gubbins led them across the floor tiled in a subtle geometric pattern, toward the one long table positioned in the center of the room. Their boots rang loudly on the tile, despite the huge, sound-dampening tapestries draping the white-oak-clad walls.

"We can fit over a dozen feasting tables in this room, depending on the event," Gubbins said.

Rasher believed it, imagining the huge space packed with tables and diners. Winning an invitation to dine with the Reapers or attend one of their social events in that famous dining room was considered one of the greatest boons a member of the Reaper legions could receive. And now he would be eating there every day.

Crystal sconces set into the walls and ceiling held golden illumination pastries, emitting a warm light and filling the room with the enticing scent of fresh-baked goodies. The extravagant expense subtly reinforced the importance of their new station. It was going to take time to get used to having everything he needed provided by a huge staff dedicated solely to that purpose.

The one table in the room was surrounded by fourteen comfortable chairs, with full place settings already waiting. Eight forks flanked each white, porcelain plate, with half a dozen knives and spoons on the opposite sides, and tiny dessert forks and spoons ranging up toward the center of the table. Cups, glasses, and tiny plates were arrayed all around. Rasher had never seen such a setting, even at the fancy lunches he'd attended with Kitan.

"Are all of those forks for one person?" Quarce asked in an awed voice that echoed across the chamber. "In the mines, we only ever had one, and sometimes we had to share."

Kucheesa shrugged. "One is enough for me. Lick it clean between courses."

Bibble winced, looking at her aghast. "You wouldn't insult one of the gods so casually."

"Better than using the wrong one, isn't it?"

As they approached the table, Gubbins angled toward where a mature woman wearing a pristine white chef's coat and a tall toque chef's hat stood waiting for them. Impressive to see four colored bands ringing her hat. Only two saucier chefs resided in all of Afitur, and one was always stationed in the Food Court, serving as an assistant to the head chefs of the High Kitchen.

"Welcome, Reapers," she greeted them warmly, her mouth and eyes crinkling with smile lines.

She wore her straight, brown hair under her toque in a severe bun, and her hazel-eyed gaze was filled with intelligence and warmth. Where most senior chefs ended up rather chunky from years of sampling the best foods, she retained a trim figure.

"I am Redael Hambo. It is my pleasure to oversee the entire chef staff assigned to the Acropolis, and to serve as your personal chef."

Rasher grinned, while Bibble and Quarce audibly gasped. Kucheesa grinned wider than she had when her name was called in the plaza and gushed, "Oh, I have so many questions!"

"I am looking forward to reviewing your recipes and augmenting them, Meat Mage Kucheesa," Redael said.

Noops said, "The revised training plan might not be ready for a couple days."

"What are you talking about?" Kucheesa demanded.

"You must have realized we will need a strict training plan to become an effective fighting squad," Noops responded.

"What does that have to do with us at this particular moment?" Kucheesa asked.

Noops shrugged. "No doubt you've concluded that with a famous saucier chef overseeing our cuisine, it is likely we will consume richer food, and in greater quantities, than perhaps we are accustomed to."

"So we'll need to work out even harder to keep from getting fat," Quarce laughed in his booming voice. He seemed to have only one volume.

"Thus the need for a revised training plan," Bibble said, stroking his thin beard, not looking nearly as pleased by the thought of even more rigorous training.

Kucheesa scowled. "Why didn't you say so?"

"I did," Noops responded.

His calm tone seemed to annoy her even more. Bibble asked, "Do you know why cheeses never worry about anything?"

She turned her scowl to him. "What are you talking about? Cheese can't worry."

"You're right," Bibble said with a grin. "Because everything is going to brie all right."

She groaned and rolled her eyes. Quarce looked from her to Bibble and said, "I don't get it."

Rasher chuckled. "Not really worth explaining that one."

Redael took a deep breath. "Anyway, back to the question at hand. I assure you my staff will provide exactly the nourishment you need for optimal performance of your duties. I will monitor your training to ensure the proper quantities to bolster muscle development without risking unnecessary weight gain."

She cast one thoughtful look at Bibble. He flushed under her gaze, then brightened and said, "You know, my wife and I recently started doing lunges as part of our workout routine."

"Really?" Rasher asked, surprised. He hadn't expected Bibble to do much exercising at all.

Bibble grinned. "Absolutely. It's not a perfect solution, but it's a big step forward."

Rasher couldn't help laughing. Noops chuckled, and Kucheesa rolled her eyes, groaning. Quarce looked from her to Bibble, a confused look on his face. Then his eyes widened and he burst into a laugh so loud Rasher winced and took a step back.

"You're a very funny man," Quarce said, slapping Bibble on the back hard enough to send him stumbling forward.

"I'm glad I managed to fool one of you already," Bibble quipped.

Rasher interjected before they got too distracted. "Redael, we are all thrilled to meet you, and eager to eat whatever you have prepared."

Kucheesa wasn't the only one looking forward to picking Redael's brain about new recipes. She might have the information Rasher needed to finalize the right recipe to overcome his blood phobia.

"Very good," Redael said with another warm smile. "One of my greatest pleasures in life is to bring joy through food. This initial feast will offer you a wide variety of choices to help us gauge your current likes and dispositions."

She lifted her hands theatrically and added in a ringing tone, "Now, for lunch."

13

THE BACON ENERGY LOOP

Redael clapped her hands sharply, the single note echoing around the large chamber. Rasher was startled to see four doors that had blended perfectly with the walls fly open, and men and women in the green and blue livery of the Heart staff poured into the room, each carrying a silver tray, covered by smoky glass domes.

The Heart was proving to be more exciting than Rasher had anticipated. Hopefully lunch would prove less surprising.

Eight demi chefs and four tournant chefs followed in pristine white jackets, hats bearing the two or three stripes of their rank. Seven Porters followed, wearing portable documentation desks on chest rigs, full of parchment, inkwells, and quills.

"If you will please seat yourselves, we can begin," Redael said, motioning Rasher to take the head chair and his team to sit to either side.

Servers swarmed around the table, depositing platters and whisking away the unused place settings. Others poured glasses of various drinks. It was early for wine, but Rasher noted three different fruit juices, plus tall glasses of fresh milk, and confectioner hot chocolate. He wondered what enhancements they might be imbued with.

Quarce lifted a hand, and Redael spoke before he could even ask the question. "We have seven different coffee brews for you to sample. I look forward to discussing your personal recipe and incorporating it into our menu, along with meats prepared by Reaper Kucheesa."

The dwarf grinned. "I did most of the cooking for my crew in the mines. I'll share the recipes they liked most."

"I'm sure that will be wonderful," Redael said, although her smile faltered a bit. Quarce swelled with pride.

Bibble rubbed his hands together eagerly, then snatched up a steaming cup of coffee just poured by one of the staff and took a tentative sip. "Fit for the gods," he breathed, drinking more deeply.

"Wait till you taste mine," Quarce said, tapping the carafe attached to his hat before also sampling a mug, while a porter stood nearby, taking notes.

Rasher noticed the dwarf's hands shook a little. That was unusual. Most coffee wizards gained advanced immunity to negative aspects of regular coffee consumption. Did that mean Quarce was new?

He'd find out as soon as they made more detailed introductions. He noticed Gubbins had not sat with them and asked, "Won't you join us?"

"At future meals, I will," he promised.

Rasher was about to protest, but at another sharp clap from Redael, two dozen servers snatched covers from the various platters in perfect unison. Aromas assaulted Rasher's nose in a wonderful medley of mouth-watering scents.

He scanned the long table with growing wonder. Everywhere he looked, he spotted meals prepared with a level of artistry he'd only ever seen in the halls of the highest houses.

Delicate stacks of pancakes, drizzled with syrup and sprinkled with sliced strawberries stood near a literal tower crafted from various flavors of mini muffins. A platter of baked eggs and salmon in avocado half-shells sat near egg and crab bakes, shaped like legion helmets. Twelve types of eggs, each prepared differently, sat on separate trays, ready to be paired with just as many meats, grilled or fried or baked to perfection.

Then there were the desserts. Spectacular towers of delicate sugar, fashioned into arches and loops, lorded over cookies and cakes and puddings. Noops was right. If the rest of the team joined Rasher in consuming all of that, they were going to have to exercise all day to work it off.

Of course, his gaze settled on a platter full of bacon-wrapped egg cups. As soon as he focused on it, a demi chef served three of them to his plate. It turned out the eggs sat on thin slices of fried potato, forming small cups of pure deliciousness. Rasher breathed deep, savoring how the scents of the egg and potato mixed with the bacon, which was coated in maple sugar.

He'd eaten a similar dish once back in his home town of Estone in Taradiddle, and as he popped an entire bacon-egg-cup into his mouth, the memory flashed into his mind. His family was celebrating his acceptance into the bacon master guild in the grand city of Weghiv, the seat of the Takmor house. The joy of that day washed through him, magnifying the rush of bacon-infused power that coursed into him, quickly replenishing his reserves.

The rest of the team dug in with enthusiasm, laughing and chatting as servers and chefs piled their plates with every dish they indicated. The tournant chefs closely monitored their choices or made subtle suggestions.

Redael oversaw everything, a little smile on her lips, and her gaze missed nothing. She made gentle corrections or reproved servers who moved too slowly, and they jumped to obey her will.

The porters took copious notes of everything. As chefs-in-training, they often worked physical jobs, scullery chores, and very basic tasks under the lowest-level chefs. Other porters were assigned administrative recorder jobs, which they fulfilled at every level of society.

Unfortunately, since they were studying to become chefs, most of their documents ended up taking the form of recipes.

Rasher let himself simply enjoy the feast, trying to consume as many dishes as possible. Every one tasted better than the last. Eating that well every day was a perk he could definitely sink his teeth into.

"I don't see any roast mutton," Quarce said around a huge mouthful of breakfast sausage.

"For breakfast?" Kucheesa asked.

"Is that a favorite of yours?" Redael asked, glancing at a porter standing near Quarce, who started jotting a new note.

"Not really," Quarce said with a shrug. "We always finished any scraps from the last evening's meal with breakfast, but I guess this is our first meal, so we won't have any scraps, eh?"

Redael smiled faintly, and the porter scratched out the last line they'd been writing.

As the rest of the group began slowing from their initial rush, Redael noted Rasher's undiminished appetite. He was wolfing down everything he could get his hands on, and loving every morsel of it. Three chefs had positioned themselves near his chair, and he kept them all busy serving more food.

Rasher loved feasting, loved the taste of fine-crafted dishes, and wanted to laugh at the feeling of so much raw food energy sizzling into his system, converted by his bacon as soon as it reached his stomach. Maybe he could eat enough to prove his theory that with enough food energy he could overwhelm the blood phobia and immunize himself from it.

Redael approached, smile widening. "You've unlocked the bacon indirect transfer of energy synergy?"

"The what?" Rasher asked, swallowing a huge mouthful of chocolate-covered waffle.

"I like to refer to it as the Bacon Energy Loop principle," she amended.

Noops frowned. "Then why call it the bacon bacon indirect something something?"

She sighed. "Allow me a little creative license, please."

"Oh, sure," Noops said with a knowing smile. "Like when we tell kids eating broccoli will make them strong."

"It will," Kucheesa said. "As long as it's been prepared properly by a vegetable shaman."

Noops tapped the side of his nose and said in a conspiratorial tone, "Exactly."

She deliberately turned away from him and said, "I prefer Bibble's terrible jokes."

"That's a first," Bibble said with a grin. "But I guess there's a thyme for everything."

Kucheesa sighed.

"Speaking of interesting vegetables," Redael said, gesturing at a small platter on the far side of the table, one that no one had sampled yet. "These are an example of experimental cuisine we'll often introduce for your feedback and assistance in testing."

The platter contained squat, round vegetables with reddish skin and wrinkles, as if someone had taken a potato and bred it with a prune.

"I've never seen that one before," Rasher admitted.

"It's an oca tuber," Redael said, picking one up and bringing it to Rasher to inspect. "It's been recently discovered that they are ideal for gravity manipulation, even better than the gravity spike carrots currently used by the rail lines. These oca tubers can twist gravity in several ways, depending on the direction they're pointed after the end is bitten off."

"Fascinating," Gubbins breathed. Rasher agreed. They sounded fantastic. The tuber was hard, and the skin looked tough. He was very tempted to bite off the end of it and try it right there. "We'll be happy to help test them."

"Very good," she said. "But that is a matter for later. Back to the bacon energy loop."

Rasher said, "I call it sizzle."

She smiled. "Sizzle. That's appropriate."

"Has anyone else discovered it?" Rasher asked.

"Only one person that I'm aware of. Back in the Keto era, nine generations ago, Bacon Master Rampion Saeculum discovered that higher form of bacon power."

"I've never heard of him," Rasher admitted. "Why isn't this principle taught to every bacon master?"

"Because Rampion quite literally ate himself to death. He consumed so much food that he exploded from an overdose of raw energy."

"Oh," Rasher said, eyeing the mountain of food still on the table, wondering if he could reach the blood phobia defense level before he reached the internal combustion death level. Only one way to find out.

Quarce laughed. "You've discovered a new way to kill yourself? Fantastic!"

"Perhaps not on your first day on the job," Gubbins cautioned.

"I'm not anywhere near the limit," Rasher assured him, although could he know the limit before he reached it?

Redael said, "I look forward to discussing your experience with the bacon energy loop at another time, captain. Right now, my chefs will come around and interview each of you to round out our understanding of your preferences and to confirm our notes. We will craft a menu based on those results."

"Excellent," Rasher told her. "I think we'll also use this opportunity to get to know each other and our abilities better so we can begin to build our plan for becoming an effective team."

Gubbins said, "I expect we'll soon receive a visit from your seamstress too."

"Oh, which one?" Kucheesa asked excitedly.

Gubbins was interrupted as one of the doors burst open and Lugubrious rushed into the room, followed by half a dozen guards. They all looked worried, and Rasher suddenly wished he hadn't just eaten enough to make his stomach feel painfully full, despite siphoning most of it off as sizzle.

"What is it?" Gubbins demanded.

Lugubrious saluted and said in a breathless tone, "Sir, we just received word that all of the legion battle cuisine is missing."

"What?" Gubbins and Rasher and Redael all exclaimed together.

"I don't know specifics, but the preliminary word suggests our entire food arsenal is gone."

"How is it possible?" Kucheesa breathed in the shocked silence.

"It shouldn't be," Gubbins said with a frown. "Those stockpiles are protected in a special walled-off area of the Acropolis, under a separate guard."

Rasher had instinctively released half a slice of chewy bacon and added some sizzle to accelerate his mind. The magnitude of the disaster only grew worse the more he thought about it.

"The legions cannot battle the largest horde ever seen without our food."

"We'd be annihilated," Bibble said, his voice squeaking a bit.

"It has to be a mistake," Gubbins said, but not even he looked like he believed it.

Rasher rose, his chair scraping loudly against the tile. He pocketed the oca tuber and said, "We have to go and prove it is, or discover what happened. We are the new Reaper team, and we have a job to do."

14

THE FOOD WATCH

The battle cuisine warehouse sector was located in the northwest corner of the Acropolis, separated by its own wall. Given the strategic value of the foodstuffs, the wall had been coated in a special fish sauce that glowed with soft, blue light even in the daylight. That coating would flare brightly at the slightest touch, instantly illuminating anyone who might try to climb up.

The foodstuffs were guarded by a separate unit called the Food Watch. Most of them were assembled just inside their open gate, a full platter standing at attention in neat rows. Their hats, tall and round like cooking pots, shone silver in the bright morning light.

As Rasher's group approached, the entire company saluted smartly in unison at the command of a junior sergeant.

"Where are your officers?" Noops asked.

Only then did Rasher realize he saw no officer with a higher rank than that junior sergeant. That man stepped forward, saluted again, then removed his hat, wringing the brim in his hands. "I'm sorry to report, but we cannot find our officers."

"You've managed to lose all of your officers?" Rasher asked. Losing one's hat or one's armor was considered bad form. Losing an entire command bordered on recklessness.

Gubbins asked, "Did you not receive the order of assembly?"

Kucheesa rolled her eyes and nodded toward the assembled soldiers. "Obviously."

"I mean, who received those orders? They were sent to the senior officer," he amended.

The sergeant said, "I receive them, Sir. I sent runners to notify the officers while I assembled the men, but we haven't been able to find them."

"When was the last time you saw them?" Rasher asked.

The sergeant looked down at his hat and said softly, "Sometime last night, the best we can tell. They were not with those of us who attended the assembly this morning, or those who maintained the watch."

"And when did you notice all the food was missing?" Bibble asked.

"After the assembly, Sir. We received orders from the general to begin preparing a caravan in support of the mobilization effort." He nodded toward a row of several empty wagons parked to the side of the square.

"You don't check on the food every day?" Quarce asked.

"No, Sir. Foodstuffs are maintained in climate-controlled warehouses, and we guard the perimeter. No one enters the warehouses except for quarterly inspections and for food rotations, which generally happen on every other inspection."

The situation was sounding worse and worse. Rasher asked, "When was the last inspection?"

"Two months ago, Sir. All foodstuffs were present and accounted for."

Gubbins interjected, looking flummoxed. "You mean that the food might've been stolen as much as two months ago and no one would know until now?"

The sergeant looked startled by that. "Of course not, Sir. We maintain the perimeter. I've already double-checked the logs. There is no evidence of unauthorized shipments of any food either in or out of the compound in the last month."

Rasher asked, "Is there any evidence of authorized shipments out?"

"I honestly don't know, Sir. Those would be kept in a different logbook, but that book was checked out by the captain yesterday, and he has not yet returned it."

"Now we may be getting somewhere," Bibble said, stroking his thin beard. It was the one part of him that was thin, and he seemed to be trying to highlight it whenever possible.

Rasher turned to Gubbins. "It seems likely the captain and some of the officers may be involved in the question of the missing foodstuffs."

The sergeant looked horrified, clapped his pot-shaped hat back onto his head, and snapped to attention. He spoke in a very formal tone. "Reaper Captain . . . Ah . . ."

"Dilskin," Rasher offered.

"Thank you, Sir." Again he set himself and continued. "Reaper Captain Dilskin, Sir. Am I to understand your intention to malign our good captain and his officers as potential conspirators in the theft of the very foodstuffs they dedicated their careers to protecting?"

The rest of the assembled watch muttered angrily, suggesting the captain had been either above reproach, or an even more talented liar than Rasher had started to think.

Kucheesa interjected. "Sergeant, the best way to resolve unfounded suspicion is to find the truth and make sure everyone knows it. Trust me."

The sergeant started to relax and she added, "You have to admit the situation suggests something foul has happened here, and your officers may have become victims of the crime. We'll need your help and the full cooperation of your troops to discern the truth and to aid them if they are in peril."

That brilliant little speech totally transformed the mood of the assembly. Men and women who had been ready to fight to defend the honor of their captain now looked eager to do everything in their power to help save him from whoever was responsible for the disaster.

Noops said, "Exactly right, Kucheesa. Should have known you would see the truth so quickly, with those circles under your eyes."

She looked at him, mouth partially agape, for once speechless, which Rasher was already realizing was a rarity for her.

He interjected before the two of them could start arguing, "Sergeant, I want to inspect one of those warehouses. Have your troops check every entrance for possible break-ins. Make sure no one comes in or out of the sector without authorization, and give the inquisitors your full cooperation when they arrive."

The sergeant snapped a salute, spun, and started bellowing orders.

Kucheesa rounded on Noops. "What were you talking about? I don't have circles under my eyes."

"Of course not," Noops said with a knowing look that seemed to infuriate Kucheesa even more. She turned away, patting gingerly at her face.

Rasher had no idea what point Noops had been trying to make, but they had work to do.

"Let's split up and check a few warehouses. I want to see if there is any evidence of what might have happened."

"Shouldn't we wait for the inquisitors?" Gubbins asked.

"They'll inspect everything even more thoroughly, but when facing a clever enemy, it makes sense to walk where they tread," Rasher said, quoting Rules number forty-two.

Within moments, soldiers were assigned to lead each of them to different warehouses. There were dozens of the long, fortress-like buildings packed into the sector in regular rows.

Rasher sent the rest of his team ahead and said, "I plan to search places the rest of you might miss."

After they left, he turned to Gubbins and asked, "What do you make of this?"

Gubbins shook his head. "I have no idea. Nothing like this has ever happened before. The Food Watch is chosen out of the most trustworthy troops in the legion. Their officers have proven themselves through years of service and dedication. I've met Captain Spoonfolley, and I never would've imagined he might be a traitor."

"Which would make him the best traitor. Unless he has indeed become a victim of something bigger."

"The captain and all of his officers?" Gubbins asked incredulously.

Rasher considered that, accelerating his thoughts with a bit of chewy bacon. "Separating the officers from the rest of the troop would not be easy. Have the inquisitors explore scenarios where it might be possible, either because they were involved, or because they knew something and had to be silenced."

Gubbins nodded but added, "That still leaves the question of how they could transport tons of heavily guarded foodstuffs right out from under all of our noses without anyone catching even a whiff of the deception."

"The timing is suspect too," Rasher said. "The one time in twelve generations all our battle cuisine is stolen, it happens on the same day we need to begin our mobilization against an unprecedented Gloaming horde."

"You suspect the horde has allies here in the Acropolis," Gubbins said.

"Given that the best-ever Reaper team was sidelined yesterday, how could they not? That was impressive, but this is unbelievable. And it happens while we're facing a horde so large it suggests the Bitter and Savory Courts might be working together."

"Don't even suggest that," Gubbins whispered.

"We can't afford to be willfully blind," Rasher countered. "None of this can be a coincidence, and it suggests unprecedented planning and coordination with traitors or agents concealed among us."

"The Rumpus Cabal," Gubbins suggested.

Interesting idea, and preferable to thinking that traitors lurked among them. The Rumpus Cabal was an organized crime network of thieves, villains, disenfranchised chefs, drunkards, and many of the confused souls who took up the worship of Lahanasi and his disgusting, unwholesome foods.

The Rumpus Cabal lurked in the shadows of every major city, but they were leeches, criminals, and chefs with no morals. They had never seen profit in outright attacking the empire. Anonymity and not drawing too much official attention were their greatest defenses.

"They have the only known human settlement in Whisternfeet," Gubbins reminded him.

"That's just a rumor," Rasher said.

"A very persistent rumor. What if the city of Bogan is real? It suggests some kind of alliance with the glowan."

"If Bogan existed, someone would've found it."

That argument usually worked, but now Rasher wondered if the Rumpus Cabal might be more than anyone suspected. Maybe they'd been something more for a long time.

"Unfortunately, I have no better idea yet," Rasher said. "We need to figure this out before the legions can march. Have the inquisitors compile every possible theory, and then we'll look for facts to confirm which might be true. In the meantime, I'm going to scout the area."

He jogged across the paved courtyard toward the long rows of food warehouses but kept going until he reached the fourth row. In the shadow of the buildings, it was quiet and shaded. No doubt it would feel spooky at night. Rasher scampered up the side of one of the buildings, using the uneven edges of the stonework for hand holds. When he reached the gently sloping roof, the entire sector opened up before him, a great space filled with the regular rows of brick tile roofs.

Rasher jogged along the roof, scanning for anything unusual. He spotted several soldiers patrolling along the sector wall, and he was clearly visible to them. None of them looked in his direction, suggesting they rarely spent time looking inward for intruders who might have already penetrated their security.

The outer wall would glow much brighter at night, which would illuminate the area, but weaken their night vision. Even so, the rooftops did not seem an ideal path for any thieves trying to move tons of stolen food.

Rasher made a slow circuit of the roof, spotting nothing out of the ordinary, then vaulted across the narrow alleyway to the next roof. As he continued his inspection, he wondered how all that food might have been spirited away without anyone noticing. If the theft was indeed coordinated with the glowan invasion, a fact that seemed indisputable, might some glowan creatures with powers that they did not know about have infiltrated the area?

That seemed more likely than the other ideas he'd considered. Some glowan could step into shadows and disappear. Others could fly or were little more than disembodied spirits. But despite all the horror stories, he'd never heard about any that could consume vast quantities of food in a short period without leaving any evidence.

Then again, he had discovered that very ability as a bacon master, so it might be possible.

His musings were interrupted by the arrival of a man soaring up out of the alleyway he'd just passed, flames from a fast-burning poppy seed muffin driving him upward. Rasher blinked, recognizing the man as one of the muffin mages he'd seen earlier in the entryway of the Heart, working on the replacement chandelier.

"Hello," Rasher said. "How did you get into this sector?"

Something about the man made him feel suddenly wary. The fellow said nothing, but just marched straight toward him, one hand dipping into the pocket of his jacket. Then Rasher realized what was wrong.

The man's eyes were pure black but seemed to glow softly in the light.

Glowan-glamoured.

He'd read about how powerful glowan could overwhelm the minds of mortals. Seeing it was a lot freakier.

The muffin mage extracted a mini cake, covered in crimson frosting. Without preamble, he flung it at Rasher's face.

Rasher easily ducked, but as the cake soared past his head, it detonated in the air. The blast tumbled him to the side, knocking his lucky hat flying and coating his entire back with flaming pastry.

Rolling with the blast, Rasher bit back a cry of pain from the searing heat. The cake hadn't been large, but still the explosion seemed weaker than it should have been. He wasn't sure why, but thanked the gods the cake hadn't blasted him unconscious. As he rolled, he managed to extinguish the flames while also releasing a bit of chewy bacon into his mind to shift gears faster and push aside his surprise at the unexpected attack. He didn't have time to question.

The muffin mage was charging, black eyes fixed on Rasher, expression calm as he drew a curved pastry blender from a pocket. The five parallel, curving blades, affixed to a wooden handle, glinted in the light. They looked far sharper than normal pastry blades.

Usually Rasher appreciated folks who took pride in their tools, but he really didn't want to find out what those blades could do to pastrify his face.

The muffin mage rushed in, blades slashing.

Rasher grinned. This kind of conflict was his daily bread and butter. He swayed aside, slipping the strike, and jabbed the muffin mage in those black eyes.

The man might be enthralled by a glowan, but no one could ignore a good eye jab. The man blinked but did not cry out. That momentary pause was enough.

Rasher yanked at the man's arm, planning to apply an arm lock, but the arm barely twitched.

Crumpets. He'd never read that englamoured people were somehow granted superhuman strength. The muffin mage shook him off and slashed again, a backhand that would have opened Rasher's throat.

He ducked, falling back onto his hands and kicked out with both feet.

The muffin mage might be strong, but he lacked superhuman balance. The blow sent him staggering back, right off the edge of the roof. He fell out of sight, still eerily silent.

Rasher rushed to the edge just as the man lifted back into view, holding a pair of muffins behind him that were erupting into long tongues of flame, propelling him upward.

Rasher set himself, released two entire slices of bacon, and punched the man right in the jaw with every ounce of strength he could muster.

The blow landed in the sweet spot, snapping the muffin mage's head back and casting his brain into unconsciousness. The muffin fires winked out, and the englamoured mage fell limply and silently to the cobbled street below. He landed hard, and Rasher clearly heard one of his legs snap.

Good. If what he'd read was true, sharp pain could often yank a person out of their glamour. Rasher jumped from the roof and rolled with the landing. The stones were hard, and he got a couple bruises for his trouble, but nothing serious.

Glancing at his fallen attacker, he muttered to himself, "No, things have just gotten very serious."

15

APOCALYPSE O'CLOCK

By the time the muffin mage woke up, Rasher had dragged him to the gate and emptied his pockets of six more muffins, another small explosive cake, and strangely, a pouch of glittering powdered sugar.

When the rest of his team saw that, they muttered in disgust and Bibble said, "He has to be under a glamour. No self-respecting muffin mage would walk around with powdered sugar."

Rasher was tempted to taste the sugar, but resisted the urge. He bet a full plate of bacon it was highly doctored to weaken the mind.

Noops asked, "I wonder if he was already an addict, or if the glowan encouraged the habit as a way of increasing their hold over him."

"So we definitely have glowan among us," Kucheesa said grimly.

Bibble blanched but said, "You know, I've never liked those glowan nesting doll toys they sell in the markets sometimes."

"Why not?" Kucheesa asked.

"They're so full of themselves."

Rasher couldn't help laughing again and appreciated how the laughter helped calm his mind.

At that moment, Gubbins jogged up with the newly-arrived squad of inquisitors in their black, flat-topped hats. The leader of the inquisitors, a severe-faced woman who wore her hair in a bun so tight, it looked like self-torture, nodded at the unconscious, bound form of the muffin mage. "What is this?"

Rasher explained what happened and what he suspected about the glowan glamour. The inquisitor snapped her fingers, and four burly inquisitors rushed over to haul the slumbering muffin mage away.

"We will interrogate him and discover the truth of your accusations," she assured Rasher.

He appreciated her efficiency but had to suppress a shiver at the thought of what kinds of interrogations they would use. Stories abounded about the terrible tactics sometimes employed by the inquisitors in their single-minded pursuit of truth.

Some claimed they would force prisoners to eat the worst of Lahanasi's evil foods, like anchovies, mushrooms, or, gods forbid, blood pudding.

Worse, if the prisoner was a bacon master, they'd grant him a bit of turkey bacon. Rasher shuddered to think of that vile anti-bacon horror. No bacon master would willingly consume turkey bacon. Just thinking about it made him want to vomit.

Quarce jogged up just then, face flushed with excitement. "We found something!"

"The food?" Kucheesa asked. None of the rest of them had found anything but empty, cavernous warehouses with not so much as a crumb left behind.

"No. Some paving stones had been ripped up in one of the alleys, as if someone had dug a great hole."

"Or tunneled in from outside the wall?" Rasher asked.

Quarce shrugged. "It's filled in now, but maybe."

The lead inquisitor snapped her long fingers and said to her subordinates, "Get vegetable shamans here on the double, and see if we can get a contingent of dwarven miners."

She eyed Quarce, but Rasher wasn't about to let her abscond with one of his team members on their first day. So he told her, "We'll leave you to your work. Send us regular updates."

The woman nodded, made a rather vague salute, and turned to her officers. Rasher let her go. The less one interacted with the inquisitors, the better. They were legendarily sour, and he shared the common suspicion that they secretly sucked on rotten lemons to improve their scowls.

Bibble asked, "Did you hear about the three holes?"

"Wait, three holes?" Kucheesa asked with a frown.

"Well, well, well," Bibble said with a grin.

Rasher chuckled, and both Noops and Quarce joined in. Kucheesa glared at them all and said, "I had expected to leave little boy jokes behind when I joined the Reaper team."

"Hey, dad jokes are nothing like little boy jokes," Bibble protested, then added, "But since you are so intent on focusing on the bad news, I've been trying to calculate how many supplies might remain scattered around the rest of the Acropolis and among the guilds. I'm sure it's enough to keep us going under normal situations, but we would burn through every morsel in the first small engagement with the enemy."

Noops said, "The legions can't fight without food."

Kucheesa looked at him, as if expecting him to add something confusing. When he didn't, she scowled.

Rasher said, "Good point. We need to work on rebuilding stockpiles immediately."

Gubbins said, "I sent runners to the general and the guilds to inform them of the crisis and request estimates for how quickly the guilds can produce enough supplies for the mobilization."

"Good. Let's hope somebody uncovers clues about what happened. Best case, maybe we can recover some of the food," Rasher said.

A courier raced through the gates, running with sugar-enhanced speed, the long tube rollers of his wig flapping wildly. He skidded to a halt in front of Rasher, throwing a quick salute even as he pulled a message from a tube roller in his wig and handed it over.

Rasher broke the seal as the others gathered around and scanned the brief message.

"Casu Marza," Quarce muttered. Then he noticed their blank looks and asked, "You don't use that curse?"

"No," Rasher said. "What is it?"

"Maggot-ridden cheese."

Kucheesa looked disgusted, and Bibble paled. "You eat maggoty cheese?"

Quarce shrugged. "I tried it once, but didn't care for it. In some circles, it's considered a delicacy."

"Delicacy," Noops repeated with a scowl. "Have a care how you use that term in Afitur. Usually it's an excuse for trying some of Lahanasi's evil foods. If you want to curse here, just say black pudding, crumpets, or fish sticks."

"Okay," Quarce said with a grin. "We should practice swearing at each other so I can get the local curses right."

"Sure," Noops said.

"Later," Rasher interrupted. "Right now, let's discuss this report about glowan blocking the Gewgaw."

"I thought they were besieging Ehverr," Bibble said with a frown.

"This appears to be another force," Rasher said, scanning the text again. Forces from Tookus, mobilized to aid Ehverr, had been turned back by a sizable force of water glowan at the great bridge over the Gewgaw River.

Rasher didn't know a lot about the water sprites, fairies, and other glowan of the depths. Had the Bitter Court summoned some fell demon from Dyspepsia Sea to help them? If so, the situation was even more dire than he'd thought.

"Another Gloaming horde," Kucheesa breathed, looking somber. "Strong enough to stop the might of Tookus. I wouldn't have thought they could muster another force that large with the biggest horde of all time already at Ehverr."

"It's going to be a long walk," Noops said with a resigned look.

"Walk?" Kucheesa asked.

"The Sugar and Spice express crosses the Gewgaw," Noops said with a shrug. "Glowan this well-coordinated will have blocked the line, so we may not have enough trains to carry the legions."

That would definitely slow their deployment.

A second courier rushed through the gate, nearly colliding with the first, who was leaving. The new courier, a young woman, delivered a second message.

"They did block the train line and disabled several trains," Rasher read with a scowl.

A third courier skidded to a halt in front of him even before he finished reading the last message. The new scroll shared even more bad news.

"They've disabled the garlic tower?" Gubbins exclaimed.

"That's just rude," Quarce muttered.

"But brilliant tactics," Rasher grudgingly admitted.

Holding the Gewgaw was a bold move. The Gewgaw chasm separating Rubric from Occiput was famously difficult to cross. The bridge was one of the wonders of the world, imbued with magic from the highest of the secret recipe books, making it all but indestructible.

The empire had built a garlic tower above the center of the great bridge. It served as the nexus for the entire garlic tower communications network that connected Rubric with most of her vassal nations. The loss of the tower would cripple the ability of the far-flung cities to rapidly communicate.

Noops asked, "Do couriers get bonuses for how many messages they deliver?"

The latest courier blinked in confusion. "What? No, sir."

"Could you not have combined those messages into one, or were you looking for more dramatic impact by arriving in close succession?"

"I don't . . ." The man looked to Rasher for help.

"Don't mind him," Kucheesa told the man. "He's only had one lunch so far today."

The courier saluted and bolted away. Noops added, "The ploy worked remarkably well."

"I don't think they did it on purpose," Gubbins said. "The messages probably came from different stations."

A fourth courier arrived, and Noops chuckled to himself as the woman handed over her message. At least that one contained some better news. "They're working on updating the Acropolis garlic tower to establish direct shout links to as many cities as possible."

"I wonder if we should close that gate before any more couriers can get in," Quarce suggested.

If only that would help. Rasher asked, "How bad is the loss of the Gewgaw tower?"

Gubbins said, "We already have direct connections with the major cities of Rubric, but that's about it. We'll have no reliable links to anywhere in Occiput, Taradiddle, Gravlax, or Oxter with the hub down."

"We need that communication to coordinate our defenses," Rasher said. "Without the ability to get word to the great cities of the vassal nations, it was likely they wouldn't mobilize to help Ehverr, but keep their forces close to home, each city focused on their own defense."

A fifth courier arrived, and Quarce breathed, "How do they all know where to find us? Impressive networking skills."

Rasher scanned the new message, trying not to feel surprised by yet another bit of bad news. "Another horde has attacked Piffle. Looks like they won't be able to send aid to Ehverr either."

Quarce snatched for the paper. "Are they holding? What word on casualties?"

"Relax," Rasher soothed. "It looks like the horde is smaller than the others. Piffle is holding. The rest of Gravlax is mobilizing to secure their borders."

Bibble frowned and asked, "Are these reports all trustworthy? We have the largest horde ever seen at Ehverr, another powerful horde holding the Gewgaw, isolating us from the rest of the empire, and now a third horde large enough to challenge Piffle? Don't they have the biggest garrison in Gravlax?"

"They do," Quarce said.

Bibble had a good point. Rasher asked, "You're thinking maybe some of this might be part of some kind of misinformation campaign?"

"Easier to confuse than to mobilize so many glowan," Bibble said with a shrug.

"If it's all misinformation, how do you explain the glamour on that muffin mage that just attacked Rasher?" Kucheesa asked.

"Fair point," Bibble conceded with a sigh.

Gubbins said, "At this point, we cannot rule out anything, but we can't afford to disbelieve these reports either. Given these highly coordinated strikes, our enemies are demonstrating a level of planning far beyond anything they've ever done before. We are facing a clear and present danger to the continuing existence of the empire. By any definition, we have indeed reached apocalypse o'clock."

The team exchanged somber glances. They already knew they would not get a gentle transition period, but the challenges were piling up faster than dirty dishes at a new year's feast, and it was still day one. They couldn't even rely on the legion officers to back them up.

"No boring transition for us," Quarce grinned, rubbing his hands together eagerly.

"That's the spirit," Rasher said. Fear wouldn't help, so bold optimism seemed a far better choice. He glanced toward the gate to see if any more couriers might be coming.

"So what are we going to do?" Bibble asked, pulling a small pouch of spices from one of his many pockets and sniffing it. Afterward, he straightened, looking less terrified.

"We're going to have a team meeting and get to know each other better," Rasher said.

"I was sort of imagining something more active," Quarce admitted.

"We'll get to action, but I think life is about to get very busy, and we barely know each other. The legions need a team of Reapers, so we'd better figure out how to become that team."

16

CULINARY WIZARDS WITH A TWIST

The distant clock tower chimed eleven bells as they returned to the Heart. Rasher pulled a courier aside and dictated a note for Kitan. He couldn't wait to find a moment to talk with her. What would she think when she heard the news?

A woman in the colors of the Heart staff reported, "All of your personal belongings have been moved to your new quarters on the top floor."

"That was fast," Kucheesa said.

"I need to speak with my wife," Bibble said. "She must be wild with worry."

Rasher said, "We'll find time for that after our meeting."

The female staffer led them to the third-floor Reaper conference room. It was a vaulted, airy room with a long table, comfortable chairs, a window overlooking the plaza, and a huge slate board on one wall with chalk for planning. It reminded him of the smaller one he'd used in his old office.

As they all took seats, the door opened again and a dozen staff members carried in silver platters, placing them on the table. When they removed the covers, they revealed beautifully designed plates of finger foods, cold cuts, sliced fruit, and tiny desserts.

"With Redael's compliments," one of them said before they left.

While the team reached for snacks, Rasher said, "It's been a busy morning, and I'm sure the pace will continue to be crazy. We have a job to do, and the legions need us to show we can do it."

Noops look pleased by the little speech and seemed at ease in his chair, munching on a tiny ham sandwich. Quarce looked eager as he chomped a pile of sliced pears, and Bibble nodded approval as he sampled a delicate pastry shaped like a swan.

"You better believe we can do it," Kucheesa exclaimed with a determined expression, skewering a grilled sausage with one of her knives. "We're the gods-chosen Reapers, for Pevnir's sake."

Bibble said, "I hate to assume the voice of reason, but everyone is going to expect us to lead the war, and I doubt any of us can find our way out of this building without asking directions."

He was probably right. Rasher doubted any of them had memorized the layout of the Heart or remembered much of what Gubbins had told them about it during the meal with Redael. He'd absorbed everything through the use of a bit of chewy bacon, which dramatically improved his memory. He'd quickly memorized the map of the Heart Gubbins showed them too.

"We started the investigation into the food theft," Quarce reminded him. "And captured an englamoured muffin mage."

Bibble regarded him calmly, again stroking his thin beard. "You think that means we can run a full-scale war?"

He had a point, but they had to avoid negative thinking, or else fear could easily paralyze them and guarantee failure. Rasher said, "I know we've gotten a series of shocks today, but we would not have been chosen if we did not have the skills and abilities necessary to succeed."

Kucheesa banged a fist on the table. "Absolutely! Becoming a Reaper is my lifelong dream. This isn't the way I expected it to happen, but we can't afford to mess this up, so let's figure it out."

"We can do this," Rasher agreed. He was looking forward to understanding the reasons behind Kucheesa's determination. He hoped her skills proved as impressive as her words. "We start now. We need to know each other and start piecing together how to become an effective unit."

When none of them said anything, he said, "I'll go first. I'm Rasher Dilskin, previous leader of the third-string Acropolis paint battle training team. I'm also captain of the Bacon Bits. We won the paint battle championships for the last three years in a row, and I've placed first each time. I've also participated on the inter-legionary council tasked with studying worst-case apocalypse scenarios."

"Did you ever consider a scenario worse than this one?" Bibble asked.

"I did once suggest we consider the scenario of an entire Reaper team getting defeated or killed, but the committee considered that proposal so unlikely as to not merit further attention."

"Good thinking on their part," Kucheesa quipped.

Rasher shrugged. "Even the best miss the mark sometimes."

"Depends on where you set the mark," Bibble responded. "I usually prefer missing high rather than missing low."

Noops said, "Speaking of higher things, Captain, are you experienced with higher forms of bacon power, like temporary invincibility?"

If only he knew. Rasher thought back to his face-first meeting with the side of that building the other day. "I am."

"I hadn't known bacon masters could do that," Bibble said.

Noops said, "That's just the first level of the classified bacon master powers. They can also temporarily become immune to other gods' magic."

"How do you know about that?" Rasher asked.

"You'd be surprised what one picks up while working the Watch," Noops said with a shrug.

"We're Reapers now," Rasher said. "So we need to learn all the higher forms of food fighting. Higher bacon powers are tricky, and require enormous expenditures of bacon."

Bibble leaned forward, expression fascinated. "You can absorb another god's power?"

"In a sense. Gods don't play well together," Rasher stated the obvious. That was why no one received powers from more than one god and why chefs could only enhance one element of any recipe. "But Domuz is very protective. He grants the ability for us to essentially borrow one other god's power for a short period if we are attacked by it, and then redirect it."

"That's amazing," Quarce boomed.

And it had been used to turn the tides of important past battles. Smoot Blatherskite had used it during the famous incursion into Whisternfeet. He'd absorbed one of the Bitter Court queen's most powerful spells, then redirected it against her forces.

"Trying it instantly consumes a full third of my entire bacon reserves," Rasher explained. "It's worth the price because not only am

I protected from that power, but I can redirect it against someone else, then copy it and release it a second time within five minutes."

"Wow," Quarce grinned. Even Kucheesa looked impressed.

"Unfortunately, using such a high bacon power would leave me exhausted, and I can't use it again for a week."

"Still pretty amazing," Bibble said.

He suspected there were ways to speed up that recovery like he'd discovered with the temporary invincibility power, but hadn't experimented with it enough to know for sure.

Since they were discussing his abilities and weaknesses, he considered telling them about his blood phobia. He hesitated, though. That was his big secret, and if he could find the right recipe with Redael's help, he might beat it anyway.

"Bibble, why don't you go next?" he asked.

"Okay. I'm Bibble Widdershins, senior spice wizard, with particular emphasis on close proximity air shielding and gastrointestinal manipulation."

Those were excellent credentials. It felt good knowing they had such an experienced spice wizard on the team.

Bibble added, "I've participated recently in efforts to modify the air blast engine from the Sugar and Spice Express cars to retrofit them into carriage-sized vehicles."

"Is that possible?" Kucheesa exclaimed, eyes wide.

"Not yet," Bibble said with a shrug. "But I suspect someone will figure it out soon. When they do, it will revolutionize transportation even more than the Express did."

That was amazing. Rasher had first ridden the Sugar and Spice Express from Taradiddle to Afitur, and the memory still awed him. The sleek, plush passenger cars moved several times faster than a horse along their fixed rails, but inside the journey felt quiet and comfortable. Each of the long freight cars linked to the end of the last passenger car could transport ten cargo wagons' worth of supplies.

The completion of Express lines between every major city of the Rubric Empire was one of the major contributors to the renaissance period of rapid growth five generations ago during the Paleo era.

The smaller trains used inside Afitur for public transportation were built on similar principles on a smaller scale. They used a closely guarded spice recipe from one of the classified cookbooks to produce gale force winds that drove the engines, while the wheels were coated with a special blend of sugars that dramatically reduced friction. That blend was the precursor for the latest generation of the gingersnap wheels everyone was clamoring to get.

Of course, the fastest of the express trains, reserved for the primi and secondi house members, included a secondary propulsion system of a huge rocket muffin that drove those trains several times faster than the normal express. There was talk of adding anti-gravity vegetable mixes to make them so light the wagons would all but fly across the realm.

Now that they were Reapers, he hoped to find an excuse to ride in one of those someday. It boded well that the team had such an experienced spice wizard on board. If Bibble moved in those high circles, participating in top-secret research projects, his spice powers must be among the strongest of his guild.

"I'm glad to hear that's in the works," Rasher said.

The portly spice wizard added, "Ah, until today, my wife and children lived with me here in the Acropolis. You've already seen my love of good jokes."

"Good?" Kucheesa asked softly, but Bibble only shrugged and continued. "I've never deployed on any active campaigns." He patted his ample midsection and grimaced. "Now I'm starting to regret that lack of field experience."

"We're glad to have you on board," Rasher assured him. The jokes would be welcome in stressful moments, and dealing with his physical fitness issues would be simple compared to most of their other challenges.

Quarce went next. "First, let me say I'm proud to be the first dwarf or any soldier from Gravlax to become a Reaper. I intend to prove to the world that we should be considered more often."

Rasher liked motivated team members. He would definitely face some opposition from some segments of the legions.

"And you're a coffee wizard," Bibble added, looking meaningfully at Quarce's hat.

Quarce smiled. "My brew is one of the best. I've spent years developing the perfect blend of beans and supplemental ingredients to maximize the energy boost, reinforced with a blend of confectioner sugar and healing creams that keep it elevated longer, and smooth the after-coffee slump."

He detached the sturdy coffee carafe from his hat. A curl of steam drifted into the air when he uncapped the spout, filling the room with a subtle aroma of fresh-brewed coffee. From the leather satchel on the floor he withdrew several clay mugs and started pouring.

Bibble looked giddy with excitement as he took the first mug. "There's nothing quite like a bracing coffee in the morning, or any time of day, for that matter."

Rasher was an occasional coffee drinker, but when he tasted Quarce's brew he decided he needed to reconsider that choice. It was perfectly blended with cream and sugar. He decided not to ask more about how Quarce ensured the sugar dosages, but would trust Quarce knew what he was doing and wouldn't risk exposing them to dangerous levels.

The beverage was a perfect counterpoint to the snacks on the table. Having a top quality coffee wizard on the team would guarantee access to energy-boosting brews on campaign whenever they needed it.

"Nothing feels better than when folks appreciate your craftsmanship," Quarce said proudly.

Bibble leaned forward and asked, "Can you craft metal with imbued coffee powers too?"

That would be an enormous boost. It was difficult to acquire quality dwarven-crafted, coffee-imbued armor or equipment. It was very expensive and closely controlled, but offered powerful battle enhancements.

Quarce shook his head and declared, "Nope. I don't work in metal." He held up his large hands and added, "I get the coffee shakes so bad, I've taken a different path."

That was disappointing, but Rasher understood what it was like to have a frustrating weakness that one could not control. "Don't worry about it. Just having access to your coffee every day will be a huge help."

"You have access to more than that, Captain. Try these."

Quarce pulled from his leather satchel an intricate little figurine of a frog. It was rendered in beautiful detail, and at first Rasher thought it must be made of silver.

Kucheesa reached down and plucked it off the table. "Paper?"

Quarce nodded happily. "It is called the art of origami. I find my shaking fingers are perfectly suited to the fast-folding of paper, and I can imbue these little origami creations with energizing coffee power. Each one can boost your energy, vitality, and stamina for short periods."

That was unexpected, but might still be useful. The dwarf extracted several more frogs and passed them around. Rasher got a red bullfrog that looked remarkably realistic.

"I feel it. How do we access it?" asked Bibble eagerly. He definitely had an intimate relationship with coffee.

"Like this." Quarce hefted his frog, regarded it with a look of pride, then shoved it up one wide nostril. He inhaled deeply, and the little frog flashed into a cloud of brown particles that disappeared up his nose.

"That's something you don't see every day," Noops commented, looking totally unfazed by the bizarre move.

Kucheesa gaped open-mouthed, then exclaimed, "That's disgusting."

Quarce shrugged. "It works, so is it wise to knock a working tool?"

She leaned back in her chair and folded her arms. "I refuse to shove an origami animal up my nose to get a little energy."

"I will," Bibble said, happily crumbling his little frog and shoving it up his nostril. He breathed deep and the little brown frog flashed and disappeared. He leaned back in his chair, smiling, and sighed. "That burst of strength is amazing. I feel like I could run for a full mile."

Rasher concealed a chuckle at Bibble's idea of feats of great strength.

Bibble added, "What kind of frogs have horns?"

No one bothered to guess, and after a brief pause, he said, "A bull frog!"

Quarce laughed far louder than that joke deserved. Rasher smiled as Noops tried his frog, then nodded, but said nothing. Rasher gave it a try too, and although the experience of shoving something in his own nose was unusual, it did not hurt, and the discomfort evaporated as soon as he inhaled and the frog disappeared.

A rush of energy coursed through him, intense but short-lived. He appreciated that the tool was available, but wouldn't bother using it himself. As long as he never ran out of bacon, he had all the energy he needed. It lasted longer too.

Besides, as a bacon master, he could not utilize other magical powers or enhancements at the same time as his bacon. To utilize the dwarf's coffee energy, he would need to release bacon and only return to it after the coffee power exhausted itself.

"Thank you, Quarce. Make sure you get plenty of paper on hand for when we deploy. Kucheesa, why don't you go next?"

She sat forward, her annoyance at the frog experiment evaporating. "I am Kucheesa Beeshee from Taradiddle. Yes, my great-grandmother was a Reaper, no she was not a traitor. I do not wish to speak of it further. I will restore my family's honor."

By the set of her jaw, she was ready for a fight. Rasher would wait for a more appropriate time to cautiously inquire for more details.

Her glare faded and she actually sort of smiled. "I am a meat mage, and I've explored capabilities that no other meat mage that I know of has ever attempted."

"You transformed your nose into a beak. That's advanced meat magic," Rasher acknowledged, hoping the compliment would help ease some of her tension.

"What raptor meat did you use to produce that effect?" Noops asked.

"I don't use raptors. I use chicken." She stated it like a challenge, smile fading as she tensed.

Quarce blinked a couple of times, and Bibble just gaped. Rasher wanted to ask a thousand questions, but waited to see if the other team members would ask them first. She seemed quick to dislike him, and until he understood why, he did not want to stoke those fires.

"Chicken is an interesting choice," Noops commented, still not displaying any surprise at probably the oddest get-to-know-you meeting Rasher had ever heard of.

"I thought meat mages only used predators," Bibble commented.

"You can't use predators when you're barred from accessing the meat palace in your homeland, can you?" she snapped.

"Why would you be barred from using predator meats?" Quarce asked.

She sat back, scowling again. "It happens when your grandmother is accused of being a traitor, and your father manages to insult the local high lord."

Quarce whistled softly, and even Noops looked impressed. It was a wonder she had managed any kind of acceptance in the Acropolis.

Rasher was starting to understand why she had that enormous chip on her shoulder.

"So who taught you the techniques?" Bibble asked, his expression curious, his tone void of any sort of mocking.

That seemed to startle her, as if few people bothered to ask her anything after they understood her family troubles. Her scowl faded and her eyes seemed to come alight as she spoke of her powers.

"I'm self-taught. I learned on the farm. The only meat I had access to was chicken since the bacon masters refuse to let anyone experiment with pork." She cast Rasher a glare as if he had any input into that policy.

"We didn't have enough cows, so I only rarely experimented with beef. I couldn't seem to get any good attributes out of it."

"What attributes can you get out of chicken?" Quarce asked, looking as shocked by her tale as she had been by his.

"More than you would think," she shot back. "I'm the only one who's ever developed that beak transformation trick. Plus, chickens have a lot more attributes than most people realize."

"Like gliding," Rasher said as he thought back to her long, graceful float down from the statue to the square the other day.

She nodded with a little smile. "That took a while. A lot of chicken meals to get that one right, but you've seen how useful it is."

"How about actually flying?" Bibble asked eagerly.

That would indeed be an amazing ability, but Rasher had only heard of the most powerful meat mages reaching those heights.

"Not yet," she admitted. "But in addition to the beak, I can grow my fingernails and toenails pretty long, I've developed advanced agility, I can survive on very little food if I need to, and I always know the direction of the sun."

Rasher wanted to ask if she felt an inexplicable urge to crow at sunrise, and dearly hoped she did not. That could prove really annoying. He also wondered if in times of danger she had the instinct to try to hide children under her coat. The thought made him smile, which made Kucheesa scowl at him again, as if guessing what he was thinking.

"We'll have to explore those abilities as soon as possible. Work with Redael and her team to incorporate your best dishes into her menu plan," Rasher said.

Kucheesa was not the only one who looked surprised by the suggestion. Bibble said, "I figured she'd focus on requisitioning some of the most powerful predator meats. We are Reapers now, after all."

Kucheesa glared, but he had a point and Rasher could not afford to ignore any advantage. He also did not want her shutting down and refusing to work with the team. "Different people react better to different meats, right?"

When she nodded he said, "Work out a schedule with Redael. Let's experiment with chicken and see if any of us can see any benefits. We may not be able to float, but if we could acquire some additional agility, that would be beneficial. We can experiment with other meats too and see which of us receive the best benefits from which meats."

She grinned. "I'll speak with her before dinner."

Bibble suddenly brightened and said, "Oh, wait. What do you call a chicken possessed by a glowan?"

"Can they do that?" Quarce asked.

"A poultry-geist!" Bibble laughed.

That got a smile from everyone. Even Kucheesa seemed to struggle to maintain her scowl.

Rasher said, "All right, Noops, your turn."

"And please explain about that shovel," Bibble added.

17

THE WAY OF THE SHOVEL

Rasher couldn't help smiling as Noops drew his spade shovel from the sheath on his back. The curved blade of the shovel was made of fine steel, polished to a shine, sharpened all along its length. It was longer and narrower than usual, but still clearly a shovel.

The three-foot-long hickory haft was covered with a waffle pattern for better grip and was capped with a knobby steel counterweight. Rasher had never seen a shovel configured quite that way before.

Noops reverently placed the shovel on the table in front of him and said, "I am Noops Finsterwallies, knight of the Acropolis Watch, born and raised in the farmlands north of Afitur. And this is my shovel."

All of the team stared at the magnificent shovel for a moment, clearly not sure how to respond. Rasher finally said, "Ah, I see you're also armed with a short sword. Is that sometimes your primary weapon?"

Noops looked at him like he was daft, and he felt like an idiot for even having to ask the question. Noops tapped the shovel. "The short sword is but a token of victory. This is my weapon, Captain."

Rasher tried to figure out how to phrase the next question carefully, but Kucheesa jumped headlong into the conversation. "But, that's a shovel!"

Noops sighed, giving her a long-suffering look. "Why is it that no one seems to understand the power of a good shovel?"

He picked it up, rose, and stepped back from the table. He expertly spun the shovel in his hands, moving with easy familiarity as he worked its wide blade through an intricate sequence that combined forms Rasher recognized from swords, axes, and polearms.

Suddenly the shovel seemed a very potent weapon. Quarce and Bibble looked impressed, but Kucheesa just gaped. "You're serious? You really fight with that thing?"

Rasher was glad she asked the question so he didn't have to. She seemed very comfortable saying ridiculous things.

Noops rolled his eyes, clearly annoyed with a question he must get all the time. "Of course. Haven't you ever heard of the shovel knight?"

Kucheesa glanced at Rasher, forgetting for a moment that she had decided to dislike him. In the face of armed shovel combat, other grudges seemed to take a back seat. Rasher shrugged.

"I have," Bibble said, leaning forward. "I heard some guys talking about betting on your matches. How many other knights have you defeated now? Twenty?"

With a final whistling spin of the blade, Noops easily sheathed the shovel and said with a shrug. "The number now stands at thirty-seven."

That was right! Rasher suddenly remembered rumors of a crazy knight he'd heard in some of the taverns. "Hold on? Are you the guy who defeated a couple of knights using a plow?"

Kucheesa started to laugh, but it faded into more of a groan when Noops grinned and nodded happily. "That was an important day." He patted the short sword on his belt. "That's when I started choosing which of the weapons of my opponents I would carry as my second."

Bibble laughed and slapped his ample belly. "I knew it." He glanced at the others and explained, "This fellow is famous. He's renowned as the deadliest knight to have ever taken up the shovel."

"Has anyone else taken up the shovel?" Rasher couldn't help asking.

"Not as far as I know," Noops admitted. "Although I've heard of some small groups attempting to duplicate my techniques in secret. I have seen no evidence to confirm the rumors."

"I knew a guy who preferred a shovel," Bibble said. "His name was Doug."

"That's a weird name," Quarce said before he got the joke and guffawed.

"Why take up the shovel at all?" Kucheesa asked, pointedly ignoring Bibble's latest joke.

Noops sat again and spread his hands on the table. "Like I said, I grew up in a small town north of Afitur. Even there, all young men are required to enter the fighting academy at age ten to identify best candidates for conscription. Our town is very poor and only had a few precious practice weapons."

He paused for a moment before adding, "I broke mine."

"So they made you use a shovel?" Rasher guessed.

Noops nodded. "I was small for my age, and as punishment for my mistake, our instructor ordered me to use my own shovel to train. He did not want to waste another expensive training sword on a recruit he feared would not pass muster."

"But you did," Kucheesa guessed.

He nodded. "I might not have hit my growth spurt yet, but I was very strong. My father was trying a new type of irrigation on our property, which required the digging of many trenches. I knew shovels better than anyone, and I welcomed the chance to train with my own."

"So even after you entered the regular academy, you kept the shovel?" Quarce asked.

Noops nodded. "I am proficient with most weapons, but I never found another as perfect as the shovel."

Rasher grinned, fascinated by the tale. He liked to teach his students to find the weapon that worked best for them, then master it. He'd never had anyone end up with a shovel before.

Noops said, "For some reason I have never understood, my choice makes other knights think me daft. Some have made the mistake of teasing me. When they heal, the foolish ones challenge me to a duel."

"And you started taking weapons from the men you defeated?" Bibble asked.

Noops nodded with a grimace. "Unfortunately, two knights created a devious plot. The first challenged me and arrived with a plow. He surrendered quickly, but they knew my habit of taking the weapon of my defeated opponent to my next duel."

"So his friend challenged you, thinking you'd be easy to defeat," Rasher guessed, trying to imagine Noops wielding an ungainly plow. Knights took their duels very seriously.

The shovel knight smiled. "Now I choose which of their weapons to carry as my victory token, and if I will wield it or my shovel in battle. The number of duels has dropped off lately."

He patted the haft of his shovel again and said, "I guess it's like the whole question of the rooster and the egg."

Kucheesa scowled. "It's the chicken and the egg."

"Which one?" Noops asked.

"What?"

"Which one? The chicken, or the egg? And how do they tie into the rooster?"

"You're bonkers," she stated, crossing her arms and glaring.

Noops nodded sagely, tapping the side of his nose. "You are the expert with chickens."

Her expression softened. Maybe Noops wasn't so clueless after all.

Then he added, "Should have seen it earlier. Look how petite you are."

"What is that supposed to mean?" she demanded.

"You've got those tiny hands too."

She reached for her knives, but Rasher intervened. He had no idea what point Noops was trying to make, but wouldn't risk a duel between the two on their first day.

"Enough. I think that's a good start for now."

As he surveyed the team, the beginnings of ideas on how best to leverage their unique blend of strengths started coalescing in his mind. He assembled ad hoc teams for paint battle tournaments all the time, so he had lots of practice building successful teams on short notice. This situation was admittedly unique, but he felt confident he could whip them into fighting shape quickly.

He wished the squad was larger, including a wider complement of guilds. They lacked several of the most vital guild representation, including muffin mages, cheese wizards, confectioners, and vegetable shamans. Those missing guilds created gaping holes in their capabilities they would need to fill with Gleaners.

They were not the squad anyone would have chosen, and were clearly not the squad General Nide or even the hero finders had planned, but it was their new reality. Their surprise nominations might actually suggest divine favor, but in the short term it promised no end to headaches, obstacles, and danger.

Rasher rubbed his hands together, drawing upon a bit of sizzle and embracing the challenge. As Reapers, new opportunities also existed, and he planned to capitalize on them.

First challenge, unite this team as an effective Reaper squad. Second, squash the doubts of those who didn't want them to succeed.

Overseeing the investigation into the missing battle foods would help with that.

Third, don't die. They needed to figure out how to work with the general and win her to their side so they could mobilize the legions and deal with the Gloaming hordes.

But his team needed time to adjust to their new reality. He couldn't give them much, but the cost of a little was worth the price. "Let's take a short break, make sure your rooms are set up right, and Bibble you can visit your family."

He doubted anyone had spotted that stranger who had attacked him in his rooms, but he hoped to get an update on that englamoured muffin mage soon. Could the two attacks be related? He needed to make sure Gubbins had spread the alert about glowan in the Acropolis. There couldn't be many, or the wards and spells protecting the area would have triggered, but clearly at least one glowan had slipped inside to englamour that mage.

As the team stood, he added, "Meet back here in an hour so we can prepare for our meeting with General Nide and her staff this afternoon."

His plan lasted about three seconds.

When he opened the door, he found a crowd of half a dozen secretaries and twice as many administration officials clustered there. They surged forward, shouting for his attention. Most of them wore the low hats with short front brims common to administrative units, but a couple wore the extra wide-brimmed hats over long wigs full of messenger scrolls like couriers.

Most of the men and women pressing around Rasher waved official-looking scrolls they wanted him to read or sign, some with looks of near desperation on their faces. It seemed the Reaper captain was responsible for a lot of decisions about the running of the Heart and how the legions assigned to support them were managed. Gubbins had not mentioned any of that.

As if he had any idea how to make those decisions yet. Besides, after what happened to the last Reaper team, he would never sign anything without first reading it very carefully.

"Is there any way I can meet with Captain Youlate?" he asked.

One old fellow in an immaculately pressed uniform stood at the front of the crowd with an air of authority. He was tall, his thinning, gray hair perfectly groomed under a very small, black cap. A whisper-thin, oiled mustache shadowed his lip. Despite the pushing and jostling among the others, they gave the old man plenty of space.

The fellow executed a perfect salute, the movement crisp, and spoke in a cultured accent of one schooled in the best academies of Afitur. "Captain, if I may take the liberty of introducing myself. I am Shemo Medjamo, your personal assistant and manager of the secretarial corps assigned to the Reapers."

"It's a pleasure," Rasher said, relieved. He took Shemo's hand in a firm grip.

The old fellow looked shocked and said, "Normal protocol does not include handshakes, Captain."

"Ah, sorry. I'm new here."

That was a stupid thing to say, but Shemo only said, "Indeed, Captain. As you can see, there are many actions requiring your attention. Unfortunately, Captain Youlate has left the Acropolis and is barred from performing any of his former duties. Repercussions of inadvertently breaching the new contract would be quite severe."

Rasher shuddered to think about the horrors of the cream cheese clause. "I know things must be hard on all of you, but I have some things to take care of today. Can we just decide to keep things running in the same manner that the previous Reapers had established?"

Most of them sighed, looking immensely relieved, as if he'd said something extremely wise.

"An excellent choice, Captain," Shemo said, then glanced at the assembled crowd and added, "Off with you, then. There is work to be done. I expect updated reports on my desk before the end of the day."

Rasher already decided that Shemo was gods-sent, and planned to set things up to have the experienced manager take care of as much of the day-to-day operations as possible.

As most of the crowd hurried off, some already jotting notes with portable ink and scroll sets, Rasher said, "Shemo, can you prepare a list of things we're going to have to talk about, as well as a list of all forces assigned to the Acropolis? I'd also like to know the status of remaining supplies and stockpiles."

"Of course," Shemo said, his calm expression never changing. "I will have the reports compiled and awaiting you in your office."

"Great. I'll see you later."

Shemo saluted again, turned and marched off, every movement exact, as if he were at a parade assembly.

That's when Rasher spotted a tall woman dressed glamorously in the highest fashion, marching toward them with a purposeful, if prancing stride. She wore the biggest, most garishly colored hat Rasher had ever seen. The wide, gauzy brims stretched nearly three feet, dipping around her beautiful face and ornately braided black hair.

The crown of the hat rose in multi-tiered waves, each level a different vibrant color. The center was hollow, filled with bright summer flowers arranged in a gorgeous bouquet. Her dress was a complex layering of silks in bright reds, blues, and golds. She stood so tall that Rasher suspected she had to be wearing very high heels. A dozen men and women dressed in pastel colors, wearing hats that could have graced the heads of the richest primi nobility followed, marching in perfect unison in close ranks behind her.

"Captain Rasher Dilskin?" the woman asked in a rich, sonorous voice.

"I am," he said with a bemused smile. He had not expected such a colorful character in the Heart. She looked like she belonged up on Nutmeg Hill.

"Looks like I got here just in time," she said, her gaze taking in their appearances.

"Just in time for what?" Kucheesa asked.

"For your first official makeover, of course."

18

SAPKA'S FIRST MAKEOVER

"Our what?" Rasher asked.

"Your first makeover," the woman declared grandly. "I am Sapka Ayakkabi, senior seamstress of the wardrobe guild, and I am now the Reaper team's official fashion consultant."

Noops and Quarce gaped, Bibble looked impressed, and Kucheesa eyed the woman suspiciously, one hand drifting toward a dagger. Rasher suppressed a laugh. With so many weighty matters to deal with, he hadn't given his wardrobe a second thought. Only then did he realize the awful truth. As a Reaper, he would need to wear a different hat.

He reflexively reached up to touch his golden frying pan hat and said, "It's a pleasure to meet you, but we don't have time for this."

"Do you have no idea who I am?" she demanded. "I design fashion for half the primi houses."

Rasher fought down a flash of irritation. "Look, Sapka, I appreciate your skills, but we're Reapers, not nobles. We can't go into battle wearing those hats." He nodded toward the huge, floppy hats her people wore.

"Of course not. I custom design every client's wardrobe. By the looks of you, we have a lot of work to do. You weren't going to your next appointment looking like that, were you?"

"We don't actually have any clothes to change into," Kucheesa admitted.

She was right, Rasher realized with a jolt. Even if their old uniforms were transported to their new quarters, as Reapers they needed new clothing.

"You do now," Sapka declared grandly, clapping her hands together sharply, and turning to gesture down the hall.

Her attendants split apart, making a path for them to pass through. Sapka started walking, clearly expecting them to follow. Since that was the way they needed to go anyway, he did, with his team close behind. As they passed between the attendants, many of them withdrew measuring tapes from pockets and swarmed around them, taking measurements even as they walked.

"What are you doing?" Rasher protested as one nimble fellow hopped sideways next to him, crouched low to measure the outer length of his leg while he walked.

"This won't take long," Sapka promised.

She led them down one flight of stairs to a hallway Rasher remembered from the map he'd memorized, but it had not been labeled. Two open doorways faced each other across the hall, followed by fourteen closed wooden doors, packed close together.

"Quick now, into the showers," Sapka said, gesturing Kucheesa toward one of the open doorways and the rest of them toward the other.

Rasher sighed. They had so much to do, but they did need new uniforms. Kucheesa entered the opposite doorway, flanked by two female attendants, while several male attendants urged Rasher and the other men forward.

Quarce looked close to panic, but Rasher gestured him on. "Just do it. We'll make it fast."

Inside the doorway, they entered a long tiled room with small, frosted glass doors marching down one side. Behind each door was a tidy, fully appointed personal shower space with a low-sided, flat basin to stand in and a wide copper spout protruding from the roof, already releasing a gentle cascade of hot water.

That looked a lot nicer than the shared officer baths he usually used. Rasher stepped inside the first one. A male attendant took his clothes, and another offered to help him wash. That was weird, and Rasher waved him back. He did enjoy the hot water, and used the soaps and hair creams waiting inside the shower to quickly wash.

In the other showers, he heard Bibble speaking, followed by someone laughing. Quarce was shouting at someone not to touch his hat. He chuckled to himself. The experience might have seemed very weird on any other day. When he finished showering, he found his clothes had been replaced by clean underclothes that fit perfectly, and a simple, white tunic and trousers.

He was the first to finish, and when he returned to the main hallway, he followed directions from another attendant into the first of the wooden doorways spaced down the hall. He entered a brightly lit square room with a tall mirror on one wall, and two more wooden doors facing each other to either side. The air was warm and smelled faintly of soap.

Three tailors wearing short, floppy green hats waited for him with measuring tapes. They gestured him onto a low platform in the middle of the room and swarmed around him, measuring every possible angle and length on his body, jotting quick notes in a pad that was whisked away by a runner. That was pretty efficient work. Those tailors could teach some fists of the legion a lesson on focus.

"I just need something simple," Rasher told one of them.

"The seamstress will have your new outfit ready in moments," the tailor assured him before the three exited through the left side door.

A young man stepped through the opposite door and asked, "Would you like some food, or a refreshing beverage?"

"Absolutely," Rasher said with a grin. He'd never turn down free food.

The young man disappeared, returning seconds later with a tall glass of cold milk, with little beads of condensed water dripping down the sides. He also carried a plate piled with bite-sized rolls of candied bacon.

Rasher munched a few bacon rolls, then took a long drink. The milk carried a gentle healing enhancement that complemented the growing sizzle of the fresh food revitalizing his body.

He was tempted to test the young man's resourcefulness by requesting a cookie to go with the milk, but resisted the urge. He didn't like eating cookies from strangers. There was no way of telling what types of sugars might have been used in the baking.

Just as he finished the snack, Sapka swept into the tiny room from the opposite side, followed by the three tailors. She had changed her entire outfit, including her hairdo. She now wore a simple dress, cut to accentuate her lithe figure, colored in bright greens, golds, and blues. Her hat was much smaller, perching on the top of her head like a glittering tiara. Her long, black hair hung in waves, with slender braids looping low around her head, and she stood several inches shorter than before in simple leather flats.

"Captain, I am so excited to work with you and your team to develop your brand and style. I have some initial ideas for today's fitting, but we must find more time for a proper wardrobe creation."

"That'll have to wait, I'm afraid. We'll be heading out on campaign soon, and we have a very full schedule."

She waved away his concerns. "I will be joining your entourage on the road. We'll find ample time to develop your wardrobe needs. May I ask if any of your duties might include formal affairs, such as a visit to Nutmeg Hill?"

"I don't think so, but we will be meeting with General Nide and her command staff in a couple hours."

"Then we will focus on the base uniform first." She extended a hand and a mannequin the same height and shape as Rasher popped into existence next to her.

Rasher startled, hand reflexively grasping for his battle staff before he reminded himself that Sapka was a full seamstress. At her level, she could maintain an extensive wardrobe of complete outfits, including jewelry, hats, and hairdos in an invisible space. He'd once heard it described as a magical closet, sort of like a giant, invisible hollow pastry filled with clothing instead of cream. She could also keep dozens of mannequins in that space, available at her beck and call.

He'd never experienced it firsthand and had to admit it was impressive. If he could have his own space pocket, he'd prefer something more like a hot pocket, an invisible kitchen he could use to summon a grill, complete with already-sizzling bacon. Now, that would be some magic.

The mannequin Sapka had summoned was dressed in black trousers with a form-fitting leather jacket colored bright blue, sporting bright silver buckles up the front. The Reaper butcher knife emblem proudly shone in bright white on the left breast. It would have looked wonderful if not for the color.

Beside the mannequin appeared a tall hat rack with a massive leather hat colored the same shade of blue. The wide brim had a graceful arc, and a dozen feathers flared from the crown, each a different shade of red and emblazoned with one of the guild emblems.

"For today, I figured we'd start with something subtle," Sapka said with a warm smile.

"That's subtle?" he chuckled. Maybe that word meant something different in primi circles where she usually worked.

"Indeed. As Reaper captain, your fashion must make a statement."

He'd never heard of Absquatch Youlate or Sumwinkle, or even Otamot wearing hats like that. His impatience returned. He'd never bothered much with fashion and appreciated the fact that most soldiers just had to worry about keeping their uniforms clean.

"I think we need to go more basic. Why can't we just use similar uniforms to the last Reaper team?"

Sapka gasped. "Reusing fashion is a sign of a weak mind, Captain. I will not allow such a thing to be associated with either your name or mine."

"Fine. The outfit's nice, but blue's not really my color."

He had no idea what color might be 'his' color.

"That is not an issue." With another wave of her hand, several more identical mannequins appeared, each wearing the same outfit in a different color. Rasher blinked. Even with her invisible closet, how had she crafted so many so fast?

His gaze lingered on one jacket colored dark green, and instantly Sapka snapped her fingers. The other mannequins disappeared, leaving the green one. "An excellent choice, Captain."

"I can't wear that hat," he told her, gesturing at the green hat with all the feathers. Imagining that hat on his head insulted the memory of his favorite hat.

She pursed her lips, snapping her fingers a couple times. Several additional hat racks appeared. Rasher was tempted to ask her for a traditional bacon master skillet hat, but doubted she'd go for it. He'd already accepted the fact that he needed a different hat, and no other skillet hat could replace his lucky hat.

So he chose the least ostentatious of the hats she offered. It was another wide-brimmed hat, but far more sensible than the others. Dark brown leather, with a gold band and a single black feather bearing the Reaper butcher knife.

Sapka flashed a brilliant smile. "I'm starting to get a sense of where you stand now, Captain. Never fear, I will shepherd you along the way to fashion greatness."

"I am so relieved," he muttered.

She smiled again, either not picking up on the sarcasm, or not caring.

"I will see to the rest of your team," she said, then swept out of the room, leaving him with the tailors.

Despite his protests, they insisted on helping him dress in the new outfit, fussing over every seam, ready to make any last-minute adjustments. They needn't have worried. Everything fit perfectly and was far more comfortable than he'd expected. They even produced a pair of new boots that hugged and cushioned his feet like fresh bread. They were tall, made of supple leather the same color as his jacket. In that new outfit, he actually looked like a Reaper captain.

The tailors led him through the side door where the young man had brought his snack. They followed a narrow corridor that ran behind the other dressing rooms, and eventually entered a wide sitting room, with windows in the rear wall of the Heart looking toward the command staff quarters.

Rasher settled into a plush, overstuffed chair and asked one of the attendants for a courier. A young woman in a courier wig-hat appeared in seconds, and Rasher asked her to go to his secretary, Shemo, and request the location of the current prophet of Arkadas. She bolted from the room at a full sprint. It was nice having motivated help.

Over the next few minutes, each of the team members emerged. Kucheesa looked astonished by the experience and a little annoyed. Rasher had heard her yelling several times, but Sapka had not entirely lost the argument.

Kucheesa's brown hair was styled into gentle waves, with a pair of braids looping from her temples back to the nape of her neck. She'd switched to a much larger hat. It was still pointed in the front, but rose much higher. The sides flared out wider, and instead of ending in a chicken outline, several chicken feathers adorned the crown. A series of red shapes ringed the center, some looking like cheeses, others like chickens.

Her uniform looked very similar to Rasher's, and she gave him an annoyed look. "Really, Captain? Choosing the team color for all of us?"

He hadn't realized by picking the green jacket he was making a team-wide statement. "This is just the first attempt. Looks like we'll have time to try different ideas. How about you choose the next one?"

"Really?" she asked excitedly.

"Sure." How much harm could that do?

When Bibble exited his tent, he too wore a new green coat, but it looked much like his old one, full of pockets. His pocket-laden hat was unchanged, but he said, "Sapka promised she can make me a hat with pockets that integrate into my jacket. It's got a concealed pulley to rotate through more pockets without increasing the length. Should double my available inventory."

"Wow," Rasher said. That could prove useful.

"Ever hear the term, when one door closes, the other opens?" Bibble asked.

"Sure," Rasher said.

"Wish I'd paid more attention to the assembly instructions for the wardrobe," Bibble deadpanned.

As they groaned, Bibble smiled and added, "I wish my wife were here. Did you know Sapka is one of the most famous seamstresses in Afitur? My wife follows all the high fashions, and Sapka is considered one of the most influential disciples of Panoply alive today."

"So she helps design all the hats?" Rasher asked. That explained a lot.

When Quarce emerged, clutching his old hat, he looked wide-eyed and laughed with window-shaking volume. "A bath and new clothes on the same day! And Sapka promised she could get me a hat carafe with double the volume and heat retention. Unbelievable."

"That's wonderful," Bibble said, then gestured at his old hat. "Still have any coffee in there?"

"Of course," Bibble said, producing cups from his satchel and pouring out.

Noops joined them, his freshly polished armor gleaming under a new green greatcoat. He'd changed his helm for a hat exactly like Rasher's and said, "Sometimes a unit has to make surprising sacrifices."

Sapka emerged with him and looked over the group with a smile. "It's a start. Consider this first uniform a blank tapestry we'll use to craft your unique personas."

"I love these," Kucheesa said, apparently deciding she was thrilled more than annoyed. "This is our first team uniform. It makes me feel so official."

Sapka dabbed at her eye makeup with a little white cloth, looking at Kucheesa like she was a half-drowned kitten. "Oh, my sweet child. You have no idea the wonders in store. You're the only woman on the Reaper team, and before I'm finished with you, everyone in the world will know your name."

Kucheesa grinned.

The young courier woman returned, looking a bit flustered. She saluted and said, "Apparently there is no registered address for Arkadas' prophet. They have not attended the annual prophet's banquet in generations and are banned from the Acropolis."

"Really?" Bibble asked. "We hear about the prophet all the time."

"And Borborygmus represented the prophet at the assembly, didn't he?" Kucheesa added.

"You could ask him," the courier suggested, gesturing behind her. "He's waiting in the hall."

"Why would he do that?" Noops asked.

"Let's find out," Rasher said. First, he turned to Sapka and said, "Thank you for your fine work. You accomplished more than I imagined possible this fast."

Sapka smiled, looking delighted. "I will leave you to your next meeting. I'll find out who's being assigned to craft your battle armor. Don't worry, I'll have wonderful samples ready for our next session."

She swept out the door, calling for cloth, and Borborygmus rushed in. The big, fat man looked harried. His expensive, dark suit looked rumpled, and his simple black cap hung askew on his head.

"Captain, please! You have to get the hero finders off my back."

Before Rasher could answer, the courier said, "Oh, one more thing, Captain. I know the guard who was stationed outside your room upstairs after the incident this morning. He was downstairs on break."

Rasher frowned. "Is that important?"

"It might be, sir. He said another guard arrived to relieve him, but I also spoke with the guard captain on my way back into the Heart, and he said no one had been dispatched to replace the first guard."

"Another intruder?" Bibble exclaimed.

Rasher was already running for the door.

19

Look Before You Leap

R asher sprinted toward his rooms, ignoring the calls from
Borborygmus to wait. The rest of his team trailed after him,
but he soon left them behind. Hopefully it was the same unknown
intruder. He owed that guy a good crack on the side of the head.

Rasher also wanted answers. Drawing deep from crispy bacon, he
burned through extra sizzle to strengthen his muscles and increase
his speed and reflexes to the point where he sprinted up the winding
central staircase in a blur.

In seconds he reached the top floor, his footfalls muffled by the thick
carpeted runner, and shot down the long Reaper residence hallway.
No guard stood outside his door, which hung slightly ajar.

Rasher slowed and gently pushed open the door, grateful it did not
squeak. This time he would be the one doing the surprising.

He stepped into the large entry room and prowled inside. It smelled
clean, as if an over-enthusiastic crew had washed everything and
spritzed the air with a hint of lemon. His belongings had already been
moved in, and he spotted his paint battle staff in a rack beside the door.

With a smile, he took up the weapon and moved inside. Doors to
the left and right led off the main room, and both were slightly ajar.
The intruder had come out of the door to the left the last time, so
maybe he'd already finished searching that area. Rasher turned right
and slipped through that door.

It led to a large bedroom with an enormous four-poster bed, a
walk-in closet to the right, and a door to a private wash room. A chest
of drawers was recessed into the wall next to the bed, near the huge
window in the left-hand wall.

A tall man wearing a guard's uniform and hat was gripping the ornately engraved wooden panel that acted like molding above the drawers, at about chest height. With a click, the panel folded forward, revealing a hidden compartment.

How could the intruder know about that? Intrigued, Rasher advanced silently.

Somehow the intruder sensed him. The man spun, again wearing that concealing white mask, and flung a handful of glittering sugar crystals into the air between them.

No way Rasher would risk stepping through a sugar cloud. They could be imbued with all sorts of weakening enchantments.

"You've trapped yourself now," Rasher said, running to the right to circle around the bed.

The intruder said nothing but turned and opened the window.

"Why the hurry?" Rasher asked, diving across the bed. He bounced and somersaulted off the center, landing with battle staff already swinging.

The intruder had already planted one boot onto the window sill. Before Rasher could grab him, he leaped out, kicking with admirable force, as if he thought he could fly.

Maybe he could. Unlikely, but the highest-level meat mages had been known to unlock flight.

"Not this time," Rasher growled, diving out after the man as soon as his feet touched the floor.

The thrill blazed through him, making him grin as he launched out over the four-story drop above the long porch on the front side of the Heart. He was moving slightly faster and would catch the intruder before they hit the ground. The intruder wasn't flying, or even soaring like Kucheesa. Rasher had no idea what he'd planned to do when he jumped, but maybe it was just desperate suicide.

It looked like he'd succeed. Maybe he could use the man's body as a cushion. Rasher had fallen enough times to have a good sense of how much punishment he could handle without needing to apply the higher forms of bacon power to make himself temporarily immune to harm.

The intruder didn't scream, didn't flail, but kept his body extended horizontally. He extracted a slender rod that had been concealed down one leg of his pants and snapped it out in front of him. The rod expanded to either side, releasing a billowing sheet of bright blue fabric. Additional rods snapped into place, and in the blink of an eye, a full courier hang glider took shape.

Holding to that hang glider, the man banked away, coasting far out over the plaza.

"Amazing," Rasher muttered as he fell past and he plummeted toward the ground below. He'd been wanting one of those courier gliders but hadn't realized they could fold down so small. Now he really wanted one.

As the porch rushed up to meet him, Rasher prepared to again use the invulnerability bacon power, but then got a better idea. Maybe he could still catch the intruder.

He pulled from his coat pocket the oca tuber Redael had given him at the initial feast and bit off the end. It was tough and hard like a sweet potato, but he chomped down and forced himself to swallow. Redael hadn't specified if it needed to be consumed, or just bitten, and he didn't have time to make a mistake.

A weird fluttering sensation rippled out through him, and hoping he wasn't making a really stupid mistake, Rasher shuttered his bacon powers so they wouldn't interfere with the tuber, lifted it out in front of his face, and twisted it.

Redael hadn't explained the mechanics of its use but just said it could alter gravity depending on how it was turned. Since he was half a second away from splattering on the porch, he gave it a pretty big twist, laughing with the intensity of the thrill.

Gravity twisted with the tuber.

His downward momentum turned into a horizontal flight, fast enough to easily catch the fleeing intruder.

Except for the fact that he'd twisted the tuber the wrong way. So Rasher crashed feet-first into the side of the building hard enough that his legs buckled and he crashed full-length against the stone exterior with painful force.

And in the process, twisted the tuber again.

For a second, he flew straight up, scraping along the stone face of the building, rocketing back toward his window. He kicked off from the stone to avoid scraping off all his skin and twisted the tuber again.

This time he flew out from the building like an arrow and laughed with exhilaration. This was amazing!

His epic flight lasted about two seconds, just long enough to shoot out over the plaza. He was still pretty low, barely fifteen feet above the stones, flashing over the heads of surprised legionaries in the plaza.

Then the tuber disintegrated in his hands, its powers consumed.

"Crumpets," Rasher muttered, somersaulting in the air as he fell toward the stones. He didn't have far to fall, but he was moving with pretty impressive horizontal speed. He released bacon to enhance his reflexes, hoping to simply land running. He could see it in his mind, a fantastic end to a remarkable flight.

He touched down hard, and one foot caught on an uneven stone, sending him somersaulting forward. His victorious smile turned into a grunt of pain as he tumbled end over end a dozen times before coming to a painful halt.

"Ow," he muttered as he sat up. Several nearby soldiers rushed to help, and he allowed them to pull him to his feet. "I'm okay," he assured them, searching the sky for the intruder. The frustratingly clever fellow was already sailing past the distant admin buildings.

"I didn't know bacon masters could fly," one bright-faced young woman in a courier's uniform exclaimed.

"Most days we can't," he admitted. "Just, ah, experimenting with top-secret battle cuisine. Don't tell anyone about this."

"Of course not," she said, echoed by the others standing close.

"I knew I could count on you," he told them before trudging back toward the Heart, trying to ignore his protesting muscles. Definitely needed to try the tuber next time over the lake so the impacts wouldn't hurt so much.

Up in the window of his room, Noops stuck his head out and called, "What are you doing down there?"

"He got away," Rasher called back.

Kucheesa joined Noops and said, "Captain, I'm not sure you understand how meat enhancements work. You have to actually eat my food for a while before you can hope to start gliding."

"Very funny," Rasher said. "What's in that hidden compartment?"

Bibble took Noops' place. "It's empty, Captain."

Rasher frowned. Did the intruder get whatever was in there, or had someone else already taken it? He called up to his team. "Grab my staff and meet me back in Sapka's salon. I want to speak with Borborygmus. And send someone for Gubbins."

Amazingly, Colly Wobbles met him at the door to the Heart. She was breathing heavily as if she'd run all the way across the Heart to reach him.

"I heard you fell," she panted.

"How? It just happened."

"There's a set of speak tubes embedded in the walls of the Heart. Standard protocol is for news of injuries to be immediately passed up to my office."

Rasher had never heard of that, but milk mages were legendarily efficient, so he wasn't surprised. He would need to see how those speak tubes worked.

Colly produced some trauma yogurt. Strawberry. It was kept chilled in a little cooler pack run by a muffin mage heat scone that sucked the heat out of the interior. As Rasher ate the yogurt, Colly rubbed some whipped cream on an abrasion on his cheek.

The trauma yogurt spread a delicious warmth through his system, healing his bruised and battered shoulder and legs. Whipped cream was more effective on external injuries, but nothing matched trauma yogurt for healing internal injuries.

"Thank you," he told her when he finished.

"Try not to get hurt so much," she urged, handing him a packet of emergency yogurt ampules in a small box. "Supplies are getting low, and we have a full mobilization to deal with.

Rasher bowed to her, and the move surprised her so much she blushed. That rosy coloring against her pale skin was quite lovely. "I promise to be careful. I doubt anything more dangerous will happen today."

20

PROPHECY, INCORPORATED

Back in the salon he'd left just moments before, Rasher found his team already waiting for him, along with Borborygmus, who sat in one of the many comfortable chairs.

"Did you catch the intruder?" Borborygmus asked.

"No," Rasher said. "But we may have gained a new clue. I'm glad you came to see us. I was hoping to speak with you."

"Good," Borborygmus said, wiping his sweaty face with an orange cloth. His hat was askew, and he was still breathing heavily.

"What happened?" Bibble asked, offering the big man a glass of water from a nearby table. He took it and gulped some down.

"The hero finders are badgering me to death," Borborygmus exclaimed, leaning back in the chair. "They're convinced we somehow altered the names of the Reaper candidates, even though I've proven our records perfectly demonstrate there is no way the fault could be ours."

He leaned forward and added, "They are threatening legal action, despite our generations of perfect service. Please, Captain. I came to implore you for help."

The man's plight did seem dire, but Rasher didn't fully understand it. "Tell me about your company, Prophecy Incorporated."

"Of course. You wouldn't know the details, would you?" Borborygmus chuckled. "We are a wholly-owned subsidiary of We Can Make The Masses Love You, Incorporated."

"What does that mean?" Kucheesa asked.

Borborygmus hesitated, his expression turning suddenly guarded. He glanced around as if just realizing where he was and said, "Ah, perhaps my actions were a bit rash after all. It is highly unusual to discuss our business with members of the Reaper teams, so perhaps we could meet in private, Captain."

"I think this morning's events override normal protocols," Rasher replied.

"We're not going anywhere," Kucheesa stated, crossing her arms and looking determined. In her uniform, she did look quite intimidating. The others looked ready to back her up.

The big man rubbed a meaty hand across his face and laughed a bit wildly. "Why not? It's not like things could get much worse. I never should have approved the additional services on such short notice."

"What services do you offer?" Rasher asked, sensing Borborygmus could give them some much-needed answers.

"Listen, my organization has fulfilled every letter of every contract we've ever taken. We've performed flawlessly for eleven generations. There's not a single addendum or clause that covers the situation we've been dealing with this week. We were asked to extend our activities far beyond our normal focus. We usually provide a new prophecy every generation and ongoing public relations activities in the interim. That's it."

Rasher blinked, drawing upon a bit of sizzle and a partial slice of chewy bacon. "Hold on. Exactly what role has Prophecy Inc. been hired to perform for generations?"

Borborygmus sighed and said, "I warned you." Then he sat up straighter and continued in a more formal tone. "As members of Reaper Team Twelve, you are indeed entitled to access privileged information, although that clause has heretofore never been activated. We are the oldest and most respected public relations firm anywhere on this continent."

"Public relations?" Rasher asked, confused.

"They help you work on your image and branding, and help you make sure people are getting the right message about you," Noops said.

"Exactly," Borborygmus said. "It's nice to converse with people who know what's going on."

As the rest of the team stared at Noops in surprise, he asked, "What? I consulted with one after my tenth duel. I wondered if maybe everyone was issuing duels because of something weird I was doing. Turns out, a lot of knights have unresolved self-confidence and self-esteem issues."

Kucheesa barked a laugh, and Bibble asked, "That's the reason the PR firm gave you for people wanting to bash your face in?"

"You should get your money back," Kucheesa laughed.

Borborygmus asked, "Which firm did you consult with?"

"The Image Chefs."

He grimaced. "Reaper Kucheesa is right. You should get your money back. At best, they're nothing but half-baked image cookers."

"What services do you provide the legions?" Rasher asked, not wanting the conversation to drift too far off course.

"Prophecy, of course," Borborygmus said, looking surprised by the question. "Eleven generations ago, the prophet of Arkadas issued a rather pessimistic prophecy about the future of the empire. The Imperial Chef, in council with the First Course Assembly, decided that making the prophecy public would impede the progress of the empire and incite negative consequences. So they fired the prophet and contracted with our firm to produce more . . . upbeat prophecies."

He leaned back and spread his hands wide, smiling. "And we have fulfilled that contract perfectly, with nary a complaint until today."

"Are you serious?" Kucheesa exclaimed. "You've been making fake prophecies since the founding of the Reapers?"

Borborygmus winced. "Please, fake is such a nasty word. We like to think we represent the future Arkadas wants us to have on days she's feeling most optimistic."

The ramifications of the deceit perpetrated upon the people of the empire was staggering. "Have the other Reapers known about this?" Rasher asked.

"As I said, access has never been requested before now."

"How would anyone know to request access?" Bibble demanded.

"That is not my company's concern. Communication with the Reaper team falls upon the hero finders."

Rasher breathed, "All this time? Everything we've ever known about the apocalypse, the Reapers, and our entire purpose has been a lie?"

He knew from personal experience that one could not trust a high noble as far as one could throw a bucket of lard, but this was insanity on an entirely new level.

"It's not like that," Borborygmus said quickly, although by his eyes Rasher could tell it was just like that. "The prophet was insane. If the high houses had let the prophet rant and rave about the inevitable nature of the apocalypse, the Rubric Empire would have crumbled generations ago."

As Rasher considered that, the big man added, "Clearly the prophet had to be a fraud, or we would not have been successful all this time in blocking each apocalypse."

That was a good point, and Rasher grasped it like a man seizing a noodle lifeline after falling in a vat of hot lard. The stories of the prophets and how their prophecies always came true were still told to every child, but before this they had always been comforting. He had thought the prophecies and the Reapers were all products of Arkadas' will. Could they really be nothing more than the attempts of desperate houses to cling to power, despite a prophecy of doom?

Could a prophet be wrong for so long and still be a prophet?

Well, like most important questions, the answer was probably, "It depends."

"That's why there's no known address for Arkadas' prophet," Bibble said.

"Is there even a prophet?" Quarce asked, for the first time all day looking dejected.

"Of course," Borborygmus said. "That prophet was fired, but no one dared kill a prophet, and Arkadas keeps one around. They're not allowed on Nutmeg Hill and are barred from the annual prophet barbecue rally, but there's one around somewhere."

"Do you know where they live?" Kucheesa asked.

"No. We avoid interacting with any known prophet to avoid accusations of collusion."

"Do you know the exact wording of the prophecy the empire didn't like?" Rasher asked.

"Again, no. Sorry. We also have a strict policy to avoid exposure to prophecies produced by any outside prophet or agency. If we don't know them, we cannot be accused of borrowing any of their language or intentions."

"Where would I find a copy of the prophecy?" Rasher asked.

"You'd have to ask the hero finders. They may have a copy somewhere, but I doubt it. They have worked tirelessly for generations to produce the very best heroes. They find Reapers to protect us from darkness, lead our forces, and rally our spirits and our hope against the evil that threatens to consume our world. The Reapers have never failed, and never will."

The little speech might have been more powerful if he hadn't spoken the words quickly, as if reciting a marketing slogan.

"Would anyone else have a copy?" Bibble asked.

"Maybe the archives on Nutmeg Hill," Borborygmus said after a moment's consideration. "Or maybe the current prophet of Arkadas."

If they could find whoever that might be. It was astonishing how effectively communication had been controlled at every level to maintain the fraud.

Maybe it wasn't fraud. Maybe the prophet had been crazy, and the leaders had done what had to be done.

So why hadn't Arkadas chosen a new prophet who wasn't insane? There was no way to know unless he could get his hands on the actual prophecy.

He asked, "Why is everyone protesting our appointment?"

Borborygmus spread his hands. "Change is hard for everyone. Many are upset that the hero finders didn't simply cookie-stamp the team recommended by General Nide. Turning to the Mixing Bowl of Divine Intervention was a bold move, one that Gubbins insisted upon over all objections."

"Why would Gubbins do that?" Kucheesa asked with a frown.

"He is perhaps the most devout follower of Arkadas I've ever met," Borborygmus said. "He made it clear he felt we must turn to Arkadas in this time of trial."

"But he knows the truth," Bibble said.

They all exchanged confused looks. Before that meeting, Rasher would have been pleased to hear the leader of the Hero Finders was so devout in his duty. Knowing the fraud, and knowing that Gubbins knew the fraud, why would he push the false devotion so far? Something didn't add up.

Borborygmus added, "Now that we used the Mixing Bowl and results are not as expected, there's confusion and fear and anger. I believe it stems mostly from the fact that no one wants to admit that someone within the hero finder ranks botched handling of the names."

"On purpose, or by accident?" Rasher asked.

"I have no way of knowing, but Captain, it doesn't really matter. You've been chosen and recognized as Reapers. You have a job to do, so why worry about if your appointment came at the will of Arkadas or not?"

It was a good question, but questions seemed to be all he had. "We're a very small team. Is there any way we could arrange to call a few more names?"

Borborygmus shook his head. "I'm afraid you have all the Reapers you're going to get. We can't amend the team after the choosing, not for at least twelve months. That's why all the additional verification checks were implemented after Team Three faltered."

Rasher had never heard about that. Borborygmus said more gently. "If it makes you feel better, the only other explanation for how you were chosen as Reapers was that Arkadas herself took a direct hand in the proceedings."

He added softly under his breath, "We could increase fees another thirty-seven percent if we could prove divine guidance."

Quarce clapped his big hands, the sound like a thunderclap in the room. He barked a laugh and shouted, "Chosen by the goddess! I knew it. We sit at the feast of grand destiny."

Rasher wasn't sure what to believe, but he appreciated Quarce's enthusiasm. Better to embrace their roles and choose to believe in divine intervention than think someone had screwed up or planted their names as some kind of epic practical joke.

So he said, "We'll go with that for now."

"You have to order the hero finders to relent their attacks," Borborygmus insisted. "I told you everything you wanted to know. Probably a lot more than Gubbins or Lugubrious would have wanted me to."

"I'll see what we can do," Rasher said.

Then the door burst open, and Gubbins stepped inside, glowering. "There you are, Borborygmus!"

21

THE ENEMY IN THE KITCHEN

Borborygmus recoiled from Gubbins, but Rasher rose and lifted a calming hand. "Gubbins, glad you could join us. Any news?"

Gubbins took a deep breath, controlling his emotion. In a moment, he looked as calm as always and said, "I apologize, Captain. Borborygmus fled his offices before the inquisitors arrived, creating quite a stir. He is privy to a high level of classified recipes, so he cannot disappear like that."

Borborygmus rose to face Gubbins. "I came to appeal to the Reapers for relief from your false accusations."

Gubbins looked from the big man to Rasher and his team, as if trying to tell how much they'd discussed. Rasher wanted to confront him about the lies, but sensed there were other aspects to the situation they didn't yet understand. Turning Gubbins against them wouldn't help.

So he said, "We were just beginning our conversation."

Gubbins relaxed a bit and said, "Very well, Borborygmus. If you agree to return to your offices and cooperate with the inquisitors, I'll make sure the process is quick, efficient, and fair."

"Quick would be good," Rasher agreed. "We need the inquisitors tracking down those missing officers and interrogating the muffin mage, not wasting time at Prophecy, Incorporated."

Borborygmus looked relieved. "I'll get back there now. Thank you, Captain." He gripped Rasher's hands and left. Gubbins stepped out with him to converse with a courier.

"We should demand the truth," Kucheesa hissed.

"Not yet," Rasher cautioned. "I want to find a copy of the original prophecy first."

"How will that help?" Bibble asked.

"I'm not sure, but I've seen enough of Food-Court-level intrigue to suspect there's more going on than what Borborygmus told us. I don't want to tip our hand until we know as much as possible.

"I never knew you hunted quail," Noops said, looking pleased.

"What does that have to do with anything?" Kucheesa snapped.

"Quail will bolt before one gets into range if the hunter approaches directly," Noops explained. "The hunter must approach at an angle, their view fixed on a different point. In that way, the quail is tricked into believing they are safe until it is too late."

"Oh," she said, frowning. "There's got to be a simple way to say all that."

"It was simple until you made it complicated," Noops responded.

"Let's just hope we're the hunters and not the quail," Bibble muttered, then smiled. "There were two hunters—"

"Stop," Kucheesa interrupted. "I can't deal with another stupid joke right now."

"Fine. Tell me this," Bibble responded. "What do you get when you combine a rhetorical question and a joke?"

She glared, and neither one spoke for a few seconds.

Rasher couldn't help chuckling. Noops joined him a second later, making Kucheesa glare. She demanded, "What?"

Bibble only smiled.

Gubbins returned and took Borborygmus' seat. Kucheesa whispered, "What?" again, then her eyes widened and she leaned back, rubbing her face with one hand.

"I apologize for the interruption," Gubbins said. "As important as that matter is, I have an intelligence update to share."

"News of the missing officers?" Quarce asked excitedly.

"Unfortunately, no. They have not been found anywhere and are officially listed as missing in action. The hunt has expanded, but neither they nor the missing food has been found. There have been a few other disappearances as well, and it appears three of the members of the previous Reaper team are also unaccounted for."

Rasher blinked in surprise. "Aren't they all being housed on Nutmeg Hill?"

Gubbins nodded. "The Junior Toque has personally offered his hospitality. Apparently Dollop Aberdeen, Clootie Dumpling, and Juusto Panjandrum are unaccounted for since this morning."

"How is that possible?" Kucheesa whispered as they all exchanged incredulous looks.

Dollop was one of the most powerful milk mages in the empire, Clootie a renowned confectioner, and Juusto a mighty cheese wizard. Rasher couldn't imagine how the three famous Reapers could disappear.

"Perhaps they just left," Bibble suggested. "It has to be hard to deal with getting booted out of your job like that. Maybe they just want some space."

"Without telling anyone?" Kucheesa asked.

Noops shrugged. "An unexpected storm can cast the sturdiest boat onto strange shores when it is left untethered."

Quarce grinned. "I like that anatomy."

"Analogy," Rasher corrected.

Bibble grinned. "Speaking of anatomy, what kind of flowers can you find on any face?"

When no one answered, he added, "Two-lips!"

Rasher appreciated his attempts to keep things light. Gubbins just ignored the joke and said, "The disappearances are being investigated, but we have a new problem to deal with."

"Are you talking about the intruder I caught trying to loot a secret compartment in my bedroom?" Rasher asked.

"No, actually," Gubbins said.

"Do we all have secret compartments?" Quarce asked eagerly.

Gubbins nodded. "The compartment in question is where Absquatch Youlate kept his personal battle cuisine armaments."

"What kind of armaments?" Rasher asked, intrigued.

"Did the intruder get them?" Bibble added. "We found it empty."

Gubbins shook his head. "No, it was all removed when we cleared out Captain Youlate's belongings. I was planning to refresh your stock after explaining it all to you."

"So it's specialty magic cuisine?" Kucheesa asked.

Gubbins nodded. "As Reapers, you have access to the highest levels of battle cuisine. I'll get into specifics once the new batch is ready. At the moment, it is a distraction."

"Who knew about it?" Rasher asked with a frown. "That intruder was looking for something specific. If we know what was in there, it might give us a clue as to who he was."

"I will have a full list prepared," Gubbins promised. "But we have other matters to discuss."

"Has Ehverr fallen?" Rasher asked, imagining the Gloaming hordes swarming through a city on fire, slaughtering the people who had been hoping for help from the Reaper legions.

"No, thank the gods. This new problem strikes closer to home, I'm afraid," Gubbins said. "There's been a major explosion in the confectioner Sugar Palace."

"No," Kucheesa breathed, and Noops cursed softly.

Quarce leaned in and whispered, "What was that, and why did you choose that one?"

Rasher gestured for them to pay attention as Gubbins continued. "The entire guild was in the palace working overtime to produce new battle enhancement sugars. Casualty counts are incomplete, but many were wounded, a few may have been killed, and every one of them was overwhelmed by severe levels of enhanced battle-level sugar."

Rasher's mind spun as he considered the horrific magnitude of the disaster. "Are there any sugar stockpiles left?"

"Very few," Gubbins said grimly. "Anywhere else and that level of sugar disaster would have claimed hundreds, if not thousands of lives. The confectioner leadership managed to limit exposure outside of the palace. They're going to need at least two weeks to purge the sugars from their people and the palace."

"Two weeks?" Bibble exclaimed.

"I'm afraid so. The entire palace is cordoned off. As a safety precaution, the spice wizards have set up an updraft to pull any particles up and away from populated areas. The muffin mages are also moving most of their production from their palace which is on the edge of the danger zone to one of the empty warehouses that used to store the Acropolis food stockpiles."

"Any word on how it happened?" Rasher asked.

"Nothing definitive yet, but we have to suspect it's the work of the same group of traitors who stole our food stockpiles."

"We need to isolate and eliminate them," Rasher growled.

"Agreed," Gubbins said. "Everyone will be looking to you all for leadership."

"This is worse than a fried brain sandwich," Quarce muttered.

"A what?" Kucheesa asked with a look of disgust.

Quarce shrugged. "It's a term we use in Gravlax."

"And you actually eat fried brain sandwiches?" Bibble asked.

"No. That's why if something is worse than that, it's really bad," Quarce said, looking from him to Kucheesa. "You don't use that phrase here either?"

"Most people blame Lahanasi's anchovy pits," Noops offered.

Quarce grimaced. "That's a revolting mental image."

"Not as bad as fried brain sandwiches," Kucheesa retorted.

"Proves my idea works better," Quarce said with a grin.

"Unfortunately, it's not the only disaster," Gubbins interjected.

Rasher wanted to feel surprised, but bad news had been traveling in packs of late.

"The cheese wizards have sealed the Cheese Palace and barred anyone from entering until they complete an internal audit. They claim there must have been some kind of foul play to slip that addendum language into the previous Reaper team contracts."

"That's a good thing though, right?" Bibble asked. "I mean, if we can discover how it was done, maybe they can undo it, or discover who was responsible."

Getting the previous Reaper team restored to active duty would be fantastic. Rasher would love to join Absquatch Youlate and his Reapers.

"Unlikely," Gubbins said. "But contracts are not my specialty. The bad news is that for now, we won't have any cheese wizard support for the upcoming campaign."

That was bad news. Cheese curses and poisons were among the most effective battle foods against many of the glowan monsters.

"Worse, General Nide is demanding answers and access to the palace. She wants information by tomorrow, or she threatens to assault the Cheese Palace," Gubbins added.

"That would be dumber than shoving your face into a demolition cake," Rasher said. How many legionnaires would die needless gruesome deaths in such an assault? They needed to unite against the greater enemy, not fall to internal squabbling.

Internal division was common among the six tiers of the high houses, but it was virtually unheard of within the Acropolis and the ranks of the Reaper legions.

"This is a disaster," Kucheesa exclaimed.

"More like several disasters," Noops interjected.

"I mean all of them together," Kucheesa clarified, waving her arms for emphasis. "Battle cuisine is missing, along with the Food Watch officers, the Sugar Palace suffers the worst catastrophe of all time, and now the Cheese Palace is closed to us."

Looking at the broader picture made one thing clear. Rasher said, "We have traitors among us, and they're coordinating with the glowan."

"We won't be able to march until we root them out," Gubbins agreed. "We cannot have sabotage among our ranks during a campaign."

"It's already going to be difficult to field a fully stocked legion arsenal," Bibble added.

"What about other legions?" Quarce asked.

"Bad news there too," Gubbins said with a grimace. "We've received reports that some of the stockpiles in Tookus have been stolen too. Not sure if they were taken before or after the siege began at Ehverr, but without that battle food, they're facing the same limitations we are. They cannot hope to launch another attack against the glowan holding the Gewgaw bridge."

"So we need to get the situation here in the Acropolis resolved, resupply our battle cuisine, and prepare to mobilize to defeat the hordes, possibly without the help of the rest of our strongest armies," Rasher summed up.

Gubbins nodded, his expression earnest, "I know today's events surprised everyone, especially all of you, but who are we to question the voice of prophecy? Arkadas established the Reapers, and she has ensured our success for eleven generations. We can trust that and move forward with full confidence that a path to victory will become clear."

The inspiring words might have helped more if they hadn't just spoken with Borborygmus. Were they really fulfilling the will of Arkadas, or were they simply pawns in a great, mysterious game?

He was sorely tempted to ask Gubbins about that, but held his tongue. He still felt they needed more information. So he changed topics.

"Any word from the inquisitors about that muffin mage who attacked me?"

"Very little," Gubbins said with an apologetic shrug. "Apparently his mind was addled badly by the powdered sugar. They suspect that someone did indeed dose him with that sugar to send him to attack you without realizing what he was doing. They are trying to track down the sugar to its source since the enhancement seems pretty unique, but with the Sugar Palace in quarantine, that's probably a dead end too."

Rasher grimaced. "In that case, the interrogation may not find anything useful at all."

"They did discover that the man is a member of the Lahanasi restoration cult," Gubbins interjected.

Quarce asked, "Who are they?"

"A waste of time," Kucheesa said with disgust.

Bibble nodded. "Agreed. They're cultists who worship Lahanasi in secret and claim to want to restore him to his previous powers."

"What previous powers?" Quarce asked.

Rasher blinked, and Bibble asked, "You really don't know?"

"Don't know what?" Quarce asked.

"We'll talk about that later," Rasher said. The meeting had already gone long, and they didn't have time to get distracted by non-pertinent discussions. Involvement in the Lahanasi cult couldn't be important. They weren't a threat.

Quarce shrugged. "Sure."

"For now, Gubbins, any advice on dealing with the hostility from the legion officers?" Rasher asked. They had to prepare for the meeting with General Nide.

Gubbins sat back in his chair, steepling his fingers. "I will continue to work on the officers and remind them of their place in the chain of command. The shock of losing the Reapers hit them hard. They had drawn up extensive plans based upon leveraging the particular skills of that team."

He sighed and continued. "Now those plans are moot, and new ones will have to be devised as they learn your strengths and how best to work with you. Unfortunately, that process usually takes time unavailable to us. Sometimes even career soldiers who train and plan for the unexpected struggle to cope with significant change."

That made sense, and Rasher dedicated a lot of training on his students' mindsets, helping them to remain flexible. He would have to consider how to apply some of his lessons to the legion leadership. He'd never imagined they might need it, but he knew by experience that it was not uncommon for officers to believe only their teams needed training.

"I'll share new intelligence when it arrives, as well as during our daily briefings. May I recommend you use the time until we meet with the general to consider ideas for ferreting out the secret traitors hiding here in the Acropolis? I expect we'll also be discussing our imminent deployment."

He then excused himself. Kucheesa leaned her chair back to the point of almost falling over, and exclaimed, "This is insane! Where do we even begin? The hordes are attacking everywhere. We might be Reapers now, but we don't command the powers of the gods, or anything."

Bibble looked solemn but again sniffed something from a little pouch that seemed to calm his nerves. He glanced at Quarce questioningly, and without a word the dwarf extracted the coffee pot from his hat and produced some collapsible cups to pass around. He'd somehow replenished the coffee again, and it was hot and delicious.

Noops, looking as unflappable as ever, drummed his fingers on one knee and said, "I knew a man who lost his sight to a muffin explosion, one leg to advanced confectioner addiction, and suffered from palsy in both hands that the milk mages could not cure. Yet, he was still one of the happiest, upbeat people I ever knew."

The words had captured everyone's attention. Rasher was impressed. He could see several inspirational turns Noops could take with that story.

"How did he manage it?" Bibble asked.

Noops looked the spice wizard in the eye and said, "He went insane sniffing aged cheddar."

Rasher sighed. That was not where he had hoped that story might go at all.

Kucheesa dropped her chair flat with a thump and exclaimed, "That's it? Why did you tell us that stupid story? You want us all to start sniffing poison cheese so we don't have to face our problems?"

"Of course not. That would be ridiculous. I was thinking it's not our problems that define us, but which friends we choose to allow to cook for us."

Kucheesa leaned back, hands covering her eyes as she groaned. "Please stop."

Rasher tried to salvage the moment. "Well, we're a team, and we can trust each other to cook for us." He glanced at Kucheesa, who dropped her hands and met his gaze, the steel returning to her spine. She nodded.

"Or to mix blends to enhance our abilities." He glanced to Bibble, who also nodded.

"Or to brew fantastic potions to help us push beyond our natural limits." Quarce raised a fist, grinning widely.

"Or watch the backs of those less capable of defending themselves," Noops declared. He looked from Quarce to the pudgy spice wizard, who looked very happy with the promise. Then he glanced at Kucheesa, who bristled at the suggestion she might need any kind of assistance.

Rasher continued. "Our top priority must be working with the legion commanders to flush out the traitors hidden among us."

"We also cannot ignore the fact that we are no doubt now among their primary targets," Bibble said. "We should begin to take precautions. Among those, I propose to place some protections around our offices and quarters to alert me if anyone again tampers with our space while we're gone."

"Good idea," Rasher said.

"And I think you should move your family out of the Acropolis," Kucheesa told Bibble.

"I agree," Rasher said. He never would have imagined thinking the Acropolis might not be among the safest places in the empire, but the enemy had somehow infiltrated their home, and until they rooted out the traitors, no one was safe.

Bibble looked relieved. "I'm glad you think so. I've been worrying about them all day."

"One thing I've been wondering is how they've managed to infiltrate the Acropolis so well," Rasher said. "If the traitors are in league with the glowan, they may be using changelings."

The others exchanged serious glances. There were more stories about changelings wreaking havoc among the people of the Rubric Empire than any other type of glowan. They could transform into different animals, and even take the form of at least one human, usually after killing the one they chose to impersonate.

"How can we deal with them?" Kucheesa asked. "The enemy's in the kitchen."

"Hats," Quarce said. "We've dealt with more glowan in Gravlax than you have here, and we've got a rule during times of trouble that everyone must wear a different hat every day. Changelings can't handle wearing too many hats before they break down. Sometimes Ruzgar smites them for wearing a hat they haven't dedicated properly, revealing their true nature."

"I never heard that," Bibble admitted.

Rasher knew that changelings didn't like wearing hats, but never heard that Ruzgar would punish them. The mysterious glowan god of the evening winds granted them a variety of strange powers, but he realized he knew far too little about him. He would need to rectify that as soon as possible.

"I think that's a great idea," Rasher said. "Let's implement it here in the Heart immediately, and recommend General Nide extend the order across the entire legion."

They were interrupted by a quick knock on the door, which was thrown open and a courier rushed inside. He looked tired, his face and clothes surprisingly dirty.

"Here we go again," Noops said.

Instead of handing over a note, the courier saluted "Reapers, there's been an attack at West gate!"

"Details?" Rasher demanded.

"I just came from there," the man said, wiping his face with a shaking hand. "The gate is destroyed, along with at least a hundred yards of wall to either side. Casualties are high."

"Black pudding," Quarce swore. Noops gave him an approving smile.

"What is the disposition of enemy forces?" Rasher asked, releasing chewy bacon and some extra sizzle to deal with the shock of the news.

The messenger shook his head. "There are no enemies, or at least none we could see. The ground under the plaza just erupted without warning. It rose like water in a boiling pot, shattered the gate, the wall, and every building in the first two streets nearby."

"Invisible glowan," muttered Bibble.

"Perhaps," Rasher said. "Sounds more like we now know what happened to some of the vegetables stolen from the Food Watch."

"Anchovy lickers," Kucheesa growled.

A second courier rushed in through the open door, message already in hand.

"Should have locked the door after the first one," Noops said.

Rasher took the note and grimaced. "Most of the legion siege weapons suffered catastrophic wood rot today."

"All of them?" Bibble asked. "That has to be another attack. Probably some of the stolen cheese stockpiles."

"Or more glowan infiltrators," Quarce added.

Neither possibility was good.

A third courier rushed in, a young woman, face flushed with exertion. She fumbled with her message tube for a moment, earning scowls of disapproval from the other couriers.

"Please go shut that door," Bibble told one of them.

It wouldn't help, but Bibble was looking queasy, so Rasher didn't object. The closed door might offer the illusion of protection from bad news. He read the latest report and cursed.

"Someone tried to attack the Cheese Palace. Looks like they were thwarted, but suspicious figures have been spotted near two other palaces. They escaped capture."

"Not good," Kucheesa said. "While we've been sitting here in meetings, our enemy have been escalating their attacks."

"Who would have imagined they'd attack the Acropolis?" Bibble objected. "It's unheard of."

"Not any more," Rasher said. "Kucheesa is right. We need to respond, or we won't have a legion to lead." He pointed at one of the couriers. "Take word to General Nide to send one of the legions to support West Gate. Special emphasis on milk mages. Go."

Hopefully supplies of healing cream and trauma yogurt weren't too low. The courier sprinted away, and Bibble muttered darkly about the fact that they left the door open again.

"We aren't staying anyway," Rasher told him. "Noops, I want you and Quarce to go to West Gate and meet the general's forces there."

Noops nodded, and Quarce jumped to his feet, looking eager. Rasher added, "Let the legion commanders manage the site and oversee aid efforts. I want you two hunting for clues. Noops, you know the Watch. Find out how the enemy might have launched the attack. If it was battle cuisine, how could they get the foodstuffs under the plaza? See if anyone witnessed anything suspicious before it went off."

Noops nodded again. Quarce asked, "What about me?"

"You're a miner, and you know glowan tactics better than the rest of us. See what you can find."

"I swear it will be done," Quarce declared, voice booming.

"And the rest of us?" Kucheesa asked.

"You and Bibble are coming with me," Rasher said. "We need answers, and the only people who might know anything are hiding in the Cheese Palace. We're going to pay them a visit."

Bibble paled, but Kucheesa said, "Good idea. We'll prove to everyone we can do this job!"

Rasher hoped she was right, and they didn't just get cheesed for their trouble.

22

Cottage Cheese and Legalese

As they walked up Guild Way toward the Cheese Palace, Kucheesa asked, "Do you really think Arkadas intervened to choose us?"

Rasher glanced to Bibble, who considered his answer for a moment. Ahead, the road widened into a stately boulevard, lined with grand palaces of the eleven guilds of magic, each housing their contingent of wizards, mages, and shamans.

The legion had no dedicated palace to Panoply, goddess of clothing. The wardrobe wizards resided in their main palace on Nutmeg Hill, and most spent far too much time creating ridiculous high fashion and ever-larger hats. There was also no palace to Lahanasi, god of disgusting food. Everyone feared him, and few admitted to openly worshiping him. The Lahanasi restoration cult was an annoying but usually harmless exception.

The Acropolis guilds prided themselves on being independent of the central palaces on Nutmeg Hill, providing all of the magical support and supplies the Reaper legions required.

Glancing north, Rasher focused on the tall spires of the Sugar Palace rising above some of the other palaces. It looked like a giant sugar creation, all graceful lines and sharply pointed towers, shining white against the blue sky. A faint sheen of light surrounded the palace from the spice wizard spell that created a steady breeze, carrying potentially dangerous sugars up and away from people.

The sight reminded Rasher of how high the stakes were for their mission. With the confectioners out of commission, they needed to get the Cheese Palace opened. Not only to find out information about the conspirators who tampered with the Reaper contracts, but to gain access to the vital battle cheeses they would need for the campaign.

Bibble said, "It's unusual, but not unheard of for the gods to intervene. If she has, it suggests that Hilekar is indeed behind this invasion."

"How could he not be?" Kucheesa asked. "We're facing a definite apocalypse scenario, one of the worst ever."

Rasher said, "From what Borborygmus said, Hilekar has been trying for generations. He doesn't seem like the kind of god who gives up easily." He must be furious that it was his own sister who inspired the prophet to warn the empire of the impending apocalypse.

"What god would give up easily?" Bibble asked.

"Is that another lame joke?" Kucheesa demanded.

"No, but I could turn it into one if you prefer."

Rasher said, "Not right now. We might be dealing with intrigue between the gods, or intrigue among the hero finders."

"It's less scary to think maybe one of the hero finders, or one of the traitors swapped our names," Bibble admitted. "Otherwise we've drawn the attention of the gods. Makes for great stories, but short lives."

Rasher said, "I like to hope we have some kind of divine blessing, but even if we don't, we can't doubt ourselves."

Kucheesa added, "I like to focus on the opportunity we have to make some positive changes too. Maybe we don't need a full apocalypse to correct some things."

"Like what?" Bibble asked.

"It's not like the empire is perfect. Many of us are from vassal kingdoms. We've all faced discrimination and difficulties that no native Rubric citizen has to deal with." She glanced at Rasher and frowned. "Well, most of us."

She had a point. Rasher said, "Good idea. Reapers are supposed to help in every way we can. Once we uncover the traitors attacking us and lead the legions to drive out the Gloaming hordes, I like the idea of focusing on a different kind of good."

They both nodded assent, so Rasher added, "For now, focus. No one has been in or out of the Cheese Palace since it was sealed, not even the high cheeses from the head palace on Nutmeg Hill."

"They're hiding something," Kucheesa said.

"Are we going to bash our way in?" Bibble asked nervously.

"Of course not," Rasher said. Battling cheese wizards in their own palace was one form of suicide he definitely didn't want to consider. "We need to find another way to get them to let us in. We can't allow the general to declare war on them."

"And what better way to begin establishing our credentials than by accomplishing the impossible?" Bibble asked.

Kucheesa blew out a breath. "So we start proving we're heroes, or we die trying."

"I like to avoid dying," Rasher said as they rounded the last corner and approached the imposing Cheese Palace. "Keep an open mind. We can't approach this like General Nide has, or like anyone following the normal chain of command would. We need to find a creative approach."

Most of the palaces reared high above the street, all lofty towers, stained-glass windows, and breathtaking architecture. They were all buzzing with activity, with couriers rushing in and out, while long wagons of raw food were hastily unloaded right through the main doors. With the stockpiles gone, they had a lot of work to do, and not nearly enough time to do it.

The Cheese Palace was different. Located halfway up the wide street, it looked deserted and blockaded against a siege. Designed like a miniature castle with no outer wall or moat, it did have small towers on each corner and a central tower rising high above the main building. The four-story edifice of heavy gray stone looked grim and threatening.

The wide, arched wooden doorway set in the center of a long entrance porch was closed, and every window shuttered. The street was blocked off by two entire platters of armored soldiers, their long pikes rising like a sharp forest.

The captains of the soldiers guarding the Cheese Palace saluted smartly. They looked impressed by the new team uniforms.

"Any word from the palace?" Rasher asked, hoping the cheese wizards had decided to come out and talk.

"Nothing, sir," said one of the captains. "What are your orders?"

He and his men looked nervous, but were trying valiantly to hide it. They probably feared orders to charge the palace.

"Stand your ground. We'll handle this."

"Of course. Good luck," the captain said as his men relaxed.

Rasher passed them, Bibble and Kucheesa trailing, leaving a growing murmur of whispers as the men talked among themselves. Rasher could imagine them wondering what the Reapers might do, or more likely betting on how horribly they were about to die.

As they approached the palace, Rasher noticed a thin sheen of creamy white coating the door and across every window. "Is that cottage cheese?"

Bibble paled, his mouth opening to speak, but no words came out. Cottage cheese could be fashioned into horrible acids.

"Look at the porch," Kucheesa exclaimed.

Only then did Rasher notice the faint lines of complex script flowing across the floor of the entire front porch. No one could approach the door without treading on it.

No one would be that foolhardy.

"We should not have come," Bibble moaned.

Rasher glanced back at the soldiers. Those elite legionnaires would charge into battle against terrifying odds, but not even they would storm a Cheese Palace locked down and protected with such extensive legalese.

Rasher had never heard of anything like it. Who knew what breaches of contract anyone trying to walk across that script would inadvertently trigger? There was almost no limit to the havoc that could be unleashed with that much script.

"Locking the place down so tight does not suggest a guilt-free conscience," Bibble said.

"Can any lawyer have a guilt-free conscience?" Rasher asked, trying to lighten the mood a little.

Bibble tried to chuckle but only managed a strangled sort of whimper. Kucheesa was peering at the script intently, a thoughtful expression on her face.

Rasher paused well short of the porch and its floor covered in dangerous legalese. "Well, we can't go in through the front door. I wonder if the back door is clear of legal script. Thoughts on how to get in there?"

Silence.

He turned to see Bibble staring at the legal script with open fear. Kucheesa had backed up. At first, he thought maybe she was afraid of getting closer.

Then she started to run, sprinting straight at the script.

"Wait!" Rasher shouted.

Too late.

Expression determined, Kucheesa dashed past. Just before reaching the cheese-enhanced legal script, she jumped. Her leap turned into a graceful glide, and she soared over the porch, hair blowing under the wings of her hat.

Soldiers along the perimeter shouted in surprise, and some began to cheer. Kucheesa landed softly right in front of the door. The script covered every inch of the porch, so she touched down on some of it. Rasher tensed, expecting to see terrible vengeance wrought upon the impetuous girl.

Nothing happened.

Kucheesa glanced back at them and grinned to see their astonished faces. "I told you, I come from a family of cheese wizards. I can't read much of the script, but I don't reall have to. One of the first lessons about legal documents is that specifics are important. I doubt any of these terms include an addendum to ward against someone floating over."

"Brilliant," Bibble grinned.

Rasher smiled. Very impressive. That was the kind of reckless action everyone expected him to do. He would need to ratchet up his thrill level to keep ahead of Kucheesa. Just thinking about that made him shiver with anticipation.

Kucheesa rang the bell. A distant gong echoed through the Cheese Palace. Rasher half expected her to get obliterated by touching the bell, but again she was fine. Kucheesa could be annoying and abrasive, but he appreciated exhibitions of bravery taken to self-destructive levels.

The door opened immediately, as if someone was waiting just inside. A middle-aged cheese wizard poked his head out. His cheese wheel hat declared him a senior cheese. "About time."

"Thanks, but did you expect people to just nonchalantly walk over the nastiest looking legal script anyone has ever seen?" she asked.

"Eventually," he admitted.

"Well here I am. We need to talk."

The man grinned. "I had my doubts when I heard about the new Reapers, but you've got spunk, lassie. Maybe there's hope left in the world. Come on in, and invite your captain to join us."

"Captain, get over here," she bellowed, waving mightily.

"Good luck," Bibble said, taking a step back.

"Thanks," Rasher said dryly. Then with a final furtive glance at the intricate script, he squared his shoulders and marched forward, forcing himself not to cringe as his foot crossed the line. He prepared to unleash most of his bacon reserves in a single rush of higher-level bacon powers if need be.

A flash of light, and a loud, disembodied voice declared loudly, "First man to risk the path of curses! Good thing we're not dealing with an invasion, or anything."

Rasher nearly jumped out of his skin when the voice started shouting around him. He was proud that he only flinched a little and didn't break stride.

The soldiers around the perimeter raised a great cheer, and some began chanting, "Reaper Captain Dilskin!"

He'd been taught to fear death by cheesecake, but now he added death by legalese to his long list of unpleasant deaths to be avoided. When he reached the porch, he smiled. The pudgy fellow in the doorway looked unimpressed, and Kucheesa scowled.

"What?" he asked softly as they followed the cheese wizard into the mansion.

"Why is it that you get all the credit for coming over here after I already did the hard part?"

"You said yourself, you avoided stepping on the curses."

She glowered, so he said, "I'm very impressed you did it."

Her scowl softened and he said, "Did you really want some invisible voice bellowing at you while you crossed to the door?"

"Probably not," she admitted.

23

CHEESE AND SUGAR DON'T MIX

The cheese wizard led Rasher and Kucheesa through a spacious entry room to a large office on the far side. A huge desk, overflowing with scrolls and parchments consumed the middle of the room, flanked by bookshelves along the walls packed with more books and papers. Thick carpeting covered the floor, a bubbling cheese fountain stood in one corner, and a heating brazier set into the left-hand wall held a gently burning chocolate muffin. The office looked like the quintessential picture of a wizard's man-space.

A very tall, very round older gentleman in flowing green and yellow robes rose from an overstuffed chair to meet them. His tall hat in the shape of a pot of liquid cheese with symbols of terrible curses ringing the outside declared his status as a high cheese.

His name was Sardoodledum Squelch, and Rasher had heard good things about him. His fluffy white hair and beard against his sallow skin gave his face the appearance of fresh cheese glistening in candlelight.

"Finally, someone made it through," Sardoodledum said, striding to meet them and shaking their hands with a firm grip.

Renowned for his work in multi-layered curses, Sardoodledum had won his appointment as head of the Acropolis Cheese Palace through brilliant research and fantastic results.

Kucheesa grabbed Sardoodledum's hand in both of hers and gushed over it. "Oh, I'm so happy to meet you! I've heard so much about you. You knew my grandmother."

After a moment of startled surprise, Sardoodledum's eyes widened and he laughed, a jolly sound that shook his ample belly. "By Peynir's fires, you must be little Kucheesa. Look at you, all grown up and . . ." His smile faded when he looked at her hat. "What happened, child?"

Her smile evaporated and she sniffled. "After granny was marked traitor and disappeared, it was awful. We weren't allowed to study cheeses. Meats were kind of an accident."

"Oh, child, I am so sorry," Sardoodledum said, enveloping her in a hug. She nearly disappeared from view under his voluminous robes, and she clutched him tight for a long moment.

Rasher watched in astonishment. That was a side of Kucheesa he had never expected to see. "Always happy to reunite old friends," he said cheerfully.

Sardoodledum released Kucheesa, who wiped furiously at her eyes and refused to look at Rasher. The old cheese wizard said, "I was indeed a close friend of your grandmother's. I never understood how her team could turn on her, but now I'm facing the same ignominy." He chuckled ruefully.

That seemed to cheer her up. Rasher said, "I'd be happy to leave you two to catch up on old times, but we've got the pressing matter of the contract manipulations to lay to rest."

"Indeed," Sardoodledum said, growing solemn. "I'm glad it's you Reapers who dared the script first. I feared we'd face angry soldiers with no concept of the complexities we're dealing with."

"Why lock yourselves away, then? You must know how that looks," Rasher said.

The surprisingly warm welcome had eased some of his fears, and he hoped the visit could conclude without hostilities. Kucheesa might be an old family friend, but the situation could turn ugly if Sardoodledum grew annoyed.

"I saw no alternative. I could not allow anyone to enter or exit the palace until we conducted a comprehensive internal audit to determine how our procedures were compromised."

"I knew it wasn't on purpose," Kucheesa said happily.

Sardoodledum looked pained. "Even suggesting such a possibility gives me heart pains. No, my child, we dedicate ourselves to exactness and honor in every aspect of shepherding the Reapers through their complex contracts. It is our duty to protect them from manipulation and legal danger, not to inflict it upon them ourselves."

He blew out a breath and wiped a white cloth across his meaty face. "It's been rough, but we've worked tirelessly to discover the treachery that has embarrassed our livelihoods and curdled the name of cheese everywhere."

"What did you find?" Rasher asked.

"Many questions, and perhaps a glimmer of truth," Sardoodledum said. "Turns out, it was a good thing we took the precautions we did."

"You mean the attempt at breaching the palace?" Rasher asked.

He nodded. "The intruders were detected and fled before we could capture them, but had we not locked down the palace, they might have succeeded."

"In what, exactly?" Rasher pressed.

"I suspect they intended to remove the one witness who might help us uncover part of the truth. Come." He headed for the door.

Sardoodledum led them upstairs to a long hallway lined with carved wooden doors. A couple were open, showing glimpses of simple, private rooms inside. At the end of the hall, they reached a padlocked door, guarded by three low-level cheese wizards with tri-pointed cheese hats, armed with wicked-looking cheese knives.

"How is she?" Sardoodledum asked.

"Unchanged, sir," one of the men said.

"Hopefully help has arrived," he said, gesturing toward the door. They quickly unlocked it and swung it wide.

Sardoodledum led Rasher and Kucheesa inside. They entered a small bedroom, empty but for a small, steel-framed bed. A middle-aged woman lay on it, softly groaning.

"We've scoured all logs, drafts, and signatures, and narrowed down the crime to authorizations approved by Ulotrichous here. Unfortunately, she's been stuck in this confection-induced haze for the past two days. Nothing we've done has cleared it, and we have been barred from bringing in outside resources to resolve her stupor."

Rasher asked, "Why didn't you inform the guard that you needed healing supplies to revive a potential suspect?"

"Because they would have insisted on whisking her out of our custody. I cannot allow anyone else to interrogate her until I know the truth. There's a chance that other conspirators would intercept her and finish her off before she could reveal any information."

That was a good point.

Kucheesa said, "We're here now. We'll help."

"Do you have a healer with you?" Sardoodledum asked.

"No, although we could requisition one if needed," Rasher said. "Let's see if we can come up with any ideas first. I agree that we should keep this as quiet as possible until we have more informtation. Can our other teammate get through to the door?"

Sardoodledum grinned. "Of course. That script may look intimidating, but it's just copied from an old treatise on the importance of balancing meats and vegetables in a healthy diet. It actually contains no damage clauses, just warnings of increased fat deposits if one fails to exercise regularly."

"Really?" Kucheesa asked, hands on hips, looking affronted.

He spread his hands wide and said, "What? We needed time, but we couldn't go around killing people. That would have confirmed the worst."

Rasher said, "Just don't tell anyone else, please."

"Why not?"

"We're trying to build our reputation. No one will celebrate the brave Reapers who dared getting fat in the relentless pursuit of their mission."

Sardoodledum laughed and sent for Bibble. When he arrived, Rasher explained the problem. Bibble crouched beside the bed and examined the woman. "This does look like a sugar overdose."

Sardoodledum grimaced. "Consuming sugars while part of the active contracts team is strictly forbidden, but I've since learned that she had a known addiction. Punitive consequences will be meted out to the supervisor who allowed her to participate anyway."

"Recreational sugar is more common than most people suspect," Rasher said. "Does that explain what happened?"

Sugar addiction was all too common, even within the ranks of the elite forces, but it was rarely discussed. Just a silent plague eating away at their ability to perform their dangerous duties. Turning that blind eye to the problem had given the enemy an opening to attack the very heart of the legions.

"Not really, but anyone suffering addiction will sometimes go to extremes to get a fix, or they may be manipulated by specially doctored compounds," Sardoodledum said.

"Another sugar-addled victim," Bibble said thoughtfully.

"Starting to see a pattern," Rasher agreed.

At Sardoodledum's raised eyebrow, Kucheesa explained briefly about the muffin mage. The high cheese considered that for a moment, his expression grave. "If these cases are indeed connected, it suggests a clear alliance between glowan forces and traitors among us."

"I can't see how the glowan could have infiltrated so deeply into our organization without inside help," Rasher agreed.

Bibble began pulling spices from various pockets of his coat and hat, mixing them with a small mortar and pestle he produced from an inside pocket. "I may be able to awaken her mind enough to speak with us, but I strongly recommend we bring in a healer from the Creamery. They specialize in these types of maladies."

"Wait," Kucheesa said, face bright with enthusiasm. "I have an idea that might help speed things up." She extracted from a pocket the exquisite origami frog she'd refused to shove up her nose earlier.

"You kept that?" Rasher asked.

She shrugged. "I didn't want to try it in front of everyone, but one can't ignore a potential tool."

Quarce would be so thrilled to hear she'd taken his words to heart.

"Fantastic work," Sardoodledum marveled.

"Our coffee wizard is a unique fellow," Bibble said.

Kucheesa leaned over the unconscious woman and shoved the frog up her nose.

"What are you doing?" Sardoodledum exclaimed.

"This is how it works," Kucheesa said as the frog disappeared, dissolving into pure coffee magic that rushed up the comatose woman's nose.

She gasped and sat up in one convulsive heave, eyes opening wide. She tried to run while still sitting up, but her legs were under the blankets, and she only managed to tangle herself badly and fall back down, gasping.

"Nicely done," Rasher said.

Bibble added, "Quarce said he considered opening an origami business . . . But it folded."

Kucheesa rolled her eyes, and Rasher chuckled. Sardoodledum blinked, then guffawed, making the woman on the bed scream and tie herself even worse in the sheets.

It took a moment to straighten her out, and by that time Ulotrichous seemed to have recovered most of her composure and was able to sit up with Sardoodledum's assistance. Her hands shook and she couldn't stop blinking, but seemed coherent. At first she was deeply offended at finding them all in her room when she wasn't wearing a hat, and very upset that all of her other personal belongings had disappeared.

"We'll sort that out momentarily," Sardoodledum assured her. "For now, I need you to concentrate. You approved late addendums for the Reaper contracts, did you not?"

She frowned, her brows creasing. "I did, didn't I?"

"Are you telling me, or asking me?"

"I'm not sure."

"I need you to be sure, and to tell me everything you can remember," he urged.

Rasher waited anxiously as she hesitated. Finally she said, "My memory is all fuzzy, like a crazy dream."

"Confectioner sugars sometimes have that effect," Sardoodledum said gently.

She seemed to wilt under his stare. "Oh, sir. I never intended harm. I just partook sometimes on the long night shifts to keep awake, that's all."

"Perhaps that's how it began, but you did something more than that to the last addendum. I need to know what, and why, and who else was involved. Tell me true, and the consequences will go better for you."

She paled and started stammering. "I don't remember much."

"Remember something, please," Rasher said. "It's very important."

Ulotrichous gasped and clutched Sardoodledum's hand. "Wait! I do remember something. Like a shadow of memory."

She clutched her face and moaned. "Oh, no. Did I really approve an addendum no one had ever read?"

"I fear that you did," Sardoodledum said. "Who gave it to you?"

"I don't . . ." She trailed off, fingers digging at her cheeks, eyes distant as she tried to remember.

Rasher wanted to shake the truth out of her and had to clench his hands to keep from reaching for her. The answers were so important, it was maddening to have to wait.

She began to speak softly. "I took the final shift before the addendums were approved. Wait, why was I alone in the final processing lab?"

"We found Pestiferous unconscious and stuffed into a closet," Sardoodledum said. "But it was too late by then. Do you know who knocked him out?"

She shook her head, but paled further. Her hands shook more violently as she scrunched up her face in concentration. "Someone entered the room, but it wasn't Pestiferous."

"Who was it?" Rasher urged, earning an annoyed scowl from Sardoodledum.

She shook her head. "He was cloaked. That was odd, but he gave me something." She gulped and looked up at Sardoodledum. "It was sugar."

"You took sugar from a stranger during a shift in the final processing lab?" the big man demanded, losing his cool for a moment.

She slunk lower in her bed. "I can't believe it, but I think I did. I sort of remember suffering a terrible withdrawal headache. I had only taken a tiny lick earlier that night, just to stay awake, but it felt like I'd been on a week-long bender with the coarsest kinds of sugars."

"Sounds like they doctored her dose, as we suspected," Bibble said. "Do we know who her dealer was?"

Sardoodledum scowled. "We did. Turns out it was Pestiferous."

"So he couldn't have been the one who gave her the changed contract," Kucheesa said.

"He might have, then conked himself out in an elaborate scheme to confuse the truth, but he was groggy when he woke up, and we fed him some munster."

Ulotrichous gasped, staring at her leader in shock. "You didn't!"

"Perhaps now you understand the seriousness of the situation," he said coldly.

"I didn't mean any harm!" she cried.

"Perhaps not, but harm was done. Great harm. So speak truthfully so we don't have to bring out the munster again," Sardoodledum said.

She nodded vigorously, clutching her sheet to her chin in obvious terror.

Rasher nudged Kucheesa, who looked extremely grave. He mouthed the word, "Munster?" Bibble leaned in closer too.

She whispered, "It's a nasty cheese with multiple uses. In addition to creating a wonderful poison acid cloud, it can be treated to induce extreme abdominal pain, with a side-effect that makes the subject very eager to answer questions truthfully."

Sardoodledum added, "And if they lie, the pain intensifies."

"A truth poison cheese?" Rasher asked. "Wow. I've never heard of it."

"It's a closely kept secret," Sardoodledum warned. "Used very rarely." He turned back to Ulotrichous. "I hope we don't have to use it again."

"I can't remember the person, but I remember that I didn't want to approve the contract," she promised quickly. "Something in the sugar overcame my reluctance. I don't know how, but I can remember going through the full approval process, even though I was screaming inside not to."

"I've never heard of such an effect," Sardoodledum said.

"This sounds like something I need to research," Bibble added. "It's possible she suffered some type of glowan glamour like the muffin mage."

"Glowan?" Ulotrichous gasped in horror.

"A long shot," Bibble soothed, even though it seemed extremely likely the glowan and the traitors had been cooperating. Bibble added, "Perhaps the archives might have a note about such an effect. I would submit a query to the confectioners too, but they suffered a catastrophic accident today."

"I hadn't heard about that," Sardoodledum said.

"A lot's been going on, and little of it good," Rasher said.

"Junior Toque!" Ulotrichous suddenly exclaimed, then squeaked, as if startled by her own outburst.

"What did you say?" Sardoodledum asked slowly as shocked silence settled over the group. Rasher barely breathed as he studied the terrified woman.

She stammered so badly she could barely get the words out. "I don't know why, sir. I didn't see him, but there's something there, something in the fog the sugars made of my mind, something about the Junior Toque."

"What about him?" Sardoodledum pressed. "We cannot throw that out without more to go on."

"No, we can't even let those words leave this room," Rasher said, glancing at everyone sternly.

Junior Toque was the title of the crown prince, the heir apparent to the Imperial Chef's throne. Hamurisi van Moraluvver dan Afitur was a name they could never even hint at associating with traitorous actions. Even a rumor that they were insinuating that Hamurisi might be involved in nefarious activities would probably get them all executed.

"What about him?" Sardoodledum roared down at the cowering woman.

Breathing fast, looking on the verge of fainting, she shook her head wildly, her curly hair shaking out across her face. "I don't know! Something about him. Maybe a threat against him? It was something the cloaked figure said after he thought I had passed out. I barely remember it, but he definitely said that name."

They all looked at each other in astonishment.

Kucheesa said, "So the conspirator who drugged you was a man? That's not much to go on."

Rasher took a deep breath, mind whirling with bacon-enhanced speed as he considered the ramifications of the woman's words.

"Sardoodledum, get a Creamery healer to see to Ulotrichous. On my authority, requisition all healing supplies required to restore her mind. Keep her here under guard and go over everything with her as many times as it takes to get a full account. We need as many details as possible."

Sardoodledum nodded. "Of course, Captain."

"What are we going to do?" Kucheesa asked.

He hated to say it, but couldn't think of any other option.

"We're going to Nutmeg Hill to see the Junior Toque."

24

THE PRICE OF EGGS

Before heading to Nutmeg Hill, they returned to the Heart and found Rasher's office. It was a huge space on the top floor, with a large window overlooking the plaza. It contained a beautiful mahogany desk fashioned into the shape of a giant piece of bacon. No doubt that was a recent change. A platter of candied rolled bacon strips waited on the desk, along with several reports from Shemo.

The room also sported a private fireplace on one side, with a fresh cinnamon roll in the hearth, ready to be ignited. Several overstuffed chairs faced the fireplace, with a soft rug between them. A small bookshelf stood against the rear wall, while a rack for weapons and armor stood to the right of the door.

Rasher was surprised to find his paint battle staff there and gasped when he spotted his crumbhorn.

"Blessed bacon," he muttered as he took up the precious instrument. Thankfully it looked undamaged by the move from his old quarters. He didn't like to let others handle it.

"What is that?" Kucheesa asked as she and Bibble explored his office.

"This is my crumbhorn," he said proudly, holding it up.

About eighteen inches long, the end was curved, making it look like a long letter J. It had a metal collar on the end he could use to secure it to the top of his battle staff. He used it that way sometimes for battlefield communications.

"So you play it?" she asked.

In response, Rasher lifted the crumbhorn to his lips and played the first part of a lively tune he loved. Kucheesa looked startled, but Bibble grinned and drew closer.

With bacon enhancing his learning curve, Rasher could play most instruments. The crumbhorn always felt best, though, and he loved its unique sound. Known as a closed-reed instrument, it produced a rich sound that he liked to think of as the fun-loving cousin to the clarinet.

"That's a unique sound," Kucheesa said when he finished.

Kitan had once teased him that it sounded like an oversized kazoo from the Schlepp Confederacy, but had never explained when she'd gotten a chance to listen to one. There was limited trade with the Schlepp nations, and with international tensions running high, few got to interact with Schlepp traders outside of the western ports of Oxter.

"It grows on you," Rasher assured her. Crumbhorns were not as popular as lutes or fiddles or flutes, but his team would have to get used to it. He played most nights before bed.

"Why do most musicians eat breakfast so fast?" Bibble asked.

"Why?" Kucheesa asked more enthusiastically than usual.

"Because they have to finish in four movements."

They both laughed, and even Rasher grinned. That one was better than a lot of his jokes.

Shemo Medjamo, the elderly secretary, knocked and entered the room carrying a stack of papers. His uniform again looked perfect, although he was using his hat like a paperweight on top of the stack of papers. "The reports you requested, Captain."

"Thank you. Please leave them on my desk," Rasher said.

Shemo looked unhappy about cluttering the desktop, but Rasher doubted he'd have time to read through all that information before they left for Nutmeg Hill. Shemo carefully positioned the papers and took his hat in his hand. The fastidious old man probably planned to wipe it clean before donning it again.

"When Reapers Noops and Quarce return, please send them to join us," Rasher added.

"Of course, Captain," Shemo said.

Bibble explained to Shemo the plan to have everyone change hats every day, starting immediately. The old man looked surprised and asked, "Are you sure that is wise, sir?"

"It's just a precaution, but an important one," Rasher said as Shemo looked down at the hat in his gnarled hands. Rasher had made an effort to like his new hat and not think about his favorite golden frying pan hat he'd been forced to leave behind, but he understood Shemo's reluctance. A hat was an important personal religious symbol.

"I will see it done, Captain," Shemo promised.

The door abruptly opened, and Noops and Quarce rushed inside. Their new uniforms bore smudge marks, and Quarce's face was smeared with soot.

"Perfect timing," Bibble said. "How did it go?"

"Please send for some refreshments," Rasher told Shemo, who saluted with crisp perfection and slipped out of the room.

Noops said, "The price of eggs will definitely be going up."

"Is that another crack about my father?" Kucheesa demanded.

"Crack," Bibble chuckled. "Didn't even need me to bring up that one."

She glared at him and he stroked his thin beard again. Noops regarded her calmly and said, "Is your father in the city?"

"Why would he be here?" she asked.

"I don't know. You're the one who brought him up."

She sighed. "What did you mean about the price of eggs?"

"I only referenced eggs as a way to quickly communicate the severity of the devastation at West Gate," Noops said, settling into one of the comfortable chairs, unsheathing his shovel, and starting to rub the gleaming, rounded blade with a soft cloth.

"How bad was it?" Rasher asked as Kucheesa stared at Noops in bewilderment.

"Bad, Captain," Quarce said, dropping into another chair and shaking dust from his beard. "The courier was right. It blew up big. Casualty counts are still incomplete, but a lot of people were injured. Deaths were low, thank Icmek, but the entire area was devastated."

"Did you see any eggs?" Kucheesa asked.

"Not a one," Quarce confirmed, disconnecting the carafe from his hat and producing mugs from his satchel. Without a word he began pouring and handing mugs to everyone. Rasher eagerly accepted his. Quarce's brew was just that good.

Rasher asked, "Did the legions arrive to help?"

Noops nodded. "Commander Moist himself led them."

That was good news. Commander Irriguous Moist was a celebrated soldier with a brilliant tactical mind. He served as General Nide's second in command.

"They've secured the area, set up field creameries for tending the wounded, and began removing rubble," Quarce added.

"Any sign of glowan?" Bibble asked.

Quarce shook his head. "Nothing definitive."

"We explored some of the watch tunnels, but found no evidence of how the foodstuffs were smuggled in," Noops added.

"Watch tunnels?" Rasher asked.

"Tunnels used by the watch," Noops confirmed. "With entrance points throughout the Acropolis."

"Really?" Bibble asked. "I've never heard of tunnels under the Acropolis."

"Gives the watch quick access points and mobility without cluttering the streets. Dug over eight generations ago," Noops explained. He smiled to himself and added softly, "Secret tunnels."

"Amazing," Rasher said. "I had no idea."

"Few do," Noops said. "But the Reapers use them often when they wish to travel without fanfare. Tunnels are so secret, they usually don't even post guards at the entrances."

"So anyone could have slipped inside with the explosive battle cuisine, and no one would have noticed?"

"It is possible," Noops confirmed.

Quarce added, "I inspected the tunnels on the outskirts of the blast zone. The explosion was definitely triggered in the tunnels, but they could have entered from any of several connecting tunnels. There's no way to know for sure. Some of the tunnels even lead under the Afitur outer wall."

"Do the Afitur city watch know about those?" Rasher asked. That didn't sound like something they'd appreciate.

"They do now," Noops said. "Afitur watch is involved in the cleanup efforts. The blast damaged the train tracks along the Afitur wall."

Not good. The city elevated train was a wonder of the empire, and very popular. Any interruption of the rail would draw a lot of ire from every tier of high houses. Unfortunately, they'd probably just blame the legions.

"We need to secure those tunnels," Rasher said. The more he considered the ramifications of secret tunnels spanning the Acropolis, the less he liked it.

Bibble nodded. "We've got traitors and potentially glowan among us, and they've discovered the tunnels."

"They might be using them to slip through the Acropolis to launch their attacks," Kucheesa gasped as she caught up with their line of thinking.

"And we might be able to catch some of them if we monitor the entrances carefully," Rasher agreed.

Noops said, "I've already issued those orders, Captain. The watch will send us updates once the entrances are secured and monitored."

"Good work," Rasher said, impressed.

He shrugged. "I know the tunnels and I know the watch. They'll appreciate extra rations when prices spike."

"Why do you keep talking about prices?" Kucheesa exclaimed.

Rasher was starting to suspect why, and guessed. "With so much disruption to the food supply and fear of attacks here in the capital, people might start hoarding food."

"And the glowan will likely continue to attack food supplies," Noops agreed. "I would."

"Shortages mean higher prices," Bibble said, glancing down at his ample stomach sadly.

"Oh," Kucheesa said, mollified. "You know, sometimes you leave out a few steps and just start talking about conclusions that make it kind of hard to follow what you're thinking," she told Noops.

"Exercise of the mind is as vital as exercise of the body," he replied calmly. "But you knew that—"

"Don't you dare say I've got tiny hands or something," Kucheesa interrupted.

"Why would I say that?" Noops asked, looking puzzled. "Your hands have nothing to do with your fitness level. Sometimes I worry about you."

She reddened, but another knock came at the door. It opened, and Kitan hurried through.

For a moment, time seemed to stop as Rasher drank in the sight of her. Her smile set her beautiful face aglow under the wide curve of her vibrant green hat. She wore an elegant taupe-colored dress, trimmed in crimson.

Rasher's heart sang as he rushed to her, and all the troubles he'd been worrying about melted away under the touch of her arms as she embraced him.

He laughed with pure joy, then kissed her quickly but passionately.

She glanced from his new hat to his Reaper uniform and asked in a breathless voice, "It's really true?"

25

SPAGHETTI WEAVING

R asher teased, "Never imagined I had it in me?"

Kitan gave him that annoyed look he found so adorable and said, "Of course not."

"So you didn't think I could do it?"

"No. I meant I didn't think you couldn't do it," she objected.

Noops interrupted the exchange. "Do you two always start conversations with double negatives?"

Rasher turned to the team and introduced Kitan, who greeted them all with her usual warmth and graciousness. Within seconds, she'd won them all over. Even Kucheesa's normal suspicious bluster faded to a low simmer.

Bibble interrupted the exchange after a moment. "We should give you two a moment."

"Good idea," Kucheesa said. "I need to go talk with Redael about recipes for dinner."

"I'll join you," Quarce said. "I'm curious to hear what she thinks about the proper levels of pepper in refried pigeon stews."

"That sounds like a dish Lahanasi owns," Kucheesa said with a grimace.

The two left, arguing about the proper table etiquette for eating gruel with bread. Noops marched out, headed somewhere unknown, but with purpose.

"I'll take care of adding those spice wards to our offices and quarters," Bibble said, excusing himself with a courtly bow.

After they left, Kitan said, "The makeup of your Reaper team seems a bit, ah, unusual."

Rasher led her to a couple comfortable chairs by the cold fireplace. "Unusual is probably a tame word for it. We're not the team anyone expected, but I'm getting a sense of their strengths, and I have some exciting plans for how to leverage them."

"You're going to need it," she told him gravely, her smile fading. "Rasher, news of your team is the talk of the entire city. The highest houses are taking an interest."

"Good interest?"

"Not really," she admitted with an apologetic grimace. "General Nide is filing an official protest with the Food Court."

"They never interfere with Reaper business," Rasher protested, stifling a flash of anger at the general's meddling. Why couldn't she just accept the results and let them get to work?

"There's never been a situation quite like this," Kitan replied. "Rasher, news of the Gloaming attacks across the empire has everyone spooked, and reports of disasters here in the Acropolis aren't helping."

"Do you think they'll try to interfere?" Rasher had enough to worry about without having to deal with high house meddling.

"It's possible," she admitted, leaning back in her chair and chewing on a strand of her hair like she did when deep in thought. "Times of upheaval present unusual opportunities. Nutmeg Hill is buzzing with news of the invasion. Houses are scrambling to find ways to leverage the emergencies to secure more funding for their houses and their favorite initiatives. They're like kids squabbling over a tray of fresh sweets."

Rasher groaned. "Seriously? That's their first reaction?"

"Of course," she said calmly. "They haven't seen the fighting firsthand, and every high house has a strict policy of not allowing any good emergency to go to waste. My father is nearly beside himself with excitement. He keeps talking about new opportunities."

"What kind of opportunities?"

"I don't know any more details about the plots he's running, if that's what you mean. The First Course Assembly has been in session all day, and from reports I've heard, arguments are already heating up, with accusations flying about whose fault the lack of warning is."

"I don't care whose fault it is. I just want them to send us support," Rasher griped.

"But they do. Whoever gets any of the blame for such a public disaster pinned on them will lose enormous influence, and could face funding shortfalls, or even sanctions. That could totally change a house's fortunes," she warned.

Not good. The intrigue of the six tiers of high houses was notoriously brutal, and more convoluted than braided spaghetti. Anyone caught up in it as a pawn in those political games usually got squashed like a grape under a hammer.

"Can you get more details from your father?" Rasher suspected he'd know a lot.

Kitan considered that for a moment. "Perhaps. I thought I knew all of his plots, but I'm realizing there is much he hasn't told me."

That didn't surprise Rasher. An ambitious man like Niffum would have to be good at keeping secrets and deft at weaving spaghetti plots. A single slip, the wrong word spoken to the wrong ears could spell disaster for a man preparing to topple a primi house.

"Do you think he'll drop his request that I leverage my family to strike at the Takmor house for him? If the high houses want to draw the Reapers into their plots, I might be able to provide better information for him that way."

"We'll have to wait and see what offers you receive, but I doubt he'll relinquish that claim on you until he's sure he can get something more valuable in exchange." Kitan leaned forward and took his hand, searching his gaze. "Rasher, be very careful."

"I'm always careful."

That made her laugh out loud in a very unladylike way. She leaned back, rubbing one hand over her eyes and said, "Oh, Rasher. You've never been careful. You can't afford to be."

That was true. He needed that rush only danger provided, or his blood phobia would eventually siphon away enough of his power to . . . Well, he wasn't sure exactly what would happen, but he feared it would cancel out his bacon powers entirely.

Kitan fixed him with her gaze and asked softly, "How are you holding up?"

"I haven't had any episodes since the duel against Balter, but we haven't seen battle yet."

"How can you even contemplate going to battle?" she asked, not hiding her worry. "Rasher, do they know?"

He shook his head. "Not even my team."

"You have to tell them."

"I know," he admitted. "I just want a little time to build their trust first."

"You may not get much time."

"It's just, what if . . ." He trailed off, not quite able to voice his fears, even to her.

Kitan moved to him, dropping to one knee beside his chair, and cupped his face with her warm hand. "Rasher, they will follow you, I know it. But you can't build an effective team on lies. You're the one who taught me that."

Rasher sighed. "I know. I will tell them, but not yet. We need to go to Nutmeg Hill, and I can't afford any distractions."

"Nutmeg Hill? Are you sure? This might not be the best time to go there."

"It can't be helped," he said, rising and drawing her up beside him. "There may be a plot against the Junior Toque. I need to speak with him."

Kitan paled. "Rasher, I usually love how daring you are, but the Junior Toque? He stands at the center of more plots and intrigue than anyone."

They were interrupted by a brisk knock at the door. A second later, Shemo stepped in and announced, "Captain, General Nide has arrived with a retinue of commanders and seeks a meeting. She is not on the schedule."

"It's all right," Rasher said, schooling his features. He had always held the general in the highest esteem until that day. He could not afford to allow her to see his anger at her games. Was she there to announce her appeal against their choosing, or for some other reason?

Shemo saluted and held the door open. General Nide marched in, followed by several armored commanders of the legions. Rasher recognized the burly Commander Moist but did not know the others by sight.

"Perhaps I should go," Kitan said.

Rasher wanted to urge her to stay, but as much as he liked the idea of annoying General Nide, Kitan was not part of the legion command structure. So he nodded and kissed her cheek.

General Nide stopped a few paces from Rasher and saluted, her expression stoic. "Captain Dilskin, we need to talk."

"Of course, General," he said. "One moment, please."

He turned back to Kitan, who added, "I'll wait for you. I would like to join you on your visit."

That was a brilliant idea. Kitan knew Nutmeg Hill far better than Rasher. She'd be like a guardian angel, hovering over his shoulder with an illumination pastry to guide his steps. He smiled and said, "Great idea."

She nodded to the general and her staff, then withdrew. Rasher asked, "General, would you like to sit down?"

"Thank you, but no," she replied, her posture stiff, her tone formal. "We lack time for niceties, Captain."

"Very well. What reports do you have on the recent attacks we've suffered here in the Acropolis?"

Commander Moist stepped forward and spoke in a deep, powerful voice. "Captain, Second Legion Gherkin Guard is in control of the West Gate area. All wounded are being treated in the field creameries. Healing supplies are low."

Rasher grimaced. "Casualty counts?"

"Not complete yet," reported another commander, dressed in the uniform of the Watch. He was a tall fellow with broad shoulders and a scar on his chin.

"You're Commander Welkin, right?" Rasher asked.

"Yes, Captain," the man said proudly. "Tenirak Welkin, commander of the wall."

"I am sorry this surprise attack hit your men the hardest."

"Thank you, sir. We serve and protect," Commander Welkin said, meeting Rasher's gaze, clearly grateful for the comment.

"I received a report that Reaper Noops issued commands to monitor and guard entrances to the watch tunnels," General Nide said.

Rasher nodded. "I support that decision."

"As do I," she surprised him by saying.

"I'm glad to hear it."

She added, "I still think your team is the wrong choice, and I will pursue any avenue I deem necessary to replace you with a team I deem fitting for your high post."

That crushed the moment rather effectively. Rasher sighed. "General, I did not ask for this position, but I cannot allow you to undermine the authority of the Reapers. I expect you to do your duty in every particular."

"You dare question General Nide?" Commander Moist asked in a dangerous tone.

Rasher held his gaze. "Like she just said, we don't have time for niceties. Should the Food Court decide to interfere in legion business and remove me and my team, you are welcome to work with Gubbins and the hero finders to submit replacement candidates. But until that unprecedented move happens, I expect you to do your duty with the same exactness you have always shown. I don't have time for insubordination, and I would hate to replace you or any of your commanders on the eve or marching to battle."

General Nide's face reddened, and Commander Moist's hand slipped to the hilt of his sword. Rasher hoped he didn't do anything foolish. They didn't have time for internal bickering.

He added, "My team and I are following an important clue we picked up at the Cheese Palace, so my time is short."

That surprised her. "You breached the Cheese Palace?" She glanced back at her commanders. "Why was I not informed?"

"Just happened half an hour ago," Rasher said. "You were busy dealing with other issues."

"What did you learn?" The general asked.

"I believe most of the cheese wizards are innocent, and that they were infiltrated by at least one traitor, who may be in league with the same glowan who placed a glamour on a muffin mage to attack me at the Food Watch compound earlier."

"I had not heard of that either," General Nide said, casting an annoyed glance at her commanders.

"I captured him, and the inquisitors are interrogating him. In both cases, the traitors used doctored sugars to influence their victims. In the case of the cheese wizards, they used the compromised woman to corrupt the addendum process. Sardoodledum Squelch, the high cheese at the palace, is following that inquiry."

"If they've uncovered proof of foul play, could the addendum be reversed?" Commander Moist asked hopefully.

"I don't know yet," Rasher said. "I would welcome the return of the previous Reaper team to join mine."

"Let us all pray the gods grant they can return," General Nide agreed. Her face revealed nothing, but he bet she would prefer Absquatch and his team simply boot Rasher's team out of their positions. He couldn't entirely blame her for that, but they'd ice that cake when it came out of the oven.

"In the meantime, my team is following up on another lead, so unfortunately we need to cut our time short," Rasher said. "Let's meet together at five bells to compare notes and work on a plan to root out the traitors hiding among us."

"And plan how to get this deployment moving," Commander Moist added.

General Nide nodded. "We've sent word to Nutmeg Hill to request supplemental battle cuisine, but chances are slim we'll receive much."

Rasher wasn't surprised by that. Afitur was the jewel of the empire, and the city dedicated enormous portions of their foodstuffs to keep the city's famous magical features running. He doubted they would sacrifice those wonders unless the war grew protracted, and danger threatened the capital itself.

"Very well. Keep me posted, General. Dismissed."

They actually saluted, and he only barely managed to conceal his grin until the door shut behind them. He could get used to ordering General Nide around.

26

A Good Time To Hold Your Thumbs

As Rasher led his team toward the terminal to board the Reaper Express train that ran to Nutmeg Hill, he attached his crumbhorn to the end of his battle staff. He'd decided to take the weapon and the instrument along for the visit. An unarmed Reaper might not send the right message to the political leaders.

He was surprised to see the same pretty vendor who had given him the fortune cookie the other day. Food carts weren't allowed that close to the Heart, but she didn't have her cart.

The woman approached with a warm smile, her tall, orange hat flapping slightly, even though he didn't feel any wind. She held out a fortune cookie and said, "Congratulations on your appointment as Reaper. To celebrate your good fortune, you get a free cookie."

"I love cookies," Quarce said eagerly.

The woman smiled at him, but her eyes never left Rasher's. He wasn't sure if she was simply a really good marketer, trying to secure a recommendation from the Reaper team, or if something else was going on, but he had too much on his mind to play her games.

"Thank you, but we're in a hurry." He started moving past, but Kitan said, "Oh, Rasher, fortune cookies are so fun."

She took the proffered cookie, and the woman handed everyone else a cookie too. Rasher sighed. He didn't want to look petulant, so he took one too and said, "Thank you."

"Enjoy it," the woman said before turning away.

"You know, Prophecy, Inc should use fortune cookies," Quarce said as he bit the top off of his cookie and extracted the little note.

"How do you know they don't?" Kucheesa asked as she examined her fortune cookie.

"Prophecy what?" Kitan asked.

"I'll explain on the train," Rasher said. His cookie was still somehow warm, as if the woman kept them in a bread-lined pocket. He extracted his fortune and offered the cookie to Quarce, who happily munched it down.

His fortune read, "The greater the betrayal, the greater the thirst for vengeance."

"Hmm, not as upbeat as usual," he said, showing it to Kitan.

She frowned at his and said, "Mine was nice. It said the bonds of family will overcome the pull of ambition."

"Usually they just say things like you will find a reason to be happy today," Kucheesa said. "This one was dumb. Just said all cats aren't always cats. Doesn't make sense."

Quarce grunted. "Mine tried to tell me my favorite color should be silver."

"Mine said when in doubt, take the stairs," Bibble added with a glum expression. "Even my fortune is telling me to get into better shape."

Rasher glanced at Noops who smiled and said, "Mine simply told me to choose the shovel way."

"It didn't," Kucheesa exclaimed, taking his paper and scanning it disbelieving. "That has to be a joke."

"It's a great waste of time, if nothing else," Rasher said as they reached the train terminal. One of the sleek express trains was preparing to depart, all eleven passenger cars colored cheery pastel shades. The train was not very full, and they got an entire car to themselves.

A moment later, it smoothly accelerated away, the gingersnap wheels barely making a whisper, while the roar of the air-powered propulsion at the rear made a distant rumble. As much as Rasher preferred riding on the roof most of the time, he could appreciate the more comfortable ride on the plush seats, with excellent views over the city with Kitan at his side.

The elevated train rolled east, and Rasher sat with Kitan, holding her hand and talking about the different high houses. They discussed their known alliances, and their likely positions on General Nide's petition. She might not be as conniving as her father, but Kitan possessed a sharp intellect, and she had paid attention. She knew an astonishing amount, and Rasher was glad she'd offered to join them.

The track eventually turned south, paralleling Carrot Boulevard, and the elevated train's large windows offered panoramic views out over the grand city.

Afitur was the crown jewel of the Rubric Empire, a vast, sprawling city built across a series of low hills that descended toward the northwest tip of Cockalorum Lake. It was packed with marble and granite buildings, with the most majestic on Nutmeg Hill.

To their left, they started passing one of the sectors of the city that vied for second place in grandeur. It was packed with stately mansions of the secondi and contorni tier houses, built as close to Nutmeg Hill as possible. Their expansive grounds were exquisitely tended, including grand fountains, many shaped like fish or lobsters, spewing crystal clear water high into the air.

"Have you all seen Bisque Boulevard from up here?" he asked his team, who were already enjoying the view. Bibble and Noops had let Kucheesa and Quarce press closer to the glass since they hadn't ridden the train to Nutmeg Hill before.

"Wow," Quarce whispered as he gazed at one of the wonders that made Afitur so famous.

The city had served as the seat of the Rubric Empire for over twelve generations. Every generation, leaders had tried to outshine their ancestors. Not only was it a renowned seat of all types of learning and culinary excellence, but also famous for its grand stone architecture and its conveniences.

Every building enjoyed running water, and the city boasted the only city-wide sewage treatment system in the known world. Additionally, Bisque Boulevard had become one of the most famous attractions outside of Art sector, down on the southwest side of the city.

Rasher gazed at the gently flowing water of Bisque Boulevard as it ran beside the stone-paved Carrot Boulevard. Brightly painted passenger barges moved faster than trotting horse carriages, while individual crafts slipped along even faster. Powered by highly classified seafood recipes, the boulevard flowed all through the city, running uphill as easily as down.

"Oh, look at that," Kucheesa cried as one passenger stepped from a moving barge onto the surface of the moving water. A little eddy separated, lifting the well-dressed woman with stately grace to the road, depositing her completely dry.

"That's the reason we probably won't be getting any seafood supplies from the city," Rasher said.

He loved the grandeur of Afitur but had to wonder how bad things would have to get before the First Course Assembly would order the cessation of food-expensive wonders to fuel the war effort.

As the rest of the team marveled at the sights, Kitan drew Rasher's attention, leaning close and whispering. "Be careful, Rasher. As much as I know about the positions of the families, even my intel might not be accurate."

"Why not?"

"The invasion is already triggering changes. Just over the past day, some of the long-term alliances are giving signs of maybe shifting."

"In what way?"

"The Takmor house publicly agreed with the Hapyr house, and the Toffers and Moores sounded positively united with them. That's an unexpected shift that gives the faction calling for more funding of houses on the other side of the Gewgaw a lot of momentum, especially since they're the ones who will need to face the horde in the short term."

Rasher whistled softly. He knew enough to understand some of the ramifications of that news. If that faction could leverage the invasion, they might finally win concessions from the 'old' high houses based out of Rubric to shift greater power to the houses located in the vassal nations. Even though they held primi seats, those houses were still treated as lesser.

Kitan continued. "So, of course, the core Rubric houses are at least temporarily dropping some of their usual squabbles to strengthen the faction to block those efforts. They are instead calling for increased funding for their military budgets."

That was a powerful argument. Most of those old Rubric houses had close ties to the military, and the empire did need to increase funding for troops, equipment, and battle cuisine.

The hordes had timed their invasion well. Spring planting had not yet happened, and food stores were at their lowest level of the entire year. Coupled with the theft of so much battle cuisine, he feared the empire might not be able to produce enough food for the guilds to fuel a large-scale conflict.

"So, do you think they'll send us reinforcements for our mobilization, or will they choose to interfere in Reaper business?" Rasher asked.

"It's not clear. That's why we have to tread carefully today. Your actions could push them in either direction."

Not good. Rasher sat back, brooding about politics. He couldn't fool himself into believing he was ready to dive into that seething cauldron of tangled spaghetti.

Kitan squeezed his hand and gave him an encouraging smile. "Don't worry. We'll figure it out, and I'll start feeling out some of the high houses to identify potential allies for you."

"I never thought I would need high house allies," he admitted.

"You're a good man, Rasher, and good men need help to survive in high society. I've got your back."

Bibble dropped into one of the seats facing them, his expression grave. "You realize this is a terrible idea, right?"

"It's not ideal," Rasher agreed. "I'd be a fool to ignore the danger we're walking into."

Kucheesa poked her head over the seat. "Is there something I need to know?"

Quarce stepped around to stand next to Bibble, his expression curious too. Rasher realized neither of them knew much about the issues he and Kitan had been discussing. They didn't need all that detail, but they could easily make foolish and potentially costly blunders in their ignorance.

"You do need to know at least a little about the political situation on Nutmeg Hill," he said.

"Since we're about to walk up to a hornet's nest and whack it with a stick," Bibble added.

"You don't actually seem nervous," Quarce pointed out.

Bibble shrugged. "We're acting on the captain's orders. He's the one who has to know what he's doing."

"Thanks," Rasher said dryly. "What Bibble is alluding to is that the invasion and the attacks in the Acropolis are likely to exacerbate existing tensions between the primi houses."

"They're still quarreling over the Wurse family rise from mini to primi house last year?" Kucheesa asked.

Rasher nodded, happy she understood that much.

"When they booted the van Evanmor lam Danothurs house from primi down to mini status and took their place, the van Wurse dan Anhiothr house shook the First Course Assembly deeply. Partly because no primi rank family had fallen from the assembly in two generations, but the Evanmor family was one of the old ruling families. It's considered especially tragic for one of them to lose the 'dan' designation from their surnames and drop to 'lam'."

"What does that mean?" Quarce asked with a frown.

Rasher hadn't realized he understood so little about the high houses. Kitan spoke up before he could.

"Each high house surname includes four parts. The 'van' defines them as one of the six tiers, followed by their original surname. Then comes the declaration of which tier they belong to. Dan are the primi, highest tier houses, Yur the secondi, Mon the contorni, Hav the antipasti. After that, are the fifth and sixth-tier mini high houses. Bar for fifth, and Lam for sixth."

"Oh," Quarce said with a happy nod.

"The final part of the house name is the city they are based out of, which produces the bulk of their wealth," Rasher finished.

"So the Evanmor house dropped from primi all the way down to a mini lam house," Quarce asked. He'd definitely spent too much time in the mines.

"Exactly," Bibble interjected. "Such a fall is extremely rare, especially for an old family."

"Old family?" Quarce asked.

Could he really understand so little of Rubric high society?

Bibble took the question in stride. "Means their main city is located in the original nation of Rubric. They think they're better than the new high primi families from the vassal nations."

His tone made it clear what he thought of that, which reminded Rasher that the Wurse family were now the patrons of the spice wizards. Bibble would probably not react well to any disparaging remarks about them, no matter how justified they might be.

Rasher said, "Originally all eleven seats in the assembly were old families, but now three of those seats belong to new families. The

Wurse family used to be considered an old family, but fell from primi rank three generations ago. Now they've deposed another old family to get back."

From the rumors Rasher had heard, the Wurse family were ruthless and determined to win back all of their previous glory, no matter the cost.

Bibble said, "More and more of the empire's wealth is coming from vassal nations, so there's growing pressure from other new families to win seats in the Food Court."

Rasher hoped they succeeded. His patrons, the van Takmor dan Weghiv house were one of the few new families who made it to primi level but were still pushing for full equality. And now Kitan's father was threatening to force him to help destroy them so he could rise and take their place.

"So what does this have to do with investigating the attack on the Reapers?" Kucheesa asked.

"The Junior Toque is the crown prince and heir apparent to the Imperial Chef's throne," Bibble explained, looking like that should make it clear. By Kucheesa's and Quarce's expressions, it didn't.

Rasher added, "Erinaceous van Moraluvver dan Afitur is growing old, and his grip on power is weakening." He was glad they had the train car to themselves for the delicate conversation.

He still lowered his voice. "In some circles, his son Hamurisi is not considered the strongest candidate for the next Imperial Chef."

Kucheesa's eyes widened, and Quarce sniffed an origami frog. Noops remained as impassive as ever.

Bibble whispered, "Even a hint of scandal could be the gust of wind that collapses the cake."

Kitan said, "There is always political scheming going on among the high houses, especially at the primi and secondi levels, but it's particularly intense right now. With the invasion, some families will no doubt see this as their chance to snatch for power or unseat rivals."

"They should be uniting against a common enemy," Noops muttered.

Rasher nodded. "Twenty years ago when the Imperial Chef was younger, they would have, but not now with succession so close."

"So we have to avoid suggesting the Junior Toque is involved in the attack on the Reapers," Bibble said. "With the other Reapers staying in his family palace, it would be awkward. Plus, such an unfounded accusation would be tantamount to treason, even for us. He would see it as a direct attack on his chances for ascension."

"And we have to avoid letting any of the other members of the First Course Assembly know what we're up to, or they'll make up their own rumors," Rasher added.

"Why are we doing this again?" Kucheesa asked. "Why don't we just go deal with the Gloaming threat?"

"We can't yet," Rasher said. "Not only are our food stores too low, but at every stage of their attack, the hordes have had internal assistance from traitors within every city. That means a sophisticated organization is backing them."

"Probably the Rumpus Cabal," Noops said, reaching the same initial conclusion that Rasher had.

"Perhaps. I bet they're involved," Rasher said. "But I'm not convinced they could orchestrate the theft of the magical stockpiles or corrupting the Reaper contracts. Now we have a clue about a potential threat against the Junior Toque. He may have insights into what factions might be willing to ally with the Rumpus Cabal and the Gloaming in order to push their chances at succeeding in a coup."

The group considered that for a moment in grim silence. The Reapers had dealt with uprisings and coup attempts before, but never one coordinated with a Gloaming attack. Rasher doubted any of the previous Reaper teams had been dumped so fast into such deep water. Any misstep could destroy or discredit them right when the empire needed them the most.

"So all we have to do is interrogate the Junior Toque, gather information about who might have committed treason at the highest levels of the government, but make sure no one realizes what we're doing," Kitan said with a smile.

Quarce grinned and said, "We'll hold our thumbs that it works."

"What?" Kucheesa asked as they all stared.

"You know," Quarce said, lifting his hands and interlocking his thumbs. "For luck."

Kitan laughed. "Oh, you mean crossing your fingers." She held up two slender fingers and demonstrated.

Quarce chuckled, waggling his thick fingers. "Can't do that, m'lady, but I get the point. Either way, we've got this!"

27

NOT SUCH A SPRING CHICKEN AFTER ALL

The train stopped just outside the gates to Nutmeg Hill, and Rasher led his team out. The gates were open, but two dozen imperial guardsmen positioned there checked all visitors. Rasher didn't stop, but raised a hand in greeting and the soldiers all saluted smartly and allowed them to pass unchallenged.

High position definitely had some wonderful perks. He bet no one would question him if he climbed up that wall and jumped off. It was tempting. A new shot of thrill would feel good, but he resisted the temptation.

Inside the walls, every building seemed grander than the last. The main boulevard was split in half. The left side was a normal, stone-lined street, while the right half flowed in another waterway, crowded with people. The water route was more popular, but Rasher decided to walk.

Stately trees lined the road, shading the finest shops anywhere in Afitur, catering to the richest clientele. People flowed around them on all sides, dressed in expensive, bright colors. Both men and women strutted in the ridiculously huge hats that were so much the rave at the moment, and that helped thin the crowds since no two people could walk within five feet of each other.

Many storefronts were bursting with colorful high fashion clothing, and one clever hat merchant whose sign read "Peptic Premier Hats" had posted their huge hats on stakes of varying heights to showcase their wares without consuming all available space inside.

Kitan walked gracefully beside Rasher, with the rest of the team flanking them. Noops alone looked unaffected by the grandeur and finery everywhere. Bibble walked with a wide smile, while both Kucheesa and Quarce gaped.

Rasher nodded toward the hat shop and said, "Did you hear about the woman visiting Chef's Walk whose hat got her into trouble?"

"Chef's Walk?" Quarce asked.

Kitan said, "I can't believe you haven't visited Chef's Walk yet, Quarce. We must make time to go there as soon as possible. It's the most famous attraction in Art sector. It's lined with restaurants, grills, cafes, bakeries, and sweet shops. It's where student chefs produce nearly every food imaginable from the public-level cookbooks."

"They're amazing," Rasher agreed, smiling at the memory of the last time he and Kitan had visited there. "World-class cuisine for a fraction of its normal cost."

Bibble smiled and interjected, "As long as you understand they're still students. Sometimes their recipes fail spectacularly."

"That's what I was thinking about," Rasher said. "That woman I mentioned was wearing an extremely fashionable hat with a six-tiered brim. She sampled a spicy quiche that accidentally unleashed a mini tornado strong enough to lift her by the hat high into the air and fling her way out into the lake."

"No," Kucheesa breathed.

"It's okay," Kitan said. "Turned out to be a big win for her. Somehow people decided her hat was touched by the hand of Bharat."

Rasher chuckled. "Yea, she ended up selling it at the exclusive cuisine auction for five thousand golden spatulas."

"Five thousand?" Quarce cried, his voice echoing between the stone buildings, drawing many surprised stares.

"You could buy a lot of hats with that," Noops commented.

Kucheesa grunted. "And more. That's a fortune."

"One of the top twenty most expensive hats of all time," Kitan confirmed.

"We need to go to Chef's Walk," Quarce said eagerly.

"Eventually," Rasher said. He doubted their busy schedule would allow much sightseeing. "Now's not the best time. I heard there was a riot by Lahanasi restoration cultists. They caused a lot of damage."

"Really?" Kucheesa asked with a frown. "Those idiots again? Why can't they live up to everyone's expectations and just get drunk and puke on each other?"

"That's usually all they do," Kitan said. "But in recent months, they seem to have been getting better organized. That wasn't the first riot they'd caused."

Rasher wondered about that, thinking about the muffin mage who had attacked him on that rooftop. The man was a cultist. Could that connection somehow be more important than he'd realized?

"I hope we don't get sent to deal with those weirdos," Bibble said. "Their eggs are definitely scrambled."

Bibble was right. Rasher doubted they'd have to worry about the cult directly, but filed those questions away for further consideration.

Soon the street opened to a wider view as they entered the guild district. Eleven spectacular palaces, each housing the headquarters of one of the principal guilds of magic, marched off in grand majesty to either side. They formed a belt along the waistline of Nutmeg Hill.

Rasher wished they had time to visit. Each palace was an architectural wonder, reflecting the guild it housed. To their right reared the palace of the drupe wizards and their god Tohum. Built like a giant sprouting seed of grain, with towers rising from the peeled open roof, it celebrated the central role of the Sons of the Seed in maintaining imperial prosperity.

To their left stood the palace of Sut and her milk mages. Sheathed in stainless steel and shaped like an upside-down milk pail, the palace gleamed in the sunlight, radiating simple majesty.

The other palaces stretching away in the distance were as varied as their gods, but Rasher did not slow to study them. They could return when they had more leisure.

As they walked deeper into Nutmeg Hill, they had to merge with heavy traffic of horses, fine carriages, and even a couple muffin mage fire-driven magical carriages. Many people noted their passage, but in Nutmeg Hill it was commonplace to see the most important men and women alive. Reapers merited notice, but not cheering.

"I'm glad we got new hats," Kucheesa said, adjusting hers slightly.

Rasher was surprised she would care. Usually she seemed eager to make a scene and cause a confrontation. As he studied her, he realized she was nervous.

Smart girl. Rasher was far more comfortable around high society, but only a fool wouldn't feel concerned by their current mission.

Beyond the guild district, they entered the primi section, lorded over by the identical palaces of the ten ruling houses whose representatives made up the First Course Assembly. Beyond those, the palace of the Moraluvver house, led by the Imperial Chef, stood alone closer to the Food Court and was significantly larger than the others.

No house formally claimed association with Lahanasi's evil foods, and no house from Gravlax had yet won a seat at the primi level, so the final two gods of the pantryon lacked representatives in the Food Court. Rasher doubted those seats would ever be added. Too many powerful families wanted seats in the Food Court to give a seat to Gravlax.

Lahanasi would never again win a seat. If a new one opened up, more likely it would be for one of the lesser food gods, like Tinapay, the fluffy god of bread, or Sudd, goddess of juices. Rasher doubted even that would ever happen unless the Food Court faced a truly dire situation.

Externally identical, each of the ten palaces served as the administrative and political headquarters for the ruling houses. Rasher had never entered any of them, but Kitan had explained that they looked so alike on the outside to represent that each ruling house wielded identical power. That was supposed to foster equality and declare to all their people that their leaders worked tirelessly for their benefit.

"The interiors are wildly different," Kitan had added. "I think that more accurately represents the reality of the ruling houses than the exteriors."

The streets were clogged with functionaries, nobility, and officials, all dressed formally and hurrying to or from important meetings. Couriers flew by overhead, secured to giant kites that glided along perpetual high currents maintained by the spice wizards.

Rasher watched them with interest, thinking back to the annoying intruder who had escaped him twice. He needed to get his hands on one of those flyers. Just thinking about launching out over vast open spaces made the thrill shiver through him.

"I feel stronger than ever, even though we've been walking for a while," Kucheesa commented.

"I'm glad you noticed that," Kitan said. "All the streets on Nutmeg Hill are imbued with low levels of vegetable powers to enhance strength and stamina." She nodded to ornate planters nestled close to the trees, filled with early-season vegetables. Rasher recognized mature carrot tops and beanstalks.

"But it's barely spring," Kucheesa protested.

"Between the various guilds, they've layered enough recipes over those planters to keep the vegetables in full bloom year round," Kitan said.

They slowed when they entered the great expanse of the Plaza of the Pantryon facing the grand edifice of the Food Court. Thirty-foot statues of the gods reared into the air along the near edge of the plaza, spaced regularly apart. The collection of mighty gods made the Way of the Gods in the Acropolis look puny in comparison.

Rasher glanced from the portly, laughing statue of Domuz, lifting a tankard in one hand and a fistful of bacon in the other, to the other gods of the Pantryon. He tipped off his new hat and placed a small offering of bacon bits from a pocket. The food evaporated a second later, and Rasher smiled as he returned his hat, feeling better about the new hat.

As the rest of the team followed his lead, Rasher glanced around the plaza, wishing there was a statue of Arkadas. Their entire purpose was dedicated to her service, after all, and if there was a statue, they might find a way to locate the prophet.

He led the way across the plaza. A squad of soldiers guarded the wide marble steps leading up to the grand Food Court building rearing seven stories above the ground floor.

The first five floors were each constructed out of different stones to represent the five nations of the Rubric Empire. The top two floors gleamed with pure white marble and were carved with huge statues of the gods, their main foods, and the favorite dishes enjoyed by Imperial Chefs of generations past.

There Rasher was finally challenged. He relayed the request to meet with the Junior Toque on important Reaper business. The sentries sent a courier rushing up the steps.

While they waited, Rasher's eyes were drawn to workers carefully unloading boxes from a large wagon with a muffin mage guild crest on the side.

"They must be part of the crew preparing the Food Court for a special assembly tomorrow," Kitan said. "It'll be a rare full assembly with the Imperial Chef planning to attend."

"I wish we could see that," Quarce said, wide-eyed.

"Unlikely," Kitan said. "It's even hard for me to get a ticket for a full assembly like that. Not only will they be debating plans to deal with the Gloaming invasion, but the Imperial Chef rarely makes personal appearances these days with his declining health. Everyone with any political pull will be fighting to get a seat."

Rasher was glad he wouldn't have to be there. The thought of squeezing into the giant assembly hall with so many high nobility made his skin crawl.

The courier returned and beckoned the team inside. They ascended the stairs, then turned to follow a grand hallway around the outskirts of the assembly hall. Through wide entrance openings spaced every fifty feet, Rasher studied the tiered seats, all facing the distant stage where the First Course Assembly would meet.

Sure enough, he spotted the work crews replacing the brightly glowing pastry lamps with larger pastries. Odd that the larger illumination pastries seemed to glow softer than the nearly spent ones. Maybe they were going to install more of them. With the dimmer light, they would no doubt last a lot longer. Or maybe the leadership hoped to calm the worries of their people by setting up a cozier ambiance.

As he watched, one worker on a high ladder fumbled and dropped the old pastry he'd been extracting from the lantern housing affixed to the balcony at the base of the higher tiers of seats. The still-burning pastry could have caused a huge mess if it had burst on impact, but another worker snagged it out of the air with a rope, using a classic lasso move popular among noodle warriors.

Unusual to see a manual worker with such highly trained skills. Maybe contractors on Nutmeg Hill were held to a higher standard than elsewhere. As Rasher passed, he could hear the distant shouting of the supervisor and shook his head. Some things never changed. The supervisor seemed to be tongue-lashing the man who saved the pastry as much as the man who dropped it.

His thoughts were interrupted as the courier led them to a wide shaft that pierced the building, extending high into the air and dropping into darkness below them. Air whistled up the shaft in a constant stream.

"Try to stay relaxed, and look for the exit point. Just step out like normal," the courier said, then stepped off the edge into the open space. He barely dipped before the rushing wind coalesced under his feet into a mini tornado and pushed him quickly upward.

"I've heard of the air elevators, but never ridden one," Rasher confided to Kitan.

"It's fun," she said with a grin. "Watch your hats."

Then, clapping her hand over her hat, she jumped lightly into the shaft. Again the air condensed around her and she shot up even faster than the courier had. The wind barely rustled her skirts, and the opaque whirlwind protected her modesty from anyone looking up from below.

"Amazing!" Quarce shouted, jumping headfirst into the shaft.

He spread his arms and legs wide as the wind caught him and threw him upward, his booming laugh echoing back down the shaft as he began to rotate.

Bibble said, "I prefer the old-school approach." He turned and fell backward into the elevator shaft, dropping a bit farther than the others had before the wind caught him and lifted him. He ascended half reclined like he'd settled into a comfortable chair.

"Showoff," Noops smiled, then stepped into the shaft. He dropped nearly ten feet before the wind caught his armored bulk. He laughed, an open, innocent expression on his face. As the wind carried him aloft, he called out, "Kucheesa, stop scowling and let out your inner chicken."

"I am not scowling," Kucheesa muttered with a very definite scowl.

Rasher was surprised to realize she was nervous. She could float, by the gods. What did she have to be nervous about?

She noticed him looking and her scowl deepened. "What?"

"Just wondering what's making you nervous? Can't be the flying, and you said you have excellent vision in the dark, so it's probably not the shadows in the lower shaft."

"I am not nervous," she insisted. Rasher only cocked one eyebrow, and she sighed. "My brother fell down a well when I was young. I've always hated them since."

The shaft did look a little like a well. Kucheesa added, "If you tell anyone, I'll feed you a dish that will turn your hair to feathers. Ugly ones."

"You can do that?"

"Oh, yes," she said with an evil grin before taking a deep breath and jumping into the shaft. She must have activated her float ability because when the air caught her, it flung her upward several times faster than anyone else.

Rasher jumped into the shaft to follow, just in time to see an arm reach into the shaft high above and snag Kucheesa mid-flight and yank her out of the shaft.

The whirlwind under his feet felt remarkably solid, and the wind barely rustled his hat. Rasher had experienced spice wizard air shielding powers before, but never coupled with high winds. It was a remarkable advancement in their recipes. Could it somehow be applied to his blood phobia?

When he stepped out of the elevator, he found himself in a wide hallway on the sixth floor. The courier ushered them into an opulent lounge. Noops was still laughing softly, and Kucheesa fuming at him for having to pull her out of the shaft.

"It caught me by surprise," she protested for the fifth time.

"Flying caught a chicken expert by surprise?" Noops asked with another chuckle. "Maybe you're not such a spring chicken after all."

That made the rest of them laugh as Kucheesa reached for her knives.

28

Not All Cats Are Cats

"Relax," Rasher urged Kucheesa. "This is not the place to quarrel."

Thankfully she let it go, turning to pace away across the huge room. It had to be fifty feet square, with twenty-foot ceilings and enormous windows showing a panoramic view to the southeast across Afitur, all the way to the distant brilliant blue of Cockalorum Lake.

One wall was draped in expensive tapestries detailing the prestigious history of Rubric's expansion across the continent. Famous paintings of old cities crowded another wall, while groups of comfortable chairs and lounges were scattered across the tile-paved floor.

The room was empty of occupants, but the courier who led them inside pointed to a small table piled with food. "Please avail yourselves of refreshments while you wait. The Junior Toque will arrive shortly."

Kitan followed Kucheesa, and the two began to speak softly. Bibble wandered over to admire the paintings with Quarce, who sipped a huge mug of coffee he produced from his satchel. He handed a second mug to Bibble without even needing to be asked.

Noops headed for the table and piled a plate high with a powder-coated chocolate muffin, a handful of tiny carrots, a pile of fried shrimp, and half a dozen little spice cakes.

Rasher followed him over. The food did look amazing. Noops began wolfing down his food, raising each item high for a brief moment in thanks to each god before consuming it.

"Do you have a patron god?" Rasher asked as he selected a grilled sausage wrapped entirely in a bacon weave, then added a couple hammer-shaped cookies.

He avoided anything with powdered sugar. No doubt all the food was harmless, but why take the chance? Once one started down the sweet road to sugar addiction, there was usually no going back. Look what happened to poor Ulotrichous, or Kitan's cousin, Alevler, who was currently in rehab in the Creamery.

"None have seen fit to bestow a gift upon me yet," Noops said between mouthfuls. "So I don't want to offend any of them by not respecting their foods. I try to keep a balanced diet honoring all of the gods."

"Not a bad idea," Rasher said, savoring the delicious bacon-wrapped sausage. It was hot, as if just taken from the grill, flavored with a hint of brown sugar, hickory smoke, and a subtle, tangy sauce that sent him back to finish off the platter. In seconds it all transformed into fresh sizzle.

In a surprisingly short amount of time, the door opened, and Hamurisi van Moraluvver dan Afitur strode in. The Junior Toque was a tall man with strong features and perfectly groomed black hair. His eyes seemed to glow with an inner light, and his intense stare carried a supernatural weight as he scanned the group.

Most primi men and women built up animal enhancements through meat mages, and Rasher had heard that Hamurisi's eyes were improved from several specialized raptors. He could even see extremely well in the dark, thanks to meats from the Tawny Frogmouth.

"Welcome Reapers," Hamurisi said in a cultured, sonorous voice. Rasher's team assembled, and they all saluted.

Hamurisi smiled, his teeth white and smooth, but lacking the enhanced canines preferred by so many soldiers. Politicians liked to lull their victims into a false sense of security before striking.

"No need for such formality," Hamurisi said, extending a hand to Rasher. His grip was firm, and Rasher sensed great strength. That shouldn't surprise him. Probably used ginger bear meat. It was a favorite among high nobles for enhancing strength without some of the side effects so common from hunting cats.

Hamurisi shook every hand in turn, openly welcoming them all, despite their heritages. Even Kucheesa's usual distrustful look softened in the face of his charisma.

Could he be a secret bacon master too? Unlikely. Rasher could usually sense other bacon masters. Spice wizards could produce charisma boosts with their blends, so he'd do well to remember that.

"I must admit I'm surprised to find you here at the Food Court so soon. I had expected your duties dealing with the attacks on the Acropolis and preparing the legions for deployment would consume all of your attention."

"We have teams working on that," Rasher assured him. "We are also investigating the contract manipulations that sidelined the previous Reaper team."

"Excellent," Hamurisi said, gesturing them toward a cluster of chairs. "Such a tragedy. Have you managed to enter the Acropolis Cheese Palace?"

"Yes. Today, in fact."

Hamurisi gave them an approving smile. "That is good news. Leave it to the Reapers to succeed where no one else can."

"Thank you, sir," Rasher said. "It seems traitors incapacitated the cheese wizards working the contracts with confectioner sugars."

"Animals," Hamurisi muttered darkly.

"Indeed. We are pursuing all leads."

"Thank you for the update, although I am surprised you felt the need to share it with me in person," Hamurisi said.

"Can you tell us if you've had any news of the three missing Reapers?" Rasher asked.

If the abrupt question surprised Hamurisi, he showed no sign, but shook his head, expression grave. "Nothing. The rest of the team insist they should be allowed to search for them, but I've kept them sequestered in the palace. There's just too much risk they'll make a mistake and suffer as poor Sumwinkle did."

"What happened to Sumwinkle?" Kitan asked before Rasher could.

Hamurisi hesitated, then said, "Perhaps we can discuss that later."

"All right," Rasher said. "We encourage you to keep a close eye on the rest of the team."

"Why?" Hamurisi asked, bright eyes narrowing. "What are you getting at, Captain?"

"There have been several other disappearances we are investigating. The enemy seems to know many of the secrets of the Acropolis, and I wouldn't want anything to happen to any more of the previous Reaper team."

"Don't worry about them," Hamurisi said confidently. "I have ordered increased security throughout Nutmeg Hill, and they are on guard." After pausing for a moment, he added, "But that is not the reason you came to see me, is it?"

"No, sir. One of the cheese wizards attacked by the conspirators said she heard them mention your name," Rasher said, drawing on a little bacon to keep his voice and demeanor calm.

He watched Hamurisi's reaction carefully, but the man only showed astonishment. "What does that mean?"

"We don't know," Rasher said, intensely aware of the tightrope he was walking with his words. "Healers are working to restore her mind, but we came here at once to warn you. You may be an additional target."

Hamurisi sat back, frowning. "I don't see how targeting the Reapers could relate to me. I have nothing to do with the contracts."

"It might be a simultaneous attack," Bibble interjected. The rest of the team seemed more than happy to let Rasher do all the talking. "We've been struck on several fronts. The attacks are clearly designed to weaken our morale and delay our mobilization, but also serve to keep us distracted. With so many prongs to their plan, might they not have one more?"

"I appreciate the warning, but every day in the Food Court, I face dangers from rival houses, so am familiar with threats to my person. I assure you I am well guarded."

A gust of cool air rustled the tapestries on the wall. Rasher turned with a frown. "The windows were all closed a moment ago."

At first, he assumed a servant must have entered while they were talking and opened a window, but the room appeared empty. One of the huge windows had indeed been cranked open slightly, and at that moment, a sleek, black cat slipped into the room through it.

"Oh, what a beautiful cat," Kucheesa exclaimed, jumping up and rushing to the cat.

She moved so fast, Rasher wondered if she was suffering homesickness. She'd lived on a farm before coming to the Acropolis, so no doubt she had a lot of cats there.

He didn't blame her for rushing to that cat. Something about it called to him. Even though he wasn't usually a cat person, he felt an instant affection for the sleek animal and wished he was the one scooping it into his arms to pet it.

Kucheesa grinned as she lifted the large cat in her arms. It purred loudly as it rubbed its face across her chest, then up to her neck. She giggled, stroking its sides.

Hamurisi frowned and said, "That's odd. I don't own a cat."

The cat's loud purring suddenly changed pitch and shifted into a long, very human-sounding sigh. It said, "Oh, you have no idea how long it's been since I've been held by a pretty young human."

29

THE CRUMBHORN OF DESTINY

"Changeling!" Rasher shouted as the cat transformed into a man, dropping out of Kucheesa's startled arms to land on the floor. She stared at it in shock, her eyes slightly glazed, her reaction strangely subdued.

As Rasher leaped to his feet, he felt slightly off balance and released both crispy and chewy bacon to stabilize himself. His mind cleared, as if awakening from a half doze and he realized with a shiver of cold dread that he'd fallen under some sort of glamour from the cat glowan.

Glancing at his team, he found them rising sluggishly, blinking in surprise, slower to throw off the spell. Only Hamurisi seemed unaffected. He pulled a small, glass sphere from a pocket and hurled it at the door. It shattered into a glittering cloud of tiny black particles. A deafening voice bellowed forth from the cloud.

"Alarm! Alarm!"

Rasher had never seen a spice globule quite like that but appreciated it. The brutal sound shook his team out of their stupor. Noops drew his shovel with a practiced move. Quarce drew a tiny hammer from his satchel. It wasn't much of a weapon, but looked more like something he might use tapping on crystals or working with engraving tools.

Then he gave it a shake and a twist, and it grew, segmented plates sliding over each other until the head was bigger than both of Rasher's fists combined and the haft stretched to two feet long. Happy to see Quarce possessed a rare dwarven-crafted weapon, Rasher hefted his staff and rounded the chairs, heading for the changeling and Kucheesa.

The changeling leaned close to her and said in a soft, purring voice that still somehow carried through the room, "I like women who are so quick to show affection. If we had more time, I'd let you scratch my tummy."

He licked her cheek.

"Eww!" she cried, snapping out of the spell. Her nose transformed into a chicken beak and she pecked him in the face.

He tumbled back, yowling very much like a cat, and transformed back, landing on his cat feet. A dark cloud erupted from him, rolling over Kucheesa and then to Rasher before he could slide to a stop.

He held his breath as the blackness pulsed against his skin, chill to the touch. Faint voices called to him from the darkness, like distant wails of souls who had lost all hope.

An image flashed unbidden into his mind of a restaurant packed with hungry patrons, all eagerly awaiting a great feast. Only there was no food. All the dishes carried forth from the kitchen were covered in blackened scraps, as if they were weeks old, but never washed. The crowds all wailed with hopeless hunger they could never satisfy.

That was freaky.

Rasher released more chewy bacon, strengthening his mind and pushing back the disturbing image. What a nightmare. He retreated and thankfully escaped the dark cloud that had stopped expanding after consuming about half the giant room.

A shape raced past him, and he turned to look. It wasn't the cat.

It looked like a dwarf. A little taller than Quarce, he was covered in dense, coarse hair the color of undiluted coffee. He wore a boiled leather jacket with spikes sticking out all over, and he raised high a huge butcher knife and a long, viciously serrated machete.

He was sprinting straight toward Hamurisi.

The Junior Toque saw him coming and backpedaled toward the door. His skin grew rougher, using a defensive enhancement Rasher had only rarely seen outside of the Gleaners. Taken from rhinoceros meat, it took a long time to develop but hardened the skin until it was almost as tough as plate armor.

Noops leaped right over the chairs to meet the attacking dwarf, shovel whistling through the air in a mighty overhand blow. The dwarf dove into a roll, barely avoiding the shovel, his eyes never leaving Hamurisi as he continued pursuing.

Quarce barreled into him in a spectacular shoulder check that stopped Quarce in his tracks and sent the dwarf tumbling sideways. He blasted right through a long couch but bounced right back to his feet.

He did look at Quarce, hatred in his eyes. "I've slaughtered many of your men-loving brethren, Zayif. Today you join them."

Quarce faced him, his features twisted into a mask of hatred. He spat at his opponent's feet, hefting his hammer. "You Pislik filth!"

They rushed at each other, both howling deep-throated battle cries that echoed through the room.

Neither of them noticed Noops. The knight intercepted the pislik dwarf, sweeping his shovel in a horizontal strike that caught the surprised dwarf across the legs.

The shovel barely slowed as it shattered bones and tumbled the evil dwarf off his feet. He screamed, his weapons flying from his hands.

Another dark wave boiled off the fallen dwarf, rolling over Quarce and Noops as they closed on him. Rasher saw them stagger under the onslaught of the dark power and kept his distance.

A cry of pain drew his gaze to Hamurisi. The Junior Toque was staggering back against the wall, hands raised against the slashing claws of the changeling cat. Somehow the cat had crossed the entire room and was savagely tearing at Hamurisi, leaping up again and again to rake at his arms. If not for his hardened skin, his arms would have been torn to pieces already.

Kucheesa stumbled out of the first dark cloud, face white and eyes wide, but determined. She held two daggers with white-knuckled intensity, and her gaze locked on the cat.

She started toward Hamurisi at the same time Rasher did, but the evil dwarf's dark cloud was still expanding and it blocked their access. Rasher didn't want to step into it, and Kucheesa hesitated too. Without the protective power of bacon, he couldn't imagine the nightmares she must have suffered pushing through the first cloud.

"Rasher!" Kitan called from the far side of the trashed sitting area. He caught sight of her near Bibble as she snatched up a broken piece of chair leg, expression determined. Her entire body was glowing bright blue, her intense light keeping the black cloud back from a short area around her.

"Can you circle to me?" Rasher called. With her light, maybe they could penetrate the darkness to Hamurisi.

"Coming," she called immediately.

Bibble, his voice squeaking with fear, said, "Captain, I'm working on dispersing it. Just a moment."

Hamurisi might not have a moment. From outside of the room, shouting was growing closer fast. Help would arrive soon, but perhaps not soon enough. He was tempted to plunge into the dark cloud and trust his bacon to see him through, but if he got turned around, he wouldn't help anyone. Better to wait for Kitan.

He glanced down at his staff, mind whirling. He could not throw the staff with any hope of doing enough damage to matter. Then his eyes fixed on the curved length of his crumbhorn, and his bacon-enhanced thoughts seized on an idea from an obscure reference he'd forgotten about.

With no time to think, he twisted the crumbhorn free and lifted the instrument to his lips.

Hamurisi screamed from the dark fog. The repeated attacks from the changeling cat must be finally tearing through his skin. A grunt of pain and a heavy clatter suggested he'd slipped on the smooth tile and fallen over one of the chairs.

The cat would go for his throat next.

Rasher needed to get through the cloud, but couldn't see anything. He'd heard that Smooth Blatherskite had used his enhanced hearing in darkness to navigate through a forest like a bat. Rasher had never tried it, but the skill might give him an edge.

So he blew, fingers finding the holes and playing notes without any particular plan. He just wanted noise to create echoes. Instead, as his fingers danced across the holes, he produced a wild tune that erupted from the crumbhorn with remarkable power. The instrument vibrated in his hands from the force of his breath. The sound grew in volume and echoed across the room, seeming to multiply with every echo.

Rasher tried concentrating on those echoes to map a path through the darkness, but the tune distracted him. He didn't even know what tune he was playing, but he played with all his might, following the inspiration that seemed to flow through his fingers without conscious thought.

The blackness abruptly dissipated, and he spotted the cat standing on Hamurisi's upraised arms, claws raised as if it had been preparing to strike. Instead it spun to stare at Rasher, its yellow eyes glowing like fire egg yolks. It shuddered and stumbled off of Hamurisi, staggering as if drunk on too much curdled milk.

The crippled dwarf lay unmoving on the floor, eyes also locked on Rasher, a look of shock on his face.

Was the song really that bad?

The outer door burst open and a squad of enhanced imperial guards charged into the room.

"Changeling!" Hamurisi shouted, pointing at the distracted cat.

The soldiers lunged with the speed of lions, blades whistling toward the monster.

It leaped straight up to the ceiling, spitting in rage, and landed feet-first up there, as if the ceiling had become its floor. With a yowling cry, it raced across the ceiling, dodging thrown knives and spears. It gave Rasher a wide berth, crossing the room in a flash and diving through the still-open window.

Several of the guards surrounded Hamurisi, shouting for a milk mage, while others vainly pursued the cat. The rest joined Noops and Quarce standing over the fallen evil dwarf.

Rasher lowered the crumbhorn, feeling as exhausted as if he'd sparred at full strength and full bacon burn for half a day.

"Bring shackles for that creature," Hamurisi ordered, rising to his feet, clothing shredded, a look of towering fury on his face as he studied the crippled dwarf. He strode closer, his guard poised to strike down the dwarf if it made any move.

The dwarf glared up at Hamurisi, naked hatred on his face. "Your crimes will not go unpunished, human."

"Like the crime of defending himself from assassination?" Bibble asked. He was trying to appear calm but kept glancing around, eyes wide.

"What is this guy?" Kucheesa demanded.

The dwarf turned his glare to her and said proudly, "I am a true dwarf, not one of these man-lackey zayif."

He sneered at Quarce, who glared back as soldiers shackled the evil dwarf's wrists and ankles. "This sorry creature is one of the Pislik, the dark dwarves sworn to serve the Bitter queen."

Hamurisi looked composed again. His clothing might be savaged, but a milk mage was already smearing whipped cream along his arms, and a manservant on short stilts was quickly styling his hair back into perfection.

The Junior Toque said, "Pislik are nasty creatures. I would never have thought to find one in the Food Court. They trade much with the other glowan, providing raw materials in exchange for enchanted armor and weapons."

"Because they've lost the skill to craft their own," Quarce said, disgust heavy in his voice.

"I'll harvest your soul!" the Pislik shrieked, earning a kick in the ribs from one of the soldiers standing guard over him.

Hamurisi turned from the angry creature to Rasher and asked, "What magic did you use to disable the glowan like that? I've never heard of food powers delivered through an instrument."

"This is just my crumbhorn," Rasher said. "Not enhanced."

"Not enhanced?" Quarce laughed his booming laugh. "That's the crumbhorn of destiny, Captain!"

Crumbhorn of destiny. He liked that and smiled. "I hadn't expected to get such a reaction from the glowan, although now that I think about it, I did hear once that they are exceptionally affected by music. I guess when they don't like a song they really don't like it."

Hamurisi chuckled. "Indeed, Captain. Again, the Reapers show their worth. Well done. I owe you a life debt."

"The debt of a life of villainy!" Chortled the Pislik. "Do you secretly worship Ruzgar?"

That earned him another kick from a guard and a scowl from Hamurisi.

"Why is this guy so angry with you?" Bibble asked.

Hamurisi shrugged. "Who can explain the motivations of creatures of darkness?"

"Darkness glows within your soul," the Pislik snarled. "And you will pay the blood price!"

Another kick. That didn't seem to accomplish anything. Rasher was amazed the creature was so coherent and so full of rage while so badly wounded. Most humans would be so busy screaming, they'd lack the focus to insult their captors.

"Why travel so far from the rest of the horde to attempt an assassination here?" Rasher asked.

The Pislik snorted. "You are blind in the light of the moon. You who call yourselves Reapers shall be reaped by Ruzgar's winds. You think you're a hero. You're marked now, and we always exact our revenge."

"What kind of revenge can you exact when you're the one shackled?" Rasher asked.

He felt like there had to be more going on than what they were seeing. If they could ferret out a little more truth, maybe they could finally get some answers.

The dwarf laughed and looked directly at Kitan. "I see his mark upon you, woman."

She gasped and took an involuntary step back as the dwarf turned to sneer at Bibble. "And I've seen your family. You probably think they're safe."

Rasher fought to control a flash of wild fury at the threat implied in those words. Bibble looked nearly panicked with fear. Rasher shouldn't let the deceitful creature bait him, but he still took an angry step forward.

Surprisingly Noops responded first. "Really? You're going there as your first volley?"

The evil dwarf frowned. "Of course. Go for the throat. That's my motto."

"I thought glowan lived a long time," Noops muttered.

"I've lived for centuries," the evil dwarf proclaimed proudly.

"And you haven't learned yet to be a little more creative?"

"What are you doing?" Rasher asked.

"Threatening your girlfriend is a pretty basic ploy," Noops explained.

"It usually works," the evil dwarf objected.

"Don't you have any imagination? Every dark story about evil glowan uses some variation on that same threat. I figured you'd get tired of living up to the cliches all the time."

The evil dwarf looked thoughtful. That couldn't be good.

The creature laughed, an actual hearty sound. "You're right. I fell into the classic pattern without even thinking about it."

"Self-awareness is the first step toward better hygiene," Noops declared.

Kucheesa rolled her eyes, Hamurisi looked confused, and Rasher sighed. Leave it to Noops to take the weird turn in every conversation.

The evil dwarf grinned evilly at Rasher. "I'll tell you what. Thanks to your friend's timely intervention, I'll leave your girlfriend alone."

"Ah, thanks," Rasher said.

"Instead, I'll tell my master that you want special treatment and offer your soul to him as tribute."

"Not thanks," Rasher amended.

Kitan joined Rasher and took his hand. She stared down at the shackled dwarf with no concern on her expression. "Your threats are as empty as choux pastry."

"Wait till the pastry is filled with my vengeance," the dwarf shot back without missing a beat.

He sure was clever for such an evil little guy. Rasher wondered if they trained in witty banter in the long, dark winters of Whisternfeet.

Kucheesa added, "Seems to me, you're in no position to be making any kind of threats, little guy."

"You can't keep me prisoner!" The evil dwarf shouted, his face transforming into a mask of rage. The chains fell away from his wrists and ankles and he leaped into a nearby chair, vaulting toward Rasher, black-clawed hands reaching for his throat.

Rasher snapped up his staff in a defensive move, but Noops' shovel intercepted the creature first, crashing down over him with thunderous force. The impact drove the evil dwarf into the floor with a resounding crack. The stocky glowan's neck snapped on impact, and he lay motionless but for an occasional twitch from one foot.

Most of the group took a reflexive step back. Hamurisi looked sick, Kucheesa disappointed, and Bibble turned away, pulling out his little bag of smelling herbs with shaking hands.

Rasher held Kitan close and turned his gaze away from the fresh blood oozing from the body as Noops prodded it with a boot and said, "It's easy to threaten. Not so easy to make threats real, is it?"

"So it was all a bluff?" Kucheesa asked.

Noops shrugged. "Looks like even a glowan can't always deliver on their promises. Should have seen that coming, with his choice of boots."

"What?" Hamurisi asked, frowning.

"Where do you come up with those?" Kucheesa exclaimed.

Noops gestured toward the evil dwarf body. "Can't you see his boots are scuffed? Looks like he's never once bothered to clean them."

"So?" Kucheesa demanded.

"So a person who cares so little for their equipment is unlikely to take the time to plan a good revenge plot, are they?"

That actually sort of made sense.

Rasher turned to Hamurisi. "Sir, do you have any idea why these glowan would have targeted you?"

"They're probably part of the force attacking you in the Acropolis. It appears Reaper Bibble was right. They are seeking to broaden their assaults," Hamurisi said angrily. He turned to the soldiers ringing him. "Raise the alarm. Lock down the building and secure the members of the Food Court. I want every resource hunting that changeling."

His guards rushed off, and he strode purposefully after them, shouting orders. He paused at the door and turned back to them. "I apologize for this unpleasantness. You will join me for some replenishing refreshments."

"Thank you," Rasher said, and the others echoed his words.

Hamurisi smiled. "We'll keep it small, but I might invite a few others to join us. I'll send someone to lead you."

Then he turned and marched out of the room, surrounded by guards and attendants.

"Sign of a good leader," Noops said with approval.

"Inviting us to dinner was nice," Kucheesa agreed.

"That's just a sign of good breeding," Noops said. "Didn't you hear how clearly he issued those orders? Miscommunication is one of the leading causes of inefficient workplaces. Good leaders avoid it."

She sighed and turned away.

"Are you okay?" Rasher asked Kitan, who was rubbing one hand across her face, suddenly pale.

She managed a weak laugh, examining the chair leg she'd picked up and still held in one hand. She tossed it aside and sighed. "I'll be fine. I promise. It's not every day you get threatened by a glowan."

"His threats were empty," Rasher assured her.

"I know," she said, then flashed a mischievous smile. "Father won't be able to keep denying my request to carry some knives now."

Rasher chuckled, appreciating her indomitable spirit. "Good thing we're planning to practice knife throwing again soon."

Kucheesa rushed to Kitan and grinned. "I saw you glowing. That was amazing!"

As the two women began talking excitedly together, Quarce kicked the evil dwarf's body and said, "We should dispose of this."

Rasher glanced down just as a stream of crimson blood bubbled out of the dwarf's destroyed neck. He tried to look away, but couldn't seem to. He reached for bacon, trying to draw the strength to overcome the terrible weakness, but his concentration wavered.

His vision tunneled in on that stream of crimson blood, and his head pounded with a sudden horrible ache. His legs felt woozy, and he couldn't seem to breathe.

He needed to fight it, needed to . . .

Rasher blinked his eyes open and found himself on the floor looking up at his team. Concern and surprise showed on every face. Kitan knelt beside him, gently stroking his hand.

"Are you all right, Captain?" Bibble asked, dropping to one knee beside him next to Kitan. He couldn't have been out more than a few seconds, but his body ached, his thoughts felt like they were swimming through cold molasses.

"I'll be okay. Usually blood doesn't make me faint so badly." His mind caught up with the words a second too late, and he cringed. He hadn't wanted the truth to come out like that.

"That's what happened?" Quarce asked with that look of disbelief Rasher had been trying to avoid since he was a child. Seeing it on his team members made him wilt inside.

Rasher shrugged and gave them a self-deprecating smile. "We've all got our weaknesses."

"Sure, but we told you ours," Kucheesa said, looking disgusted. "We didn't hide what we were, Captain."

She stormed out of the room. Rasher watched her go with a crushing sense of defeat. He hated people knowing his weakness, but it was worse to see his team thinking he'd lied to them.

He glanced at the others and said, "I had planned to tell you. It just hadn't come up yet."

"Are there other things that haven't come up yet?" Bibble asked quietly.

"Not that I'm aware of."

Noops said nothing, his expression thoughtful. Rasher couldn't even begin to guess what the strange knight might be thinking.

Bibble squared his shoulders and said, "Captain, I'd like to ask a dozen questions, but we don't have time. Come on. That dwarf might be dead, but the cat got away. He threatened my family."

As Kitan helped Rasher to his feet, an older servant with streaks of gray in his hair entered the room. "If you will please follow me, I will lead you to the dining room."

Rasher gripped Bibble's shoulder. "We'll send word for the Gleaners to watch your family until we return, but we can't ignore this invitation."

"I know," Bibble said with a sigh. "It might have been an empty threat, but it still worries me. I'll feel better once the Gleaners are there."

30

THE CREAM CHEESE CLAUSE

Rasher wasn't surprised to see that the small dining room turned out to be large enough to seat two hundred. His boots rang on the tiled floor, which was covered in an intricate mosaic depicting the map of the Rubric Empire.

One entire wall was made up of huge windows overlooking the southern cliff of Nutmeg Hill. The views over the lower city and across Cockalorum Lake were truly breathtaking. The bright afternoon sun sparkled off the distant waves, and just enough puffy white clouds dotted the sky to highlight its deep blue expanse. Along the distant horizon, the sky and lake seemed to meld into one, broken only by the tiny shapes of trading ships.

Instead of one giant feasting table, the room was broken up by fifteen tables that could each seat a dozen. Gilt-edged place settings were already in position, and softly glowing illumination pastries in crystal chandeliers filled the room with warm, bluish light. They were the first to arrive, and as they wandered deeper into the room, Kitan and Kucheesa moved to one side, talking quietly. Kucheesa still looked angry, but her expression slowly softened as they talked.

"Look at this," Quarce called, drawing Rasher's attention. Both he and Bibble had lingered near the door, each lost in thought. Noops had moved to the windows, standing at parade rest, hands clasped behind his back as he surveyed the incredible view. Rasher immediately noticed the life-sized statue on a low pedestal standing in the center of the room. It depicted a man standing proudly, one hand raised in defiance. He looked like he should be grasping a sword, but the weapon was missing.

As he drew closer, admiring the incredible detail in the white statue, he exclaimed, "Hey, that's Sumwinkle!"

"You're right," Bibble said, pacing around the statue, which looked like a perfect image of the man, every detail correct, right down to the wrinkles on his Reaper uniform.

"Interesting," Noops said. "Usually they wait a bit longer before making statues of the previous Reaper teams.

Quarce reached out to touch the statue's shoulder and recoiled in surprise. "It's soft, like it's made out of cheese instead of marble."

"Don't touch it again," Rasher ordered, leaning closer, studying the statue intently, heart sinking as his new suspicions grew. He sniffed, applying some bacon to his nose to sharply augment his sense of smell.

That confirmed it. He breathed a heavy sigh. "Oh, no."

"What is it?" Quarce asked.

"Don't touch that!" snapped a familiar voice.

Rasher spun to find Otamot striding quickly toward him, his expression stern. Behind him came the rest of the original Reaper Team Twelve. Well, all but the three missing Reapers. Despite their civilian attire, they couldn't help still looking mighty.

Absquatch Youlate called, "Take it easy, Otamot. I am sure they meant no disrespect."

"Their very presence here is an insult," Otamot said, his eyes locked on Rasher's, his expression even less friendly than when they'd met briefly at the Bubble and Squeak.

It was unfortunate that Otamot had chosen to hate him, but their positions had changed, and Rasher found he had no patience for the angry fellow.

"What happened to him?" Bibble asked as Rasher turned from Otamot to give Absquatch a sharp salute.

Absquatch smiled sadly. The man who had been the captain of the original Reaper Team Twelve looked weary. He had been the most famous spice wizard alive, a living hero. Now . . . Rasher wasn't sure what he and the others would do.

"Please don't," Absquatch said softly, his voice deep and smooth. "We cannot engage in any acts of leadership among anyone associated with the legions."

Bibble snatched his hand down. "I'm so sorry."

"It's been a difficult few days, and we are still adjusting," Absquatch said as the rest of his team gathered around. Kitan joined Rasher, slipping her warm hand into his. Kucheesa stood near Quarce, who was grinning at the newcomers with an awed expression.

Absquatch looked up at the statue of Sumwinkle and sighed. "Poor Sumwinkle. He could not let go. He refused to accept that we could no longer help and serve the legions. He tried to protest, tried to make one last speech."

"Fat lot of good it did him," Otamot growled.

Quarce gaped, glancing back at the statue. "You mean, that's . . ."

Absquatch nodded as the rest of the old Reaper team placed hands over their hearts, facing the statue. "The cream cheese clause manifests in different ways. This time when he triggered it, he transformed into a statue of cream cheese. It's hard like it's been set in a mold, but we worry it could be easily damaged."

"I've never heard of such a thing," Kucheesa breathed.

Neither had Rasher. He was appalled to see the fate of the heroic man. Sumwinkle had epitomized all the greatness of the Reapers.

Absquatch Youlate faced Rasher and said, "We have not yet met, but I hear you now lead the Reapers."

"Yes, sir. My name is Rasher Dilskin. I'm honored to meet you." He extended a hand, and Absquatch took it with a firm grip.

Otamot hissed something under his breath and marched off. Absquatch said, "It is rare for members of one Reaper team to meet the next. Some of us have not yet reconciled ourselves to our new reality."

"I can't imagine how hard it must be for you all," Kitan said.

Absquatch bowed over her hand, and Rasher introduced her, then the rest of his team. Absquatch greeted them all warmly. The rest of his team did likewise.

Otamot returned to them and scowled. "So we're all going to play the game and pretend everything is fine, even though we're out without so much as a protest, and the new team was given our same team number?"

"I was as surprised as you," Rasher assured him. "I consider our team the caretakers of these positions until we can get to the bottom of what happened to your contracts and get you reinstated."

"And then what? You'll relinquish command and go back to a life of obscurity?" Otamot demanded.

"We are preparing to mobilize against an unprecedented horde invasion. I believe there is a need for all of our service," Rasher responded, using half a slice of bacon to fortify his self-control and remain calm in the face of the constant harassment.

Otamot opened his mouth to respond, but Absquatch gestured him to silence and said, "If only such a partnership could be possible. Any leads on how the contract breach happened?"

"We're working on it," Bibble interjected.

"Good," said Saeculum Wyrd, the old team's vegetable shaman. She was a mature woman with earth-browned skin and deep brown eyes. She was famously powerful with earth magic, which would be extremely helpful in the upcoming campaign.

"And what of your missing team members?" Noops asked.

Absquatch said, "We have not heard from them since our first night in the Junior Toque's palace. Searches are underway."

He didn't look hopeful. Rasher wondered if someone would discover three more cream cheese statues somewhere. That would be a better alternative than another insidious idea that had begun creeping into his mind. He refused to think about it yet, but couldn't shake it either.

The Junior Toque swept into the room just then, followed by a retinue of fifty other nobility and staffers, along with a full fist of elite Nutmeg guard. They positioned themselves around the room, maintaining a vigilant watch. Chefs followed, along with an army of serving staff, bearing a mountain of food that made Redael's first feast in the Heart seem like appetizers by comparison.

Hamurisi declared that he wanted to keep the event informal, so instead of sitting, they each took up a plate and mingled. The servers set up eight entire tables that groaned under the weight of the food. Rasher forced down growing impatience to get back to work. They had tight deadlines. Chatting with nobility was a necessary part of the Reaper office, but it still annoyed him.

The food was fantastic, but that created another point of annoyance. He would usually consume as much as possible to top off his sizzle, but he felt acutely aware of Otamot watching him. If the man had treated him better, he would have happily shared the secret of the sizzle.

Even eating with as much restraint as possible, he had to fight to resist returning to the food tables again and again. Everything was so good! Pork ribs dripping with spicy, dark sauce took his breath away, while a quiche bursting with delicately spiced vegetables gently replenished his sense of well-being.

Kitan kept at his side, politely nibbling on a salad, followed by a chocolate-filled croissant with a subtle enhancement to nimbleness of mind. She then switched to a fresh fruit smoothie. The blend of strawberries, bananas, and other ingredients was supposed to magnify self-confidence and was hugely popular among high-society women that year.

That success significantly boosted the position of the van Tribble mon Toos family, a contorni house that sponsored the guild to Sudd, the lesser goddess of juices. Kitan told him all about it as they mingled.

Eventually, Hamurisi sent a servant to request her presence. Rasher wasn't surprised. Kitan was well known among all the nobility, and her father was neck deep in much of the intrigue of Nutmeg Hill. As Rasher turned away from watching Kitan glide gracefully through the crowd toward the knot of nobility clustered around Hamurisi, he noticed Otamot speaking with a couple other officials. His back was to Rasher, and with a start, Rasher recognized him.

He couldn't help staring, mind racing with bacon-enhanced speed as he processed the revelation. Otamot's stance, bearing, and height were exactly the same as the intruder he'd twice intercepted in his apartments.

What did it mean? Rasher forced himself to turn and replenish his plate at one of the food tables, barely noticing what the servers chose for him. He started munching, hardly recognizing the delicious chocolate cake as he mulled over the revelation.

Why would Otamot risk returning to the Acropolis? Why sneak into Absquatch's rooms and search them? He'd been seeking specialty self-defense cuisine the second time, but had he been searching for something else too? The implications triggered a web of new thoughts, and Rasher drew deeper on chewy bacon, using a trick he'd mastered over the past few years while working on solutions to his blood phobia.

As he joined in conversation with several other members of the primi and secondi houses, he loosed his subconscious mind on the problem of Otamot. His thoughts would percolate in the background, like a simmering pot set over a low flame. When he pulled those thoughts to the forefront of his conscious mind, any conclusions would snap into place.

It seemed everyone wanted to speak with him and congratulate him on his appointment as captain. Rasher wished Kitan hadn't been called away because although most of the dialogue seemed innocent, he suspected there were layers of meaning he might be missing. More than one person mentioned General Nide's petition to strike down the new team and choose new Reapers. Most kept the conversation light as they discussed the odd request, but they all eventually asked his opinion.

He tread carefully, expressing confidence in his new team. Yes, they were small, but they were extremely capable, and they had access to fully staffed Gleaner teams to fill in the missing guild slots. A member of the Fathar family shouldered his way into the conversation Rasher was having with an exquisitely dressed elderly woman from the Morstyl family. The newcomer was a beefy, middle-aged fellow. The Fathar family were patrons of the vegetable shamans, based in the besieged city of Ehverr.

"Captain Dilskin, I hear mobilization has been delayed," the man declared loudly. "How is this possible? Our city is besieged! We need the Reapers to march post haste."

"We are preparing the legions," Rasher assured him. "Unfortunately, we suffered several mishaps in the Acropolis that have undermined our battle readiness."

The man snorted. "You were attacked, Captain! We heard about West Gate, about the so-called accident at the Sugar Palace, and the loss of the battle cuisine. How have the Reapers become so lax?"

So much for downplaying the dangers. If Kitan had been with him, Rasher bet she could have helped keep the conversation calm, but he lacked the will or the time to milkwash the conversation.

"You are correct, sir. We've been attacked. We suspect traitors allied with the glowan invaders. We are actively hunting them down, and we will march as soon as possible."

"That's not good enough," the man cried, loud enough to draw several stares from nearby knots of conversations.

Rasher met his gaze calmly and said, "Then I am sure you will aggressively support our request for battle cuisine aid from the Afitur stores."

"I wholeheartedly support the requisitioned supplies," he continued loudly. "Although I admit there are some factions in the Food Court who prefer to play politics in this time of need instead of supporting cities under siege. Traitors, the lot of them, wouldn't you say?"

That drew even more attention, and quite a few scowls from other nobility nearby, including several from the old family houses of Rubric.

One of the Toffers, a rather short woman with a tall muffin hat on her head, said loudly, "Just because we won't all surrender our entire net worth to you the moment your city is attacked does not mean we are traitors."

As the two of them started arguing back and forth, drawing several of the other nobility into the heated exchange, Rasher turned, hoping to slip away from the argument, only to find Otamot standing close behind him.

He should just nod and walk by, should pretend he hadn't recognized Otamot. Now was not the time or place to trigger a confrontation.

But he couldn't help it.

"Planning to try hitting me over the head again?" Rasher asked softly.

Otamot feigned surprise. "What are you talking about? If I hit you over the head, you'd wake up in the creamery."

Rasher smiled. "And yet, it was you who fled like a coward both times." He nodded toward the huge windows in the outer wall. "Think you could dive through one of those and escape again?"

Otamot scowled. "You enjoy playing at being a hero, Rasher, but we both know you're a fraud. I plan to make sure everyone knows just how useless you are."

"What were you looking for?" Rasher pressed. "A scrap of honor, maybe?"

Otamot's expression relaxed. No doubt he had released some chewy bacon to master his emotions. "What do you know of honor? You cannot succeed, yet here you are, pretending to be a hero."

"Who else did you attack?" Rasher asked, ignoring the barb. "Are you working with the traitors striking the legions?"

That got under his skin. Otamot flushed and hissed, "I am a patriot, a Reaper! You honestly think I'd ally with traitors?"

Rasher shrugged. His blood phobia had forced him to learn discipline and self-control. Most bacon masters enjoyed far easier roads to success. Otamot's pride might make him reveal more of what he was doing.

"You attacked me. Makes sense you'd be willing to attack others."

Otamot leaned closer. "The legion tossed us away like garbage. They can rot under their own corruption. I will not help stop the traitors from tearing down your world. You can't stop them, and soon the entire world will know your failures."

Rasher regarded the other man for a moment while the arguing nobles behind them grew so rowdy that a staff member had to urge them to quiet down.

"I hope you find a way to reconcile with your new life," Rasher said. "It's sad to see a once-great man reduced to this."

Surprisingly, Otamot smiled. "I look forward to seeing if you can remain witty to the bitter end."

Then he turned and strode away.

Rasher watched him go, puzzling over the conversation, but just then Quarce started singing a boisterous dwarven drinking song. He was holding two enormous tankards of beer, one in each hand, taking turns gulping from each of them between short verses.

His performance drew everyone's attention, and many scowls from nobles. Rasher appreciated Quarce's enthusiasm, but a high-class social mixer wasn't the right time for it. He headed for Quarce, hoping to avoid a big scene.

Noops arrived first. With a big smile, the shovel knight lifted his own tankard to clink hard with Quarce, spilling a fair amount of the amber liquid down the sides.

"To the glorious dead!" Quarce shouted, raising both tankards high in salute to the cream cheese statue of Sumwinkle.

Noops raised his tankard as well, repeating the phrase loudly. The toast to the fallen Reaper helped quash some of the annoyance his boisterous singing had created, and most of the gathered lifted delicate glasses of wine in turn.

Noops spoke more softly into the quiet. "It must be fun to celebrate death feasts in the great halls."

"It is!" Quarce bellowed, face a bit flushed. "How did you know?"

"We don't usually have to shout so loudly to get a good echo in these little dining rooms," Noops said.

"Oh, right," Quarce said, glancing around at the gathered nobles with a chagrined look. "Sorry."

"It's fine," Rasher told him as he joined them. "Sumwinkle was a great man. He would have loved such a loud toast."

"Indeed," Hamurisi said. He'd approached the other side of the statue, followed by his ever-present knot of followers. "I did not recognize your tune, Reaper Quarce."

"Really? It's the only appropriate song for such an occasion. A death feast of a great warrior, complete with the bounty of Calobogus. Best beer I've had since leaving Yaffle." He raised his tankards high again.

"We import the finest drinks from across the realm," Hamurisi said with a smile. "I am glad you appreciate good beer."

"I do," Quarce declared, loudly enough to make some of the noble women wince. "I am a devout follower of Icmek, but every dwarf loves Calobogus too. Honor to the god of beer!"

That elicited some smiles, but many of the gathered started to look decidedly nervous. Otamot called from across the room. "Silence that fool before he says something stupid."

"Are you afraid he might take that honor from you?" Kucheesa asked, generating a round of polite laughter.

"You're all country bumpkins," Otamot stated with a glare, then turned to the large group of nobles who had been arguing about the war and efforts to succor Ehverr. "You still think the legions have any hope of success following these idiots?"

"Enough, Otamot," Absquatch said with a frown.

Otamot scowled and turned away. As polite conversation picked up again, Quarce asked, "What was he so upset about? Is he not a beer drinker?"

"He probably drinks prune juice," Kucheesa muttered as she joined the group. Rasher was glad to see she'd stood up for Quarce, but she still didn't look Rasher in the eye.

"Many in the city follow both Calobogus and Sarap," Rasher told Quarce. Indeed, the dwarven god of beer was more popular among the lower classes, even though the goddess of wine held far more sway among the nobility.

"We just don't talk about it much," Bibble said as he rejoined the group.

"Why not?" Quarce asked.

"You really don't know?" Kucheesa asked.

Quarce shrugged, taking another long pull from one of his tankards. "In the mines we worship all the gods, but Icmek and Calobogus are the most popular. Why pretend they're not."

"Because of Lahanasi," Noops said.

"Back to the evil god of disgusting foods," Quarce noted. "Is this that topic we didn't have time to discuss in that meeting with Gubbins?"

"It is," Rasher said. "I believe we should make time now.

"Good. So what does Lahanasi have to do with good beer, and why is there a cult trying to restore him to some other powers?" Quarce asked.

Rasher asked, "You do realize Lahanasi used to be the god of all alcohol, right?"

"Really?" Quarce asked.

Bibble looked shocked. "I can't believe they don't talk about this in Gravlax. Lahanasi was so powerful, he threatened to take over the entire Pantryon and become a higher god over them all."

Kucheesa took up the tale. "So all the other gods banded together against him and corrupted his power. Now instead of fermenting drinks, his power is more sinister. He can only create the most disgusting of foods and produce the vilest of results."

Quarce looked down at his tankard. "But Calobogus is god of beer."

"He is now," Rasher said. "Once Lahanasi fell, other lesser gods took up pieces of his fallen powers. Calobogus won beer and ale, Sarap wines and finer spirits, with a few others picking up the rest."

Bibble said, "The important thing to know is that none of them can be allowed to become too powerful, or they risk drawing the ire of the Pantryon again."

"Best not do that," Quarce agreed grimly. "I'd hate to see beer destroyed, even though I'm a coffee wizard by day."

"Just keep that in mind," Rasher said.

"I will," Quarce promised. Then he turned back to Noops. "How did you know about the great feasting halls?"

As they talked, a hand touched Rasher's arm. He turned to find Jaggery van Takmor dan Weghiv standing beside him. He'd spotted the ambassador for the Takmor house earlier but hadn't found time to speak with him yet.

Jaggery was an older gentleman with silver hair and a well-groomed beard of stately salt-and-pepper. Rasher had never met him, but Kitan had told him he was well regarded in the highest circles of power and was reputed to be one of the most adept at the high-stakes intrigue of the Food Court.

"Come, Captain Dilskin," Jaggery said softly. "We need to talk."

31

WEAVING CAKE INTO A HAT

Rasher followed Jaggery to the back side of one of the food tables, one mostly full of sweets, desserts, and dozens of fruit dishes. As the old ambassador made a show of sampling a colorful fruit salad, he spoke softly.

"Congratulations on your appointment as captain of the new Reaper team. Your abrupt rise in prominence reflects well on house Takmor."

"Thanks," Rasher said, following the old man's lead and piling a few slices of bright green melon onto a small plate. They were far enough from any of the others to enjoy a brief moment of near privacy without looking suspicious. Jaggery had timed his approach well, while most of the other guests were occupied with other conversations.

The old man met Rasher's gaze with steady eyes. "However, it has come to my attention that your relationship with the young daughter of the Ihlget house has progressed beyond a casual dalliance."

How had he learned that? Rasher had not tried to conceal his growing affection for Kitan, but neither had he broadcast to the world his intentions to marry. It seemed Kitan's father was not the only high noble with a far more extensive network of spies than Rasher had ever realized.

Keeping his expression calm he said, "Kitan is wonderful."

"Indeed," Jaggery glanced toward where Kitan was still conversing with other nobles among Hamurisi's inner circle. Rasher instantly found her beautiful face within the crowd and his heart sang anew to see her smiling and chatting, her full charm on display.

"Is there some kind of problem?" Rasher demanded, feeling annoyed that everyone seemed to feel entitled to mettle in his life. "Her father is one of your strong allies, isn't he?"

Jaggery took a slow spoonful of his fruit salad before answering. "Lord Niffum is indeed a staunch ally, but it is no secret that he is an ambitious man."

Rasher wasn't sure what to read in that. Did they know about Niffum's plans to supplant them, or did they just assume every ally was ready to betray them if the opportune moment appeared?

"I don't know Lord Niffum well yet," Rasher admitted.

"Ah, but you will," Jaggery replied. "If you are indeed intent on marrying his daughter, he will require some advantage from that association. Until now, you had very little to offer, but as captain of the Reapers, your status has changed significantly."

"I appreciate your concern for my success," Rasher said, pleased that he managed to sound sincere.

"We look after our own," Jaggery responded. "And we expect the same courtesy in return."

Rasher took another bite of the sweet fruit to gain a moment to think. They couldn't know of Niffum's proposal, could they? He instead chose to focus on the comment about looking after their own. They had not treated him well, and that memory stoked his anger.

That helped him deal with the irritation at having to speak so carefully. Talking with nobility was more convoluted than trying to weave cake into a hat.

"Forgive me, Ambassador, but I am new to politics. What exactly are you saying?"

"New players in the field always provide fresh insights and opportunities. I will do my best to help guide you as you navigate the primi circles. For starters, keep your eyes and ears open. Pay attention to what you learn about Niffum and his plans. He is a skilled player, and any insights you can offer us would be well rewarded."

Rasher couldn't help staring. "You want me to spy on Kitan's family?"

"We all spy on each other," Jaggery said with a smile that did not reach his eyes. "I recommend you keep your voice down. We all play the game, but it is considered poor manners to blurt out details so loudly."

He wondered if it was also considered poor manners to throw corrupt old nobility through windows.

Jaggery took his silence as acquiescence and added, "Furthermore, I have an offer for you to consider. Your family provides important meat resources to our house, and we wish to reward them for their excellent service. Please communicate to your father that if his house will commit to a long-term, exclusive contract with our house, the arrangement could benefit all of us greatly."

"How so?" Rasher asked, even as his mind raced. It could not be a coincidence that the crafty old man was making the same connection that Niffum had. Did they know about Niffum's offer, or were they merely hedging their bets?

"Your family will reap significant financial benefits, and I would commit to personally assisting your father in leveraging the relationship to further improve the family's position in society. I could see house Notda rise to the fifth, or even the fourth tier within the next couple years."

"That is generous of you."

Jaggery inclined his head with another little smile. "Your marriage to Lord Niffum's daughter would further our alliance with his house even more, and I am authorized to offer you a significant bonus should such a union come to pass."

Apparently, outright bribery was not considered poor manners.

"It sounds like a wonderful offer," Rasher said.

"It is, my boy," Jaggery told him with a fatherly smile, if snakes could present themselves as warm-hearted fathers. "Consider it, and we will discuss it further when you return from your upcoming campaign."

Jaggery walked off, leaving Rasher alone to ponder the old man's words. Kitan's father thought himself very clever, but it sounded like the Takmor house was aware of at least some of his schemes and was actively preparing countermeasures to ward off his ambitions. Rasher would bet breakfast for the next month that the Takmors were also preparing their own schemes to topple Niffum if he caused too much trouble.

High society intrigue gave him a headache. Rasher didn't see Otamot, so he risked piling a plate high with as much fruit and desserts as he could and wolfing it all down. As he converted it all into sizzle, the pulsing energy coursing through him helped ease his worries.

He might not like the scheming and politics of the high houses, but if he wanted to marry Kitan, he would need to secure his place among them. Jaggery was right about one thing. With his new position, he finally had a chance to at least try.

A few minutes later, Kitan slipped away from the other nobles clustered around Hamurisi and joined Rasher just as he finished a conversation with a very ample-bodied dowager of house Hapyr. She had been the first woman from that distant house based in the city of Ishudbe that he'd ever met, and he'd found her coastal accent endearing.

"How is it going?" Kitan asked as she kissed his cheek.

"Well, I think. More of the nobles have offered support to my team than support of the general's petition to have us canned. Helping save Hamurisi from glowan helped convince some that we're worth giving a chance. If I can believe them, I think we should be okay."

"I am hopeful too," she said, glancing around the room full of important people. "By the way, I met one of Hamurisi's newest tournant chefs tonight. He was very charming. I think he has a crush on me." She spoke with a mischievous twinkle in her eye.

"Are you trying to goad me into hurting someone before we leave?" he teased.

"As fun as that might be, no, my love. It's just, he seemed eager to share higher-level recipes with me when I mentioned my interest in them."

"I bet he would," Rasher said. Some of the famously bad pick-up lines young chefs seemed compelled to try out included, "Want a tour of my kitchen?" or "I've got a recipe I know you'll love."

"Relax," she said, kissing his cheek again. "I know how to handle myself. With even a hint of encouragement, I'll gain access to some of the other recipes you wanted to try."

"I could use a break," Rasher admitted. "I've asked Redael to try some energy-boosting recipes to see if we can push my sizzle to the point it can counteract my weakness."

Countering the blood phobia weakness still seemed like the best idea to him, but he was willing to try just about anything.

"Good," Kitan said. "I'll steer my new friend toward other options. Don't worry, my love, we'll figure this out."

Hopefully before embarking on the campaign against the horde. If he couldn't find one, his chances of surviving a major battle were slim at best.

Kitan changed the subject. "Hamurisi did you a big favor by inviting you to this gathering. I've already started feeling out some of the houses about supporting you and your request for food aid. I've got three follow-up visits scheduled. They may lead to offers of real support. That's a good start."

"How much will they want in return?" Rasher asked.

She gave him a dazzling smile. "You're learning quickly. I take it the Takmor ambassador made you an offer."

Rasher chuckled. "Of course you would notice him speaking with me."

"He was subtle, but I've always got my eye on you," she said with a warm smile.

Gods, he loved this woman. Rasher took her hand and led her to the nearest food table. As they sampled roasted duck slices, and chicken cubes floating in a spicy orange sauce, he told her about the conversation with Jaggery.

Kitan kept her expression pleasant, but her eyes narrowed slightly. "Not good. Rasher, if they suspect my father's ploy, they'll be prepared to strike quickly."

Which meant striking at his family too.

"Will you warn him?" Rasher asked.

She hesitated. "Not yet. They may not have real intelligence, but might just be fishing to trigger a reaction. I doubt we have to worry about any of this until after the legions drive the hordes away from Ehverr. That will give me some time to secure other alliances that might change the dynamic."

"I'm glad I have you," he told her, slipping an arm around her waist to pull her closer. Barely a day as a Reaper, and already neck deep in intrigue. Looking into her beautiful eyes, he vowed to find a way through every challenge. She was worth any sacrifice and any effort.

As long as he didn't destroy his house in the process.

32

THE BENEFITS OF TRAINING RATS

O n the train ride back from Nutmeg Hill, they commandeered another private car. Most of the team was excited about the visit and chatted loudly about defeating the evil pislik dwarf, and the high-society social event.

"My mates in the mines will never believe me," Quarce chortled loudly. "Hob-nobbing with royalty. Me!"

"I'm just glad we had our new uniforms," Kucheesa said, actually smiling. She didn't even scowl when she glanced at Rasher. He doubted she'd totally forgiven him for concealing his blood phobia, but at the moment she seemed willing to overlook it.

Bibble added, "I bet Sapka will be horrified to think we met Hamurisi and all those nobles wearing nothing but . . . What did she call these?" He picked at his shirt.

"The first prototype," Kucheesa said, pulling off her hat to examine it. "I think she did a wonderful job, but we probably do need dress uniforms for our next visit to Nutmeg Hill."

She was probably right, but Rasher couldn't find enthusiasm for the idea. He sat near the others, missing Kitan. She had left them before they boarded the train, citing the need to meet her parents for an evening dinner social.

Rasher couldn't imagine flowing from one social to another like that. Such a full social schedule would exhaust him more than pitched battle.

"You're awfully quiet, Captain," Bibble said, settling into the chair across from Rasher. "I would have thought you'd be pleased by our visit."

"Yeah, no one threatened to execute us for treason, we saved the Junior Toque's life, and I think we impressed enough of those nobles that they'll tell General Nide to go suck a lemon," Kucheesa added with a grin.

Rasher nodded slowly. "That's not what I'm thinking about."

"What, then?" Bibble asked as Noops and Quarce drew closer to listen.

Rasher explained about Otamot, and that snuffed out their good humor.

"Why would he sneak back into their old rooms like a thief?" Kucheesa exclaimed.

"We should return to the palace and challenge him," Quarce declared.

"Not yet," Rasher said with a calming gesture. "We don't have enough proof, and we don't understand the full extent of what he's doing."

"Do you think he's involved in the attacks on the Acropolis?" Bibble asked softly, as if afraid to even speak the words aloud.

"Impossible," Quarce exclaimed, then glanced from Bibble to Rasher. "Isn't it? I mean, he was a Reaper until this week, for Icmek's sake. Why would he attack the Acropolis?"

"He did seem rather grumpy," Noops commented.

Kucheesa barked a laugh. "Wouldn't you be? I was amazed at how well most of the team was holding up. Their entire lives' works were crushed, and three of their team are missing. I don't know that I could handle all that so well."

"Otamot is not doing well," Rasher said. "He's bitter, but the idea that he might be in league with the traitors enraged him."

"I can't believe you said that to his face," Bibble said, shaking his head slowly.

"I had to push a little," Rasher said, focusing his thoughts on the bacon-fueled ideas he'd left stewing in the back of his mind. He hadn't come to any clear conclusions, but a couple ideas had bubbled to the top.

"He might not be actively attacking the Acropolis yet, but he didn't seem surprised by the idea of traitors. The way he talked, I have to wonder if he might know who they are, even if he is not actively working with them."

"How could he?" Kucheesa asked. "Their team was sent to Hamurisi's palace once they were kicked out of the Reapers. Who would he know that could be involved?"

Rasher looked up at the team, waiting to let them think through the logical conclusion to that question.

"The missing Reapers!" Bibble exclaimed, looking shocked.

"Perhaps," Rasher said. "Their disappearance bothers me. They are all very powerful, so I doubt the enemy would have succeeded in ambushing all three of them without some kind of fight that would have drawn attention."

"But we're back to the same question," Quarce said with a frown. "Those other Reapers were also leaders of the legions. Why would they turn against us so quickly?"

"I don't know yet," Rasher said. "I fear they must be involved somehow, even if it was because they uncovered something about the enemy and had to be silenced. I think we need to expand our investigation to focus more on the missing Reapers. If we can solve that mystery, we might finally get solid clues about the enemy attacking the Acropolis."

"What do we do about Otamot then?" Bibble asked.

Rasher shrugged. "All we can do is wait. He threatened some kind of vengeance against those who turned their backs on the old Reaper team, but I don't have enough information to make any accusations."

"At least we'll better know what to look for," Kucheesa said.

Rasher nodded. "And I need to get my hands on one of those personal courier kite flyers." If Otamot showed up on the Heart again, he didn't plan to let him escape so easily.

"Those look like a lot of fun!" Quarce boomed.

Kucheesa grinned. "I bet I could soar for miles with one of those boosting my glide ability."

"How long do you think it'll take for us to develop that too?" Bibble asked.

She shrugged. "I've already begun incorporating some of my best chicken dishes into the menu plan with Redael. Chicken seems to produce at least minor effects a lot faster than some of the bigger predator meats, so hopefully it won't take long."

As the three of them discussed the best chicken enhancements she could produce, Noops stepped toward the back of the train and gestured Rasher to follow.

He did so, and when Noops stopped far enough away for private discussion, Rasher asked, "What's on your mind?"

Without preamble, Noops said, "So you faint when you see blood. That's rough, Captain."

"Yes, it is," Rasher agreed.

"Back on the farm where I grew up, I once taught a rat to wash his paws before coming into the house."

"Why would you do that?"

Noops looked at him like he'd gone bonkers. "Do you have any idea how much filth a rat can track into the house? They bring disease too. Why wouldn't you want to teach them that trick?"

"I mean, why bother? Don't most farmers get cats to hunt the rats?"

"You'd know all about that. You've got good eyes," Noops said, nodding to himself. "But Captain, cats can't solve the problem, not entirely. They can't be everywhere."

Rasher rubbed his face. "Look, Noops, I'm sorry. Today's been long, and I'm just not seeing your point."

"Don't worry about it, Sir. You've got to do all the thinking for everyone. That takes a toll. I recommend spicy ginger barley."

"That sounds disgusting."

Noops nodded, tapping the side of his nose. "I knew you'd get it, Captain. Drink something so bad it shuts off all thought for a while. Helps rejuvenate the thinking muscles."

"I usually just use bacon," he admitted.

"I guess that works too," Noops conceded. "Back to rats. If you can't guarantee the cats can keep out all the rats, why not teach them to be better? I figured by training one to wash up first, he'd spread the knowledge around. Rat infestations wouldn't be nearly so bad if they're clean rats, would it?"

"Did it work?"

Noops shrugged. "I don't know. One of the cats ate that rat while he was wiping his paws on the welcome mat. Shame really."

Rasher forced down a growing sense of frustration. "So what does this have to do with me?"

"Simple, sir. If I can train a rat to wash his paws before entering the house, there's hope you can train yourself to react better to the sight of blood."

Rasher sighed. "Thanks, Noops. I appreciate it."

"Hold on, sir," Noops said, holding out a big hand. "I'm not finished. You can't improve your skills if you don't have a plan to practice."

That was a valid point, one that Rasher usually beat into his trainees. He'd included similar wording for his rule number seven. "What plan do you suggest? Just walking around looking for bleeding folks so I can faint in front of them doesn't sound appealing."

"Of course not. You faint because your blood slows down, right?"

"How do you know that?" Rasher asked, astonished.

Noops shrugged. "I've been in a lot of fights. Never fainted unless my blood was slow. Usually because I was bleeding a lot. More often I'm the one giving the bleeding wounds. I've seen it dozens of times. Drop enough blood and you're going to faint."

"Right. Happens to everyone, so there's no way to avoid it," Rasher agreed, not hiding his bitter frustration.

"That's not entirely true, sir. Haven't you seen people last longer than they should, fight through the blood loss?"

"Actually, I have," he admitted, finally starting to really listen. Buried under the ridiculous story, Noops might be on to something. "Enough determination, enough focus, or enough battle lust can drive a man farther than he could usually go."

Noops nodded. "I've trained hard under a lot of excellent teachers, and I've learned one of the tricks to harnessing that resilience. Every time I start feeling faint, I tense my arms and legs as much as I can. Helps keep pressure in the blood."

"Does that really work?" Rasher asked. He'd never imagined Noops might have anything useful to teach him, but maybe he'd made exactly the kind of assumptions he always insisted his trainees avoid.

Noops nodded. "Takes practice, but it does help. More than you'd think. But you need to face the problem head on, Captain. Shocking the system is harder to deal with. Regular training conditions the body and the mind."

"I know. I teach that every day," Rasher reminded him.

"So live what you teach, Captain. The best training is to put yourself in conditions of danger."

He needed to try something, especially if all of the new recipes he was planning to try from Redael or from Kitan's new chef admirer failed. If he didn't figure something out, he'd faint at the worst possible moment and die.

"Thanks, Noops," he said, clapping the big knight on one armored shoulder.

"My pleasure, Captain. And if you ever want to train with the shovel, I'm your man."

"I can't imagine training shovels with anyone else," Rasher admitted truthfully.

33

DOLLOP ABERDEEN

Balter Fopoon and a squad of tiger-enhanced Gleaners waited for them at the Acropolis train station. As soon as he spotted Rasher, Balter saluted and said, "Sir, there's been a development."

"What's going on?" Rasher asked, glad the big warrior was fulfilling his duty without making trouble. The two of them hadn't gotten along before, but hopefully Balter's respect for the office of the Reapers would overshadow his dislike for Rasher.

Besides, now that Rasher was the Reaper captain, Balter's brother might well get Rasher's old position. In fact, Rasher planned to put in a good word for Lagan. That might help smooth the transition with the Gleaner teams even more.

"The Milk Palace was sabotaged," Balter said.

"No," Kucheesa breathed. "We need those healing supplies."

"That's exactly why it made such a good target, no doubt," Bibble said with a grimace before adding, "You know, it takes talent to hit a target no one else can hit, and genius to hit targets no one else thinks about."

Rasher wasn't sure if he was trying to make a joke or say something Noops-ish.

Quarce asked, "So, are you saying you have an idea about who did the attacking?"

"No," Bibble said with a little smile. "But not to brag, one of my kids at six months old learned how to count from one to soup."

Balter blinked, frowning. Kucheesa groaned, rolling her eyes. "Really? A dad joke now?"

Rasher suppressed a chuckle. "Balter, I thought all of the palaces were under tighter security."

"They are," Balter said, casting a final confused look at Bibble. "We have Gleaner fists at every one, and the guilds have all instituted their best security measures, but it was not enough. Somehow someone infiltrated the Milk Palace and sabotaged the entire new crop of healing supplies."

"Son of a brisket!" Rasher cursed. "Did anything survive?"

Balter shook his head. "Nothing. A large batch of trauma yogurt turned rancid and somehow infected most of the remaining cream supplies. Healing materials are critically low, the production area was contaminated, and will not be available for at least forty-eight hours."

"We can't afford any more battle cuisine losses," Bibble said. Then he tilted his head to the side, his expression distracted.

"No more stupid jokes," Kucheesa warned.

"This is no time for joking," he told Kucheesa, who scowled as he added, "Captain, one of the spice alarms I had the Watch set at one of the entrances to the secret tunnels just triggered. It's located not far from the Milk Palace."

"It might be one of the traitors," Quarce exclaimed.

"Trying to flee," Kucheesa added, a predatory gleam in her eyes.

Rasher turned to Noops. "Do you know the entrance he's talking about?" When Noops nodded, Rasher added, "Assuming they're trying to flee the Acropolis, can you lead us on an intercept course to stop them in the tunnels?"

"I can," Noops said confidently.

Rasher turned to Balter. "Send messengers to notify all the other entrances to double the guard. You and the rest of your squad join us. We're on the hunt."

Within moments, they descended to the tunnels, using a nondescript door in the back wall of a bakery not far from the train station. The tunnels were just tall enough for Noops to run without smashing his head on the ceiling, and wide enough for him and Balter to run side by side. The rest of them trailed behind.

Rasher wanted to admonish everyone to keep as quiet as possible, but running in armor on stone floors was just loud. Bibble, who was struggling to keep up at the rear of the pack produced a few herbs and managed to mix them on the run. When he cast the mixture into the air, a wonderful aroma spread around them.

It was like springtime in open fields, and as the aroma surrounded them, all sound faded to silence. The stomping of boots, rattling of armored plates and mail, the clacking of swords against legs, and the creaking of leather all faded to nothing.

Rasher glanced back and gave Bibble an encouraging smile. Now their quarry would get no warning of their approach.

The tunnel branched periodically, but Noops pounded ahead without hesitation, taking one turn after another and never slowing. The rest of them followed, the tiger-enhanced warriors running with effortless grace. Kucheesa took long, flowing strides, clearly using her float ability to draw more distance from every step. Quarce kept up, shorter legs pumping fast, eager expression never wavering.

Only Bibble started to lag. No doubt after a few weeks of Redael's targeted menu and a strict exercise regime, his physical state would dramatically improve, but that improvement was still weeks away.

Rasher, who was running right behind Noops, tapped Balter on the shoulder. When the big man glanced back, Rasher gestured to Bibble. Balter nodded understanding and flashed a series of hand gestures. The last Gleaner slowed from the group to shepherd Bibble after them.

They saw no one in the dimly lit tunnels. The Watch didn't even bother with illumination pastries down there, but used traditional oil lanterns set in partially recessed alcoves high on the walls.

As he ran, Noops started to sing softly to himself. At first, Rasher couldn't understand it but applied a little bacon to his ears as Noops kept repeating the phrase. With his sharpened hearing, he finally understood.

"Secret tunnels. Secret tunnels," Noops kept chanting.

Rasher wasn't sure why Noops was doing that but didn't comment on it. Even though Bibble had fallen behind, the spicy silence still clung to them, and he didn't want to risk breaking it. Instead he strained his hearing, listening into the shadowed tunnels ahead of them for any sign of their quarry.

Noops eventually slowed as he approached another junction and turned to speak softly. "Captain, we turn right at the next junction, which will lead to an open space where seven tunnels meet. If the intruder knows the tunnels and is trying to escape the Acropolis, they will pass through here soon."

"Very good," Rasher said, then turned to Balter. "What do you recommend, Lieutenant?"

For a second, Balter looked surprised but then grinned. "I'll split my squad into two teams. We'll take two of the tunnels and wait just outside of the room. You Reapers can take the tunnel between us. When the enemy enters, we can hit them from three sides."

"Good idea," Rasher said. "Let's do it.

A moment later, he crouched in the shadows at the mouth of one tunnel near the low-ceilinged stone junction room. The rest of the team crouched nearby. Kucheesa had jumped to hover in front of the nearest lantern long enough to lift it down from its shelf. She turned down the wick and plunged the tunnel into deeper shadow.

Noops leaned against the wall, looking calm and at ease, while Quarce kept crouching for a moment before rising again. He looked like he wanted to pace, but didn't want to move his feet and possibly make any noise. He gripped his expandable hammer in one hand, the weapon already twice as large as a carpenter's framing hammer.

Kucheesa crouched on one knee, her expression eager, but a little nervous. She kept glancing from Rasher to Noops, one hand on one of her knives, the other on the top of the lantern sitting on the floor beside her.

Rasher wanted to encourage them but didn't want to talk. Instead he gave each of them an encouraging nod when they looked at him. Quarce grinned widely, a flash of white teeth in the dimness. Noops nodded, and Kucheesa looked away.

Hopefully they'd moved fast enough and could intercept one or more of the traitors. Rasher doubted there would be many of them. The enemy had to move in small numbers to avoid drawing attention.

Of course, if he was wrong about that, they might be facing a pitched battle in the tight confines of the tunnels, with no backup on the way. Maybe he should have sent a couple more messengers.

His thoughts were interrupted by a soft noise echoing from the far side of the junction room. Instantly everyone froze, every sense straining. Rasher released more bacon into his sight and hearing, and suddenly the darkness didn't impede his vision nearly as much. The soft breathing of his companions sounded loud, as did the minor creaking of armor from the concealed Gleaners.

He had also applied bacon to his nose, and he could smell them all clearly too. The pleasant smells of steel and leather blended with the lingering summertime scent of Bibble's spice mixture. It was almost enough to mask the scent of sweat and nerves.

Another sound drew his attention. It sounded like a footfall, but slow and raspy, as if someone was creeping along, dragging their feet.

Not good. Were they being cautious, or had they somehow sensed Rasher's team?

Then he heard a sniffle that ended in a snort, as if someone was wiping a runny nose.

A shadowy figure moved in the exact tunnel Noops had guessed. Another step or two, and they'd emerge into the light and reveal their identity. So focused was he on the far side of the room that he didn't even notice Bibble joining them.

The exhausted spice wizard coughed loudly and asked, "Am I late?"

The figure across the junction room stiffened and gasped.

Instantly Noops charged. At the same second, Balter and his tiger warriors boiled out of their tunnels. Together, the warriors converged on the startled intruder in a rush.

Quarce gave instant chase, while Kucheesa followed, already turning the wick on the lantern and flooding the area with new light.

"Oops," Bibble muttered, but Rasher didn't have time to chasten him for the foolish noise. He too was rushing across the room, battle staff at the ready. He'd already detached his crumbhorn and secured it to straps on his back.

By the light of Kucheesa's lantern, Rasher realized their quarry was a slender woman wearing a dark robe and a senior milk mage's double milk bottle hat.

The woman cried out in surprise and took a couple fearful steps back, but Balter and his men quickly blocked her escape. They surrounded her, an unbroken circle of blades pointed at her throat from every side.

She did not try to fight, and she had nowhere to run. Instead she just stood there, looking at them, her expression pained. As Rasher pushed through the ring of soldiers, he realized she'd been crying. Her eyes were puffy and red, her cheeks marred by tears.

Balter spoke, his voice shaking with unusual hesitation. "Lower your weapons."

As his squad obeyed his command, Rasher recognized her.

"Dollop Aberdeen?" he exclaimed.

Indeed it was one of the missing members of the previous Reaper team. She met his gaze with soft, brown eyes and sighed, as if with great relief. "Finally. I can't believe how long it's taken you to catch me."

"Catch you?" Balter asked, taking a step forward and bowing low.

"Of course," she said. "Isn't that why you're here?"

"We're here to intercept a traitor," Balter said. "Not one of the Reapers."

She sighed again. "Unfortunately, today I fear you must refer to me as the former, while I will never again be worthy to be remembered as the latter."

"What are you talking about?" Balter exclaimed.

She lifted a gentle hand to his shoulder, a sad smile on her face. "Peace, Balter. All will be explained. Know that I did not willingly betray my oaths."

"What, then?" Rasher asked, drawing her gaze again. He'd suspected somehow the missing Reapers must be involved, but he'd feared they shared Otamot's anger and thirst for vengeance against the legions he believed had wronged him. Something else was definitely going on.

Dollop stood to her full height before him and said, "Captain Dilskin, well done and thank you. Only now, facing capture can I fully cast off the glamour that has clouded my mind and forced me to do unspeakably evil things."

"A glowan took over your mind?" Balter exclaimed. "How? You were too strong, too well protected."

"Not from my teammates," she said sadly.

"I think you'd better explain," Rasher said.

"There is not enough time for a full explanation," she said. "My mind is still fuzzy, but I am finally awake. Somehow two other Reapers were taken by the glowan."

"Clootie Dumpling and Juusto Panjandrum," Rasher guessed.

"Indeed."

"How can you know that?" Balter exclaimed.

"They are the other missing Reapers," Rasher said.

"Clootie is a confectioner," Bibble said, putting the pieces together.

Dollop nodded and said again, "Indeed. How he fell to the glowan, I do not know, but he weakened my mind with powerful confectioner sugars that left me vulnerable to manipulation."

"How?" Balter cried again, looking horrified and betrayed by her words. "That takes time."

"He had time," she said. "This all happened even before the contract addendums forced us from our roles as Reapers."

"That's how they did it," Rasher exclaimed. "I knew things weren't adding up. With Reapers already compromised, they could infiltrate the contract process."

"And that's how the battle cuisine was stolen without raising the alarm," Bibble said.

Kucheesa gasped. "Of course! They could simply order it moved, and no one would question."

"Powdered sugar never lies," Noops said. "The Muffin Mage who attacked you, and Ulotrichous both fell to sugars."

Some of the mysteries might be making sense, but it didn't make Rasher feel better. To think of some of the Reaper team compromised right in the heart of the Acropolis meant every member of the legions had failed.

Balter reached the same conclusion. He dropped to one knee, looking close to tears. "How did we fail you? Who did this?"

"I do not know the glowan that was controlling us, but they have to be close, and by now they will have realized their hold over me is broken."

"Do they still hold Clootie and Juusto?" Rasher asked.

"I believe so," she said, taking a sip from one of the milk bottles attached to the brim of her hat. "But the glowan hold is not perfect. As they pushed me to commit worse and worse crimes, I began to resist."

She sighed again. "Unfortunately, I could not break free before obeying the order to sabotage the Milk Palace, but as soon as I saw the destruction I had wreaked, my horror gave me the strength to begin to awaken."

Rasher didn't know details about how glowan glamours worked, and he filed that information away. "So you're saying it's possible the others can also break free?"

"Yes."

"But now that the glowan has fewer targets, their hold will be that much stronger," Bibble said. "Assuming there is one glowan managing them all."

"We need to find out who it is," Balter exclaimed.

"You must hurry," Dollop said. "My memories are all twisted, but I recall enough to fear poor Clootie and Juusto have been ordered on another mission even more devastating than my sabotage of the Milk Palace."

"What mission?" Rasher asked.

"To destroy the Heart."

34

The Dangers of Too Much Cake

As they raced through the tunnels toward the Heart, Rasher's mind whirled. Clootie and Juusto knew the tunnels and knew the Heart as well as anyone. Assuming Dollop was right, would they really attack their home, the great cornerstone of the Reaper legions? The Heart stood for so much more than the home and office space of the Reapers. It was a beacon of hope and a symbol of the might of the Reaper legions.

Could any glamour force them to commit such an atrocity? Hopefully the attempt would give them the strength to break free of the glamour.

Unfortunately, he had to assume they would go through with it like Dollop had. He wished they had more time to interrogate her, but that could wait until they stopped the attack on the Heart. One of the Gleaners was escorting her to the Cheese Palace and would hold her under guard there.

How would the englamoured Reapers plan the attack? They could simply walk through the front doors and no one would try to stop them, but their arrival would draw too much attention.

If they tried masks like Otamot had, the guards would stop them. Rasher had left clear orders not to allow anyone else to use that trick.

"Balter, what will be their primary target?" Rasher called to the big soldier, who was running silently, expression a thundercloud.

"If you were there, I'd say you. Since you're not, your offices, your staff, and the highest-ranking officials they can attack."

"We're supposed to be meeting General Nide and some of her commanders very soon," Kucheesa reminded him.

Fish sticks. Could the glowan know about that meeting, or was the timing merely a coincidence?

Balter blanched. "They'll definitely attack the general if they can."

Killing General Nide and some of her commanders would hurt the legions as much as depriving them of their battle cuisine, or destroying the Heart itself. Such an attack could effectively cripple the legions for long enough that they'd never succor Ehverr before the hordes overwhelmed the city.

Running in front of them, leading them toward the exit closest to the Heart, Noops said, "I once knew a cheese farmer--"

"Not now!" Kucheesa cried. "I cannot take another meaningless analogy from you, or I swear I'll curse you with one of my grandmother's worst curses."

Noops looked disappointed, but Rasher said, "Wait a minute, can you use your grandmother's curses?"

"Sure. They're old family recipes. I've been cursing gophers and rabbits out of our garden since I was a little girl. We've got one gouda cheese curse that would drop those pesky critters in their tracks." She grinned with pride. "Never mess with a cheese wizard's garden."

"How?" Bibble called from the rear of the pack where he was clinging to an improvised sled made out of leather armor, towed by two of the Gleaners. "No one is blessed with powers from more than one god."

"It's not like that," Kucheesa said with a shrug. "I've always been good with curses, but I'm not a cheese wizard. I'm a meat mage." She tapped her winged hat for emphasis. "I haven't even made any curses in months."

Bibble didn't look convinced, and Rasher made a note to follow up with her on that later. The ramifications of her story could be huge if she wasn't exaggerating.

Now was not the time. Noops took a sharp turn to the right and led them pounding up a narrow stair that emerged on the edge of the huge plaza facing the Heart.

They'd run hard, but the time was growing late. Rasher bet the general and her officers were already in the conference room, impatiently waiting for them. As he ran across the wide plaza, he started planning their response.

"Balter, get upstairs to the general and warn her of the danger. Barricade them in the conference room until we send reinforcements."

"Noops, notify the Watch. I want everyone they can get to form a perimeter around the Heart until we verify it is secure."

"Kucheesa, you and Quarce with me. We'll rouse the Heart guard and lead the search for any intruders."

Thankfully, no one argued. Rasher needed to get word to Gubbins as soon as they reached the Heart. He knew the compromised Reapers far better than Rasher did and could help us set up the best plan to capture them.

Sprinting across the plaza drew attention from the few people there, but Rasher didn't have time to pause. He led the way quickly up the stairs to the porch but paused when a window on the second floor exploded outward.

A man fell shouting to the wooden porch and hit with a loud thud.

Rasher grimaced as he ran toward the fallen man. His team followed, but Balter and the Gleaners didn't pause. They raced into the Heart and disappeared.

Balter might be right. They needed to secure the building, but the fallen man might have clues about the attack. Falling from that height probably wasn't fatal, but it probably broke bones.

The man's dark hair was streaked with gray, and he wore the white baking jacket of a muffin mage. He'd lost his tall, muffin hat somewhere.

"I don't see anyone else up there who might have pushed him," Kucheesa said as Rasher dropped to his knees beside the fallen muffin mage.

Other soldiers and officials were rushing toward them from every side, but Quarce and Noops urged them back. Bibble dropped to his knees on the other side of the fallen man, looking for signs of life. As soon as he touched him, the muffin mage gasped, rolling onto his back with a painful groan.

His eyes blinked open and he focused as Rasher leaned closer and asked, "What happened?"

With one hand, the man seized the front of his uniform with desperate strength and yanked him closer. He looked terribly injured, his other arm hanging at an unnatural angle, his face bloody from his hard landing, but he spoke through blood-soaked teeth.

"Get everyone out. It's going to blow!"

Rasher's heart fell even as he made sure to avoid looking at the blood. He hadn't expected a bomb. The enemy was moving too fast.

"Get them out of the Heart. It's all going to blow! I couldn't stop him."

Rasher met Bibble's horrified gaze as the spice wizard whispered, "Balter just went in there."

He didn't want to believe they were too late, that anyone, no matter how englamoured, could place a bomb in the Heart, but the panic in the man's eyes was too real.

"Get everyone out!" he shouted.

The words were drowned out by a massive explosion on the ground floor of the Heart, two-thirds of the way down the building from where they crouched. Glass and stone and wood exploded outward as a twenty-foot section of wall disintegrated. A fireball blasted out the opening, spraying flames.

Another explosion rocked the second floor, vaporizing the room where the muffin mage had been. The concussion from the blast flattened them all to the ground, the sound crashing over them with stunning force. Fiery debris rained down around them.

Rasher flung himself over the injured muffin mage to protect him from more damage. He needed information and that man was the only one who might have some.

More explosions rocked the building as each floor blasted apart in rapid succession. Rasher's ears rang and the world shook and rattled and rained fire. Everywhere he looked people lay prone, stunned or injured or covering their heads as they screamed in fear. Others crawled or ran for their lives.

His team crowded in close around him, helping to shield the injured man. He felt a rush of pride that they reacted exactly as he had instead of succumbing to the panic.

Echoes from the final explosion bounced back and forth between the other administration buildings surrounding the square several times before fading. The giant copper-bottomed pots banged like thunder on their hooks, and one fell off, clattering to the cobblestones with an explosive report.

Then for a brief moment, smoky silence settled over the square, as if the world had to take a breath.

A second later, with a mighty groaning of timbers and sharp reports of shattering stone, the Heart began to implode.

"Go!" Rasher shouted. Noops and Quarce heaved the wounded muffing mage into their arms and they all sprinted for the stairs down to the plaza.

Several men leaped from one of the windows. It was Balter and his team. They landed gracefully, rolling with the impact, already running for the safety of the plaza. Rasher was glad to see they hadn't died in the initial explosion.

Other people jumped from windows, but most landed hard, screaming on impact. Rasher hated that he couldn't slow to save them. He had to get away, or he would die too. Every step he took felt like a betrayal of his oath, and he wanted to howl with anger and horror.

The implosion started slowly, ponderously, as the famous tabletop roof sundered and collapsed down into the building below. As they ran, the cascade of timbers and stone accelerated, blasting out a choking, blinding cloud of dust and debris in every direction.

They all kept running, not slowing until they reached the center of the square. There they lowered the muffin mage again. The man had passed out, but Rasher could not escape the horror of the moment.

"See if you can revive him," Rasher told Bibble through a cough. The spice wizard looked on the verge of panic, the whites of his wide eyes looking particularly huge against the dust-covered gray of the rest of his face.

Bibble shook himself and pulled a tiny pouch from one of the long pockets hanging down from the left side of his hat. He flung a bit of the black powder into the air and made a mixing motion with his hand. A gentle breeze blew around them, pushing the smoke back, forming a dome of clean air about a dozen feet across.

Nodding with satisfaction, Bibble began extracting jars and bags of herbs from various pockets in his coat and hat. He opened one and sniffed it deeply, holding his breath for a moment, eyes closed. That seemed to calm him, and he tucked that one away before getting back to work.

Kucheesa crouched beside him, and he gave her a small pewter bowl to hold the items as he began a mixture.

"Noops, see if you can find a milk mage," Rasher said. The sounds of collapse were subsiding and a breeze was already beginning to thin the billowing cloud of dust.

The full extent of the disaster would emerge momentarily. He released the power of chewy bacon, accelerating his thoughts and prioritizing the immediate needs. First, verify the area was secure. Second, search for survivors.

Scores of other people milled about the square, visible as shadowy figures in the murk. Many were wounded, and all were stunned by the disaster. Cries of pain and anguish echoed through the murky gloom.

Rasher glanced down at the pale, bloody muffin mage. Third, get some answers.

Noops hurried off, followed by Quarce, who offered to find cloth to use as bandages.

Rasher paced around Bibble as the pudgy spice wizard quickly concocted a mixture in the bowl. He took it from Kucheesa, worked the spices with a tiny pestle, then paused, head bowed, concentrating over it.

He was about to urge Bibble to hurry when his accelerated thoughts locked onto the truth he'd been unconsciously trying to avoid thinking about. Horror seared his mind like fire in a pan of bacon grease.

General Nide and her commanders were supposed to be waiting for him in the Heart, along with Gubbins and most of the hero finders. He turned to stare toward the Heart as if he could see through the still-billowing clouds of dust. Had they all just died?

The saboteurs had destroyed the Heart, the symbol of the Reaper might. Had they just decapitated the legion leadership in one fell deed at the same time? The idea threatened to lock up his mind.

He looked for Balter but didn't see him through the clouds of smoke. If the explosion had been caused by the englamoured Reapers, had they known the general would be there?

Had they expected Rasher and his team to be there too? If not for getting distracted by the chance to catch Dollop, they would have. They would have probably died and been buried under that huge pile of rubble.

If the timing wasn't just chance, then the enemy must know their current schedule. That suggested the glowan might have corrupted someone in the administration. Rasher rubbed his temples. He had a pounding headache and his eyes burned from the stinging dust.

The muffin mage coughed, pulling him back around. Bibble was holding the spice mixture under the man's nose, and as the man gasped in another breath, he coughed, then groaned, his eyes blinking open.

Rasher dropped to his knees again, leaning close. Bibble and Kucheesa pressed in on either side.

"What is your name?" Rasher asked. He wanted to demand answers but forced himself to start slow.

The man blinked his eyes a couple more times, but they seemed unfocused. He groaned again and whispered, "My name. My name is . . ." He giggled, then groaned again. "Alevler Yakmak."

Bibble gasped. "I've heard of Alevler, but would not have recognized him. He's a senior muffin mage. One of the most respected patissiers in the Acropolis."

Alevler giggled again, then groaned. "Make it stop. It's not funny any more."

"What's wrong with him?" Kucheesa asked with a frown.

"I fear he's suffering a sugar overdose," Bibble said, reaching for more spices.

"Sugar overdose like Ulotrichous," Rasher muttered angrily. "More of Clootie's handiwork. Can you get him stabilized enough to give us some answers?"

"I believe so."

Alevler's eyes started to wander, then snapped into focus again and he again seized Rasher's jacket. "Must stop him!"

"Who?" Rasher asked, impressed by the man's ability to even temporarily break through sugar euphoria.

"Clootie Dumpling."

Rasher sighed. He hated being proved right. The thought of the famous confectioner committing atrocities under the command of a secret glowan was the worst kind of insult to his entire life's work.

Alevler's eyes rolled back and the hand gripping Rasher's jacket dropped back to the cobblestones. The man started singing whisper-soft to himself.

"Has to be the sugar euphoria," Bibble said, returning to work.

Rasher sure hoped so, but his mind was racing. It appeared Dollop was right. If only they'd captured her sooner! A matter of minutes, and they might have intercepted those bombs.

Or died in the Heart while trying.

In the distance to the north, someone screamed. Rasher glanced through the still-billowing, choking clouds of dust pulsing against their clean air shield and asked, "What now?"

"Throw me, and I'll see what I can find out," Kucheesa said.

Rasher cupped his hands and crouched. Kucheesa jumped forward, planting her foot into his hands, and leaped. Drawing upon two entire slices of crispy bacon, Rasher heaved with all his strength.

Kucheesa was a slender girl, but she must have already activated one of her chicken enhancements because she felt lighter than a child. When he heaved, she flew upward with astonishing speed. He nearly lost sight of her in the churning dust.

More shouts came from the north, but he couldn't see anything. He realized he'd somehow lost his new hat somewhere, and scowled anew.

"Someone's on the ground bleeding. It's fresh, as if they were just wounded. More people are falling over. Might be another sugar attack."

Before Rasher could respond, she added, "I see a cloaked figure running away. There!"

Either Alevler's desperate escape out the window had forced Clootie to detonate the cakes early, or he'd just hung around to enjoy the carnage. Bad idea. Now that he had a target, Rasher focused all of his horror and all of his rage onto it. He would not allow the villain to escape.

"Which way?"

"West, toward the edge of the square." Kucheesa's shadowy form started gliding down in that direction.

Rasher gave chase and almost ran right into Noops and Quarce, who were returning with a harried-looking milk mage in tow. Rasher pushed the milk mage toward Bibble. "Heal that muffin mage first. Bibble, help him. Noops, Quarce, on me. We may have a lead on Clootie."

Together, they plunged through the billowing clouds of dust, with the cries of the wounded on every side urging them on to greater speed.

35

SPRINKLE CHEESE

T hankfully the billowing haze lessened by the time Rasher reached the western edge of the plaza, with Noops and Quarce close behind. Kucheesa landed nearby and rushed after them, her strides long and graceful.

He slowed near the corner of the admin building on that side of the plaza to scan the crowds. People were rushing in by the scores to help the wounded, while others were stumbling away, coughing and dazed.

There. He spotted a lone, dark-cloaked figure turning the corner to the north. No one paid them any heed, all focused on the disaster. So many people were screaming and shouting, he didn't even bother calling for others to help.

He would deal with them.

Rasher accelerated again, using his bacon-enhanced agility to weave through the press. Kucheesa kept pace right behind him, while Noops and Quarce lagged a little. Rasher didn't have time to wait.

The previous Reapers may have been under a glamour, but they were wreaking terrible havoc among the legions they had led and inspired for so long. Rasher needed to stop them now, then figure out who their handler had been and destroy that evil glowan.

He rounded the corner at a full sprint just in time to see the tail end of the cloak disappear into an alleyway between two senior officer housing units. Battle staff at the ready, he rushed down the alley after their quarry.

The alley was packed with carts laden with heavy, cast-iron grills and all their associated paraphernalia. As Rasher leaped up onto the first cart, he remembered there was supposed to be a big cooking challenge between champion barbecue chefs as part of a feast celebrating the new Reaper team. He'd totally forgotten about it.

He feared they'd never hold that cook-off now. The thought angered him as much as the destruction of the Heart. The building was a symbol of the Reapers, and many important people might have died. The vast scope of the disaster was still so new, he couldn't quite wrap his mind around it.

Losing out on one of the famous chef cook-offs was a far more personal loss, one that struck right in the gut. One more reason for the cloaked figure to pay severely.

Their quarry was running lightly over the heavily laden carts, moving with remarkable agility. Rasher gave chase, drawing deep from bacon to increase his agility. Kucheesa bounded easily beside him, making the strenuous effort seem easy.

"Clootie was famous for his performance-enhancing sugar cookies," she called. "Looks like he ate a couple dozen himself today."

"Won't be enough," Rasher promised.

Behind them, Noops and Quarce paused at the entrance to the alley. Noops shouted, "We'll go around and try to head him off."

Good plan. They'd never keep up through the carts. Rasher focused on moving as fast as possible, sliding into that bacon-fueled trance of pure instinct where he didn't have to think about moving, but let his muscles and the unrivaled awesomeness of bacon do the work.

He pulled ahead of Kucheesa, flying over the carts, barely making contact with each step before leaping off again. Several times he jumped sideways and ran along the walls to get around particularly high obstacles.

Then Kucheesa launched into the air and glided over the entire next cart, catching up with him. She flashed a grin and called, "No one outruns a chicken that easily."

As they approached the end of the alley, they had halved the distance to their quarry and he finally noticed them. He glanced back, but the wide brim of his black hat obscured his face.

"In the name of your oaths, stop!" Rasher shouted, filling his voice with the commanding power of bacon.

He hadn't expected it to work but hoped to reach that core inside of the man that remembered his honor. If Dollop had broken the glamour's hold over her mind, maybe this conspirator could.

The man actually stumbled, shaking his head, and slowing.

"No way," Kucheesa breathed. She had a dagger in each hand and looked ready to throw them.

Their quarry shouted, "Tell them I didn't mean--"

His words broke off in a choked cry and he spun and leaped away again. Whatever moment of clarity he'd managed to find was gone.

Kucheesa threw one of her knives, but the cloaked figure dove off the final cart, barely avoiding it. The man rolled and raced around the corner. They exited the alley seconds later and raced after him. Their quarry was turning down another alley on the far side of the street, this one wider and without any debris clogging it.

The street was almost empty as everyone rushed toward the Heart. Rasher spotted Noops and Quarce rushing around the far end of the building and gestured them to continue. He and Kucheesa raced after the fleeing figure and had nearly reached the mouth of the alley when movement up on the roof caught Rasher's attention.

He glanced up and spotted another dark-cloaked figure leaning over the edge. The figure threw something into the air over the alley. Rasher saw only glittering points of light settling slowly toward the ground.

It took a critical second to understand what he was seeing, and when he did he reacted on pure instinct.

"Look out!" he shouted, diving at Kucheesa who had pulled slightly ahead of him while he was distracted.

He tackled her just shy of the alleyway entrance, knocking them both tumbling into the side of the building. They hit hard and his shoulder protested the abuse.

"Get off! What are you doing?" Kucheesa snarled, one knife raised as if barely restraining herself from stabbing him.

"Sprinkle cheese!" he shouted, leaping to his feet.

"What?" She turned to look at the alley mouth that was full of the gently falling flakes of deadly cheese. The air had turned a foul yellowish-green color, barely inches away.

Rasher grabbed her by the shoulders and hauled her away. They didn't have time to talk about it. She squawked in protest, but then her body shuddered and she twisted in his grip, vomiting explosively against the side of the building.

Rasher kept going, dragging Kucheesa. The stench hit him a second later, and he almost fell. Gagging, barely holding back his own bile, he staggered several more paces before escaping the area effect.

Once they were safe, he lowered Kucheesa to the ground. She had stopped vomiting but continued shuddering. Her face had turned pale, her eyes wide and afraid.

"I grew up on a farm. I thought I knew bad smells, but that was horrid," she gasped, spitting vomit from her mouth.

From the whiff he'd gotten, Rasher understood just how close they'd come to a gruesome death. "Munster. They grated it to increase potency. Look."

The alley mouth was blocked by a stinking cloud of yellowish green. The air shimmered from the stench, and the cobblestones had begun to blacken.

"You saved my life," she breathed, glancing at him with an unreadable expression. He couldn't tell if she was impressed, or just disappointed that maybe she couldn't hate him as easily.

Rasher flashed a grin and said, "Find Noops and Quarce. See if you can track Clootie from the far side of the alley. I'm going after Juusto."

Without another word, Rasher released three entire slices of crispy bacon and drew deep from the sizzle thrumming through his limbs. Bacon power erupted through every sinew, and he grinned as he ran straight at the wall.

With a series of acrobatic jumps, Rasher climbed the side of the wall, moving from window sills to thin strips of molding to cracks between the stones of the facade. In seconds, he reached the roof.

He spotted a dark figure on the next roof, a lovely garden complete with small trees and an octagonal-shaped greenhouse. The figure ducked behind the greenhouse too late.

Rasher rushed across the roof and easily leaped the twelve-foot span to the next building. He called out, "You've violated your oaths and betrayed your people. Surrender now and maybe we can make things right."

A man stepped from behind the greenhouse, no longer cloaked.

It was not Juusto.

It was Otamot.

36

BACON OVER BACON

"That wasn't you who tried to kill us with the munster attack," Rasher said.

"No," Otamot agreed, stepping farther from the greenhouse onto a small patch of soft, green grass.

Most of the roof was tiled in terra cotta colors, with small potted trees and bushes ringing much of the outer edge. They faced each other across a square open grassy area about fifteen feet across. Otamot was dressed in a standard legion uniform, wearing an unremarkable wide-brimmed hat. Instead of his signature double swords, he carried a wooden staff slightly longer than Rasher's.

"So you are in league with the others," Rasher said.

Otamot gave him a disgusted look. "As if I would ally with fools too weak to break free of a glamour."

"But you knew they were compromised," Rasher pressed.

Otamot shrugged, giving his staff an experimental spin. "I figured it out the first night after we were cast from the Acropolis."

"Why didn't you say anything?" Rasher demanded, unable to conceal his anger.

"Why would I?" Otamot sneered. "We dedicated our lives to the legions, and you cast us out without hesitation. They gave our positions to you rabble the very next day!"

He was shouting by the time he finished, and only calmed himself with visible effort. His voice dropped back to a conversational level. "I watched and figured a little retribution was in order. I foolishly expected you all to intercept them almost immediately, but you are useless, weak, and vulnerable. You deserve the punishment you received!"

"And the Heart? Did you help them plant that bomb?" Rasher asked, his anger settling into white-hot fury.

For the first time, Otamot looked pained. "The Heart was my home, but you have polluted it. General Nide and her commanders needed to pay, and this was the best way to do so. I would have preferred some other way, but justice this way has proven far too poetic to ignore."

"You are a traitor to every vow you ever made," Rasher declared, taking a step closer. "The others were compelled, but you participated willingly."

That struck a nerve. Otamot lunged across the distance in a blur, staff striking like a snake at Rasher's head.

Perfect.

Rasher easily deflected the blow and side-stepped the rush, returning with a sharp rap against Otamot's thigh.

With a shout of rage, Otamot unleashed a barrage of strikes against Rasher, staff blurring with the speed of his assault.

Rasher grinned as the two of them flowed around each other, staves cracking so fast the sound was like never-ending thunder. Otamot might be a famous warrior, but he'd focused most of his training on swords. The staff was Rasher's world, and there he reigned supreme.

As they fought, the tempo increased faster and faster until they both moved on pure instinct. Rasher released three more slices of bacon and dedicated most of his remaining sizzle to strengthen his body and accelerate his reflexes. He also released two slices of chewy bacon to speed his perceptions.

The two of them surged back and forth across the roof, staves striking like lightning at an ever-increasing tempo, forming a blurring fog between them.

Rasher met everything Otamot had to throw at him, reveling in the absolute concentration of the fight. He loved battle, loved to test his might against worthy opponents, and he hadn't faced another competent bacon master since he'd left the training academy at Weghiv.

His anger faded to the centered calm of battle, his entire being focused as the world contracted to nothing but their fight. The scent of wood seemed to magnify the sharp staccato of their battle, and Rasher smiled as the familiar scents and sounds washed through him.

After a moment, Otamot's wild assault faltered, and Rasher easily read shock on his opponent's face. Rasher doubted anyone had stood against Otamot successfully in years.

"You're a failure," Rasher taunted. "At least tell me you learned who the glowan is so we can destroy them after I drop you in a holding cell."

"You dare insult me?" Otamot hissed, unleashing a brutal strike at Rasher's face. If it had connected, it would have split his skull in half.

Rasher ducked and whipped the base of his staff across Otamot's knees. The double crack sounded loud in the hazy air, and Otamot stumbled back with a cry of pain. The bacon master would have fallen, but used his staff to catch himself.

"Fighting in anger grants your enemy power to control you," Rasher said, quoting his rules of engagement number twenty-five. He stalked after Otamot, disgusted to see such a great man fallen so low. "Now tell me who the glowan is."

"I don't know," Otamot confessed.

"Really? What was your plan, throw a tantrum for a while and hurt a lot of people, and then just run away and leave your sworn teammates in the power of a glowan to die?"

"I would have discovered the foul creature," Otamot promised, taking a step with a hiss of pain.

"Sure," Rasher said with abundant sarcasm. "You were supposed to be a great man, but you haven't learned anything about honor or the heart of what it means to be a Reaper, have you?"

"I deserved more!" Otamot shrieked, drawing a small knife and slashing it across the back of his other hand. "And you deserve death, thin slice!"

Rasher turned away, but the bright blood spilling from the cut on Otamot's hand seized his vision.

No. No no no, he couldn't let the vile traitor exploit his weakness.

Rasher forced his eyes closed as he staggered, his blood pounding in his ears. He had used most of his sizzle, so lacked the energy to fight the blood phobia.

If he fell, Otamot would butcher him like a pig.

That thought triggered a vivid memory of Rasher as a boy running along the catwalk above the blood vats in his family's slaughterhouse.

Huge pools of blood spread beneath him, awaiting processing into the myriad purposes the family had developed for it.

He hadn't fainted at the sight of that blood, hadn't cared about the precarious narrowness of the catwalk. Rasher couldn't remember what he'd been doing up there. The memory had been lost for years.

He sensed somehow that memory might be important, but it disappeared in a flash, and he was again stumbling on the roof, blood pounding, head spinning, fighting for his life as Otamot hobbled after him.

Rasher panted for breath but felt his mind succumbing to blackness. He raged against the weakness, and Noops' words returned in a flash.

Rasher tensed his limbs, fighting with all his strength to solidify the muscles and reinforce his blood flow. The blackness did not leave, but its progression over his mind slowed just long enough for Rasher to look up at Otamot, who was closing on him, murder in his eyes.

"You cheat like a little girl," Rasher wheezed through lips that barely worked.

Then with the last of his strength, he hurled himself backward over the edge of the roof.

Otamot's surprised cry chased him into blackness. Rasher's mind whirled, but he didn't think he passed out before he struck the ground.

He hit something, but it almost felt like he started falling sideways for a second. Death was supposed to hurt a lot more than that.

Weird.

37

You Should Eat More Chicken

Rasher awakened lying on cool stones of the street. He felt battered and disoriented like always after a blood fainting episode, but he didn't feel the sharp pains of broken bones like he should after falling four stories.

Not feeling the pain was supposed to be a really bad sign.

Dark shapes loomed over him, and for a second he feared Otamot had jumped over the wall after him. But a second later his vision cleared and he smiled to see his team.

"Are you all right?" Quarce asked.

"I think so," Rasher said, his voice rasping from a dry throat.

"You should eat more chicken," Noops said.

"What?" Rasher managed to sit up and was surprised to see Kucheesa crouched beside him, helping to steady him.

"You tried to fly," Noops said. "Didn't work out so well. Eat more chicken before you try again."

Quarce grinned and added, "Noops caught you right out of the air."

"Thanks," Rasher said, rubbing his head before looking up at the roof he'd just jumped from. "Did you see anyone else?"

"No," Kucheesa said with a scowl. "Lucky for you we lost Clootie. We were returning to report when we saw you fall. What happened?"

Rasher sighed. They'd lost all of the conspirators, but at least he'd learned some things that might prove useful. He said, "Otamot was waiting for me up there."

"He knocked you off the roof?" Quarce exclaimed.

"Sort of. When he couldn't beat me with staves, he cheated."

Kucheesa looked at him with new respect. "You beat Otamot in a duel?"

"If he'd had his swords, it might have gone differently, but the staff is my weapon," Rasher responded.

"Then you should stop losing yours," Noops said, lifting Rasher's battle staff and handing it over. Rasher took it gratefully, happy to see it looked undamaged.

"My crumbhorn," he cried, reaching back and pulling the precious instrument from the straps on his back. He inspected it briefly and was relieved to see it undamaged.

"Should we chase them?" Quarce asked.

"No." Rasher climbed to his feet. "We know who we're hunting now, but we need to get back to the plaza and assess the damage."

And the casualty counts. He didn't want to think about the fact they might have lost General Nide and some of the highest commanders, or Gubbins, or Shemo, but they had to know. When they reached the plaza, the billowing dust cloud had dissipated, driven by a steady wind conjured up by a trio of spice wizards.

The Heart was destroyed, the majestic building reduced to a huge pile of rubble. Only a small section of the front porch remained intact. Rubble had spilled out onto the square, and some of the debris was still burning. Fire brigade squads were working on it, assisted by a handful of muffin mages.

Rasher slowed as he pushed through the crowds of responders, heading toward Bibble. Hundreds had come to help, and the wounded were already being organized in long rows, attended to by a full company of milk mages. Scores of milkmaids assisted, along with even more soldiers pressed into service.

"They don't have enough cream," Kucheesa said softly as they surveyed the devastation. Many of the wounded groaned in obvious pain, waiting for their turn with the milk mages.

The milk mages were focusing on the most severely wounded, but still doled out their precious healing whipped cream and trauma yogurts with miserly precision.

"No wonder Dollop broke free of the glamour," Rasher said. "She would have realized the terrible price the legions would pay for her sabotage."

He spotted Bibble crouching over the injured muffin mage, but the milk mage was already gone to help other patients. They hurried toward him, Rasher keeping his eyes moving, avoiding looking at any bleeding wounds. He felt tired and empty and wasn't sure if he could even suffer a second episode so soon, but this wasn't the time to test the theory.

Many people spotted them and some cheered, drawing even more attention. Several officers intercepted them with questions and reports. Rasher told them to hold and follow until he dealt with another matter.

When they arrived with a growing entourage of followers, Bibble looked relieved to see them. "Any luck?"

"They got away," Rasher said with a scowl.

"Who were you chasing anyway?" Bibble asked.

"In a minute." Rasher glanced down at Alevler, who was still lying on the ground. His eyes were closed, his breathing regular, and his face peaceful. "How is he?"

"The milk mage stabilized him and I administered a tea to ease his mind from the effects of the sugar euphoria. Ideally, he should sleep for a couple hours."

"We don't have that much time," Rasher said. Turning to the gathered crowd he added, "Give us some room."

Amazingly, they shuffled back. Two captains took command of the group, beginning to arrange them in order of priority. Rasher appreciated their initiative.

Bibble knelt beside the muffin mage and pulled a small, stoppered bottle from one of his many pockets. Jaw set in lines of concentration, he unstoppered the bottle and waved it under the muffin mage's nose. "I prepared a second dose to shock his system. It'll tax his strength, but should bring temporary clarity."

Alevler gasped and coughed, his eyes popping open. Rasher crouched beside him as the rest of the team gathered close.

"Tell us what happened," Rasher ordered, drawing Alevler's eyes to him.

"I'm so glad you survived," Alevler said.

"A lot of people didn't, so we need to know what happened and what your involvement was," Rasher told him, trying to keep his voice calm.

It was becoming difficult to hold at bay his clamoring thoughts. Estimates of possible casualty counts kept intruding. He needed General Nide and her commanders, and could not imagine commanding the legions without them.

"I was finishing work on a large batch of three-tier cakes for the siege company when Clootie Dumpling entered my workshop."

"It was him," Quarce said sadly.

"Yes," Alevler said. "He and I are old friends, so at first I just thought he'd stopped by for a social visit."

"He was your dealer, wasn't he?" Rasher prodded gently.

Kucheesa gasped. "You're a sugar addict?"

"Quiet," hissed Alevler, glancing toward the nearby officers. "It was just a harmless habit. We'd get together on our days off, eat a few sugar cookies or truffles or . . . a twenty-four layer cake a couple times."

"How could you?" Bibble demanded, staring down at the man with pity.

"It wasn't a big deal. I never used enhanced sugars in any of my cakes or muffins, never went to work in a sugar high. I always kept it strictly controlled," Alevler protested.

"So what happened?" Rasher asked. It was far too easy to fall into a sugar addiction, but he doubted Alevler had made such a foolish mistake.

"When Clootie entered my workshop, he offered me a hit of straight powdered sugar."

"No," Kucheesa whispered in horror.

He shrugged. "I knew it was a bad idea, but he promised it was a low dose, just a final farewell. How could I refuse?"

"Except it wasn't a low dose, was it?" Noops guessed.

Alevler's shoulders sagged and he looked on the verge of crying. He shook his head slowly, his voice falling to a whisper. "Not at all. It was like tasting a bolt of lightning, but by the time I realized he'd lied to me, it was too late."

He wiped savagely at his eyes, then his expression hardened. "He's been my friend for years, but he lied to me!"

"What did he make you do?" Rasher asked, moved by the man's obvious pain, but unable to stop. They needed answers.

"It's all hazy, like a sugar dream. We loaded all the cakes into a cart and delivered them to the Heart. Somehow he had all the authorizations to get past security. We staged them with short wick timers and he left me in the room with one of them. Just ordered me to sit and gave me another hit of sugar."

"It's a miracle you didn't pass out from the double dose," Bibble said.

"I did for a moment, but something woke me up. My mind wasn't working, but I knew something was wrong. The only idea I had was to get help, but the door was locked and I could barely stand. Then I saw you through the window and had to get to you."

Rasher sighed. Alevler's story matched closely with what Dollop had said. By corrupting Clootie, the sinister glowan had gained the perfect pawn to help them subvert more minions.

"So the Reapers did turn on us," Quarce boomed, drawing way too much attention.

"Keep it down," Rasher told him. "Most folks are not prepared to deal with this truth yet."

Hearing the truth from Dollop had been bad, but the confirmation from Alevler removed any possible doubt. Three of the mighty Reapers had fallen to glowan treachery right in the heart of their own homes. It made Rasher feel sick.

Not as sick as the thought of Otamot's treachery, though.

"Our top priority is getting this mess under control and figuring out who was killed in the explosion," Rasher said. They had to focus on their mission, although he felt suddenly exhausted by the burden of his new responsibility.

Bibble looked toward the rubble, eyes haunted. "We need confirmation about what happened to the general."

Rasher gestured one of the waiting officers closer. "Does anyone know if the general was in the Heart when it blew?"

"Yes," the officer said.

"She was inside?" Kucheesa groaned, and Rasher's heart nearly stopped. The weight of his responsibilities suddenly felt overwhelming.

"No, she was not," the man said.

"Which is it?" Rasher demanded.

"I was answering your question," the officer protested. "You asked if we knew if the general was inside the Heart. Yes, we know, and no, she was not in there at the time."

"Why not?" Kucheesa asked as Rasher took a long, relieved breath.

The officer shrugged. His uniform was covered in dirt and grime like most of them and he too had lost his hat. "I was stationed in the plaza and I witnessed several commanders enter the Heart about twenty minutes before you arrived. General Nide and Commander Moist were not among them."

Rasher's relief subsided a bit as he realized what that meant. "I never would have thought I'd be grateful she decided to snub us by sending lower-level officers to the meeting."

Another officer stepped forward and saluted. "Reaper Captain Dilskin, sir, we just received reports of an explosion near South gate. An armored wagon full of grated parmesan cheese blew. Initial casualty counts are high and the entire area is contaminated and too dangerous for anyone to approach."

"They're hitting us on every side," Quarce said.

"General Nide was seen near South gate at the time," the officer continued. "She is reportedly safe and messengers have already been dispatched to inform her of the attack here."

"Good," Rasher said, trying to keep a calm expression. The enemy was hitting them on all sides, battering the legion from the shadows.

Not any longer. He now knew most of them, and knowledge turned the tides of battle.

He added, "The saboteurs will no longer find it so easy to slip among us."

"You know who some of the saboteurs are?" asked one of the officers excitedly.

"We have suspicions, but cannot make them known publicly yet," Rasher said.

Kucheesa looked like she wanted to protest, but thankfully she held her tongue. If word got out that some of the old Reaper team was responsible for all the death, destruction, and sabotage they'd suffered in recent days, the news would crush morale. It might spark riots too. He could not take the risk.

"There you are!" someone called.

Rasher turned and was shocked to see Gubbins rushing toward them. His uniform was clean and he looked healthy. A large leather satchel hung over one shoulder.

"You're alive," Rasher exclaimed, greeting the hero finder with a warm handshake. "We thought you lost in the Heart."

"I should have been," Gubbins said gravely, glancing back at the rubble and shivering. "When you were late, I excused myself from the meeting and went next door to send messengers to find you." He pointed at the nearby admin building.

"Lucky you didn't just send messengers from your office," Noops said.

"I know," Gubbins said, then his expression turned grave. "Rasher, most of the other hero finders were in there, along with several commanders, and representatives from all eleven houses in the Food Court."

"What?" Rasher gasped.

"Not the ambassadors themselves or their secretaries, but other assistants," Gubbins added quickly. "I've already sent word to Nutmeg Hill of the disaster. There will most definitely be an inquiry."

Rasher wanted to yank on his hair. The problems were compounding too fast. They had multiple disasters to deal with, wounded to help, and saboteurs to hunt down. He wanted to lash out at their enemies but had no idea where to find the one that really mattered.

Finding the glowan would cripple the enemy's plans, but for the evil creature to have remained concealed among them for so long, and to have gained access to the Reapers unaware, that meant it had to be a changeling.

Not good. Ferreting out a changeling was notoriously difficult. The last thing they needed was more Nutmeg Hill intrigue cluttering up their work too.

"The general," an officer shouted, pointing.

Rasher turned to see General Nide, Commander Moist, and a large retinue of officers and her personal guard approaching on horseback. A battered-looking Balter Fopoon and his entire fist of Gleaners trotted along on either side. Their deadly presence seemed to reassure many.

Rasher shouldn't feel so disappointed that Balter had sought out the general instead of seeking to help him chase down the fleeing attackers. With Gleaner assistance, they might have succeeded in capturing the compromised Reapers.

He turned to the nearest officer. "Make sure every possible resource is being used to search for survivors and assist the wounded."

"Yes sir," the man promised, saluting smartly.

Before General Nide arrived, another voice called Rasher's name. It was a thin, frail voice, and he was shocked to see his secretary, Shemo Medjamo, being carried on a stretcher toward him by a couple burly soldiers.

"Captain," the old man said as they drew near. "I am so happy you are safe." Shemo looked terrible. He was covered in dirt, his usually pristine uniform tattered, and his hat missing. One arm was held in a sling, and his hair was matted with dirty blood.

Rasher avoided looking at the blood as he rushed to him and gently took his good hand. "Were you in the building when it fell?"

Shemo nodded. "I was in a basement supply room, preparing the inventory you requested. Then everything came crashing down."

"We just pulled him from the rubble," one of the soldiers carrying the stretcher said. "Barely let a milk mage stabilize him before insisting we carry him to you."

"We're okay," Rasher promised. "Go rest. Take care of yourself. We'll talk later."

"There are so many reports we'll have to redo," the old man said in an anguished tone.

"We'll figure it out," Rasher promised.

Just then the general arrived with her retinue. Rasher glanced from her to Gubbins to his secretary. He was overjoyed they had all survived, but he couldn't help wondering at the miracles that had spared them all.

Any one of them could be a glowan changeling. How could he trust anyone?

General Nide pulled her mount to a halt, and Rasher barely caught himself from saluting first. The habit was so deeply ingrained that his hand started moving. He changed the movement into scratching his chin, but the general's eyes followed the move and her stern mouth twitched with the hint of a smile.

She looked down at him and said, "You've made a fine mess of things, haven't you?"

38

SNUFFED BISCUITS

Rasher sighed. He'd known the general didn't approve of him and his team, but pushing him now, on top of everything else, was a really bad idea.

Forcing calm, he said, "General Nide, thank you for reporting so quickly. I hope I can count on you to show the same level of dedication to attending our scheduled meetings in the future."

Her expression hardened, and Commander Moist leaned forward in the saddle and growled, "Watch your tone, soldier."

Rasher met his angry scowl. "Commander, I don't want to have you arrested for insubordination today. We have bigger problems to deal with, but if you ever address me like that again, I'll have you whipped in front of the entire legion."

The big commander's face reddened and he sputtered in rage. General Nide waved him down, her own glare deepening.

"I need you," Rasher told her. "I don't have time to coddle you or deal with your hurt feelings. Our chain of command must be clear and I have to know you're willing to fulfill your oaths to the Reapers, or I have no use for you."

She focused her steely gaze on him. "Captain, you've been a Reaper for less than twenty-four hours."

"Which is twenty-four hours longer than you have, General," he retorted. "Didn't you swear an oath to serve and support the Reapers?"

"Of course we did," she said through gritted teeth.

"Did your oath include following only Reapers you happen to like, or who have dashing smiles?" he continued.

"You may be a Reaper, but I will not allow you to disrespect General Nide," Commander Moist growled.

"I'm surprised you wish to break your oath to the Reapers right when your home town is threatened," Rasher retorted. Commander Moist was related to the Fathar family who ruled Ehverr.

The man reached for his sword. "I've never broken an oath in my life! I'll call you out for that."

"I'm the dueler for the Reaper team," Noops said calmly. "I would be happy to accept your challenge, Commander."

They hadn't actually assigned anyone as their duelist. Rasher hadn't ever imagined they'd need one, but he applauded Noops' decision to position himself that way. It caught the commander by surprise.

"I'd be happy to stand in for you, Commander," Balter said, stepping forward, yellow eyes fixed hungrily on Noops, who looked unfazed by the challenge.

Rasher didn't want anyone dueling, not there in the square moments after so many had senselessly died. "Your oath is to serve the Reapers. We have been chosen and recognized by every level of leadership, the ceremony witnessed by every member of the legions. Are you really going to try to convince the legions that it would be better to mutiny?"

That snuffed their biscuits, and they didn't like it. General Nide motioned the commander to calm down and gestured Balter back.

"Let me make this abundantly clear," she said. "If at any time I believe your choices are endangering the lives of the men and women entrusted to me, I will declare you all possessed by glowan spirits and order your immediate execution."

That could have gone better. Rasher changed tactics and smiled. "Now that we've all traded threats and proven just how committed we are to the cause, I think we can get down to business. Thank you for confirming your loyalties."

Gubbins laughed, General Nide snorted, and thankfully most of the command staff looked amused.

Commander Moist banged a meaty fist on the pommel, making his mount prance to one side and smiled. "By Arkadas' wrath, Captain. You've earned your bacon from Domuz today."

"Thank you. General, know that the Reapers are ready and eager to work with you and the legion commanders to save Rubric and stop another apocalypse. We have work to do."

"Very well. I believe we understand each other," General Nide said, once again calm.

"What happened at South Gate?" Rasher asked.

"We nearly got caught in a parmesan explosion," Commander Moist said with a shiver, his anger evaporating.

General Nide added, "If we hadn't stopped to deal with a horse with a thrown shoe, we would have been right in the middle of the blast radius."

"And if we had arrived on time for our meeting, we would have died right here," Rasher said, gesturing toward the Heart.

"You set the time," Commander Moist pointed out. "And yet you conveniently arrive just late enough to avoid the disaster."

"What are you implying?" Kucheesa demanded.

Rasher waved her back. "The same thing we could imply about you skipping a meeting you were supposed to be in and miraculously avoiding another apparent assassination attempt. Or the same thing we could imply about Gubbins stepping out of the meeting just in time to miss the explosion, or my secretary of being in a basement storeroom instead of his office."

He held the general's gaze and said, "We could waste a lot of time accusing each other, but we have new intelligence and a bigger problem."

He gestured at Alevler, who had sat up during their discussion. The muffin mage shrank down under the new attention. Rasher motioned the general and her closest staff to dismount and join them, ordering Balter and his elite troop to keep everyone else back.

"What is this?" General Nide asked.

"Tell them what you told us," Rasher ordered Alevler.

Reluctantly, the muffin mage did. Rasher watched their expressions as they listened to the amazing tale, but could not glean any hints that any of them knew of the plot in advance.

When Alevler finished, General Nide slammed one fist into her other palm, the only outward sign of her frustration. "I can't believe it."

"We've worked with those Reapers for years," Commander Moist added. "They were all the best of the best. No way any of them would have turned against us."

"I refuse to believe they would betray us," General Nide added.

"What if those contracts had other stipulations we don't know about?" Bibble asked.

Rasher hadn't even considered that. The possibilities were horrible.

"They would die before betraying the legions," Commander Moist insisted.

"Sumwinkle did," Kucheesa said softly.

"There's more I've learned," Rasher said. "It will help clarify what's going on."

He took a moment to explain what they'd learned from the captured Dollop Aberdeen, the chase of the cloaked figures they suspected were Clootie Dumpling and Juusto Panjandrum, and his clash with Otamot.

Silence hung around them for a moment as they absorbed everything.

"So we have a glowan changeling among us," General Nide said, coming to the same conclusion Rasher had.

"It's the only possibility that makes sense," he agreed.

Commander Moist grunted. "I can barely believe any of the Reapers could be turned, but given enough time, a glowan could work a glamour over the strongest mind."

"And they did it right here among us," Rasher said. "Whoever we are dealing with, they have access, know our schedules, and have had time to work their evil spells."

"So it could be any of us," Gubbins said.

"Perhaps," Rasher said. "Ferreting out this enemy is our top priority after capturing Clootie, Juusto, and Otamot."

"We will notify all sentries to watch for them," Commander Moist promised.

"The Acropolis Watch is already on the hunt," Noops added.

Bibble said, "We need to get word to Nutmeg Hill too. Otamot might return to the palace."

Unlikely, but he was right. Rasher said, "Our next highest priority is to marshal the legions. All of the attacks we've suffered have been designed to delay our mobilization. Clearly the glowan fear us, so we have to prepare to march. I want the legions prepared to begin the march tomorrow."

That triggered a round of surprised exclamations from the commanders and his team.

Kucheesa exclaimed, "But what about the missing battle cuisine?"

"And the loss of the healing supplies," Bibble added.

General Nide was watching Rasher carefully, her expression hard to read. She nodded toward the devastation around them. "This will not be all cleaned up by tomorrow, let alone the mess at South gate."

"We can't wait. Our primary mission is to succor Ehverr. We're being attacked by Reapers. Think about that. This is their home too. They know all the secrets, and they've had time to prepare."

As they considered that, he added, "We may or may not be able to stop them here, but if we stay, they'll keep hitting us until they weaken us to the point we become combat ineffective. We need to mobilize."

"He's right," Commander Moist said, looking astounded that he was agreeing with Rasher. "We can harden the defenses around our mobile camps."

General Nide surprised Rasher by smiling. "I agree, Captain. We will oversee the mobilization. Our combat-ready forces are reduced. We won't have cheese wizards or confectioners. We will have no performance-enhancing sugars or sugar bombs, which have usually proven particularly effective against glowan."

Commander Xigua Whomst spoke up. "Our healing supplies are critically low, along with many of our other food stockpiles, and only a fraction of our siege weapons are operational."

He was a big, grizzled fellow, middle-aged, with a strong accent from the coastal regions of Oxter. He was in charge of the legion siege corps, and relating the sorry state of their siege weapons visibly pained him.

"Do we have any?" Rasher asked.

Commander Whomst grunted. "I've requisitioned some from the Afitur legions and appealed directly to the Juscant and Fathar families for any they can spare. I'll get something, but it won't be a full complement, not by dawn tomorrow."

"I'll take care of informing the Junior Toque of our suspicions about the missing Reapers and Otamot," Gubbins promised.

"Delicately," General Nide urged. "An accusation this severe . . ."

Gubbins nodded. "Understood."

"They may not be working alone," Rasher said. "But they are the key."

"We'll get the mobilization underway," Commander Moist promised. "We recommend marching every available resource at best possible speed to Ehverr to rout the Gloaming hordes before the city falls."

Rasher agreed, but was surprised when Bibble said, "About that. I feel like I'm missing something."

"Like what?" Commander Moist asked.

"We need to succor Ehverr, but I'm not sure we should rush headlong in that direction without considering other potential dangers."

"What do you mean?" General Nide asked.

Bibble scratched his dirty beard thoughtfully. "Reports tell us that the greatest Gloaming horde of all time attacked Ehverr unawares, and although parts of the city were temporarily breached, the defenders have successfully withstood every assault."

"Ballads will be sung of their bravery," Commander Moist said proudly.

"Probably," Bibble agreed. "But we also hear of every other sizable garrison along the border suffering surprise attacks while all of the magical stockpiles have been simultaneously stolen from every large storage facility. We've also suffered unprecedented attacks right here in the Acropolis."

"Exactly. We need to hurry," Commander Moist said, but Rasher was starting to think Bibble might be onto something.

"The point is," Bibble said calmly. "With such an obviously high level of planning and coordination, why have they failed at every turn? How could they not have taken at least the outer city of Ehverr? How could every outpost withstand all of these surprise attacks?"

That got them all thinking. Rasher continued the thread. "You're suggesting that maybe they intended to fail?"

"Not even the Gloaming hordes are that stupid," one of the officers said.

"I'd never assume they might be stupid, not after planning such an extensive campaign," Bibble said. "I just wonder if perhaps there are objectives in play that we have not yet realized."

"Like all of this is some kind of smokescreen for some other impending attack?" General Nide asked.

"Perhaps."

That was a scary thought. Rasher said, "I see your point, but I can't imagine they have other armies large enough to threaten major cities."

"No," General Nide agreed. "They've already exceeded our maximum estimates. Given their unexpected numbers on top of specific reports of individual glowan confirmed to be present within their forces, it appears we are facing for the first time the combined might of both the Savory and Bitter glowan courts."

Rasher had come to the same conclusion, but Quarce said, "I find that hard to believe."

His homeland of Gravlax lay immediately to the east of Whisternfeet and they interacted with the glowan far more than men from Rubric. They even carried on trade with the less-aggressive Savory Court and had battled the evil Bitter Court glowan more than anyone.

"I would have thought the same thing," General Nide admitted. "But the evidence is overwhelming. For some reason, they've set aside their normal animosity and decided to work together."

"What would drive them to do that?" Rasher asked.

One of the reasons the glowan had never proved as dire a threat as they might have was that the Savory and Bitter courts usually warred more with each other than their neighbors.

"We do not know yet," Commander Moist admitted. "If we can figure that out, we might finally understand how to best counter them."

"Have the Godwottery Patrol been informed?" Quarce asked.

"Indeed," General Nide confirmed. "Unfortunately, it appears most of the Godwottery Patrol was trapped in Piffle with the garrison when it was attacked."

"They'll rout the glowan infesting that area," Quarce said confidently.

"Godwottery Patrol?" Kucheesa asked.

Quarce said, "Elite anti-glowan special forces and spies. They manage the Gravlax border with Whisternfeet. No unit knows more about fighting glowan than the Godwottery."

"I wish we had some of them with us," Rasher muttered.

"We've requested a company," Commander Moist said. "Unfortunately, even if they free Piffle tomorrow, they may not arrive in time to help us rout the Gloaming horde around Ehverr. I'm afraid we're it."

"And we are fairly certain we have accounted for all but a very few glowan," General Nide added. "I can't believe we could be wrong by a much larger margin."

"So any additional objectives can't be large military targets," Bibble said. "What does that leave us?"

"Targeted attacks by special forces, like the assaults we're facing here in the Acropolis," Kucheesa piped in.

Commander Moist said, "The entire city is on high alert. With what we've learned today, the rest of the original Reapers will be quarantined and effectively blockaded. They will no longer be able to pose any significant threat."

That seemed an optimistic assessment. Then again, outside of the Acropolis forces, the city of Afitur had four legions for city defense, plus the Watch, plus the largest contingents of the most powerful wizards, mages, and shamans in the empire. No one ever considered Afitur a viable target. It would be suicide to attack the heart of the empire.

And yet the enemy was still at large, still harrying them. And they'd managed to subvert some of the very Reapers against their own people.

"What about special targets?" Rasher asked.

General Nide shook her head. "The Watch has quadrupled the guard at Nutmeg Hill and throughout the Food Court. The Imperial Chef, the Sous Chef, and all of the ruling ambassadors have enhanced security."

"So we continue with the mobilization plan, but keep an open mind about potential secondary objectives the glowan may be after," Kucheesa reiterated.

"We have to," General Nide confirmed. "Despite any potential danger elsewhere, the hordes at Ehverr must be dealt with first. Even if the city were not in imminent danger of falling, the horde has to go."

Commander Moist added, "Spring planting is upon us, and the seed caravans need to leave the Drupe wizard compound within the next ten days or risk a late planting."

Of course. Rasher had forgotten about that. He exchanged a look with the rest of the team. Bibble and Quarce both looked grave and Noops was nodding to himself.

Kucheesa exclaimed, "They haven't left yet? How is that possible? The caravans should have crossed the Gewgaw weeks ago."

"Usually, yes," Commander Moist replied. "But the Sons of the Seed encountered some kind of delays this winter preparing the crop. There are significant levels of adverse meteorological forces building this year, which required an entire magnitude of additional magic to be applied to the seeds before they could be released."

That didn't sound good. Rasher asked, "What kind of delays?"

General Nide said, "It's an issue that's becoming more common than anyone likes to admit. The Sons of the Seed imbue the seeds with the power to ensure plentiful harvests, which can tweak the weather to ensure optimal growing conditions."

"They've developed the techniques over generations," another officer said. He looked young and glanced toward the rubble where the Heart had stood. "We had one commander who was an expert in the subject, but he was . . ." He trailed off, wiping at his eyes.

General Nide said, "His loss is tragic. He reported to me that the Sons of the Seed have realized in recent years that using their powers to guarantee plentiful harvests does not remove adverse weather, but just pushes it out."

"They've been pushing it out a long time," Bibble said.

She nodded. "Apparently, doing that year after year has created a magnifying effect."

Whoa. That was news to Rasher, and the ramifications seemed as severe as anything the Gloaming hordes represented.

Bibble exclaimed, "Wait, you're saying that by imbuing the seeds with the power of a good harvest, it pushes back bad weather, which makes that bad weather worse."

"And we've been doing that for generations?" Kucheesa added, looking pale.

Commander Moist nodded. "But the chefs of the High Kitchen have been working with the drupe wizards and the Sons of the Seed to develop new recipes to help."

That eased some of his worries. The Baker's Dozen who led the High Kitchen were the most senior chefs. Led by the Sous Chef himself, they were the keepers of the master cookbook. If anyone could develop the right recipes to reverse the threat, they could do it.

"How many people know about this?" Rasher asked.

"Very few, and we are all under strict orders from the Imperial Chef himself to keep it that way," General Nide stated, fixing them with a warning stare. "Severe penalties are affixed to breaking this decree."

Rasher rubbed his temples where his headache was growing worse. He'd been mostly worried about the Gloaming hordes, but had never considered danger to the harvest.

The promise of plentiful harvests was one of the greatest points of leverage Rubric had over its vassal nations. The entire empire depended on those harvests to feed its people and fuel their guilds.

For the first time, Rasher wondered if the wondrous blessing of guaranteed harvests might instead become a curse. Like a delicious cheesy bacon casserole touched by an angry cheese wizard in secret.

"The drupe wizards and chefs will solve that problem," General Nide promised. "Our job is to defeat the Gloaming hordes and clear the path for the caravans to move."

"I concur," Rasher said.

The General sighed and rubbed her temples. "Let me be clear, Captain. I applaud your attempts to step into far larger shoes, but we lack time to train your team properly. I will support your positions as Reapers, but I ask you to leave the running of this campaign to me and my staff. We know what we're doing, and we don't have time for you to muck anything up."

He was surprised when Noops spoke for the first time. "General, it sounds like you fear we are not qualified for the command we've been assigned."

"That's exactly what I'm saying."

Noops rubbed his chin. "With all due respect, General, when has qualification ever been a requirement for command?"

"What?" she snapped, flushing with anger.

Rasher was so surprised he couldn't think of a good response fast enough to cut Noops off.

"Well, ma'am, you could ask any soldier in the legions about incompetent officers who have made their lives miserable. Every one of them would have tales to tell. I've always thought it was one of those forced traditions that never made sense, but everyone feels they have to keep following anyway. Like eating lettuce with a fork."

She blinked at him a couple of times. Commander Moist growled, "Look here, soldier—"

Kucheesa cut him off. "He's now the Reaper shovel knight."

The general blustered, "I don't care what happens in some other forces, but in this army, officers have to be qualified for their positions."

"You might want to tell them about that one of these days," Noops responded calmly.

Rasher was enjoying how Noops had sidelined her objections, but they needed to move the conversation back to more productive ground or the general was going to dig in her heels and make life very difficult.

The general might not be wrong in doubting them, but he could not allow them to codify that doubt. He knew all too well that a team that doubted itself was guaranteed to fail.

"General, like you said, we lack time. We've already approved the plan to move out, and are happy to leave the day-to-day leadership of the march in the hands of your officers. That should leave us time to explore how to best work together, to train as a unit, and to train jointly with the Gleaners. Hopefully we can take existing plans you developed with the previous team and alter them to fit our new reality."

That mollified her a little, but Commander Moist said, "Your team is woefully underrepresented."

"Indeed," Rasher acknowledged. They should have at least eight more members, and no amount of posturing was going to fill that gap.

"That's why the Gleaners unit was instituted, after all, right?" Bibble asked.

"Indeed," General Nide echoed Rasher.

"Very well. We look forward to your recommendations," Rasher said.

He expected the general to grow annoyed again by the response. Instead she only said, "We'll have a list ready for your review by tomorrow evening. We can meet in our first mobile camp."

"In the meantime, assign what troops you can to the clean-up efforts," Rasher said. "Leave Balter and his fist with us."

"What are you going to do?" Commander Moist asked.

"We're going to hunt Reapers."

39

The Smallest Mistakes Can Have the Greatest Consequences

After the general and her commanders left, already issuing orders to their many underlings, Rasher surveyed the disaster scene around them. How many had died? How many of the wounded would perish due to lack of healing supplies?

"Are you sure mobilizing now is the best idea?" Bibble asked softly.

Rasher nodded. "If we don't, I fear we'll get so distracted hunting the conspirators and the glowan that we'll never march, and that's exactly what the enemy wants from us."

Like rule number fifty said, when in over one's head, what's a little more depth?

But he said, "We need to find out if Redael survived."

"She did," Gubbins interjected. "I saw her helping to tend to other wounded kitchen staff, even though her arm was in a sling."

"Good," Rasher said. "I know timing isn't great, but we're going to need a big breakfast in the morning."

"Should that be our main focus?" Kucheesa asked.

Rasher shrugged. "When the going gets tough, make sure to eat a big breakfast." That was related to rule number thirty-six.

Bibble said, "Well, while we figure out where to begin our hunt for glowan, I have a mixture that should help us withstand glowan glamours."

"Good idea, but what about that mist of darkness like they used in the palace?" Kucheesa asked.

"I'm not as familiar with that, but will see what I can do," he promised.

Rasher was glad for every advantage they could get. They all could have easily died in the palace. He thought of his crumbhorn strapped to his back. How had that worked so well against the glowan?

The power his crumbhorn seemed to possess over the glowan might prove vital, but he didn't like not understanding why it worked. For the life of him he could not remember what music he'd played. The glamour had left the memory weird and fuzzy.

They'd gotten lucky. They could not afford to count on luck in the future.

So many hadn't shared that luck. His eyes drifted to the line of cloth-draped shapes along one side of the square. It was already far too long, and work crews were barely digging into the rubble. How many more dead would they find?

Gubbins interrupted his thoughts. "Captain, there is much to do, but may I ask where you plan to begin the hunt for the elusive enemy?"

"Yeah, they got away," Quarce added. "They could be across the Acropolis already."

Rasher hoped they were, but somehow doubted they'd go too far. The glowan controlling them had to know the noose was closing. After successful attacks against the Heart and South Gate, he bet they would push forward, trying to wreak as much havoc as possible before the Acropolis defenses could solidify and begin a systematic search for the corrupted Reapers.

"We need to identify who else might have had enough access for a glowan changeling to target them. Finding the glowan is our most important goal."

"As you consider the possibilities, I can offer a little assistance," Gubbins said with a smile, lowering his satchel to the ground. "The real reason I went to the other admin building was to accept this."

He opened the satchel and began extracting bundles wrapped in cloth, laying each one carefully on the stone ground. Rasher had to admit he was intrigued as they all gathered around Gubbins.

"We discussed the fact that each Reaper was given several specialty personal defense items. This is the new batch."

He began to unwrap them, revealing first a cluster of small, red cubes that jiggled as he moved them.

"Gelatin defensive bubbles," Gubbins explained, handing them each one. The cube was barely two inches across, cool to the touch, and spongy.

Bibble laughed. "I've heard of these, but never seen one. They explosively expand into a protective globe around whoever is carrying it at the moment of severe impact."

"Correct," Gubbins said. "They are very effective against impact injuries from events like falls or crashes."

Next came squat carrots. "Gravity spikes. Throw these to the ground at someone's feet to temporarily reverse gravity in a one-foot-square space. It'll send anyone or anything in that space tumbling away into the air."

Rasher glanced at Kucheesa, who was eyeing her carrot with a glint in her eye. He bet if she dropped that at her own feet, she could soar halfway across the Acropolis. They needed to get their hands on another of those oca tubers. With a few of those, he bet she could just about manage actual flight.

Tiny bandoliers of mini muffins came next. They could be secured around arms or hats, and each mini muffin could be triggered by simply squeezing its base. "These are potent missiles. They'll fly up to a hundred feet in a couple seconds," Gubbins warned. "And they detonate as big as a sheet cake."

Rasher whistled softly as he carefully secured his around his left forearm. He'd shift them to his hat once he found one.

His hat. That thought triggered an idea, and as Gubbins continued to speak, Rasher unleashed a full slice of chewy bacon onto it, considering it in the back of his mind.

They received small, round cookies that contained concentrated confectioner dazzle bursts, sufficient to stun or disorient several enemies, especially if tossed into an enclosed space like a room. After that came compact crabcake emergency beacons that emitted a soft blue light, and half a dozen evaporated milk first-aid packets.

"String cheese," Gubbins said, lifting cigar-shaped containers. "These contain a potent acid that can dissolve locks and metal. Use them with caution."

Finally they received cubes of fried fish in paper wrappers that granted extreme breath holding for up to twenty minutes.

"These are amazing!" Quarce laughed.

"Hopefully no one here is too enthusiastic of a hugger," Noops added with a smile.

"Now we're armed, we need to get you a hat," Kucheesa told Rasher.

"I think I know just where to find one," he said. "Come on."

As they crossed the square toward the pantry-facade admin building being used to house wounded, Balter and his warriors trotted up. Behind Balter and his squad of yellow-eyed tiger-enhanced warriors came a squad of massive soldiers with enormous muscles and black eyes of bear enhancements. Beside them trotted a squad with the hardened skin of rhino enhancements.

A squad of wolf-enhanced Gleaners prowled at the back of the fist, blue eyes bright. Another squad, made up of all women with amber lion eyes, caught up with the rest of the Fist just as Balter stopped facing Rasher.

"Gleaners reporting for duty," Balter said, looking straight ahead and not quite focused on Rasher. The Gleaners all saluted, slamming fists to armored chests in perfect unison. They were an impressive sight.

"Stay close. I've got one thing to do, then we begin the hunt for the glowan responsible for causing all this."

Balter gave him a predatory smile, and his squads fell into step behind them.

"Where are we going?" Kucheesa asked, hurrying to keep up with Rasher's fast pace.

"The one person who will know if anyone refused to follow our orders to change hats," Rasher said.

Bibble said, "Shemo? I hope he accepted healing after he left us. He's also the only one who knows where my family is."

A steady stream of people moved in and out of the admin building where Rasher had seen Shemo carried to. It looked like many of the wounded had been placed in there. Bibble extracted three little pouches of spices, mixed them, then added them to a small bottle of cold tea he kept in one of his deepest coat pockets.

"Drink," he urged them.

"What is it?" Kucheesa asked before sipping. Her eyes widened and she coughed.

"It's a bit potent," Bibble apologized. "No time for careful taste doctoring.

"I like it," Quarce said after taking a sip. "We'll have to discuss how you got that flavor."

"Happy to, as soon as we have time."

When Rasher took a sip, he gasped at the fiery spice coursing down his throat and through his body. A bit potent indeed.

"This should help keep our minds alert," Bibble promised.

"Thank you. Hopefully it won't be necessary, but I like being prepared," Rasher said, then led them into the building.

Behind him, Noops took a long sip and sighed. "Tea that good reflects well on your parentage."

The inside of the building was packed, so Rasher ordered Balter and his men to wait outside and keep a sharp eye out for suspicious activity. It took only a moment to inquire about Shemo. They found him in a private room on the second floor.

Rasher expected him to be sleeping, but Shemo answered his knock immediately. The room had been an office, but all the furniture had been piled in one corner, making room for a simple medical cot and a chair beside the bed. A lantern placed precariously atop the pile of furniture cast a warm glow over the room.

Shemo Medjamo, Rasher's private secretary, sat propped on several pillows. He was dressed in a white nightshirt, his hair still matted with blood.

Rasher rushed to him. "Are you all right? Did you finally let a healer help you?"

"I am fine, Captain. Thank you for asking," Shemo said, saluting smartly and trying to rise.

Rasher motioned him back down. "Please dispense with formalities today. You're injured."

"Again, thank you, Captain," the old man said, settling back. "I am afraid I may need a day or two to compile the reports you requested."

Rasher chuckled. The man's dedication was remarkable.

Bibble said, "I need to know where my family is."

"They are safe," Shemo assured him. "As Captain Dilskin ordered, I had them secretly moved to a secure location."

"I'm afraid the location may be compromised," Rasher said. He briefly recounted their encounter in the palace.

"Incredible," Shemo said, looking from Rasher to each of the members of the team, his expression fascinated. "May I see your instrument, Captain?"

That was a surprising breach of etiquette, but Rasher didn't mind. Even Shemo could be forgiven a little slip when suffering a head wound. He quickly pulled the crumbhorn from his back and handed it over.

His secretary examined the instrument carefully, then placed it on the sheet in front of him. "I am astonished by your resourcefulness, Captain. Few know of glowan susceptibility to music, but I've never heard of any score powerful enough to so mightily affect a close general to a fell lord of the Bitter court. The knowledge of this secret would be worth a fortune in favors from the queen herself."

Bibble said, "We're not sure exactly what happened, but hopefully we won't need it in the future. I've already—"

Rasher cut him off, his mind racing as several clues clicked into place. "An interesting turn of phrase, Shemo. I had no idea the changeling was a glowan general. How did you?"

For a second, everyone froze.

Then Noops snatched for his shovel just as Rasher raised his battle staff.

The secretary's face started glowing, and an invisible force pushed Rasher back. Beside him, Noops grunted, his shovel dipping toward the ground. The rest of the team gasped under the weight of the glamour.

Patting the crumbhorn, Shemo said, "I blame the injuries. I needed to be injured in the blast to avoid suspicion, but I hadn't expected to suffer so much from the need to refrain from repairing it."

"That's why you refused healing," Rasher forced through clumsy lips. "A milk mage might have recognized you for what you were."

"Perhaps. The risk was low, but enough that I thought it prudent to be cautious. It appears I shouldn't have bothered." He sighed. "I'm impressed you caught that one little slip, Captain. I'm afraid I'll have to accelerate my plans."

"You?" Kucheesa gasped weakly.

The force of the glamour increased, pressing against them. It crept around Rasher's mind like a slowly rising dough seeking to block out the air. This time however, the fires of Bibble's spice burned back the glamour and his mind remained clear.

Noops' shovel quivered and rose an inch, but Rasher said, "Why can't we fight this?"

Shemo chuckled. "Only the strongest minds can fight my glamour. You are new Reapers, not yet grown into your full strength."

The rest of the team seem to understand that Rasher did not want to reveal that the glamour was not totally incapacitating them. He still felt lethargic, but was sure he could move when he needed to.

"You beguiled the other Reapers, didn't you?"

Shemo's smile widened, and his teeth became pointed. "They were truly strong, and it took long, subtle prodding to move them into position. Do you think the recent addendums that subverted the team were the first secret clauses I slipped into the documents?"

Rasher's rage began to grow. The smug glowan spy had wreaked horrible destruction among people who had trusted him. He'd subverted three of the Reapers and forced them to fight against the central purpose of their lives.

"I still control two of them," Shemo continued proudly. "The Reapers who could stand against armies fell to my machinations."

He sighed again. "My influence is reinforced by the very magic foods they would wield against my people. Their cheeses and sugars weaken their minds and keep them pliable. Unfortunately that hold will slip if I maintain my focus on you for too long. I'm afraid that means I won't have much time to use you the way I had planned to. I'm afraid you poor fools will have to make do with a quick death."

Such a masterfully planned assault. Shemo was positioned perfectly to know all of the Reaper plans. He ran most of the day-to-day operations in the Heart. He would know what they were doing and when they were doing it. Rasher could only guess that one of these days they would find the old secretary's body in a shallow grave somewhere.

"My family," Bibble groaned, taking half a step closer.

Shemo looked impressed. "I underestimated how much family ties would motivate you. Pity we won't have time to leverage that connection. My general's agents already requested their destruction and I had no reason to deny the request."

He regarded them with pride. "I wonder that my people feared you so much. You tear yourselves apart even as we plan our vengeance. I'm amazed we haven't witnessed your destruction by your own hands already."

"Where are they?" Bibble growled.

"You should worry about yourself," Shemo said, his expression turning predatory. "Your family will either disappear from the safehouse, or one more random building will burn down near South gate. I doubt anyone will even notice."

"Captain," Bibble said.

"Good-bye, Reapers," Shemo purred. "Know that your vaunted leaders will drown in their own filth."

Time to move. They had to get to South Gate. Rasher straightened and pointed the tip of his staff at Shemo. "You're a clever guy, but your games are over."

Surprised, Shemo focused on Rasher, his eyes glowing bright yellow. The glamour intensified, and Rasher swayed under the onslaught. If not for the fire of Bibble's spices, he would have certainly fallen.

Noops' shovel swept forward just as Kucheesa threw a knife. The shovel slammed Shemo back against the wall, severing his left arm, and the knife sunk deep into his shoulder. Blood sprayed across the wall, but Rasher kept his gaze on the changeling's eyes.

Shemo screamed, and the glamour winked out. The others surged toward the injured changeling, but Bibble shouted, "Stop!"

He lunged forward as Shemo began to softly glow. "Oh, no you don't."

Bibble shoved a little bag up the changeling's nose and squeezed hard. Little puffs of black powder wafted out both sides and Rasher distinctly smelled pepper.

Shemo's eyes widened, then he explosively sneezed. The glow faded as he sneezed again and again, his body wracked with convulsions.

Bibble seized him by the hair and shouted, "Where are they? Which building?"

It took a moment for the sneezing to subside. Shemo gasped weakly for breath, staring in fear up at Bibble. "What did you do?"

The usually calm Bibble was flushed with rage. His voice turned deadly and he growled, "I will tear you apart piece by piece, glowan, unless you answer my question right now."

He reached for another bag of spices, but Shemo gasped, "The Endless Desserts guest inn near South gate."

"Bind him," Rasher ordered.

"But what if he changes?" Kucheesa asked.

That was a really good question. Rasher wasn't sure how to effectively bind a changeling. He needed to keep Shemo for interrogation. Maybe if he surrounded the changeling with Balter's men they could keep him corralled until he could round up a chef who knew the recipes to hold him.

Shemo suddenly glowed with bright sparkles of light and his body changed into a huge, black, snarling wolf. Bibble stumbled back with a cry while Kucheesa, Noops, and Quarce all lunged.

"Wait!" Rasher shouted.

Too late.

Noops clove the creature's head with his shovel at the same time Quarce smashed it in the shoulder with his expanded hammer. A second later, Kucheesa drove a dagger into its heart.

Rasher cursed softly, averting his gaze from the gore spurting from the dying creature before he suffered another episode. He couldn't afford to waste any time.

They really needed to learn how to capture changelings. They couldn't keep killing them immediately. They needed intelligence.

"That could have gone better," Noops commented as he wiped his shovel on the sheets.

"We have to go!" Bibble cried, rushing for the door.

Rasher ran after him. He was right, they needed to get to that guest inn before more innocents died.

Outside, Balter and Gubbins were rushing toward the door. At first, Rasher thought maybe he'd heard the shouting inside, but then he noticed commotion across the square. Soldiers who had been tasked with helping the wounded were rushing toward the east side of the square, buckling on armor and weapons.

"Captain!" Balter cried. "East gate is under attack!"

"What's going on?" Rasher asked just as the distant alarm towers began tolling.

"Enemy forces," Balter said. "Numbers unknown, but we need to go now. They need aid."

"How can they have an army?" Kucheesa asked.

Rasher wasn't sure, but Balter was right. They couldn't ignore an assault on East Gate. Was that what Shemo had been saying when he warned they would die in their own filth?

"My family," Bibble protested.

Rasher made a choice. "Bibble, you and Quarce take a squad of Gleaners and get to your family. The rest of us will head to East gate, assess the threat, and assist with the defense."

He turned to Gubbins. "Please get word to Kitan to stay on Nutmeg Hill. The glowan threatened her as well as Bibble's family."

"Of course," Gubbins said.

In seconds, they were all racing out of the square in different directions. Rasher glanced back once at the devastation of the Heart and hardened his resolve.

The enemy had picked a very bad time to try a frontal assault. The legions were spoiling for a fight, and he planned to lead them from the front.

40

FOOD FIGHT EXTREME EDITION

They reached East Gate within minutes after Balter procured horses for Rasher's small team. His enhanced warriors kept pace through the fast gallop through the Acropolis, shouting for everyone to make way.

Legionnaires were boiling out of barracks, with officers shouting them into ranks while wizards, mages, and shamans scrambled to prepare their limited food stockpiles. The air rang with tumultuous noise, while the constant pealing of the alarm bells overshadowed everything, punctuated regularly by the boom towers shouting the call to arms.

Rasher pulled his horse to a stop in the square just inside the huge gate, which was already closed and sealed. Platters of reinforcements raced up the stairs toward the top of the wall to join the ranks of men and women already gathered there paused to cheer their arrival.

"The Reapers are here!" Others took up the call along the wall, and the shout was repeated over and over.

"Well, we've bolstered morale at least," Kucheesa said, then eyed Noops. "Wish we had time for some better armor too."

Balter heard her and snapped a finger, pointing at the tall woman who led the female wolf-enhanced squad. She led her squad away at a run. Balter said, "We'll see what we can find."

Rasher was impressed. If Balter remained so dedicated, he might just have to revise his opinion of the man.

"Reapers!" a soldier in a lieutenant's hat cried, rushing up to them. "The wall commander invites you to join him at the command tower immediately."

"What is the status?" Rasher asked.

"Giant possessed statue has been smashing wagons and scattering civilians in the square."

"Did you say a giant possessed statue?" Kucheesa asked, eyes wide.

He nodded. "Yes, ma'am. It appears glowan possessed the statue of Tohum in the square. It knocked a rail car from the Reaper line, and all other trains have been paused."

Not good. That statue was huge. "Passengers or cargo?" Rasher asked, shuddering to think of the casualty count if the monster had caught a passenger car.

"Cargo, thank the gods," said the lieutenant.

Noops frowned at that. "Why waste time with collateral targets? It could have hit the wall by now."

"Maybe it's waiting for reinforcements," the lieutenant suggested.

"But we're getting reinforcements too," Kucheesa pointed out.

"I hope they arrive soon," the lieutenant said. "We've gotten enough soldiers to reinforce the lines atop the wall, but our contingent of guilds is still low. We do have one chef with a single cart, but . . ."

He hesitated before adding, "Sir, we're critically low on battle cuisine. Looks like almost all the foodstuffs were rotated out yesterday, but the replacement supplies were delayed."

"Just like everywhere else," Kucheesa grumbled.

Rasher said, "I hadn't even considered double-checking the supplies on the wall. I figured it would be unaffected by the other theft."

The lieutenant said, "Uh, we also received word that most of the siege weapons were on scheduled repair this week. They're being reassembled for the mobilization, but all the wall catapults are in warehouses today."

"I wonder if they were caught up in the wood rot sabotage," Noops said.

"Let's hope not," Rasher said. "Maybe we can salvage some of them for the deployment."

"Blackened crumpets," Kucheesa cursed. "It's super annoying when traitors turn out to be this clever."

"This is clearly an assault planned well in advance," Rasher said.

Was that what Shemo had been gloating over? Maybe they were about to finally see more of the forces of the changeling cat general.

With their own forces in disarray and their battle cuisine so low, it was a perfect time to attack.

Rasher took a calming breath. "Very well. We saw guilds mobilizing on our way in. Reinforcements will be here soon."

Whether or not they had much battle cuisine available was another question. He scanned his small team and added, "Noops, take the Gleaners and reinforce defenders on the wall until enough legionnaires arrive to fill in the ranks."

Noops nodded, while Balter gestured his sergeants toward the stairs. Thankfully he didn't make any snide or negative remarks. They had work to do, and duty came first. The Gleaners headed for the stairs with Noops, but Balter stayed with Rasher.

"Kucheesa, go find the chef and take stock of guild resources and foodstuffs. That giant's going to head for the wall soon, and we'll need them to deal with it."

She nodded and rushed up the stairs after the others. Rasher followed, with the lieutenant in tow. He needed to see for himself what they were dealing with.

Rasher hoped he wasn't overlooking anything important. Everyone was looking to him to lead, but he'd only been a Reaper for a day. Still, he knew how important it was for morale for officers to keep up the illusion that they knew what they were doing.

General Nide and her commanders were busy organizing the mobilization. He assumed they'd receive word of the attack. Depending on what kind of forces they faced, he was sure the general would send them more reinforcements.

Probably.

The outer Acropolis wall stood over fifteen feet tall, and ten feet thick, forming a wide platform for defenders. At the top, he paused to scan the scene. The Acropolis outer wall had always seemed perfectly adequate, but suddenly Rasher wished it was twice as high.

"By Karides," Kucheesa whispered nearby as they stared at the towering figure in the square.

The twenty-foot-tall statue of the drupe god Tohum that usually lorded over the center of the plaza outside of East Gate was ponderously walking toward the wall. Somehow glowan fairies had brought it to life. Its stone suit flexed like cloth as the giant moved, and the sound of its enormous body creaking echoed through the square. Each footfall landed with a crashing boom that drowned out the still-clamoring alarm bells.

All the civilians had fled, leaving the huge square empty save for half a dozen smashed carts and wagons. Apparently the giant had decided it was time to assault the wall. The empty square only made the giant seem taller and more menacing. In the distance, crowds of curious onlookers peered from around buildings.

The giant moved with ponderous sluggishness but seemed to be picking up speed. Its eyes had grown enormous and glowed with sinister yellow light. Looking at them made him shiver with dread.

The heroic tales of the Reapers never mentioned the Reaper captain ever feeling small or insignificant, or secretly wishing he could just back away from a fight.

"Can glowan do that?" asked Kucheesa in an awed tone.

The giant reached one enormous hand into its basket and flung handfuls of seeds across the plaza at the wall. Those stone seeds were somehow transformed into actual seeds. Big ones.

As they cascaded down onto the ground and against the wall, they sprouted into creeping vines that spread rapidly up the wall. In seconds, tendrils began snaking over the edge, reaching for the soldiers standing there, wrapping feet and limbs. The wall guard hacked wildly at the fast-growing vines, but many were knocked down, vines lashing out to wrap them up.

Rasher always taught his classes to keep open minds to respond most effectively to enemy tricks. Even he had to blink a couple of times and used a bit of chewy bacon to accelerate his mind to avoid simply staring in dumb amazement.

As centurions barked commands to their legionnaires, Noops and the Gleaners joined the defenders. Noops' shovel sheared through vines better than any of the swords or spears of the other soldiers.

"Find that chef," Rasher called to Kucheesa, snapping her out of her astonished reverie. She flushed, nodded, and hurried toward the nearby tower flanking the gate.

A muffin mage stepped to the front edge of the wall, directly over the gate. His white baking jacket seemed to glow in the afternoon light, and his hat, shaped like a red muffin in a silver baking cup, began to glow with a dangerous, crimson light.

The mage began pulling muffins out of a large paper sack and flinging them down at the fast-spreading vines. The vines had already started digging at the gates, as if to wrench them open. The muffins exploded with brilliant flashes of crimson light and clouds of powdered sugar that disintegrated in brilliant sparkles.

The explosions tore through the vines, ripping them to shreds. The air carried a hint of charred sugar, and soldiers stationed along the wall cheered.

"He can't have more than a couple dozen muffins in that sack," the lieutenant pointed out.

Sure enough, the muffin mage soon ran out, while the giant kept slowly but inexorably casting a new wave of seeds every half minute.

He might have been out of muffins, but the muffin mage leaned over the wall, hands extended. The flames licking at vines all down the wall swelled to new life. The fire, moving like a living thing, snaked along the wall, searing vine after vine in an awe-inspiring display of fire mastery. The latest wave of seeds incinerated before even reaching the wall.

"Wow," Rasher murmured. "I might have to recruit that fellow to the Gleaners."

Usually muffin mages could manage only minor direct control over elemental fire. They needed to use the medium of pastries to work with bigger flames. The energy required from the mage was simply too great.

"Burn them all," a nearby soldier laughed.

As Rasher feared, the mage quickly exhausted himself, and the flames faded to wisps of smoke. The man staggered back and the vines resumed their fast climb.

"Reaper Captain Dilskin," shouted Captain Tenirak Welkin, the wall commander Rasher had met earlier in his offices along with General Nide. "Thank you for coming so quickly."

"Happy to help. Sorry it's not under better circumstances."

"This time we're ready to dish out some payback for the West Gate explosion," Captain Welkin promised.

Rasher nodded, gripping his hand tight. The enemy needed to know they'd lost the element of surprise and the legions were more than willing to meet them in battle.

A trio of spice wizards moved to the front of the wall. They wore standard black-and-white checkered jackets, their hats similar to Bibble's, long hanging pockets bulging with spices. Together they flung mixtures of spices over the wall.

The wind picked up as air rushed in from every direction, smelling sharp and dangerous. The wind strengthened, whipping around the square, and in moments it coalesced into a dark, roaring whirlwind that enveloped the statue.

The air grew heavier and the scent of spices intensified and tasted faintly of peppers. Through the swirling, howling wind, it looked like the outer layer of stone on the possessed statue was crumbling, while seeds the monster was trying to throw were shredded almost instantly.

"I've never heard of that effect," Rasher said.

Captain Welkin said, "I heard it's a recent development. Some kind of pepper and thyme mix."

"I'm glad they've got it, but I don't think it's enough by itself," Rasher said.

The giant monster was still slowly pushing forward, despite the clawing wind tearing at it, screaming like a tea kettle left too long over a fire.

A commotion in the square behind the gate drew his attention. Down on the God's Banquet, an enormous catapult drawn by eight draft horses rumbled up the paved street with an ominous implacability. More soldiers were pressing forward to join the defenders, but they made way for the huge, black-painted catapult. It's massive timbers and enormous basket looked sinister in the sunlight.

"That's the new Juscant prototype," Captain Welkin said.

"I've heard about that one," Rasher said. "Supposed to be three times more powerful than any they've ever produced." They'd won a lot of new investments from important houses with that one.

Balter grinned. "Well, if we can only have one catapult today, I'm glad it's that one."

Rasher nodded and asked, "Captain Welkin, any sign of additional glowan forces?"

"Not yet, Sir. The Afitur city watch has been alerted, and the outer city wall is marshaling in case this giant is being used as a distraction."

"Biggest distraction I've ever heard of," muttered one of his lieutenants.

Kucheesa rushed back toward them with a tournant chef. Together they pushed a tall, rolling steel cart and the chef said, "I've got one cart with twelve trays."

"I'm glad you're here," Rasher said.

Captain Welkin asked, "Have you got any mini muffins?"

"I do. A full tray."

"Someone find me that muffin mage and get those mini muffins upstairs to the roof of the southern tower. We've got archers gathered there, but regular arrows won't accomplish anything against stone."

Immediately a junior officer rushed off to find the muffin mage.

That was a good idea. Even a single cart full of supplies in the hands of a good chef could substantially augment their available power. He could help other guild wizards and mages craft higher forms of battle cuisine.

"What I wouldn't give for a seven-layer cake and a garden salad," muttered another lieutenant, and Rasher had to agree. A good vegetable assault could literally level the battlefield.

A moment later, just as the boom towers shouted another warning of attack, the muffin mage arrived to get the tray of muffins. Although still looking tired, he grinned and said, "Poppy seed. We've got a chance now, Captain!"

He rushed toward the nearby tower, and a moment later arrows began to fly from the roof. Instead of regular tips, the arrows had muffins nestled into tiny muffin tins screwed into the ends of the shafts.

Those enhanced arrows rained down over the monster with explosions that tore chunks of stone away. At first, Rasher felt a flash of hope, but it fell when he realized the tiny explosions didn't seem to inflict any real damage.

"How can we stop a living statue?" Kucheesa demanded.

Rasher said, "We beat it to dust if we have to, but I'm hoping one of the guilds can find its magical weakness."

"We could send a troop into the plaza to attack its legs," Captain Welkin said.

"We'll save that option for later," Rasher decided. If they had a full cohort of dwarves with hammers, they could well destroy the thing, but the wall guard would probably just get stomped flat.

Balter said, "Sir, going for the legs is a good idea. What if we wrapped them in chains? Trip it up and disable it. Then take hammers to its face."

That was a better plan. "Do we have chains strong enough?"

"Northern gate tower should have some," Captain Welkin said.

"Do it," Rasher decided. "Commandeer whatever or whoever you need. Let me know when you're ready."

Balter flashed a predatory grin as he saluted, this time lacking the hesitation he'd shown before. "We'll show these glowan what it means to tangle with the legions."

That was a good line. As Balter ran down the wall, Rasher dared hope they could find a way to work together. Balter had a lot of great skills, and they would need all of them when they faced the main horde.

A trio of vegetable shamans rushed up the stairs to the wall, along with three drupe wizards. The vegetable shamans wore low-profile, rounded caps with front brims. The white caps were covered in bright emblems representing the most common and powerful vegetables. As usual, the drupe wizards wore tall, pointy hats with wide brims, festooned with images of fruits and nuts all up the crowns.

"Can you counter these infernal vines?" Rasher demanded when the newcomers reached them.

With the help of Noops and the Gleaner squads, the legionnaires were holding their own against the vine attacks, but the constant pressure made it difficult for anyone to prepare for the arrival of the huge statue.

The leader of the drupe wizards was a tough-looking, middle-aged fellow, dressed in the usual drupe wizard mottled-green jacket. He saluted and gestured his two assistants, a young man and a young woman, to the edge of the wall. They cast their own handfuls of seeds over the wall and stood there, hands extended, brows furrowed.

Nothing happened.

Then a vine reared over the wall and swatted the young woman across the face, sending her tall hat flying off the wall. She screamed and collapsed. The other two drupe wizards dragged her back as soldiers rushed in to sever the nasty vine.

"I've never seen anything like this," the lead drupe wizard said as his young assistant tended to the girl, assisted by a senior milk mage who appeared next to them in a flash.

"Explain," Rasher said.

"The creature wields seed magic like a club. It's incredible. I've heard rumors of glowan shamans maybe accessing such potent magic, but only in short bursts."

"So they might exhaust themselves soon too," Kucheesa guessed.

"Let us hope so," Rasher said.

Nearby, the vegetable shamans were huddled over a portable stove the chef had pulled from the guard tower. One of them produced a frying pan, added some oil from a stoppered jug, and then dumped in a vegetable medley from a pouch.

The chef conferred with them as they worked and opened another drawer on his cart. It was full of chopped vegetables, spices, herbs, and sauces. He extracted several, and the shamans added them to the mix, looking pleased.

"Thank the gods we've got a chef who knows his business," Captain Welkin muttered.

Rasher eyed their fire, wishing for his lucky hat and his own frying pan. He'd love to fry up a fresh batch of bacon-wrapped pancake sticks to replenish his stores. Freshly cooked bacon strengthened him more than the cold bacon strips, bacon bits, and bacon-wrapped puff pastries he carried in various pockets.

As if reading his mind, the chef gestured him closer. "You look like you could use a few smoked pig shots." He opened a lower tray on his cart. It was filled with bacon-wrapped kielbasa chunks filled with white cheese sauce.

"You're a credit to your kitchen," Rasher said, plucking several from the tray. They were somehow still piping hot, and absolutely delicious. The bacon was right on the cusp of crispy, so it topped off both his stores of crispy and chewy bacon. The sauce must have been imbued by a cheese wizard because it radiated a pulsing warmth through his limbs.

In addition to working poisons and curses, cheese wizards could imbue their cheeses with the opposite effects. As a bacon master, he couldn't benefit as much while actively releasing his bacon powers, but he still appreciated the protection. He took a few extra shots back with him, and Kucheesa eagerly gobbled down three of them.

The drupe wizards approached the wall again, casting more seeds over the edge. They started chanting a recipe together, their voices rising above the din of shouting soldiers, rasping vines, the steady, slow crashing of the monster's feet, and the pealing of alarm bells.

"What are they doing?" Rasher asked the chef, who moved his cart closer.

"Taking a page out of the enemy's cookbook, sir. They're going to entangle the giant's feet to slow it."

"I hope it works," Rasher said, although Balter would be furious if he returned with chains to find the drupe wizards had already accomplished his plan.

He stepped closer to the edge and spotted fast-growing yellow beanstalk vines slithering over the stones of the plaza toward the statue. If they didn't find a way to slow it soon, it would reach the wall in another minute.

The vines slithered up the monster's legs, wrapping them over and over. The drupe wizards' voices shook with strain, but they never stopped chanting. Their faces were covered with sweat, but the young man lifted a mixing spoon defiantly. The young woman swayed, as if on the verge of collapse.

The giant tried taking another step, but the vines tightened around its legs, grinding its forward momentum to a halt.

A cheer erupted along the wall, and Rasher shouted along with them.

"They can't hold it for long, especially if it turns its own seed powers against them," the chef warned.

"Let's hope it's enough," Rasher said, glancing back at the vegetable shamans and their pan of vegetables.

It took only moments for the vegetable medley to start sizzling, but every second seemed to drag on for an eternity. In the square, the giant swept one huge arm down, raking the restricting vines and tearing them away.

The drupe wizards stopped chanting, and the two men caught the girl, although they looked little better. Milk maids rushed in with fortifying glasses of milk and led them back toward the tower to rest.

Meanwhile, the warm scent of stir-fried vegetables wafted over the wall, reinforcing the courage of the soldiers.

The three shamans, all mature women, lifted the pan from the flame and dumped the contents over the wall, shouting in unison, "Sebzeler, grant your might!"

Fried peppers, onions, broccoli, and cauliflower cascaded down the front of the wall, and the head shaman shouted, "Brace yourselves! This is going to get rough!"

Rasher had already grabbed a nearby crenellation, wishing he was farther away. The vegetable shamans usually unleashed their mighty powers through the siege weapons, not right in front of their troops.

When the stir-fry struck the ground, vegetables blasted forward like they'd been shot from a catapult, and a rumble of thunder shook the wall under their feet. The ground rippled, cracking paving stones, and earth rolled away from the wall, gaining speed and cresting into a ten-foot wave of multi-colored earth that crashed right into the giant.

The wave flung the god-monster back. It toppled to the plaza with a resounding crash that shook the wall again. Even as Rasher joined the triumphant cheer, the monster rolled right back to its feet, looking undamaged.

"By Sebzeler's mighty frying pan, I don't believe it," the lead shaman exclaimed. Dark circles now rimmed her eyes, and her face looked lined and drawn from the enormous expenditure of energy.

The best food magic was prepared slowly in advance. Rushing it was like trying to bake a cake in half the time. To keep it from fizzling, the effort drained far more energy from the wizards, mages, and shamans and still often produced weaker effects.

"The catapult is ready to fire!" someone shouted, and Rasher turned to look back toward the inner side of the wall, his hope renewed.

The huge catapult was in position in the street, the massive arm cranked back, with an entire nine-layer cake packed into the wide basket. The cake was already smoldering and two muffin mages were standing nearby, whisks raised high.

"Fire," Rasher ordered, riding a wave of exultation. They would show the glowan real magic.

"Fire!" the officer of the weapon repeated, and all eyes turned to watch in expectant silence to witness the mighty machine deliver a death blow.

A flash of yellow light at the base of the catapult arm caught Rasher's attention. He squinted and spotted a tiny winged figure flitting about the catapult before it zipped away.

Cold dread gripped his heart.

"Fairies!" he shouted.

Too late.

A soldier had already pulled a lever, releasing the coiled energy of the catapult.

With a thunderous crack, the base of the catapult arm splintered, rocking the entire weapon and flinging the arm high into the air.

Rasher gasped as the basket with its deadly cake somersaulted straight up as if in slow motion. Several of the soldiers around the catapult had been knocked sprawling by the disaster. Everyone else stared in horror for a split second before scattering like roaches.

They could never hope to move fast enough.

"Take cover!" Rasher shouted into the terrible silence that fell over the entire scene. One muffin mage down in the plaza defiantly held his whisk aloft, as if trying to snuff out the power of the cake. The other one fled with everyone else.

The cake-laden basket and catapult arm dropped back down onto the wreckage of the catapult and detonated with a world-shattering explosion.

Searing light, blistering heat, and a shockwave of superheated air slammed into Rasher like a hammer from the gods, knocking him sprawling. An ear-splitting crack of thunder pounded his head.

Distantly he heard screaming, but for a few seconds could not clear his vision. The hard stones of the parapet felt cool under his left cheek, while his right burned from the heat. All he could smell was burned sugar. His lungs hurt when he tried to sit up, and the world seemed strangely silent, despite the ringing in his ears.

Soldiers lay sprawled all over each other along the wall. Down on the God's Banquet, the blast had flung soldiers in every direction. Some were rolling weakly, clutching wounds, but most lay as still as death.

It had also toppled all the statues of the gods, shattering several of them into pieces. The sight filled Rasher with a sense of terrible foreboding.

The catapult was simply gone, as was the muffin mage who had tried heroically to stop the explosion. Rasher quickly looked away from the carnage. He couldn't risk his gaze lingering on the blood.

He had to act. He was the Reaper captain. So he pushed his horror aside and lurched to his feet, ignoring groaning muscles. "Centurions, get your men back to the wall! Milk mages to the square!"

His voice sounded weird to his own ears, as if he was shouting inside a paper sack, but his words shook officers from their stunned stupor.

Centurions began ordering the lines along the wall, while women wearing the pointy white hats, tan coats, and white capes of milkmaids rushed to the roofs of the two tall gate towers and began loading the fling dispensers already mounted there.

They started rapid-firing down upon the carnage in the courtyard, flinging giant, head-sized cream puffs. Each fast-deployment puff erupted upon impact, spraying heavy cream in every direction and dispensing life-saving healing. The injured who could still move rolled in the cream or scooped up fistfuls to slather over their wounds and burns.

Hopefully the cream could stabilize the wounded until the milk mages and their field teams arrived. The milkmaids were well trained and soon covered every figure with cream.

Rasher tried not to think about the huge expenditure of healing cream. With stockpiles so low, it was a wonder the milkmaids had so much cream on hand, and that they had not received orders to use it more sparingly.

Looking out across the cream-covered disaster area, he couldn't bring himself to give those orders. Maybe he should, but too many had died or been wounded already that day. He would not give the orders that might cause more to die.

The legions would mobilize with scant resources, but that was tomorrow's problem.

Outside the wall, the giant god-monster had figured out how to move faster and rushed the wall while they were distracted. Shouts of alarm rang all down the wall. For a second, Rasher feared it would try smashing right through.

The giant's previous marble-like skin had changed. Now it looked pasty white, like rotten flesh draped over a mottled, lumpy form, as if it was all broken up inside. The face was like a white mask, and now each enormous yellow eye was filled with dozens of little, glowing orbs.

Instead of smashing through the wall, the monster slammed both hands down onto the parapet on either side of the gate. The wall shook, but held. The monster did not let go. The skin along its arms and shoulders began bulging outward in dozens of places. The lumps grew to about the size of small children, then detached themselves from the whole.

Those lumps rolled up the monster's body and along the arms that acted like bridges to the parapet. As they moved, they coalesced from blob-shaped piles of whitish goo into recognizable shapes.

Some turned into dogs, while others became cats, miniature horses, and even very short people wielding wickedly notched blades.

"And now we have demons," Rasher groaned.

41

THE EVILS OF CHEESE AND CRACKERS

Bibble thanked the gods that Gleaners were resourceful as he rode on a commandeered horse, with Quarce holding tight to his back. The squad of rhino-enhanced Gleaners ran on either side of their horse, their heavy, tramping boots ringing in perfect unison on the stones. Anyone who saw them coming quickly moved out of their way.

Good thing, because for once Bibble did not worry about someone accidentally getting hurt by moving too slowly. His family was in danger, and fear gripped his heart so tight, it was hard to breathe. He was no warrior, and the sight of Shemo transforming into a great wolf had shaken him deeply.

Not as deeply as the threat against his family. The thought of those evil creatures attacking his wife and children filled Bibble with unfamiliar rage. Usually he'd recoil from such feelings, but not today.

Instead, he embraced the rage as a way to fight back his fear. He was a Reaper now, and by the gods, he was ready to unleash some smiting upon his enemies.

"Where are we going, Reaper Bibble?" asked the burly sergeant leading the Gleaners in a deep, raspy voice. His name was Orzo, and he seemed very competent.

"The Endless Desserts guest inn. My family is supposed to be staying there, but we fear the glowan have sent agents to kill or kidnap them."

Orzo nodded and turned to one of his five men. "Get to the Gleaner rallying point and fetch a full complement of guilds to meet us at South gate with all speed." The soldier saluted and sped off at a full sprint.

"Thank you," Bibble said. "But I don't plan to wait for them to arrive."

Orzo grinned in response. "Sir, my team is well trained in fighting glowan. We should take the lead."

"Are you prepared to face the Reapers you once served?" Bibble asked.

Orzo and his men had participated in the capture of Dollop, so they knew the truth, but they'd trained and worked closely with the old Reaper team.

Orzo's expression turned hard, his dark red eyes blazing. He took a couple deep breaths and said, "The vile changeling has robbed their honor. They would want us to stop them." He then spoke loudly to the rest of his men. "We're facing a scorched souffle scenario."

By their expressions, they also understood the truth. They clearly didn't like it, but it appeared they would do their duty.

Quarce spoke for the first time. "We take them alive, if possible. The glowan who subverted their minds is fallen, so we may be able to free them."

Hopefully they could. For a few minutes, they just rode. As they drew closer to South Gate, Bibble caught whiffs of a foul, pungent smell on the air.

"Fallout from the parmesan bomb," Quarce noted, shifting to cover his nose with one hand.

"We're close," Bibble confirmed. He could mix some spices to push the poison stench away but didn't want to tip off their quarry.

He slowed the horse, and Orzo said, "We'll secure the building. Team one with me on the first floor. Team two, take the upstairs."

They all saluted and trotted ahead. It took all of Bibble's willpower not to drive his heels into his horse's flanks and gallop headlong to the inn. He needed to get to his family, but if the enemy was already closing on them, he didn't want to force them into doing anything rash.

He refused to consider the fact that they might already be too late.

It was surreal, moving through the Acropolis. Even as soldiers scrambled to respond to the alarm, support personnel moved about purposefully, preparing for the impending mobilization. None of them knew of the other dangers lurking in their midst.

They trusted Bibble and the Reapers to ferret out the danger and deal with it. Many cheered and waved as he passed. Bibble couldn't bring himself to wave back, but thankfully Quarce did. The dwarf seemed to enjoy the attention and waved so mightily, he almost knocked himself off the horse.

When he caught Bibble for balance, he nearly pulled Bibble off with him.

"Do you mind?" Bibble asked, forcing a civil tone. "I'm kind of busy worrying about my family."

"If you worry, you get tense," Quarce responded softly. "When you're tense, you can't react quickly. We cannot change what might have happened, but we need to be ready to deal with what is happening when we arrive."

That was remarkably good advice, and Bibble focused on it as his horse moved with agonizing slowness down the street. Ahead of him, the Gleaners suddenly rushed around the next corner, moving with remarkable quiet, despite their huge size and speed.

Bibble cursed himself for being distracted. He could have silenced all their sounds, but hadn't even thought about it. Now it was too late.

When they reached the corner, the inn finally came into view. It was located near the edge of the cordoned-off area contaminated by the parmesan cheese explosion.

Inside that contaminated area, several buildings had collapsed, while others sagged, covered in a strange, green mold. The cobblestones were also coated in the same mold, and the air shimmered with waves of noxious fumes. One of the huge gates in the outer wall was shattered, the other hanging precariously sideways.

Even outside of the containment area, the air smelled foul, and after the bustling activity of the rest of the Acropolis, the empty street felt eerie.

"We should dismount," Bibble said.

Quarce jumped off without hesitation, and Bibble swung down, suppressing a groan. He'd ridden more horses that day than he usually rode in a month, and his inner thighs were already warning him he was going to be very sore tomorrow.

Orzo's team didn't wait for them but flowed down the street like a deadly, silent tide, weapons at the ready.

They split when they reached the inn. One pair took up positions flanking the entry door, while Orzo and the other two slipped down the alley on the left side of the building, disappearing into the shadows.

Bibble tried to move quietly, but Quarce moved like a living rockslide, armor clanking, steel-shod boots striking loudly against the stones.

When Bibble gave him a disgusted look, he shrugged and whispered, "What? I'm not a chicken or a bacon master. Dwarves are solid."

Bibble just pulled out the rest of the spice mixture he'd made for them earlier and cast it into the air around them. As the spices billowed and settled over them, their sounds faded to silence.

Quarce grinned. "Wish we had some of that in the mines. Would have made hunting rats so much easier."

As Bibble approached the inn, he studied every window but spied no movement. No lights were visible inside, so it was likely the windows were covered by drapes. Hopefully that meant no one inside had heard them coming.

His nervousness was threatening to overwhelm his rage, but he fought it back, thinking about the tortures he would inflict on anyone who hurt his family.

The inn was a grand, two-story structure with fluted columns flanking the tall main door and its roofed entrance. Only one door broke the front facade, but large windows marched down the entire length of the front wall, with smaller windows from the second floor keeping pace above.

Orzo suddenly appeared at the corner of the building. He jogged to them and spoke so quietly, his words barely reached them.

"Perimeter is secure, but I smell several people, including Clootie Dumpling and Juusto Panjandrum."

Bibble was glad he knew their scent, but his fear ratcheted higher. They were already in the building. "We can't wait."

"Agreed. My team will breach through windows in the side of the building in ten seconds."

"We'll meet you there," Bibble promised, facing the front door. Quarce softly counted down the seconds.

The Gleaners waiting there must have heard a signal because just as Quarce reached one, they lunged. The front door was not locked, so they swung it open gently before rushing in, weapons at the ready.

Quarce jumped in front of Bibble and said, "I'm the one with the hammer. You follow me."

He wanted to argue, but Quarce was already charging after the Gleaners. Bibble followed just as he heard crashing of glass upstairs.

The door opened into a large parlor, lit by dim illumination pastries in sockets high on the wall. Tiles covered the center of the floor leading to a large reception desk, while plush carpeting covered seating areas to both sides, sprinkled with sofas and chairs.

The dim open area seemed empty, and the Gleaners were already rushing toward the grand staircase circling up toward the second floor. Quarce followed, and Bibble gave chase.

It was already abundantly obvious that his new position was going to require way too much running. He'd never liked running, and would have to continue research he'd started a few years ago into the possibility of personal hover craft that would make running obsolete.

For now, he had to run. Bibble huffed as he rushed up the stairs after the others. He started hearing the sounds of splintering wood. At the top of the stairs, a single wide hallway pierced the center of the building, broken regularly by the doors of guest suites.

The Gleaners had begun systematically smashing through each door, rushing into each suite to quickly search them. Several screams punctuated their efforts, but they returned each time, shaking their heads. No one was foolish enough to exit their rooms to complain.

The hallway ended in a T-junction along the back half of the inn. Bibble had visited the inn once and knew that the best rooms were at the back. Sure enough, when he made the turn, he spotted Orzo and his two men standing three-quarters of the way down the hall facing the black-robed figure of Clootie Dumpling.

The confectioner had lost his hat, clearly revealing his identity. He stood before the door into the chef's suite, as if on guard, but his eyes looked glazed and he swayed where he stood.

Orzo was slowly approaching, sword held low, one hand extended toward Clootie. "Sir, we're here to help. Can you understand me?"

Bibble was glad they hadn't simply rushed the man and cut him down. Clootie could be extremely dangerous, but he looked unhinged, as if suffering one of his own sugar highs.

Shemo had said his glamour would fade if he lost focus for too long. Now that he was dead, his glamour should be gone, but he'd suggested he'd forced the Reapers to apply their own mind-weakening sugars and cheese poisons on themselves to make them more pliable.

It looked like he was right. Clootie might not be under a glamour, but he was still addled by the sugars. It would take time for him to recover.

A shriek inside the suite echoed through the building. The sound tore at Bibble's heart and he gasped. He recognized that voice.

His wife, Lahmacun.

The sound galvanized Bibble into motion. His wife was not a screaming type, and she sounded afraid, but also angry. That suggested Juusto was inside.

Inside with his family.

With a roar of fury that surprised even him, Bibble sprinted full speed at the addled Clootie.

The confectioner might be out of his mind, but even in that state, he recognized a threat and his hand dipped toward a pocket in his jacket.

Orzo shouted a warning, but Bibble was done waiting. He plowed into Clootie as the addled Reaper pulled a dangerous chocolate chip cookie from his robes.

Still roaring, Bibble smashed Clootie right through the locked double door to the chef's suite. The impact rattled Bibble hard, and it blasted the breath right out of Clootie's lungs.

As the two of them tumbled inside, the cookie went flying, and Bibble was surprised to realize Clootie's breath smelled sweet, as if he'd just consumed another cookie.

They hit hard, with Clootie on the bottom, and for once Bibble's heft gave him the advantage. Clootie cried out in pain as his chest took a second hit, and Bibble punched him in the jaw as they both rose.

Bibble hadn't ever been in a fight, but he threw every bit of strength into the blow. He connected, and Clootie toppled back to the floor so hard his head bounced off the carpet.

Bibble surged to his feet, hat and coat askew, hand aching from the impact, but none of that mattered. He looked wildly around for his family.

He'd crashed into the main salon of the chef's suite. The beautifully decorated room had a high ceiling with skylights, walls painted sky blue and covered in expensive paintings. A spinet piano stood against the inner wall, while the back wall had a huge window overlooking a private garden. Two couches and several overstuffed chairs were placed around the window and the piano.

Most of Bibble's children sat huddled together on one of the couches, while his wife faced Juusto, one hand outstretched in fearful supplication.

The cheese wizard had also lost his hat, which lay discarded on the carpet nearby. He was clutching the hand of Bibble's beloved ten-year-old daughter, Pilaf.

Everyone turned to stare when Bibble crashed into the room. His wife looked astounded and exclaimed, "Bibble, is that really you?"

Pilaf grinned and said, "Good tackle, Daddy." She turned to Juusto and said, "Now you're in trouble. My dad is here."

Juusto's eyes were wild, and in his other hand he held a cracker smothered with cheese. It was whitish, with dark veins swirling through.

"Blue cheese," Orzo whispered gravely.

Quarce clutched his hammer tighter. "I don't care if he's under a glamour. Any man who waves blue cheese around a child deserves to be whipped."

"Orzo, what are you doing here?" Juusto called, releasing Pilaf and turning toward them, a confused look on his face.

"Sir, we've come to escort you back to the Reaper headquarters," Orzo said, striding purposefully forward.

Juusto's eyes widened with fear and he backed up quickly, holding the cheese cracker out like a shield. "No! I won't go back and risk the cream cheese clause."

"We'll leave the Acropolis immediately," Orzo soothed, steadily closing the distance, but panic had seized the cheese wizard.

Bibble couldn't imagine what poisons and sugars he'd been forced to consume, but the famously brilliant cheese wizard was reduced to a terrified husk of a man.

Pilaf didn't wait to see what the Gleaner would do. She kicked Juusto with all her might in the shin.

Surprised, Juusto roared and staggered back. Lahmacun snatched Pilaf away, just barely avoiding a swipe from the cheese cracker.

Two of the Gleaners lunged across the room, tackling Bibble's family right over the back of the couch. It upended and they kept the screaming family hidden behind it.

In his panic, Juusto turned and dove at the window.

He bounced off.

Chef suites always used the best quality glass, and Juusto only managed to break his nose and probably give himself a concussion. He staggered back from the window and plopped down onto his backside.

Orzo reached him a second later, and as Juusto looked up at him in confusion, he said, "Sorry about this, sir."

He punched Juusto in the jaw, knocking him out.

Bibble rushed to his family and swept his wife into an embrace, shaking with fear and happiness. Lahmacun hugged him back for a long moment.

Then she pulled back and gave him an appraising look. "One day as a Reaper and you've already started crashing through doors and getting into fights?"

Pilaf and the boys cheered wildly and started chanting, "Dad is the best!"

42

CHEESE BALLS!

The swarm of summoned demon creatures swelled, fascinating and horrifying Rasher at the same time. More and more pulled themselves free of the god-statue's body and charged along its arms toward the wall.

"Repel!" Noops shouted in a basso voice that thundered over the din of the still-clamoring alarm bells. Legionnaires formed shield walls in line with Balter's squads and Noops, and the horde of small monsters swarmed into them.

Rasher hefted his staff, heart racing with battle energy, but he forced himself to hang back and survey the lines.

As soldiers hacked and stabbed and shield-bashed the swarm, monsters rushed in, raking with black claws and biting with long, black fangs. Some leaped impossibly high, trying to overwhelm the defenders. Soldiers in the next ranks skewered them, while archers atop the nearby towers poured arrows down into the nasty white ranks.

The Gleaners might not have shields, but they savaged any monsters who drew within range. Lion and tiger squads moved with feline grace and speed, slipping past fang and claw, swords and spears piercing enemy demons with deadly precision. With their heavy hammers and axes, the bear squad smashed through any demons foolhardy enough to attack them.

The intense battle raged along the wall on both sides of the gate. Legionnaires stabbed and slashed, killing the beasts by the dozen, but more kept coming. The sounds of screaming men mingled with the high-pitched shrieking of dying monsters and the constant growling and clicking sounds they made as they swarmed toward the fray.

The air turned rancid with the sharp, coppery scent of blood, overlaid with a stronger vinegar-like acid smell of monster blood. Rasher kept his gaze moving, not settling on any one scene of bloodshed. He willed himself to be strong, could not allow anyone to see his weakness.

"I'll help hold the line," shouted another soldier just arriving at the top of the stairs.

He was tall, with unusually perfect hair and square-jawed good looks. He wore full armor, and a helmet with sweeping wings along either side. He carried a dueling sword, and his voice was a deep, confident baritone.

"It's Nudge Bobsydie," Kucheesa gasped, staring at the handsome newcomer with a look of awe.

"The wardrobe wizard?" Rasher asked. "Kitan bought one of his signature hats this season." She would have loved to meet the famous wizard, but probably not under the current circumstances.

"Perfect timing, as usual," Captain Welkin told Nudge as the newcomer rushed up to them and saluted.

"Sorry I don't have more time, Captain," Nudge told Rasher. "I've been tasked with designing your new armor, but for now we'll hold the wall until you figure out how to destroy that monster." He strode toward the wild melee above the gate.

With a grand gesture, he threw his hands out wide. And suddenly there were two of him walking in perfect step together. Then four, then eight.

By the time he reached the fighting, the line of duplicate Nudges stretched to nearly a hundred. All of the duplicates lacked the fancy wings on their helms, but wore full plate armor and carried huge, square shields and short, stabbing spears. As one, they charged forward into the fray, and their arrival helped push the monsters back and secure the lines.

Rasher had never seen a wardrobe wizard use his troop ability before, and it was inspiring. With the wardrobe troop reinforcing them, the legionnaires took heart and stood firm against the horde of demon monsters.

Nudge's duplicates held the center, their shields forming a wall against the tide, short spears plunging into the horde with perfectly timed unison.

Unfortunately, the stream of monsters did not relent. The men were holding, but they would grow tired. Rasher glanced back down into the inner court. More reinforcements had arrived, but were also engaged with more monsters. It appeared they'd somehow broken through the gate without him even realizing it. There would be no relief on the wall any time soon.

The huge god monster appeared to be losing no mass, despite disgorging a steady stream of monsters. They could not defeat it this way. They needed to change tactics.

He looked around for Balter, but couldn't spot the big Gleaner through the press. Either he'd gotten caught up in the fighting or had to look farther for chains.

The god monster leaned forward, opened its mouth, and bellowed, the vast sound shaking the wall and knocking soldiers back. The sound trailed off into a laugh, like a spine-shivering sound of grinding rock. Then all the yellow points in its huge eyes grew larger until dozens of great eyes filled each socket, pressing against the outer eye, as if it was full of scores of glowan.

All the summoned monsters shrieked in response, the cacophony like a thousand steel pots tumbling off the back of a high wagon. They renewed the attack with a frenzy the soldiers would never manage to match for long.

Some of the creatures skirted the edge of the lines and came screaming toward Rasher's group. He raised his staff, but Kucheesa said, "We'll deal with it, Captain."

She trotted forward, sword in one hand, a knife in the other, gesturing a few of Captain Welkin's lieutenants to flank her. She glanced back at Rasher and said, "Well, don't just stand there. Figure out a solution."

Then she led her little troop forward with a shouted battle cry. Kucheesa skewered one with her sword and took another right out of the air with a thrown knife as it swooped down toward her.

It looked like they would manage all right, so Rasher turned to the chef. "Any word on when we'll get more reinforcements from the guilds?"

"They should have been here by now. They might have gotten delayed by the fighting down in the square."

"Or maybe they couldn't find battle cuisine ready to go," Captain Welkin said.

"How about archers?" Rasher asked, glancing up at the south tower where the archers were shooting down into the press of summoned creatures.

Captain Welkin shook his head. "No good. Arrows can't harm stone, and the giant's eyes are shielded with magic. Arrows can't penetrate."

"We need something more," Rasher said, releasing a slice of chewy bacon to accelerate his thoughts. He considered the resources at hand, but found no solution. Then, as he thought of other guilds and what they might bring to bear, he got an idea.

He knocked loudly on the chef's cart, startling the man, who had crouched to take inventory of one of the shelves. "Do you have any cheese?"

"Of course. I've got some parmesan crumble of confusion, a nasty gruyere that'll melt just about anything, and —"

"Give me the gruyere, quick," Rasher ordered, handing his battle staff to Captain Welkin.

The chef blinked in surprise. "You're not a cheese wizard."

"I know how to handle cheese without cursing myself, but that gruyere acid poison has been stewing for months. You don't need to be a cheese wizard to hit something with it."

"True, but a cheese wizard could do more with it," the chef countered even as he pulled out a tray near the bottom and carefully extracted a long, shallow dish full of small cheese cubes.

"I think it'll work just fine for what I need," Rasher said as he released twenty full slices of bacon.

The tide of bacon power swept through him with a jolt, as if he'd swallowed a bolt of lightning. While it blazed through every fiber of his being, he couldn't help laughing. Bacon made everything better, and at that moment, he couldn't help feeling amazing.

Grinning, Rasher reached down and scooped up all the cheese squares into his bare hands.

"Captain, don't!" Captain Welkins cried, his expression horrified.

The rest of the group around them recoiled in horror, looking like they already imagined his flesh bubbling and melting from the bones of his hands, then his bones sagging and falling away as he screamed out his final moments.

The chef only gave Rasher an approving nod.

The warm cheese flexed and flowed around his fingers as he mushed it all together into a ball. The mighty curse worked into it during the long months of its curing dug at Rasher's skin with all the promise of a gruesome death.

All of that bacon power burst through Rasher's hands in a tide of pure incandescent light, pushing back the poison and absorbing it all. Rasher felt it along his skin, like an oily sheen, and in his mind he sensed its power and knew how to release it.

"Higher-level bacon," the chef chortled exultantly.

Rasher didn't wait to explain to the others, but turned and dashed for the south tower. The doorway was crowded, the inside packed with wounded soldiers. He didn't try pushing through to the stairs, but drew upon two more slices of bacon from his much-depleted stores and leaped, catching the lintel over the high door.

With an acrobatic flip, he swung himself higher, then scrambled up the rough face of the tower like a spider. In seconds he reached the battlements and flipped over the edge onto the flat roof where a squad of archers was firing down upon the monsters. Luckily none of them mistook him for a target.

"Reaper Captain?" a nearby soldier asked in surprise. "What are you doing up here?"

"Hopefully proving that my lessons are useful."

"I don't think paint will help today."

"We don't need paint, but better analysis of enemy weaknesses. I want ten of you to sight on the giant's eyes."

"Our arrows just bounce off."

"Not this time," Rasher promised, hefting the cheese ball. In seconds, he moved down the line of archers, smearing cheese onto every arrow. The archers looked astounded that he risked handling raw cheese without protective gear, but held their peace.

The giant's head was turning slowly side to side as it surveyed its forces. Rasher waited, trying to calm his breathing and steady his heartbeat until the head turned in his direction, giving them the perfect shot.

He'd spent most of the curse on the arrows, but as he focused, he unleashed a second identical cheese curse over the remaining cheese. The effort left him feeling drained, but he forced himself on and drew upon yet another piece of crispy bacon to enhance his skill.

"Watch for my signal," he told the archers. "And don't hesitate."

Without waiting for a reply, Rasher rushed to the edge of the roof. Without slowing, he dove out over the long drop, shouting with his loudest voice, "Nudge, shields!"

Thankfully the wardrobe wizard heard and reacted without hesitation. Four of the duplicate Nudge warriors lifted their shields high, forming a steel platform.

They held it for three precious seconds, even as monsters rushed into the sudden gap, claws and fangs flashing with deadly intent.

Rasher somersaulted in midair and landed on the shield platform. It gave under his weight enough to absorb the brutal impact. Using his momentum, Rasher vaulted again, somersaulting right over the hordes of shrieking monsters and the valiant legionaries battling to stop them.

As he tumbled, sights and sounds and scents crashed into his enhanced senses. Screaming of men, howling and hooting of demons, the sharp scent of blood and fear, and glimpses of terrifying creatures and determined soldiers.

It all passed in a flash, too fast for the blood to seize his mind. Rasher landed on the wrist of the giant monster and without slowing, raced toward the giant's torso.

Half a dozen new demons shared the wide arm with him, already rushing forward to join the fray. Two dogs, one midget with an ax, and four feline demons. They howled with glee when they caught sight of him, teeth, claws, and ax reaching out with the promise of death.

"Captain!" Noops shouted, but Rasher didn't have time to explain his plan.

With so much bacon thundering through him, he started whistling the legion battle chant as he rushed the demons.

Two throwing knives tumbled past him, so close he felt the rush of air past one ear. They caught both of the dogs center mass, knocking them sprawling.

Kucheesa was a great shot. Rasher jumped the distracted demon dogs, knocked the midget flying off the arm with a kick, and met the lunging felines with cheese-enhanced punches.

The cat demons shrieked in agony as they tumbled off the arm, bodies disintegrating under the concentrated power of the cheese.

Behind him, the legionnaires shouted support, and a rain of spears and arrows swept the arm clear the rest of the way to the shoulder.

Rasher charged through the opening, drawing the gaze of the giant as it turned its massive head toward him. That close, he could see the dozens of smaller, glowing orbs pressed against the inside edge of the eye sliding over each other as they focused on him.

"For Rubric!" Rasher shouted, leaping high and smashing both fists into the closest giant eye.

For a second he saw the shimmering glow of the protective spell before his cheese-cursed hands punched through and plunged deep into the eye.

The eye imploded as his arms plunged through to the shoulder. The retina gave under the pressure, like a thick crust over a meat pie.

Inside, he spotted at least two dozen small humanoid fairies pressed into the eye socket. They looked like miniature men and women, who shrieked in surprise as he beat through their defenses.

Rasher seized two of them, and they instantly started to melt.

As the others recoiled from him, arrows plunged into the giant eye all around him, easily penetrating the retina and skewering most of the fairies in the first volley.

Rasher dropped and rolled down the shoulder to get out of the line of fire. The archers were very skilled, but getting accidentally killed by an unlucky shot would be a stupid way to end the battle.

"Captain!" Noops shouted again, and when Rasher turned to look, he saw the shovel knight throw the chef's cast-iron frying pan. The heavy skillet soared in a perfect arc to Rasher, who scooped it out of the air.

He hefted it in thanks. Now that he's used all the cheese, he lacked a weapon to fight off several new demons rushing onto the arm to fight him. Rasher charged them, reveling in the unrivaled awesomeness of bacon.

Riding that wave of bacon might, Rasher danced through the enemy monsters, dodging their claws and fangs while clocking each of them in the head with the frying pan. It was the perfect weapon for the job, its solid weight clobbering monsters flying off the arm.

The entire god-monster shuddered, the head rearing back. Archers cheered even as they knocked fresh arrows and fired again. More arrows struck true, and the monster staggered, releasing the wall.

Uh oh.

With the way clear again, Rasher charged for the wall, thankful that the flood of mini monsters stopped as soon as contact was broken. The monsters on the wall convulsed, melting into the stones like lumpy butter on a hot pan.

The archers had found their groove, and they poured arrows into the giant's eyes. The steady stream of arrows flashing over his head would have been distracting if he wasn't running for his life.

Rasher crossed the distance in a flash, and thankfully the giant raised its arms to shield its face as it stumbled back. Rasher raced up the rapidly rising incline, reached the hand, and threw himself toward the wall.

The gap had grown quickly, but he jumped from ten feet above the wall, throwing himself at the close-packed ranks of cheering soldiers, casting his frying pan ahead of him.

He wasn't going to make it.

Smashing face-first into another wall was not the plan, but he was out of tricks.

Balter stepped to the front ranks and threw a heavy length of chain. Rasher seized it, and Balter and four of his Gleaners hauled mightily on it, yanking him to the wall instead of splatting into the outer edge of the stones.

Rasher crashed into them, and they all went down in a heap, surrounded by cheering soldiers. Dozens of hands reached down to haul him to his feet, and heavy hands pounded his back so hard, he nearly fell again.

When he glanced back at the giant through the press of cheering soldiers, it was starting to topple backward, its mouth open in a silent scream. Half a dozen small glowing fairies erupted out of it, shooting up into the sky.

A dozen more of the little creatures fell lifeless out of the thrashing head, punctured by arrows that looked immense compared to their tiny frames.

"Get the fairies," someone shouted, and archers unleashed another volley.

Outside of the confines of the stone giant head, the fairies zipped and dodged with astonishing speed, easily avoiding the arrows. Within seconds they rose out of reach and flew directly toward the late afternoon sun, disappearing in the light.

As soon as the fairies departed, the giant's body hardened into solid granite just in time to smash to pieces in the plaza with a resounding crash.

Balter leaped right off the wall, landing atop the fallen giant. He raised his fists, roaring like a tiger, the sound visceral and terrifying. All along the wall and inside the courtyard, soldiers cheered. The Gleaner squads roared like lions, tigers, and bears.

Rasher chuckled, happy to see his men enjoying the well-deserved victory. Then he headed for the tower where Captain Welkins waited with his battle staff. Archers exited the tower in a rush and surrounded Rasher, cheering loudly.

He grinned and told them, "You're all a credit to the legion. Well done."

The archers cheered, already congratulating each other. Unlike most bacon masters, Rasher didn't like being the center of attention and tried shouting over the din. "We all share in today's glory. Bards will sing of your bravery."

Kucheesa and Noops joined him. She smiled, but leaned close and said, "You realize you're insane, right?"

Rasher started to reply, but his eyes fell upon a badly bleeding soldier being carried toward the tower by a pair of milkmaids.

He tried to look away but reacted too slowly. He'd managed to avoid looking closely at any of the bleeding soldiers through the entire fight, but now the crimson smear of blood seemed to sear his eyes. He tried to draw upon the comforting power of bacon, but it wasn't enough.

His vision swam and seemed to contract to a point around his feet as he stared toward the stones, as if through a long, dark tunnel. His head pounded, and he stumbled and would have fallen if not for Noops grabbing him.

Distantly he heard Noops calling to him to tense his limbs. He tried, but nausea flooded through him and he felt woozy and flushed with heat.

He couldn't faint, not now. The battle was done, and he was the Reaper captain.

He needed to be strong, to . . .

43

FORTUNE COOKIES OF DUBIOUS WISDOM

Rasher awakened lying on a cot in a dimly lit stone room. By the many voices outside the door, he suspected he was in a room of the gate tower. He felt surprisingly good. Well, he did until the memories crashed back into his mind of the crazy battle on the wall over East Gate, the giant, and that bloody soldier.

Rasher sat up with a start. That's when he noticed Colly Wobbles sitting in a low chair beside the cot. She smiled, her teeth flashing almost as white as her skin in the dim light.

"Hello," she said with her usual cheeriness. "Welcome back, Captain."

"How long was I out?" His throat felt very dry, and his voice rasped.

Colly was ready and handed him a clay mug full of cool milk. He sipped it, sighing with appreciation as the healing milk eased his thirst. The air suddenly smelled cleaner, as if an invisible washerwoman had just swept through the room.

"About an hour," said Kucheesa, stepping into the room through an open door. "Just long enough to skip most of the boring work."

Rasher swung his legs off the bed, grateful to see he hadn't been undressed. He instinctively checked his bacon reserves and cringed to feel them so low.

"Take it easy," Colly cautioned. "Have you ever used the higher bacon powers before?"

"Not that one, not in combat anyway," Rasher admitted. The memory of the power of twenty full slices of bacon blazing through him, absorbing the cheese curse, and redirecting it outward again made him smile.

"Its use is uncommon. You won't be able to try it again for a week, and it leaves the wielder exhausted." She hesitated before adding, "Coupled with your rare blood phobia, it's no surprise it knocked you flat."

Her words made Rasher freeze in the act of preparing to stand. He stared into her kind eyes, then glanced at Kucheesa, who lifted one eyebrow, as if daring him to deny it. "How did you know?"

"I'm your physician. I've compiled a detailed chart of all of your team, and I found a reference to your condition."

"Any recommendations on how to deal with it?" Rasher asked hopefully. Colly might be young, but she was a senior healer.

"I've begun to look into it," she admitted. "Your condition is rare, and we've never had a Reaper suffer from blood phobia before."

"Makes sense," Kucheesa said, drawing a step closer. "Sets him up for a quick death. I guess we need to make sure the second in command is clear before we march, eh Captain?"

Rasher grinned, happy she was willing to joke with him. He wasn't sure what had changed. Maybe facing a giant, glowan-animated monster together was the event they'd needed to bond better.

"I was thinking of appointing Noops," he said with a straight face.

"You wouldn't," she gasped.

Rasher chuckled. "I'm open to discussing other candidates, but let's table that for now."

Colly said, "Your condition is known as blood injury phobia, and variations of it are more common than you would think, although the severity of symptoms vary widely between subjects."

"I get dizzy, instant headache, and usually faint."

"Which pushes your affliction to the higher end of the scale, unfortunately. When you see blood, your body reacts by withdrawing. Your heart slows, which slows your blood. That's what causes the weakness, headache, and fainting."

"So how do I treat it?" he asked, hope flickering a little. He'd tried talking with other milk mages in the past, but none had even told him that much.

"Usually we prescribe exposure," she said with a grimace.

"I need to see blood more often?"

Colly nodded. "It often takes time, especially for the more severe cases, but I have heard that steady improvement can be made."

"I don't have time," he pointed out.

"I know. Let me do some more digging to see what I can find. In the meantime, take these. They will help foster quicker recovery."

Colly extracted a small box filled with little white capsules from a leather bag at her feet. Rasher gratefully took the healing doses. Even with the evaporated milk packets Gubbins had given them, he had no doubt his team would need them. With supplies so short, they were far too scarce.

"Thank you."

He suppressed a feeling of disappointment. No one else had known how to solve the problem. He'd struggled with it for years and tried many failed recipes. His blood phobia had always been his one big stumbling block.

If Colly Wobbles could indeed find a way to help him overcome it, he could finally accomplish his greatest dreams. For a moment, he imagined himself a competent Reaper, married to Kitan, with the respect of her father. He smiled to think of his parents seeing him succeed, and justifying the many terrible risks they took for him.

Too much daydreaming was unwise, so he forced his mind back to the present. "Kucheesa, what's the status?"

"Surprisingly good. We spread the word that you fainted from exhaustion from wielding a higher form of bacon. Everyone was so awed by that stunt you pulled that no one questioned the story."

"Thank you," he said again.

She shrugged. "Can't let the legions think we're following a captain who can't keep up. It would make the rest of us look bad."

"And the glowan attack?"

"Finished. Teams of Gleaners and full complements of guilds are sweeping the Acropolis walls, but the glowan are just gone. We've had an hour of peace, if you can believe it."

Rasher leaned back against the wall, considering that with a frown. "That can't be everything."

"Of course not," Kucheesa said with a grunt. "Insanity seems to be part of the job. The Acropolis is secure, and most of the legions are focused on the mobilization, but there's been an attack on the Cheese Palace on Nutmeg Hill."

"What?" Rasher exclaimed. "Who was responsible?"

"Not the corrupted Reapers," Kucheesa said. "Bibble and Quarce captured both Juusto and Clootie at the inn." She held up a calming hand as he opened his mouth to ask the next question. "Don't worry, Bibble's family is fine. It was a close thing, but apparently Bibble's got a fighter's spirit after all."

That sounded like a story worth hearing, but he'd get the full story from Bibble. He chuckled and added, "A fighter's spirit is a good start. We've got a little time to get his fighter's body ready."

"Hopefully," she said. "That's going to take some work. The attack wasn't glowan either. Sounds like a score of attackers wielding highly classified recipes. They all died in the attack, but caused a lot of damage and hurt a bunch of cheese wizards. Managed to corrupt most of their cheese vats too."

Rasher muttered a curse. "Now that we know the cheese wizards didn't intentionally undermine those contracts, I was hoping to get a better contingent from them to support the campaign."

"We might get a few wizards, but their stockpiles are as low as everyone else's," Kucheesa said grimly.

Not good. Starting a campaign with such low stockpiles boded ill for the legions. They needed to figure out how to deal with that.

"Could the attackers have been under glamour?" Rasher asked.

She shrugged. "No indication of it that I've heard."

"That seems odd," Colly said with a frown.

"I know," Rasher said. "It doesn't fit with the attack patterns we've seen so far."

"I'm sure you'll figure it out," Colly said with confidence. "I've ordered bacon to replenish your stores. They should arrive soon. In the meantime, I received these just a moment ago."

She handed Rasher two fortune cookies.

"Who delivered them?" Rasher asked.

"A young woman. She insisted you would want to eat them right away."

Interesting. Rasher handed one to Kucheesa, then broke open the other cookie and extracted the note.

"Sounds like the woman who gave us those last fortune cookies," Kucheesa said. "They turned out to be surprisingly accurate."

"It's easy to find reasons to believe fortune cookies after the fact," Rasher said. "But they did seem unusually specific to what we encountered."

He unrolled the little note and read, "Evil thrives in darkness, and manifests when the bright lights are dimmed."

"That's more ominous than most fortune cookies I get," Colly said.

Kucheesa opened hers and chuckled. "What do you get from a sick chef's first course?"

"Disgusting foods, of course," Colly said with a smile. "Silly. Maybe this one was just for fun."

"What do you think?" Rasher asked Kucheesa.

"I think mine is a joke." She held out one hand, and he passed over his note. She took a moment to study it.

"The bit about darkness and evil makes it sound like maybe our work isn't finished," she said finally.

Rasher grunted. "That's the understatement of the day." He considered the fortune as he ate the still-warm cookie. It spread a comforting warmth through his body, easing his aches, reminding him that he usually didn't eat cookies when he wasn't sure where they came from.

The fortune cookie girl seemed intent on helping them, and if her fortunes were indeed useful, then she had to be tied to a power of prophecy. He needed to follow up on that.

First, though, what did it mean?

On the surface, it seemed one of those obvious statements most fortune cookies contained. Of course evil thrived in darkness, but was that some kind of warning? Was another attack planned that night?

The second half seemed more specific. What bright lights were dimming? Something about the phrase tickled a memory at the back of his mind, but he couldn't quite find it. He risked applying a quarter slice of chewy bacon from his much-diminished stores to the problem, but the thought remained elusive, flitting just out of reach.

A knock on the door drew his attention. Colly jumped to her feet with a grin. "Must be the bacon I ordered."

It wasn't bacon, but a messenger with a small scroll. Rasher suppressed a groan. It seemed when one messenger appeared, they were about to get several.

Sure enough, no sooner had Colly closed the door after the first messenger than a second quick knock sounded. It was indeed another messenger with a second scroll.

Kucheesa's expression turned guarded. "Should I order all messengers to be intercepted?"

"If only we could get rid of bad news that easily," he said, accepting the messages from Colly. The first one was a simple note from Kitan. Rasher instantly recognized her handwriting, and his sense of worry evaporated. She always seemed to know when he needed a boost.

He eagerly scanned the note, but his good humor evaporated and he frowned over the words. "Rasher, I received your note. Sorry I'm running late, but I'll meet you at the training field as soon as I can get there."

Why would she be going to the training field, and why did she make it sound like he'd asked her there? He wanted her to stay on Nutmeg Hill, protected by the might of the Chef's Watch and all the guilds.

Puzzled, he opened the second note, then sat straighter with a start. The note was from Bungey, who he'd left in charge of the paint battle trainers.

"What is it?" Kucheesa asked, drawing closer at the abrupt change of his expression.

Rasher scanned the note, then forced himself to read it again, mind racing with the ramifications of the news.

"My old paint battle training team. They were attacked by an unknown assailant. They are all badly wounded and being treated at the Creamery."

"Who attacks paint battle trainers?" Kucheesa asked.

"Someone who really wants to get my attention," Rasher said grimly. "The attacker left a note with Bungey to tell me their beating was just a warning. Everyone I love will suffer."

"Well, that's ominous," Kucheesa said. "Who would send that? We killed Shemo and captured the corrupted Reapers."

"Not all of them," Rasher said. He didn't need extra bacon to sort out this mystery. "Otamot wants me to come to the training field to fight him."

Colly gasped, her pale face trying to grow paler. "He's tricked Kitan into meeting you there?"

No doubt. Rasher's heart chilled to think of what Otamot might do to Kitan. But his fear was quickly replaced by white-hot rage.

He tried to control it. No doubt that reaction was exactly what Otamot was trying to stoke. He wanted Rasher angry and out of control. He also understood rule number twenty-five.

"We have to stop him," Kucheesa exclaimed.

Rasher nodded as he rose and took up his crumbhorn and battle staff from where they leaned against the wall. "Find the rest of the team, and find Balter. Meet me at the training field."

"We should go together," she insisted.

Rasher shook his head. "I can't wait. Otamot wants to face me again. So be it. Get there as fast as you can."

Kucheesa met his gaze for a moment, then nodded. "It's not the smartest move, but I'd do the same thing. We really should have set up your second in command."

Then she turned and bolted from the room.

Colly placed a hand on Rasher's arm. "Captain, your bacon stores have to be very low, and you may suffer lingering weakness from the combined effects of your high-level bacon power with your blood phobia faint."

"That can't be helped," he said. Getting that bacon would have been nice, but he couldn't afford to wait. "Hold the bacon for me. I'll eat it later."

"Good luck, Captain."

He flashed his trademark smile and sprinted from the tower.

Evil indeed flourished in darkness, but this time he planned to stomp it out.

44

A Taste of Your Own Turkey Bacon

Rasher reached the paint battle arena in moments. It wasn't that far from East Gate, after all. The streets were busy as many people from all walks of life and all levels of society rushed to witness the devastation of the square and the destroyed giant statue.

Many noticed him and cheered, but he didn't slow. He had found a new hat in the tower waiting for him from Sapka, with a note that he be more careful with this one. It fit perfectly, with a wide brim and a shape similar to his last hat, except it was colored red, like the field of the Reaper crest. The band around the brim was shaped like a long strip of bacon, with another strip extending like a feather.

Rasher wouldn't want to face such a deadly opponent without a good hat, but he wasn't convinced Sapka had found the ideal solution yet. Still, he wouldn't complain, and he made a point of sacrificing half of his last handful of bacon bits into the hat as an offering to Domuz.

He found a couple of bacon-encrusted pastries in a pocket and gobbled them down as he ran. They helped a little, but his bacon stores were still dangerously low. So low, it was beyond foolish to face a bacon master of Otamot's caliber, but he could not wait.

The main entrance to the paint battle arena was locked, but Rasher let himself in through the staff entrance and slipped through the staff dressing rooms. He snatched up his leather paint battle armor on the way.

It wouldn't do much against Otamot's swords, but the familiar weight helped settle his mind. He also noticed the little box of chocolate-covered bacon Balter had gifted to him after the private lesson with Sumwinkle.

It seemed such a long time ago. Rasher's entire world had changed in the couple days since that event. Sumwinkle was gone, and now he faced a deadly foe, with the fate of Kitan and the success of his entire Reaper team hanging in the balance.

No pressure.

Rasher slipped the dubious bacon into his belt pouch beside his other personal protection cuisine, checked his staff to ensure it contained a full charge of pressurized paint, then headed for the training sands.

The arena was shaded, with long shadows from the late afternoon sun snaking across most of the sands. The air was cool and clean, with the familiar scents of wood and sand and paint. Silence reigned across the empty stands.

Rasher moved cautiously into the maze of half walls and towers of the paint battle field. His team had reconfigured it since he'd last been there. It looked like they'd planned to host a large-scale mock battle, and had added quite a few new walls and towers as a result.

"So you came." Otamot's voice came from around a long, low wooden berm.

Rasher circled it warily and found the other bacon master standing across an open space about twenty yards square in the center of the arena. He wore his old Reaper uniform, complete with the pommels of his famous dual swords protruding over his shoulders.

This time he wore no mask, and Rasher was surprised to see a bruise around one eye. Had he done that during the battle on the rooftop?

"You made the messages so obvious, you might as well have sent me a written invitation," Rasher said.

"That would lack imagination."

"So it would have fit you perfectly. I can see one of those frilly afternoon tea invitations, all fancy scrollwork and pompous words."

"A joker to the bitter end," Otamot said with a frown. "So pathetic."

"Not as pathetic as beating up a team of paint battle trainers who did you no harm," Rasher retorted, infusing his words with some of the anger he kept tightly coiled in his chest.

"As Reaper captain, you must learn that your choices have consequences and that it's usually those around you who suffer when you act the fool."

"The legions only ever gave you respect," Rasher replied. "You're the fool for needing more."

"Respect?" Otamot snarled. "Was it respect to toss us out like charred leftovers?"

"You're pathetic," Rasher said, and he meant it. "You had it all, but at the first sign of adversity, you lash out like a spoiled child."

"I earned my place among the Reapers," Otamot retorted hotly. "You're just the joker they appointed to replace the real heroes."

"Keep telling yourself," Rasher said with a shrug. Otamot's mind was so curdled, he couldn't enjoy taunting the man. "Where is Kitan?"

"She is alive, but restrained," Otamot assured him. "She proved far more obstinate than I expected from a girl of her station."

His hand flicked toward his face before he caught himself, and Rasher laughed. "Kitan gave you a black eye? That must have been embarrassing."

"I will deal with her after I deal with you," Otamot said, striding forward, drawing his twin swords with a flourish. The steely hiss of the weapons sliding from their sheaths signaled the shift from taunting to fighting.

"Smart to change approaches," Rasher commented as he circled to the right, wishing he'd watched Otamot fight with those famous swords. "You're pretty weak with the staff."

He'd heard many stories of the man's battle prowess, and although he'd fought against many dual-sword-wielding foes, none matched Otamot's legendary status.

"I fight with real weapons," Otamot sneered. "I'm not afraid of seeing my enemies bleed."

"And you're not afraid to bleed yourself to escape when you get trounced. Planning to cheat like a coward again?"

As he hoped, the insult touched a sore point. Otamot's pride would hate that he'd been forced to resort to a cheap trick to escape the rooftop.

"You're the only one who will bleed today," Otamot promised, raising the weapons in salute, and then stalking forward purposefully.

Rasher returned the salute and committed three entire slices of his tiny supply of bacon. Instead of waiting for Otamot to close, he charged, letting the euphoria of bacon drive him on.

Surprise was one of the most effective weapons in one's arsenal, and he wasn't about to let Otamot define the fight.

His opponent did look surprised for a second, but then grinned and lunged to meet Rasher, swords flashing.

Rasher ducked one blade, deflected the other, and spun around his foe, unleashing a series of fast strikes, leveraging the speed of his two-handed weapon to the fullest.

Otamot moved just as fast, swords ringing as he countered or dodged every blow. After Rasher's initial flurry, Otamot began slipping his own strikes in between Rasher's. The tempo of the fight increased until their weapons seemed to blur in the air.

Together they spun and lunged, dodged and leaped, moving without hesitation, blades and staff sweeping around and between them in a deadly dance. They battled back and forth across the sand for long seconds, neither scoring a hit, both missing by fractions of an inch many times.

Rasher grinned, his entire being focused on the battle. He saw everything, and every muscle sang loudly in his senses. He felt every movement, sensed Otamot's position in relation to his, and tracked every slash of every blade.

His mind tuned out everything but the fight, his body attuned to it, as he fought to reach his enemy.

"You're using the Truly defense against me," Otamot commented, looking confident as he fought.

"I found it fitting, considering the flat terrain," Rasher responded.

"Naturally, you expect me to attack with Cappuccino."

"Naturally," Rasher agreed. "But I find that Turnip cancels out Cappuccino. Don't you?"

Otamot lunged, driving a shoulder into Rasher and knocking him back. "Unless your enemy has studied his Arugula. Which I have."

And with that, he shifted styles, driving Rasher back among the half-walls and berms of the paint battle maze.

Rasher shifted quickly, impressed. Only the most adept warriors studied beyond the common forms taught by the various high houses that sponsored most of the troops. Otamot had mastered all the higher forms of combat, and he began shifting between them rapidly, making it impossible for Rasher to anticipate his blows.

Rasher shifted in response, choosing the styles that best matched the attacks, and meeting every stroke as they battled around, over, and sometimes through the various flimsy barriers.

As they fought back around to the open sand area, Otamot's expression grew steadily angrier. Rasher doubted he'd ever met anyone who could keep up so long.

Finally Otamot grew impatient and drew even deeper from his bacon stores.

Rasher didn't dare release more bacon for fear of running out too soon, but Otamot wasn't limited by the same low stores. The extra bacon gave him a tiny advantage, and within seconds, one sword swept in, slashing a rip across Rasher's leather armor, right over his heart.

Rasher found himself retreating, fighting to hold off the increasing tempo as Otamot's swords flashed in faster and faster. The master swordsman shifted more rapidly between the various styles, his swords seeming to strike from all sides at once.

In any other circumstance, Rasher would have applauded the display of sword mastery.

Now, with death on the line, he didn't feel so much like cheering.

Otamot's angry expression turned into a smile as he sensed the tide of battle turning in his favor.

"You have no hope—" he started to gloat.

Rasher sprayed him across the face with a blast of blue paint.

Otamot must have forgotten about the paint because the move caught him completely by surprise. He staggered back as paint splashed across his cheeks, barely missing his eyes.

"You cheater!" Otamot shouted, one sword flashing at Rasher's face, even as he wiped at his own with the other.

Rasher dove to the side, rolling under the blade and cracking Otamot on the side of the leg as he passed. It was a solid strike and must sting like a snapdragon, but he missed the knee.

"Cheater? That's funny," Rasher said as he circled, happy for a moment to catch his breath.

He checked his bacon stores. He had enough to keep fighting full speed for maybe another minute, no more.

Not good. He needed to change tactics.

He'd proven that he could hold his own even against Otamot's famous swords, which surely infuriated the man. Now he had to get Otamot to make a mistake.

Except Otamot charged back into the fight, faster than ever. He must have committed a full ten slices in hopes of overwhelming Rasher.

Backpedaling, Rasher fought with all his skill to fend off the swords. He was forced to commit all of his bacon reserves at once to avoid getting skewered.

With all of his bacon concentrated into a burst of awesomeness that would burn out in ten seconds, Rasher stabilized his defenses and held off everything Otamot could throw at him. The cracking of swords against staff echoed through the arena like a constant pealing of epic thunder, and the look of surprise on Otamot's face was like his mother's special sauce to his soul.

But he couldn't keep it up.

As Rasher retreated close to one long wooden wall at the edge of the open area, he blocked one sword stroke poorly, and Otamot twisted the blade with a shout of triumph, knocking the staff from Rasher's hands.

He didn't even pause to gloat or start monologuing about how Rasher's demise was inevitable. He just lunged, both swords stabbing for Rasher's heart.

With the last of his bacon strength, Rasher back-flipped right over the low wall, barely avoiding the striking swords.

Otamot pursued, murder in his eyes. "You're just making the end harder on yourself, Rasher. There's no way you escape this arena and we both know it."

He hopped lightly over the barrier just as Rasher threw the squat carrot Gubbins had given him. It struck the ground directly below where Otamot was about to land. Instantly the surprised bacon master tumbled high into the air.

He'd been moving forward, so he shot up and forward fast. Despite his surprise, he still lashed out at Rasher as he flew past.

Rasher ducked and shouted after him, "Looks like you're the one trying to escape."

Otamot crashed hard into the side of one of the towers, and the entire flimsy structure buckled, crashing to the ground with a very satisfying implosion.

Rasher was tempted to retrieve his battle staff, but it wouldn't help. He lacked the bacon reserves to fight Otamot. So he pretended to have forgotten about it and fled toward the staff changing rooms, as if trying to escape.

Otamot caught him ten strides before the door. With bacon-enhanced speed, he could probably run down a deer. He shouted with triumph as he closed the distance.

Rasher dove to the side, but Otamot anticipated the move, and one of his swords slashed a long gash down Rasher's leg.

He fell to the sand with a groan, making a point of not looking at the wound. That one stung. A lot.

"You're out of bacon," Otamot chortled as Rasher fell onto his back.

"But I'm not out of tricks."

Rasher extended one hand and squeezed one of his mini muffins. The tiny missile leaped away with a hiss of fire, a spray of sugar sparkles, and the scent of fresh-baked sweets, aimed right at Otamot's face.

He dodged on pure instinct, and the mini muffin missile detonated against a nearby half wall with an impressive blast, ripping the wall apart.

In quick succession, Rasher triggered all the other mini muffins. Missiles leaped from his arm, forcing Otamot to leap and twist to avoid each one.

That was really fun, and Rasher laughed, "Dance, monkey dance!"

Unfortunately, he only had half a dozen missiles, and Otamot's bacon-fueled reflexes were just too fast.

Good thing he didn't expect to actually blow Otamot's head off. He just needed a bit of space.

After the last missile zipped past his head and exploded into another tower, ripping it apart in a fantastic spray of blasted timber, Otamot glared. "Are you finished with this childish display?"

"Of course not," Rasher said, extracting two pieces of chocolate-covered bacon. He shoved one into his mouth with a smile of victory.

Before he could eat the second one, Otamot lunged across the distance and clobbered him in the side of the head with the hilt of one sword.

Rasher rolled his head with the blow, so it didn't knock him out, but it still rattled him. Before he could recover, Otamot snatched the other piece of precious bacon from his hand.

"Thanks for replenishing my supply," Otamot teased as he chomped down on the stolen bacon.

Perfect.

Rasher didn't care that his insides were churning with nausea, as if he'd just consumed one of Lahanasi's corrupted foods. A vast sense of emptiness clubbed him so hard, he would have fallen if he wasn't already lying down.

He'd already consumed all of his bacon stores. The turkey bacon concealed under that chocolate still blasted his system with its purging negative bacon effects, but he suffered only a shadow of what he would have if he'd still had bacon reserves.

Unfortunately for Otamot, he had been actively using his bacon reserves.

Two heartbeats after shoving the very turkey bacon into his mouth that he'd given to Balter after the food fight to sabotage Rasher, the effects hit Otamot too. His eyes widened in horror and sudden understanding. He opened his mouth to shout something, but then twisted and vomited every ounce of bacon from his system.

Otamot fell to his knees under the brutal savagery of turkey bacon. It was the vilest counter to a bacon master's power, and Rasher had only ever tried it once.

Once was more than enough.

Otamot coughed and heaved, his entire body curling in on itself under the intensity of the purging, as if his stomach was trying to suck in his feet to then spew them out his open mouth.

His skin turned pale, then faded to a greenish cast as he wobbled unsteadily on his knees and nearly fell to his side.

"It's just the worst, isn't it?" Rasher asked, climbing to his feet and scooping up one of Otamot's fallen swords.

"How are you standing?" Otamot croaked in disbelief. "You ate it too."

"I was out of bacon already, so what did I have to lose?" Rasher asked, spreading his hands in apology. "And to think you fell to the very turkey bacon you tried to use against me. I'd call that poetic justice on most days."

Otamot tried scrabbling weakly for his other sword, but Rasher kicked it away. Otamot's connection to bacon had been deep and active when the turkey bacon struck. It was a wonder he was still coherent enough to whine. He wouldn't be fighting for quite a while.

"Kill me, then," Otamot spat. "Cheater."

"I had to level the playing field and give you a taste of your own turkey bacon."

"Know you'll never be anything but a fake hero," Otamot promised, his face twisted with hate.

"Maybe," Rasher acknowledged. "But unlike you, I didn't choose this job. I'm just trying to help. If you weren't so jealous, you might understand that."

"Jealous? Of what?" Otamot coughed and spat another chunk of vomit.

"Your heart is poisoned like a well-seasoned limburger, and you're only destroying yourself."

"Oh, please just kill me," Otamot said, dropping onto his back like a drama cake. "Lecturing is worse torture than the turkey bacon."

"Really?" Rasher asked with a grin. "My dad used to lecture me for hours. I've got so much material saved up." He grinned down at the suffering Otamot. "I can do this all day."

"I don't think so," Otamot said, drawing a tiny knife and slashing across his other hand. He lifted the bleeding hand toward Rasher, grinning.

Rasher blinked, thunderstruck, his eyes locked on the blood.

He felt nothing.

For the first time he could remember, he looked at fresh blood and felt no nausea, no weakness, no emotion at all. The emptiness of the turkey bacon was unshaken.

Again the blood triggered that long-buried memory of himself as a boy scampering along the narrow catwalk high above the vat of fresh blood in the slaughterhouse. He was laughing, calling back toward someone. Rasher couldn't remember who.

Then he had tripped.

With a start, the memory disappeared and Rasher shivered. That was so weird, but he didn't care about strange old memories. He was cured! Somehow he no longer had to fear blood. He laughed aloud, exulting.

Otamot frowned, looked down at his hand, and shook it toward Rasher.

"It's not working," Rasher laughed.

"That's just not fair," Otamot complained weakly. "Why now?"

"Maybe because I've finally defeated an evil villain to save my true love," Rasher suggested.

Otamot made a retching sound. "You are deranged."

Rasher shrugged, finding it impossible to worry about Otamot any longer. He wanted to understand how his blood phobia had healed. What had changed?

He doubted it had anything to do with defeating Otamot, but could it? Or might it be tied to the turkey bacon?

That would be the worst kind of bad luck. The only way to avoid the sickness that prevented him from best leading the legions as a bacon master was to wipe out his bacon master powers?

No, it had to be something else, but he was interrupted by the arrival of his team. Kucheesa, Noops, and Quarce burst into the arena from the dressing room, followed by Bibble a moment later. Balter and a score of Gleaners somehow vaulted right over the outer wall and leaped down the bleachers in fantastic bounds. The rhino-enhanced team smashed right through the main gates, leading half a hundred legionnaires in a thunderous charge.

"So subtle," Rasher commented as they rushed up to him. "Almost didn't hear you coming."

Quarce bellowed a laugh. The others looked relieved.

Bibble said, "You know, they closed down the jousting arena once too. One of the knights remarked that it made him feel so very tired."

"You might say, he was listless," Bibble finished with a flourish.

Rasher couldn't help laughing. That one was so bad, and it helped wash away some of the lingering tension from the recent duel.

"What?" Otamot scowled. No surprise that he didn't get the humor.

"Listless?" Bibble asked. "Lists. Knights. Closed arena?"

"That is so stupid," Otamot groaned, then started weakly coughing.

"It was pretty dumb," Kucheesa agreed, then took a threatening step toward Otamot. "But I will not allow you to insult a Reaper."

Rasher smiled but waved her back.

Balter asked, "What happened?"

"I had to defeat him in personal combat," Rasher said nonchalantly. Everyone looked dutifully impressed.

"You did not!" Otamot insisted, but lacked the strength to even sit up.

"Of course I did," Rasher replied, waving Otamot's sword. "I'm standing, you're lying defeated on the sands, and I took your sword. Looks like defeat to me."

"You cheated," Otamot insisted.

"Sore loser," Rasher said, then turned his back on the man. "He kidnapped Lady Kitan. She should be here somewhere, bound. Find her."

Gleaners scattered in every direction. Balter was looking from Rasher to Otamot in astonishment.

"You don't believe him, do you?" Otamot begged.

Balter shrugged. "He defeated Sumwinkle and me together. Not a surprise he defeated a man with no honor."

"Bind him and take him to the stocks," Rasher said. "We'll convene a tribunal eventually. I'll inform the inquisitors. They'll have to try something other than turkey bacon on him, though."

Several Gleaners lifted Otamot and quickly bound him with strips of caramel that not even a bear-enhanced warrior could break. Otamot's struggles proved laughable, and protested loudly until Balter gagged him, then removed his hat and stomped on it.

That snuffed his biscuits. Subdued, but still glowering, Otamot was thrown onto the back of a mule and led away.

"Nice hat, Captain," Noops commented. The others hadn't even noticed yet.

"I'm not sure it's perfect, but it's far better than nothing," Rasher admitted, fingering the brim of the red hat.

"Sapka will make more until she gets the right one," Kucheesa said with absolute confidence.

A moment later, Kitan rushed out of the battle maze. She looked a bit disheveled, but healthy. Rasher's heart finally relaxed as he moved to greet her.

She threw herself into his arms, laughing, and kissed him soundly.

That reminded him that his leg was still bleeding, but he found he just didn't care. Shifting his weight a little to his better leg, he just enjoyed the moment.

"If you greet me that enthusiastically every time you're kidnapped, I might have to arrange for it to happen more often," he teased when she finally let him breathe again.

"Don't you dare," she warned, then kissed him again, gently.

"Looks like you two need some space," Bibble said with a warm smile.

As much as he was tempted to simply take time to rest and enjoy Kitan's company, Rasher shook his head. "I don't think we're quite finished yet."

"You are," Quarce said, gesturing at his leg.

When Kitan saw the wound, she made him sit down and called for a milk mage. Colly Wobbles herself arrived a moment later and quickly doctored the leg with some fresh whipped cream.

The pristine white cream concealed the blood, although Rasher again felt no wave of nausea when he looked at it. The cool, healing sensation washed away the pain. Rasher sighed and thoroughly enjoyed the moment as Kitan insisted he lean on her while he healed.

He could get used to being an injured hero. There were so many perks the stories never talked about.

He wanted to discuss his lack of sickness, but there were too many people around. Most of them knew of his blood phobia by now, but he still didn't feel comfortable discussing the nuances of his weakness in front of them all. He'd find some quiet time to discuss it with Kitan.

"What else could we have to do?" Kucheesa asked after a moment. "You defeated Otamot, Bibble saved his family, all the compromised Reapers are captured, and the glowan assault on the gate was defeated."

"And mobilization is underway," Bibble added.

Noops said, "The fortune cookie."

"How did you know we got new ones?" Rasher asked.

He shrugged and held up a tiny slip of paper. "Because I received one too."

"What does yours say?" Quarce asked.

"It says 'You're not done yet'."

"That's strangely specific," Bibble said, extracting his piece of paper. "I got another one too. It says, 'You're going to need a lot of cloth'."

"That's random," Kucheesa said with a scowl. "Almost as bad as mine."

"Hey, I want another fortune cookie," Quarce complained.

"I think these are enough," Rasher said. "Now we just need to figure out what they mean.

45

THE LAHANASI RESTORATION CULT

As his team discussed the question of what dangers they still might need to face, Rasher only had eyes for the bag of bacon pastry twists Kitan produced from a deep pocket.

They were a specialty of the Ihlget family chef, and Rasher had consumed hundreds in recent months. Each one of the delicious pastries contained a full slice of crispy bacon twisted within a light, fluffy dough that was fried, then glazed with honey and dusted with tiny bacon bits.

He lifted the first one to his mouth, but paused and glanced at Colly. "How long before the effects of turkey bacon wear off?"

They had discussed the digestion period in the academy, but since he'd never intended to try turkey bacon again, he couldn't remember the specifics.

"Did you have active bacon when you consumed it?" she asked.

He shook his head. "All my reserves were depleted."

She pursed her lips. "I'd give it an hour before it's completely safe. Probably don't want to go swimming either."

"No swimming," he repeated. That much was fine, but an hour? That felt like forever.

Reluctantly, he put the bacon twist away. Kitan insisted he keep the bag for later. There were twenty twists in there. Enough to replenish about a third of his bacon stores. He couldn't remember the last time he'd allowed his bacon power to run completely dry. He felt strangely weak, his mind struggling to focus, and his emotions dampened.

Then again, those effects might be due to the turkey bacon. He fervently hoped the blood phobia relief wasn't, though.

"What then?" Kucheesa demanded of Bibble, hands on hips. "I don't think it's a good use of our time to go wandering around the Acropolis all night, looking for more glowan who might be skulking around."

Rasher tried to focus. "No, I don't think that's it."

"What then?" she demanded again. "All the enemies we know about are already defeated. That seems like a pretty good day's work to me. I think we should go back and find Redael. She was going to commandeer one of the officer kitchens and make a victory feast."

That did sound good, and they needed the boost, but Rasher couldn't ignore those fortune cookies.

"If not the glowan, the traitors, or the corrupted Reapers, who have we forgotten?" Bibble asked.

His mind might feel like he was trying to think through pudding, but Rasher actually got an idea. "The attack on the Cheese Palace on Nutmeg Hill."

"What about it?" Quarce asked as Balter and his sergeants gathered to listen.

"It doesn't fit the pattern," Noops said.

Rasher nodded. "That's what's bothering me too. Otamot was attacking the legion leadership because he felt betrayed and wanted to punish us all."

"The glowan could have done it," Bibble said. "That cat general thing did attack the Junior Toque."

"True, but why not attack him again?" Kucheesa asked, frowning over the puzzle. "Hurting the cheese wizards doesn't affect him, and that cat had made it sound like he had a personal grudge against Hamurisi."

Balter spoke up, extracting a piece of parchment from a pocket. "The note we received about the attack on the Cheese Palace included a little more information you may not have heard. The lead inquisitor has already stated they believe the attackers were in league with the glowan invaders."

"Really? Why didn't you share that with us sooner?" Kucheesa asked, taking the parchment.

Rasher frowned at the news. "It still feels weird. Why would the glowan attack the Cheese Palace instead of going after Hamurisi again?"

"Maybe he's too well guarded now," Quarce suggested.

"And the Cheese Palace wasn't?" Kucheesa asked.

"Not good for them if they left their guard down," Noops said with a frown. "They're already seen as corrupted after the fiasco with the Reaper contracts."

"Except they've proven it wasn't their fault," Balter objected.

"True, but most people don't know that yet. By attacking the main Cheese Palace and wreaking so much damage, they've hurt the cheese wizards and damaged their reputation.

Quarce shrugged. "They're a guild. They'll get over it."

"But their patrons might not," Kitan said with a sharp inhalation of breath.

Rasher sat up straighter so they could all look at her. Her face had paled and she clutched Rasher's hand.

"Everyone is in an uproar over the invasion, the hordes, and the attacks here in the Acropolis. They're already trying to pin blame on each other, and traditional alliances are in flux. Everyone already blames the cheese wizards for the contract fiasco. Now the Cheese Palace is attacked, making them look weak and vulnerable."

"And Sumwinkle was turned to cream cheese," Noops added.

Rasher nodded. "The statue is on display right there in the Food Court. Everyone has seen it, seen the abuse of those cheese powers."

Kitan grimaced. "The van Les dan Yussless house already has lots of enemies. They've used their lawyers to twist so many contracts in their favor that everyone would be thrilled to see them lose power. My father mentioned that some people were already calling for repercussions on the cheese guild and the Les house. One more fiasco and the cheese guild may lose standing."

Even hearing the words made him cringe. That hadn't happened in a generation. Losing standing would result in closing the guild palace on Nutmeg Hill, would severely damage their reputation, as well as the position of the Les family.

If they didn't resolve their issues promptly during the review period, they could conceivably be officially labeled 'out of savor' and banned. That extreme outcome would usually be considered impossible, but not under the current circumstances. Even so, Rasher doubted the Les family could really fall out of primi status. Their contracts locked them into position deeper than a tick.

But they could lose influence. A loss of prestige for the cheese guild could dampen the influence of the goddess Peynir. That might encourage the guilds of lesser gods, and motivate the Les house rivals to strike harder.

He hated Food Court intrigue, especially when they were facing an apocalypse, but he couldn't ignore the fact that many in power like Kitan's father would never pass up an opportunity to strike at their political opponents.

Words that Shemo had said returned to mind. "You tear yourselves apart even as we plan our vengeance. I'm amazed we haven't witnessed your destruction by your own hands already."

Was he speaking about something specific and not just in grand generalities? Did he know about other traitors among the people? Had he been expecting the attack on the Cheese Palace?

Or did he know about another, deadlier plot?

Rasher frowned, wishing for bacon to enhance his thoughts. All of that intrigue and potential disaster for the cheese guild and the Les house made perfect sense, but not if the attack came from the glowan. Would they know all of the intricacies of the Food Court?

Would they care about taking down one house? Or were they just looking to foster discord?

"Hold on," Bibble asked, interrupting Rasher's thoughts. "If all the attackers were killed in the fighting, how can the inquisitors know they were traitors allied with the glowan?"

Good question.

Kucheesa passed the parchment to him. Rasher scooted over to read over his shoulder and quickly scanned the page. Balter had provided a succinct summary, and Rasher didn't notice anything else important.

"Maybe one of the attackers said something during the fighting that revealed their alliance with the glowan," Kucheesa guessed.

Quarce said, "Or maybe someone saw fairies or other glowan during the attack."

"I'll send a runner to request more information," Balter said, making a single hand gesture. One of the tiger-enhanced warriors sprinted away at full speed.

Rasher said, "If we assume the glowan aren't involved, maybe the attack really is from an inter-family plot. Kitan, who would most like to see the Les family's reputation damaged?"

She chuckled without humor. "Everyone. If they lost power, it might weaken some of their contracts. They've hurt every high house over the years, but I think the Toffer family probably hates them the most. They're constantly maneuvering to damage each other."

"Do you think they'd stoop to using the glowan invasion as a cover to attack the Cheese Palace?" Kucheesa asked.

"I wouldn't usually think so, but everything is all in an uproar this week."

Bibble looked up from the paper. "So would you consider it important to learn that one of the conspirators was a member of the Toffer house?"

"What?" Kitan exclaimed.

Bibble offered the paper. "At the bottom they've listed the attackers who have already been identified."

Rasher had seen the list, but ignored it. Kitan gasped with surprise when she scanned the list. "This can't be right. Not Tamarind."

"You know him?" Rasher asked.

She nodded. "A little. Tamarind van Toffer dan Itluks. He's a cousin, one of the outliers of the Toffer house. He's not motivated enough to be a traitor. He likes to waste time gambling and drinking and whining with other members of the Lahanasi restoration cult about the need to restore his alcohol powers."

Rasher exchanged a look with Bibble, who asked, "The Lahanasi cult?"

She shrugged. "He invited me to a couple of their parties, but they were usually really boring."

"Another link to both the Toffer house and the Lahanasi cult," Rasher said, thinking back to the muffin mage who had attacked him on the roof of the food storage warehouse.

"You can't be serious," Kitan said. "The cult is popular because they share a lot of booze at their parties. I know lots of people who go, but most of them aren't foolish enough to get involved with serious plotting for Lahanasi's return. That would be insane."

"It only takes a few radicals to stir up trouble," Quarce said.

Noops nodded. "I bet Tamarind has a lot more cousins."

"He does," Kitan admitted. "What does that have to do with anything?"

"That much drinking often results in affairs. Is he a legitimate son of the family?"

She frowned. "Now that you mention it, I'm not sure."

Interesting, but probably not relevant.

"Maybe he sees the cult as a path to accessing greater power," Kucheesa suggested.

"Either way, he's not motivated or smart enough to join the glowan," Kitan said confidently. "I wouldn't have suspected he'd get involved in something as stupid as a cult attack either."

"So why would the lead inquisitor tell everyone they're glowan traitors then?" Kucheesa asked.

"Either she knows something we don't, or she's received bad information," Bibble guessed.

Noops shrugged. "Bad information won't confuse people for long. If Kitan knows the truth, others will realize the lie soon enough."

"Could the cult be planning another attack somewhere?" Rasher asked.

"I don't see how they could," Balter interrupted. "The Chef's Watch and all of the guilds are on the highest alert, especially after the Cheese Palace attack. I doubt a single fairy could infiltrate Nutmeg Hill right now with all the active wards and defenses."

"What else could they even try?" Quarce asked. "A bunch of drunks aren't going to accomplish much."

"I don't know, something that might push the cheese guild farther out of favor. They only need one more big push, one more disaster . . ."

He trailed off as several facts snapped into place, and he felt a chill of horror.

"What?" Kucheesa asked.

"There's a special session of the First Course Assembly in the Food Court tonight, right?"

Kitan nodded, glancing at the sky, even though the sun was not visible beyond the arena wall. "It should start within the hour. They will discuss the invasion and security lapses in the Acropolis and on Nutmeg Hill. Everyone of any importance will be attending."

She frowned and added, "Usually I'd get an invitation, but my father told me there were limited seats, so only he could attend from our family."

Rasher snapped his fingers, thoughts seizing on a new idea. "Kucheesa, what was that fortune cookie you received again?"

"That dumb riddle?"

"Yes."

She extracted the paper. "I almost threw this out." She read the text again. "What do you get from a sick chef's first course?"

"Disgusting food," Colly spoke up. "Still just a silly children's joke."

"What if it's more than that?" Rasher asked with a shiver of dread trickling down his spine. "What if it's talking about the Master Chef and the First Course Assembly?"

"The Master Chef is in bad health," Bibble said, eyes wide. "A sick chef."

"First Course is the assembly, of course," Kucheesa added, slapping her forehead loudly. "Why didn't I pick up on that?"

"Because none of us expected Lahanasi's followers might attack the assembly tonight," Rasher said.

"Are we sure that's what it means?" Balter asked with a frown. "The logic seems spread pretty thin."

"And how would they do it?" Quarce asked. "They can't storm the hill. It's too well defended."

"It's got to be something to do with cheese if Lahanasi's trying to destroy one of his enemies in the Pantryon," Noops said.

That's what Rasher feared, and he remembered the worker with the noodle warrior skills who caught that falling illumination pastry.

"Workers were replacing all the illumination pastries in the entire Food Court assembly hall," he told the others. "The pastries were big, but gave off less light. I just thought they were doing some weird ambiance effect."

"Or maybe there was less actual pastry to burn," Quarce exclaimed.

Kitan looked horrified. "What are you suggesting, Rasher?"

Kucheesa spoke first. "You might be onto something, Captain. If they packed those pastries with cheese, they could get all the nasty poisons or acids they wanted into the Food Court and no one would notice."

"And they're already in position right above everyone's heads," Bibble said softly.

Rasher nodded, convinced they were right. "It would be a simple thing to include an explosive element in each pastry."

He imagined the pastries, set high above the unsuspecting assembly all exploding together, raining curses or poisoned cheese over everyone. He shuddered at the potential destruction. How many would die or be crippled?

Such a disaster could either wipe out the high cream of the empire in a single blow, or at minimum sow enormous chaos right when they needed those leaders the most.

"Crumpets!" Quarce swore.

Noops grinned approvingly. "Perfect timing for that one."

"We have to get to Nutmeg Hill and stop them!" Bibble exclaimed.

Rasher grinned. "Time to crash the Food Court."

Noops sighed. "Looks like it'll be a late dinner."

46

NEVER SEE THEM BLEED

Within moments, they were galloping full tilt toward Nutmeg Hill, with Balter's elite Gleaners running escort. The tiger, wolf, and lion-enhanced squads kept up, running lightly over the stone-paved streets. The most fleet-footed of them even ranged ahead, shouting for everyone to make way.

Even though the rhino and bear-enhanced Gleaners fell steadily behind, they made a valiant effort to pursue. They'd probably catch up easily while Rasher raised the alarm at the gate.

Balter's Gleaners had commandeered mounts from some of the passing nobility. Rasher rode a large chestnut gelding at the head of their war party. When he glanced back at his team galloping behind him, their faces set in grim determination, he should feel pride, but his emotions remained strangely void.

Bibble's face was more like a mask of terror. The chubby spice wizard was so focused on the effort of not falling out of the saddle that he didn't even try sharing any terrible jokes.

Kucheesa and Noops both rode easily, while Quarce clutched on with a white-knuckled grip, grinning so widely he was probably swallowing bugs. Kitan rode beside Rasher, the picture of elegant grace, making the tricky side-saddle position seem simple.

He only wished they had more time to prepare. He would have appreciated time to find some armor, and he wished he could delay until the turkey bacon void wore off and could restore his precious bacon powers. He hadn't gone so long without the lightning-like feel of bacon coursing through his veins and pooling in his joints since the day he discovered his powers. It should unnerved him, but again he felt nothing.

The weird emotionless void of vile turkey bacon compounded the effect, leaving him feeling like he was a spectator, experiencing events in a strangely detached way.

Was that why the blood hadn't triggered his blood phobia? He desperately needed to explore that, but he didn't have time. Like his Rule of Engagement number fifty said, when in over one's head, what's a little more depth?

A moment later they made the final turn onto Cheddar Way that ran along the north wall of Nutmeg Hill and led to the main gate in the center. The huge gates were open, but the portcullis was closed during the rare full Food Court meeting, and a long line of fancy-dressed nobility milled unhappily outside, mingled with traders, officials, and curious citizens.

Rasher's group created quite a stir as they plowed through the group, Balter's Gleaners forcibly pushing aside those too slow or too self-important to get out of the way.

The captain of the gate guard stepped out through a small sally port to the side of the portcullis and raised a hand for them to stop. He was a middle-aged fellow with a spotlessly shining breastplate, elaborately embroidered boots, and a captain's wide-brimmed hat with bits of silver thread scattered throughout the brim that gave the impression his head was exploding.

Probably not the effect he was going for, but that's what Rasher saw.

"Must be from the Morstyl house," Kucheesa muttered.

The captain recognized Balter, then blinked in surprise to see the Reaper insignia on Rasher's uniform.

"What is going on?"

"I'm Captain Dilskin," Rasher said. "Let us pass and rouse the Chef's Watch. We must get to the Food Court immediately. The Imperial Chef and everyone in the assembly is in danger."

The captain blanched and straightened his shining steel gauntlets, but glanced at Balter. "These are grave allegations, Captain, but I must apologize. I do not know you. Balter, can you vouch for him?"

Balter nodded and spoke with clear impatience. "Get out of the way, Waldorf, and do what Captain Dilskin said. We have credible evidence that traitors allied with the glowan are planning to assault the assembly."

"He speaks the truth, Waldorf," Kitan said. She clearly knew him, and Rasher was glad she was with them to give their words more weight.

Surprisingly, Captain Waldorf didn't move, but frowned and removed his hat to run gauntleted fingers through his perfectly coiffed black hair. "I was specifically ordered by Commander Cobb to not allow anyone through under any circumstances, and to hold all couriers until after the conference."

"Is that normal procedure?" Rasher asked.

Captain Waldorf hesitated before saying, "No, sir."

That didn't sound good at all.

"I've got a very bad feeling about this," Bibble muttered.

"Me too," Rasher agreed before urging his horse forward another step. "Captain Waldorf, on my honor as the Reaper captain, this threat is real. I have the authority to commandeer your men to assist in protecting the Food Court from foreign enemy attack. You will summon every soldier available and join us."

"Can you really do that?" Quarce asked in what he probably thought was a whisper, but which echoed from the stone wall.

"Of course I can," Rasher said confidently, although he had no idea if his authority trumped that of the Chef's Watch.

It probably didn't, but it gave Captain Waldorf an excuse to do what was right. As the man hesitated, Rasher added, "If we find our intelligence is faulty, I swear on my honor and every witness here to accept full responsibility and all consequences for the actions of you and your men in fulfilling my orders."

That did it. Moments later, they trotted through the wide thoroughfares of Nutmeg Hill at the head of four hundred Chef's Watch soldiers. The streets were unusually empty. It made progress simpler, but felt wrong.

"Where is everyone?" Kucheesa asked.

Captain Waldorf said, "All businesses were ordered closed during the assembly. Even restaurants. Everyone not attending the assembly was ordered inside."

"That sounds ominous," Bibble said.

"On Commander Cobb's authority?" Rasher guessed.

"No," Captain Waldorf said, then hesitated. "Well, he is the one who gave the order, but he said the order came from the Junior Toque himself."

"Convenient," Bibble said. "Is everyone higher ranked than Commander Cobb at the assembly?"

When Captain Waldorf nodded, it made sense. Rasher said, "Captain, be aware that we believe the attack is being coordinated with extreme members of the Lahanasi restoration cult. Your Commander Cobb may be involved."

Captain Waldorf looked shocked, but not as shocked as he should have. Kucheesa noted it too and asked, "He is a cult member, isn't he?"

"Yes. A lot of people are, but they just like to drink and make silly proclamations that one day alcohol will rule supreme again."

"Not so silly any more," Kitan commented.

"How many others do you know in the cult?" Bibble asked Captain Waldorf.

"Quite a few, but they can't all be extremists. Can they?"

"We don't know, but we can't assume they aren't," Rasher said.

Bibble glanced back at the troops following them. "Are any of your soldiers cult members?"

Captain Waldorf paled at the suggestion, glancing back at the ranks again. "I'm not sure. With my family connections, I attend high society parties that most of my men can't."

"Stay alert then," Rasher said. "Worst case, we may have traitors at our backs as well as to our front."

"We may need more guild support," Bibble suggested, looking nervous. "I mean, if the cult includes so many people, it's possible they've got wizards and mages and shamans helping."

"How could we not know about this?" Captain Waldorf exclaimed.

Rasher shrugged. "Everyone knows about the cult, so we're all used to ignoring their threats."

"It is easier to see danger in the faces of those we do not know," Noops added.

Rasher hoped they were wrong, but feared they hadn't brought nearly enough manpower to root out the cultists. The one thing they had in their favor was that no one would expect a strong military response before the surprise attack at the Food Court. If the enemy was relying solely on that surprise and remaining unseen so the cheese guild could take the blame, they might not be ready to repel Rasher's forces.

As they trotted past the row of high house palaces, Kucheesa pointed up. "Flying couriers."

Indeed, Rasher spotted three of the courier personal kites flying high above the distant Food Court. He hadn't spotted any couriers at all over the Nutmeg Hill skies.

"Odd," Captain Waldorf said with a frown. "They're just circling the Food Court. That is not an authorized flight pattern."

"I fear the enemy knows we're coming," Rasher said. The only plausible explanation for those couriers was as far-seeing scouts. "Let's pick up the pace."

His team and the Gleaners could easily outpace the Chef's guard, but they might need them, so they only managed to increase to a fast jog. The sound of hundreds of soldiers running, armor clanking, swords banging, and chainmail jingled created a rising crescendo behind them.

A moment later, they rounded the long curve of the main boulevard around the Junior Toque's palace and caught sight of the grand Food Court building. The huge Plaza of the Pantryon was empty, but heavy wagons had been arranged to block the road, and more blocked the gaps between the tall statues of the gods. Thick planks fastened to the front sides of the wagons prevented anyone from slipping underneath, and formed a rather formidable wall.

"That's not encouraging," Bibble muttered as they slowed their horses to give the troops time to catch their breath. Captain Waldorf quickly ordered his troops into a wide battle formation, shield bearers at the front, followed by spearmen. The few archers remained at the rear.

Rasher was disappointed to see they only had a single muffin mage and one milk mage to help Colly Wobbles. The muffin mage was followed by a pair of assistants pulling a small cart, but he couldn't hold a huge amount of battle cuisine in there. The milkmaid who attended the milk mage pulled a small, refrigerated wagon.

"Where is the guard assigned to protect the plaza?" Captain Waldorf asked with a frown as they drew to within fifty yards of the makeshift wall blocking the way.

As if in response, hundreds of people stepped out of concealment behind the statues and wagons. In seconds, they formed into loose battle lines.

They were an odd mix, including a few squads of armored soldiers wearing the uniforms of the Chef's Watch. The majority looked like men and women in the rough garb of workers, like the ones Rasher had seen replacing the illumination pastries.

Unfortunately he spotted at least three muffin mages, a vegetable shaman, a cheese wizard, and surprisingly, two milk mages.

"By Hilekar's bony knees," Kucheesa muttered.

"I think most of them are Lahanasi cultists," Bibble interjected.

She shrugged. "Either god, this is not good."

The cultists lifted weapons and cheered, the sound echoing loudly across the plaza. Some of the workers carried steel swords and spears, but most of them carried more makeshift weapons they could have easily slipped past the Watch. Cudgels, hammers, and a few longbows.

Captain Waldorf hissed in an angry breath, and Rasher followed his gaze. About halfway down the line of the enemy forces stood a larger knot of soldiers in the uniform of the Chef's Watch, led by a man with the tall hat of a Commander.

"Commander Cobb," Captain Waldorf whispered, face twisted with rage. "Traitor!"

That confirmed their worst fears, even more than the sight of the rogue army holding the Plaza with guild members openly betraying their oaths.

"Why aren't they worried about the sound?" Quarce muttered.

That was a good point. If the assembly realized a pitched battle was about to start just outside, that would mobilize all the military and guild members of the audience. Many of them were the most powerful culinary wizards alive, and their assistance would easily sweep away the cultists.

"Air shielding over the entryways," Bibble said, squinting at the distant Food Court. "I can't see it clearly, but I can feel it."

"Can you bring it down?" Rasher asked.

"Not from this distance," Bibble said.

"Okay, then. Time is of the essence," Rasher said, studying the battlefield and making a plan. "Balter, focus the Gleaners on the center, right down their throats along the road. We must punch through to get Bibble close enough to bring down those spice shields. Once we rouse the assembly, the battle will turn into a rout."

Balter banged a fist to his chest and relayed the orders while Rasher turned to Captain Waldorf. "Captain, deploy your forces to flank the Gleaners and keep the enemy distracted. Archers focus on enemy guild members. Have the muffin mage provide fire support."

Captain Waldorf nodded grimly, glancing back at the deserters from the Watch, his gaze focused on Commander Cobb. "Traitors are the vilest of evil. I swear on my life that we'll purge them."

"And us?" Kucheesa asked as the team bunched around Rasher. Noops surveyed the enemy forces calmly and Quarce had drawn his expandable battle hammer with a wild glint in his eyes. Kucheesa was trying to look brave, but kept glancing nervously at the enemy forces.

"I know you haven't seen battle before," Rasher told her. "Just try to channel that annoying side of yourself that was willing to take on an entire angry mob."

"Hey, I'm not annoying," she protested.

"That's the spirit," Noops said.

"And what's that supposed to mean?" she demanded.

He only smiled.

Rasher said, "We go in with the Gleaners. Kucheesa, see if you can float up one of the statues. Use your knives to support us. Whatever the cost, we have to get Bibble through their lines to the entries so he can take down those spice air shields."

They all nodded. Bibble gulped, already sweating, but he pulled his reinforcing smelling salts from a pocket of his hat and took a long sniff."

Then he nodded once. "I won't fail you, Captain."

"You tackled one of the most dangerous retired Reapers alive," Quarce reminded him. "You've got this."

Bibble straightened in his saddle and whispered, "For my family."

Rasher was proud of their courage. He extended a hand and said, "For Rubric, and the Reapers."

They all joined hands and loudly repeated the traditional Reaper battle cry. The Gleaners took up the call, which spread like a grease fire through bacon vats to the rest of their forces.

As one they chanted, "For Rubric and the Reapers!"

The sound boiled through Rasher's veins with almost as much power as bacon. He shouted above the din to his team, "We might not be everything the legions wanted in a new Reaper team, but we're all that stands between the empire and traitors trying to help usher in the apocalypse!"

Quarce cheered, his voice booming from his thick chest. Bibble raised a defiant fist, and Noops nodded approval.

Kitan was watching him with a proud little smile. He wished they were alone so he could steal a kiss, but Kucheesa interrupted the moment. "Captain, aren't you supposed to be trying to encourage us before battle?"

He grinned. "Rasher's Rules of Engagement number one. Never see them bleed."

"Wait, shouldn't it be never let them see us bleed?" Bibble interjected.

"Not for me," he said, raising his hand and bringing it down hard.

As one, their entire little army surged forward.

47

THE BATTLE FOR NUTMEG HILL

B alter and his two dozen Gleaners launched forward with a roar, their voices shaking the plaza. They quickly outpaced the rest of the army as everyone gave chase. Rasher and his team pursued, still on horseback, although he wasn't sure the horses would be able to get through whatever gap the Gleaners made. If nothing else, they could jump onto the wagons from the saddle to get over the barrier.

The enemy raised weapons as the first arrows flashed from the rear of Rasher's lines, striking into their ranks. A lucky shot even struck the traitor muffin mage in the shoulder, spinning him away.

Rasher wondered if Balter and his Gleaners would simply smash right through the thin ranks of the traitors. Makeshift barricades and weapons would not stand against the elite, enhanced warriors.

The traitors had brought their own surprises.

Every single traitor along their entire front simply dropped their weapons and instead drew forth a wide array of small objects, which they began throwing in impressive unison. Before Rasher could raise an alarm, sheets of small clay jars, bottles, and cloth bags rained down just in front of the charging ranks of Rasher's little army. Balter and the Gleaners were caught in a storm of projectiles.

They tried dodging or knocking items out of the way, but there were simply too many to dodge them all. With every impact, the objects shattered, releasing their contents to splash all over the Gleaners. Jars burst in a shower of clear liquid, while little round globes that looked like eggs exploded into green clouds of choking gas. Clay jars shattered to release yellow liquid.

For a second, Balter's team powered through as the rest of the army skidded to a halt right in front of the poisonous clouds of green smoke.

"Bibble!" Rasher shouted.

"On it," he said, already extracting ingredients. "Ten seconds."

A horrible stench wafted out from the cloud, and Rasher gagged, covering his nose with his arm. All down the lines, soldiers staggered and retreated from the smell.

With a roar of defiance, Balter vaulted onto the center wagon. There he stumbled and abruptly fell forward to explosively vomit over the side of the wagon. The rest of the Gleaners, still caught in the clouds of green smoke and covered in whatever vile cuisine the traitors had launched at them, also began vomiting. The sounds were horrible as the mighty warriors spewed everything they'd eaten.

The stench grew worse and Rasher didn't have to urge his horse to retreat. Snorting and shaking its head violently, the animal danced back with the others from the potent miasma.

"Look at them," Kucheesa exclaimed, pointing.

The Gleaners were trying to rise between bouts of vomiting, but they staggered to and fro, often falling.

"They look drunk," Quarce said.

"Of course!" Rasher exclaimed, realizing what they were seeing. "We should have expected something like this."

"How could you expect this?" Kucheesa demanded.

"We're dealing with Lahanasi's cult. They want to restore his alcohol powers, but right now he has power over disgusting food. I think we're seeing both."

"I've heard of alcohol bombs," said Noops, who had drawn his shovel and held it ready. "Forbidden recipes that trigger drunken confusion."

"What about the green clouds?" Quarce asked nervously.

Kucheesa's expression had turned thoughtful. "I bet they're fermented quicklime eggs. Sometimes called Century eggs."

"How do you know that?" Rasher asked.

She shrugged. "Many in the Meat Palace opposed my appointment, so they made me study with the chef researchers. I had to spend two entire weeks studying recipes by disenfranchised chefs so I never accidentally replicated any of them."

"You realize that doesn't make any sense, right?" Quarce asked.

"Of course it made no sense. That's why they made me do it."

As fascinating as that insight was, they didn't have time for it. "What do the eggs do?" Rasher asked.

"That's the stench. If it gets on your skin, it triggers body odor so foul it's been known to make skunks sick."

"That's amazing," Quarce said enthusiastically.

"And the other liquids?" Rasher asked.

She shrugged. "There are a few options, but I bet it's baby mouse rice wine."

"That's disgusting," Bibble grimaced, still mixing herbs.

"Lahanasi," she said with a shrug.

"Ready!" Bibble said, urging his horse to the front of their group. He flung the spice mixture into the air, hands spread wide.

Immediately a soft breeze picked up, blowing the clouds of green smoke back toward the traitors. The breeze intensified into a moderate wind, which pushed the clouds faster. Wherever the green clouds blew, men and women staggered, coughing and retching as the stench took hold and quickly became unbearable. Ragged lines appeared in their ranks.

"We must press the attack," Rasher said, turning toward Captain Waldorf. "Charge!"

Despite the danger and the recent display of the enemy's battle cuisine, the captain didn't hesitate, but took up the cry. "Charge!"

If only they had more time to call in reinforcements, but the assembly had already started, and the traitors could strike at any second.

As their little army charged again, the enemy launched a second volley of projectiles, but far fewer in number.

"They don't have enough!" Kucheesa cried as she leaped straight up off her saddle, floating high over the incoming barrage toward the nearest statue of the gods. Appropriately, it was Peynir, goddess of cheese.

"It's plenty," Quarce muttered as he swung his hammer to intercept incoming projectiles before they could strike Bibble.

Rasher and Noops had reacted at the same time, all three of them closing ranks around the spice wizard, staff and shovel and hammer swinging to deflect the missiles. Rasher braced for the impact with disgusting wine or eggs.

Nothing struck him.

Even as his staff, Noops' shovel, and Quarce's hammer flashed out to strike projectiles out of the air, shattering them into clouds of shards and sprays of foul liquid, the rain of destruction deflected away, as if off of an invisible barrier.

Bibble shouted, "That's how it's done in my house!"

His hands were lifted, fingers coated in spices. He'd created a barrier of air around them.

"I'm so glad you're on our team," he said with a relieved sigh.

The rest of their army was not so lucky. Men and women staggered under the new barrage, screaming from the stench, staggering in drunken clumsiness, or falling to all fours to heave out everything they'd eaten in the last week.

But many of their forces made it through the barrage. Archers at the rear kept firing, keeping the traitorous guild members dodging, while their muffin mage began unleashing a barrage of mini muffin missiles. They streaked close overhead. Some exploded against the makeshift wagon walls, while others cleared the defense and ripped through the enemy ranks, wreaking mayhem and blasting holes in their lines.

"Go!" Rasher shouted, urging his nervous mount toward the wagons. The Gleaners were still out of commission, although the rhino-enhanced warriors seemed to be shaking off the effects faster. Their thicker skin must have offered some defense.

Rasher reached the wagon where Balter was still swaying drunkenly on all fours. The bed of the wagon was slick with vomit, and the entire area reeked. Rasher leaped onto the wagon, followed by Noops, while Quarce hung back to protect Bibble until they could clear the way.

Instead of charging to repel them, the traitors closest to the wagon abruptly stepped apart to reveal a woman with a hose connected to a large bucket. Cackling maniacally, she pointed the hose at them and pulled a nozzle.

"Look out!" Noops shouted, leaping in front of Rasher and jumping forward. As he vaulted toward the woman, he flung his shovel with both hands.

A powerful jet of pressurized liquid shot out of the hose. Brown and thick, the liquid passed just above the shovel and caught Noops in the chest, coating his gleaming armor in nasty sludge and knocking him out of the air.

He fell to the ground, gagging and retching.

His shovel found its mark, though. The magnificent blade shattered the pressurized container, which exploded, blasting all the traitors around it with a thick coating of thick, brown sludge.

Rasher stared, aghast, as dozens of traitors collapsed, screaming and vomiting.

"That's Ttongsul!" Kucheesa shouted, her voice terrified. "Captain, get out of there. It's a vile mixture made from fermented child feces. It causes extreme nausea and catastrophic loosening of the sphincter!"

"Oh, you've got to be kidding me," Rasher grimaced, glancing at Noops, who was struggling valiantly to rise, despite the muck coating him.

Other ttongsul sprayers opened fire down the enemy lines, spraying soldiers who began struggling over the wagons, even as other traitors continued throwing their rapidly diminishing supply of other vile recipes.

The traitorous milk mage also appeared down the line about a hundred feet to Rasher's left. The tall fellow had an enormous gut, thinning hair, and a scraggly beard. He hefted glass spheres of whipped cream, but Rasher noted black bits inside too. Some kind of corrupting agents, no doubt. Some of Lahanasi's evil cuisine the traitor had used to poison his own healing cuisine.

The milk mage shouted, "Lactose incompetent!" and began hurling spheres at the troops led by Captain Waldorf who were beginning to swarm over the wagons, despite everything they'd already been hit with.

Glass shattered and whipped cream sprayed over the surprised soldiers' faces. They gagged and shuddered as the exposed skin of their faces and hands began to bubble into huge, nasty purple hives that popped like giant zits, spraying more filth around them.

Many of the soldiers fell, but somehow Captain Waldorf and three of his men made it over the wagon barrier unscathed. Without hesitation, the captain charged the knot of traitors wearing the Chef's Watch uniform, led by Commander Cobb.

Raising his sword, he shouted, "Oath breakers!"

Commander Cobb stepped to the front of his men and met the angry captain's charge with steady confidence. They battled each other viciously, but Rasher couldn't spare the time to watch. He had to get through the line and clear a path for Bibble. If only he had bacon! Usually defeating even a large number of unenhanced enemies would be a simple matter, but he felt slow and weak.

"Get Bibble up here," he ordered Quarce. "We'll fight through and he can follow."

"I've got this, Captain," Balter said drunkenly, surging to his feet before falling over and vomiting again. The poor Gleaner had taken more vile cuisine in the face than any of the others. His attempts to continue were valiant, but he wouldn't recover in time.

As Rasher turned to help Bibble onto the wagon, Kucheesa shouted from her perch above, "Cheese Wizard!"

He spun back around to see the traitorous cheese wizard, a skinny fellow whose green and yellow robes made him look sickly, had slipped to the front of the enemy forces.

Grinning evilly, the cheese wizard waved a hand, and several traitors pulled thin ropes that Rasher hadn't noticed lying on the ground, extending to the wagons. With a snicking sound, a twelve-inch wide band of brown cloth along the entire length of the wagon was whisked aside.

How had he missed that?

Wow, the lack of bacon was really showing.

Moving the cloths uncovered long lines of black script. The letters looked like they'd been burned into the wood, and the sight of the legalese filled Rasher with more dread than all the evil cuisine he'd seen unleashed so far.

"Go ahead, mighty hero," the cheese wizard cackled. "Step over the script and see what happens."

"You don't have authority to make any legal contract binding here," Kucheesa shouted from her safe perch atop Peynir's scales of justice.

"Test it, then," the cheese wizard said with far too much confidence. "These wagons were purchased legally and their owners approved their current use."

"Son of a brisket," Rasher cursed, retreating farther from the script and motioning Quarce and Bibble back. He couldn't risk it. They needed to find another way.

Kucheesa wasn't deterred. She threw a pair of knives at the cheese wizard, who was too busy taunting Rasher to recognize the danger.

The knives caught the man in the chest, and he staggered, screaming and clutching at the hilts.

Then Kucheesa threw an egg.

Rasher blinked in surprise, but it really was an egg. It struck the screaming cheese wizard in the face and detonated in an impressive explosion that removed his head in a flash of gore.

"What in the name of all the gods?" Rasher whispered, but Kucheesa was already moving, leaping from Peynir and floating to the next statue in the line, then on to the next.

He wasn't sure what she was doing, but didn't have time to chase her. Rasher jumped back off the wagon, pulling Balter with him. The Gleaner had recovered enough not to fall on his face when he landed, but still looked woozy. He reeked like an open sewer, but anger was beginning to replace nausea. His men were also starting to recover, and Rasher gestured them to follow as he retreated with Bibble and Quarce.

The attack had faltered, and now that the devilish legalese was revealed along all of the wagons, the Watch retreated to regroup near Rasher. Several officers hurried to him, looking for guidance as other soldiers pulled wounded companions from the battlefield.

"We can't go over the wagons," Rasher said. "It's too dangerous. We'll need to break through those outer walls and roll them over to make room."

"We've sent runners to call for reinforcements from every palace and the guilds," one sergeant said.

That was good, but it would take too long.

"Noops is over there, along with Captain Waldorf," Bibble said nervously.

"I am confident Noops can take care of himself," Rasher said. "The fastest way to get aid to Captain Waldorf is to roll those wagons." He pointed at the only other captain of the Watch in the group. "You take command of that effort. Focus all energies on breaking through. I'll have the Gleaners assist as soon as they recover."

The captain saluted and turned to begin issuing orders.

"What about us?" Quarce asked. "We need to get through to take down that shielding."

"We'll break through the defenses in time, but we don't have time," Rasher said with a frown.

His little army could easily cut through the defenders once they breached the wagon wall, but the traitors had shown far more ingenuity than he would have imagined possible. His thoughts still felt like they were moving through sludge, but he had gotten an idea.

He turned to the woman who was the sergeant of the wolf-enhanced Gleaner squad. She was filthy and stank horribly, but appeared mostly recovered. "I need hats."

"Hats?" she asked, trying to focus blurry eyes.

"Hats," he repeated. "As many of the biggest, gaudiest hats you can find, and fast. Go!"

She might not understand, but her discipline held. She barked an order and left at a remarkable sprint, followed by her entire squad.

Good, the Gleaners were recovering. It might take a week of constant bathing to get the stench out, but it looked like the evil cuisine hadn't caused any lasting damage.

"What are we doing, Captain?" Bibble asked nervously.

"Remember your fortune cookie," Rasher said.

"We're going to need a lot of cloth?" Bibble asked with a frown.

"Exactly. And we'll need some wind. A lot of wind." He gestured straight up. "I need to get up to the courier windstreams."

Kitan whistled softly. "It might work, but you don't even know who the traitors are."

"That's why you're going with me," Rasher told her.

He'd never heard her curse before. She was really good at it.

48

HOLD ONTO YOUR HAT

"You are well and truly insane," Kitan told Rasher as the two of them stood behind the battle lines.

They each wore gigantic hats. Rasher's was so big, it fit right over his red bacon-trimmed Reaper hat. Kitan's hat rose in seven magnificent tiers, the side flaring out over three feet to either side. It was simply the most ridiculous hat he had ever seen, but she made it look glamorous.

"You'll eat those words when we land safely," he told her.

"And you'd better eat some bacon before we even try," she told him with a worried look.

Two dozen soldiers stood around them, each holding aloft another giant hat. All of the hats were connected by rope, which bound them together into a multi-layered, brightly-colored net. The wolf Gleaner squad had raided them from the Premier Peptic Hats shop.

If his plan failed, Rasher would probably end up working for the rest of his life to pay off those stupid hats. He glanced at Colly Wobbles, who had paused her healing efforts long enough to see that they didn't kill themselves at the start of his crazy plan.

She asked, "How do you feel?"

"The turkey bacon void seems to be gone," he told her, and he mostly believed it. Kitan was right though, he couldn't wait.

"Ten more minutes would be safer," Colly said, "but I know we don't have that long. The traitors might have already begun the attack. So yes, I approve."

With eager trepidation, Rasher opened the bag of bacon pastry twists. He wished he'd managed to commandeer more bacon on the way through Nutmeg Hill, but all the restaurants were closed, and he didn't know which of them were authorized suppliers.

In seconds, he wolfed down all of the pastries. They were delicious, and it was a crime to eat them so fast, but he'd apologize to Kitan's house chef if they survived the stunt. The unrivaled awesomeness of bacon washed through him, and Rasher couldn't help laughing at the return of his powers. He didn't feel any ill effects of the turkey bacon void, so he applied some bacon to his mind.

The pastry twists were mostly crispy bacon, so he didn't have much, but he managed to spark an acceleration of his thoughts for a few seconds, making him grin again. It worked!

Even with his accelerated thinking, he couldn't see a faster way to reach the Food Court. Balter and the Gleaners were in the process of smashing through one of the wagons, but the traitors had concentrated their remaining supplies on holding back the advance. Vile clouds of smoke and gas and sludge poured down over the Gleaners, and a vegetable shaman concealed among the traitors had used an entire head of broccoli to create a deep moat along the inside edge of the wagons. Those were desperate, delaying tactics that would ultimately fail, but all they had to do was could keep everyone back long enough for the attack in the Food Court to succeed.

Their army's archers continued shooting into the traitor's ranks, and the muffin mage set each arrow alight before they fired. Rasher hadn't seen arrows from the enemy side in a while. Either the archers were dead or had run out of arrows.

The enemy vegetable shaman had shaken the ground a few times, but couldn't seem to generate any offensive attacks like rolling tides of earth. Kitan had said she believed the plaza was warded too well against earthquakes, so at least their little army wouldn't get buried.

It seemed that one could only remain nauseous for so long before there was nothing left to hurl. Every Gleaner still doubled over periodically, heaving empty guts and grimacing with pain. Their skin was a mask of weeping sores, and they often staggered as if drunk, but continued fighting.

They'd win through but then had to fight the traitor army. Rasher would bet his next month's worth of bacon the enemy still had at least one surprise waiting for them. Kucheesa had reported sighting what she believed was a durian fruit. He shuddered to think of the horrific stench bombs those vile, contraband fruits could produce.

So far, his reckless plan was the only idea anyone had come up with to get them to the Food Court faster. If it was just him, he'd love the idea. It was the ultimate thrill ride, and he needed the thrill today. His only hesitation came from the fact that Kitan would be with him, and he'd made sure to secure her to him with a leather harness used by kite-flying couriers so she couldn't fall.

"Let's do it," he told Bibble, who stood ready.

"Hold on to your hats," Bibble warned, flinging his hands out wide, releasing a spice mixture into the air around Rasher and Kitan. The pleasant smells of cloves, nutmeg, cardamom, and other spices filled his nose.

And a mighty gust of wind roared to life, blasting him in the face.

"Now!" Rasher cried, and both he and Kitan threw gravity spike carrots to the ground at their feet. Instantly gravity shifted and suddenly they began falling up, dragging their hat net along with them.

At the same second, an honest-to-custard mini tornado formed beneath them, driving them upward faster and catching the net of hats, which billowed majestically outward under the powerful gusts. Kitan shouted, and Rasher laughed with thrill as they both clung to the hats strapped tightly to their heads.

The gravity spike waned quickly, but Bibble's wind continued. Driven by that howling wind, the net of hats yanked them ever higher, like a flock of brightly colored birds winging away with freshly captured pies.

Rasher couldn't hear anything over the howling wind, not even Kitan's screams. The air swept across his skin, silky smooth despite its ferocity, and somehow the scent of all those spices never dispersed. Kitan kept one hand on the band holding her giant hat on, and with the other she gripped Rasher's hand so tight he grimaced. The wide net of hats thrummed under the air onslaught, but the lines held and the high-quality craftsmanship proved up to the abuse.

He'd expected it to. The story of the woman who'd been blown out over Cockalorum Lake had inspired him with the idea of using the hats to fly over the traitors' blockade. As they rose higher, the plaza opened beneath them. The lines of battle looked so thin and fragile from up there, the danger remote.

Balter and the Gleaners were just rolling aside the first wagon, while other troops surged forward with makeshift plank bridges to cross the moat. Within seconds the two forces would clash in close hand-to-hand fighting. He didn't spot Captain Waldorf, Commander Cobb, or Kucheesa until the flash of Noops' armor drew his gaze.

The shovel knight was still harassing the traitors' ranks, and Rasher easily spotted a swath of fallen enemies, writhing on the ground in pain from broken limbs or cracked skulls. Kucheesa had joined him, and even as Rasher watched, Noops threw her into the air. She soared over the plaza, heading for the shielded entrances, with Noops fighting his way after her.

Rasher was happy to see them still up and fighting. He hoped his plan worked, but it was good to see them making a separate attempt to breach the entrance. One way or the other, they needed to get in there, find the conspirators, and stop their diabolical plot.

First though, don't die.

And have an amazing time doing it!

Kitan's grip had started to loosen as she realized they weren't going to fall to their deaths immediately, and she flashed a dazzling, if nervous smile as she glanced across the plaza.

Of course the traitors chose that moment to begin firing arrows at them.

Kitan screamed again, but the archers didn't have many arrows, and their aim was terrible. A few came sort of close, but the whirlwind knocked them wide. Thankfully, within seconds they rose out of effective range and entered the stable courier air currents above the plaza.

The net of giant hats abruptly surged toward the Food Court, dragging Rasher and Kitan with them. Rasher laughed with thrill as their speed increased. In moments they would soar right over the roof.

And . . . Keep on soaring until they blew past the rest of the city and out over the lake.

Crumpets.

"Rasher, how do we steer?" Kitan shouted above the wind, realizing the problem the same second he did.

He shrugged, having too much fun to get too worked up about it. "We can't."

"What do you mean, we can't? This is your plan," she shouted, her worry growing into fear.

He grinned. She was so very beautiful with her big eyes so wide, her face flushed with excitement, her long hair blowing around her face.

"I wasn't sure we'd get this far," he admitted.

"Rasher," she warned as they cleared the outer walls and began hurtling over the various levels of roof.

The mass of the central Food Court roof rose above most of the structure, a giant dome they'd skirt but not overfly. The rest of the grand structure housed meeting rooms, administrative offices, and much more, and the sprawling expanse resulted in many different rooflines, pitches, and patios.

Rasher spotted one likely spot, calculated the distance and timing with most of his remaining chewy bacon reserves and asked, "Do you trust me?"

"I don't like where this is going?" she said with a warning tone in her voice.

"It'll be fun," he reassured her. "Like I always say, moments of great danger are opportunities to look dashing and enjoy the thrill of living."

"I've never heard you say that," she objected.

"Sure I have. Rasher's Rules of Engagement number forty-five."

She started to ask another question, but Rasher pulled her close and yanked the release straps for both of their hats. Instantly they fell free as their web of hats bobbed higher and sped away, tossed lightly on the wind.

Kitan screamed, clutching tightly to Rasher as the roof rose to meet them with alarming speed. He wanted to throw his arms out wide and enjoy the rush, but that might scare Kitan more, so he held her with one hand, smiling reassuringly.

With the other, he extracted his tiny cube of personal defense gelatin. Just before they smashed to death on the hard stones of a rooftop patio, he flung the gelatin downward. It struck the ground and erupted into a huge sphere of jiggly gelatin just as Rasher and a still-screaming Kitan plunged into the center of it.

The clear gelatin stopped their fall with remarkable gentleness. They slowed from a death splat to a standstill, shaking the gelatin so hard the outer edges blasted away.

But it caught them.

Rasher relaxed in the heart of the gelatin, exulting in the thrill blazing through him, replenishing his strength and mental agility. Gubbins had been right, the gelatin was amazing.

It also tasted great. Some of it had seeped up his nose and into his mouth, forcing him to swallow to clear his airways. It was sweet and smooth, and surprisingly refreshing after a long fall.

Kitan hadn't been so lucky. Her mouth had been wide open, still screaming, so gelatin filled it. Now she rocked side to side, hands struggling to reach up to pull at the gelatin blocking her airways, but they moved with glacial slowness in the springy stuff.

Rasher drove his hand through the gelatin to her mouth and yanked a handful of gelatin free. With that, she closed her mouth, swallowed mightily, and then gasped for breath. He couldn't hear, as his head was in a different bubble, but he grinned and patted her cheek.

In seconds, he cut them free using his belt dagger. The gelatin had sucked all the muck and filth and smoke out of their clothes, leaving Rasher feeling remarkably good. Kitan's hair gleamed from the moisturizing, but for some reason she didn't look happy.

"Rasher," she began, but he stepped close and passionately kissed her on the lips. She tasted like gelatin, and after a moment's hesitation, she kissed him back, clinging to him with all her strength.

When he released her, he grinned down at her. "Nothing like near-death adventure to spice up a boring life, eh?"

She rolled her eyes, but still laughed weakly. "Let's not do that again."

He nodded but didn't tell her about the plans he'd already started making to start a base jumping adventure group. They could combine elements of fast-rope descent and gelatin safety cubes. It would be a huge hit.

In the meantime, he led her to the doors inside. They found themselves in a fancy restaurant. The scents of fresh-baked bread and grilling meat assaulted his nostrils, and he breathed deep, savoring it. Apparently they were preparing for a fancy party after the assembly.

"Let's eat here after," he told her as they rushed to the door. He unslung his battle staff from the straps on his back and checked it, but found no damage. He'd check his crumbhorn later.

In a moment, they found the wind elevator and descended to the ground floor. Rasher stepped out, ready to fight off a horde of traitors guarding the many entrances into the hall, but the corridor was empty.

He and Kitan jogged along the gently curving hallway, their footsteps slightly squishy. They had forgotten to clear their boots of gelatin. It felt good.

When they caught sight of the exit to the outside, he realized why no one had stirred to investigate the battle. The shielding over the doors looked opaque on this side, and no sound seeped through. A couple of uniformed soldiers stood guard.

Traitors, for sure. No doubt they would tell anyone curious about the barrier that it was a new security development to protect them and the Imperial Chef. Clever.

"This way," Kitan said, leading Rasher in through one of the wide openings to the main walk that circled the hall, leading to the various tiers of seating.

They paused just inside to let their eyes adjust to the dimmer light and to take in the sight. The entire hall was packed with thousands of men and women from the highest levels of society, all dressed from soup to sandwiches in their best formal attire.

The only exception was their hats. The popular enormous hats could never fit inside, with everyone seated so closely in tight-packed tiers of seats that stretched both down toward the ground level and up into the tiers of balcony seats overhanging the central hall. Instead, everyone wore miniature versions of their hats, with tiny brims.

Far below where they stood, on the far side of the assembly hall sat the Imperial Chef on a grand throne in the center of the stage. The Junior Toque flanked him on a slightly smaller throne, while the sitting members of the First Course Assembly sat in thrones arranged in a half circle extending out to either side.

The assembly had begun. They'd already sung the Rubric anthem and cut the ceremonial cake. The Sous Chef stood at a podium at the front of the stage, as was his right as leader of the High Kitchen and the Baker's Dozen of the mightiest chefs of the realm. He was solemnly reading the Recipe Book of Ages, where the sacred text of the empire's founding was recorded.

Apparently the traitors hidden among the audience also couldn't hear the bedlam outside, so hadn't decided to accelerate their timetable. Rasher bet they would strike in just a few minutes, timing the disaster for either when the Imperial Chef spoke, or when the High Cheese gave his report about the state of the cheese guild.

For once, Rasher was happy that formal affairs were more cumbersome than a twenty-course meal. They had time. Not much, but a little.

"We need to raise the alarm," Kitan whispered to him, patting her hair self-consciously. She'd lost her hat when they fell. Amazingly, his red Reaper hat had fallen with him.

He swept it off his head and placed it formally onto hers. She sighed with relief to have that mortifying lack rectified. He gave her a reassuring smile and said, "If we save the day, everyone will forgive me the lack of a hat."

"And if we fail . . ." She said with a grimace.

Well, if they failed, his hat would be the least of their worries.

"We can't just shout a warning," he warned.

That would result in their getting arrested for disturbing the assembly. Or if they believed him, it might start a panic. It would also alert the conspirators that the game was up, and they'd probably just blow the pastries early.

Rasher scanned the area, trying to put himself into the traitors' mindset. Where would they stand? How would they do it and avoid getting caught in the disaster too?

He spotted a familiar figure and decided on a course of action. "Kitan, can you find the seafood shaman leader? They'll believe you. Have them alert security. Quietly."

"All right. What will you do?"

He gave her a reassuring smile. "I plan to improvise."

She hurried away, looking strangely nervous.

Rasher sauntered in the opposite direction, moving under the shadow of one of the overhanging balconies that extended from the walls above. His target noticed him approaching at the last moment and turned in surprise.

Rasher smiled and said softly, "Hello, Lord Niffum."

49

You Can Always Choose Breakfast

"R asher, what are you doing here?" Lord Niffum asked, clearly surprised, but not hostile. Or maybe he was just that good at acting, but Rasher didn't think so.

"I see you didn't manage to find a seat with everyone else," Rasher noted.

Where they stood gave them an excellent view of the assembly hall but would minimize potential exposure to the illumination pastry explosions. Assuming that was the attack that was planned. Lord Niffum might not be directly involved, but he was one of the few standing like that, and the coincidence seemed a little too obvious to ignore.

Niffum shrugged. "When you get a little older, you might understand the torture I face sitting in prolonged meetings. This one is likely to go for at least two hours."

That might be true, and it was a good excuse, but there were a lot of elderly people in attendance and they weren't standing. Rasher simply lacked the time to mince words.

So he met Lord Niffum's gaze and said softly, "I honestly don't care if you were involved in orchestrating the attack on the Cheese Palace to damage the Les house, but I never took you for a traitor."

Lord Niffum's eyes widened in surprise before narrowing in anger. "How dare you make such an accusation? Are you trying to guarantee I never approve your courtship to my daughter?"

His anger seemed genuine, but more important was that initial surprise. Rasher hoped his ability to read people didn't fail him now. If he got it wrong a lot of people were about to die.

It also didn't escape him that Lord Niffum had smoothly avoided the question of whether or not he was involved in the attack on the Cheese Palace. Something to think about for later.

"Please forgive me. I had to see your reaction," Rasher said. "Did you know about the attack planned on the assembly here tonight?"

Again Lord Niffum looked shocked, going so far as to glance to either side before responding, as if scanning for threats. "What attack?"

"I believe that members of the Lahanasi restoration cult were involved in the attack on the Cheese Palace."

Lord Niffum tried to suppress a laugh but didn't quite manage it, drawing reproving glares from a couple elderly women walking past. In a whisper he said, "Those drunken fools? They can barely attack the bar, let alone pull off such an advanced plot."

"Not alone, anyway. However, there is currently a pitched battle going on in the Plaza just outside the Food Court. Members of the cult, armed with contraband recipes, are fighting to block the Chef's Watch from entering here."

"What?" Niffum exclaimed, again a little too loudly, but he ignored the additional glares they were receiving.

Rasher honestly believed the man did not know about the attack. He might be neck-deep in plots and intrigue, and unabashedly eager to find a way to topple one of the high houses, but Rasher could not believe the man could fool him so completely.

So he said, "We don't have much time. Do you know anyone who might be in a position to leverage the cult's insanity to act as their foot soldiers and divert the blame from the true culprits? Someone in here is the traitor I need to stop, but I need a place to start looking."

Niffum only stared for a moment before saying softly, "By the gods, you're serious, aren't you?"

"Yes I am, and if you don't stop stalling, a lot of people are going to die, and the future of the empire is not sure."

Lord Niffum looked shaken but accepted the statement with calm honed from years of intense political intrigue. He might be a plotter, but Rasher doubted he'd ever seriously considered trying to topple the empire. At least not until he had a much better plan in place to take advantage of the chaos. Rasher wanted to shake him as the slow seconds ticked by, but forced himself to wait.

"I can't believe any of the high houses, or even the main players among the secondi or contorni levels, are ready to launch an all-out play for the throne yet. It has to be another player." His voice trailed off and he glanced to his right suddenly.

Rasher followed his gaze and for the first time noticed a tall man in a festive black cloak standing under the deeper shadows of the balcony, not far from one of the exits. Unlike the seated attendants and Lord Niffum himself, he had not adopted the mini hats for the evening, but wore a rather modest, wide-brimmed hat.

How had he not noticed the man before? Was the turkey bacon still messing with his perceptiveness that much?

"Who is that?" Rasher asked.

Niffum swallowed, and for the first time Rasher had ever seen, looked honestly nervous. He leaned closer and whispered just loud enough for Rasher to hear. "Leccino Peptic. Officially he is an extremely successful hat merchant. Unofficially, I have sources that have identified him as a key member of the Rumpus Cabal."

The Rumpus Cabal. Rasher had suspected them from the start as likely players in the chaos that descended over the city and the Acropolis, but no additional leads had come up confirming that theory.

It made sense, though. The Rumpus Cabal would definitely benefit from chaos in the empire, and might even have a treaty in place with the Gloaming hordes to seize power if they could indeed topple the current Rubric leadership.

If they succeeded in that, chaos and civil war would sweep the empire, creating a vacuum where the hordes could wreak terrible destruction. If the Rumpus Cabal played their cards right, they could even position themselves as saviors of the people and be welcomed as new leaders.

"What are you going to do?" Lord Niffum asked.

Rasher flashed his trademark smile and said, "I'm going to introduce myself, of course."

"Not a good idea," Lord Niffum whispered after him, but Rasher was already moving.

He strolled casually straight toward Leccino, who instantly noticed and shifted slightly to orient on him. His face remained shadowed under the wide brim of his dark hat, so Rasher could not get a read on his expression.

"Hello," Rasher said cheerily. "I'm Rasher, captain of the Reapers. You may have heard of me."

When Leccino spoke, his voice was a deep, rumbling whisper that seemed to vibrate across the distance between them. "I have."

"I'll be honest," Rasher said with an apologetic smile. "I hadn't heard of you until just recently, but I have to say I can appreciate master craftsmanship when I see it."

Leccino smiled, a flash of white teeth in the shadows of the rest of his face. "May I assume I've had the pleasure of providing you with a top-of-the-line hat from my establishment?"

"Not exactly. A large portion of your inventory just flew out over Cockalorum Lake. Sorry about that."

"What are you talking about?" Leccino asked, his composure cracking finally and annoyance creeping into his voice. He wasn't doing too great of a job staying in character, probably because he was too busy exulting over his impending success ahead of time. A common malady for arrogant souls.

"It's kind of a long story, but we don't have time for that. I'll sum up. We've unraveled your plot to attack the assembly tonight and to blame the cheese wizards for it. Masterful stroke, by the way, but it won't work. Right now my forces of ten thousand legionaries are mopping up the remnants of your traitors trying to block their passage into the assembly hall. Rather a pitiful effort on your part, I must say. With so much time to plan, I have to admit I expected something more."

For several seconds, Leccino stared, his body language stiff under the coat. That was all the confirmation Rasher needed. If Leccino had been a simple merchant as he claimed, the accusation would have astounded him and generated exclamations of denial.

To his credit, he did recover quickly and tried to follow the script. "Are you insane?"

But they both knew he'd reacted too late. Rasher said, "It's not going to work, Lechy. If you start running now, you might even escape. I doubt it, but I like to share hope wherever I can."

Leccino's voice turned menacing. It was nice to see he didn't waste time sticking with the pretense of his other life after his cover was blown.

"You lie. If you had ten thousand legionaries at your back, you wouldn't be standing here trying to convince me so hard. You would have just flooded the assembly hall with troops."

Rasher shrugged. "It was worth a try. Would you believe I have two thousand battle-hardened troops and twenty culinary wizards at my back?"

"No."

"How about lightning wit and indomitable spirit?"

That got a chuckle. "If you believe those are your talents."

"Oh, and dashing good looks," Rasher added quickly, snapping his fingers.

"Now you're becoming a boor. What do you want, Captain?" Leccino asked, assuming a more confident pose. "You can't stop me, and we both know it. This pitiful attempt has proven amusing, but ultimately fruitless."

Rasher smiled. He was really looking forward to braining this traitor, but he said, "Before I arrest you, there is one thing I'd like to know. Why consort with Lahanasi's followers? Have you no dignity?"

Leccino shrugged. "They are rather disgusting, but sometimes we don't get to choose our allies."

"You can always choose breakfast."

"What does that have to do with anything?"

"Rasher's Rules of Engagement number thirty-six. When all hope is lost, eat a memorable breakfast."

"You're more clever than anyone expected," Leccino said with a little nod of respect. "But you're too late. Nothing can stop me now."

Just then, one of the illumination pastries on the far side of the assembly hall abruptly winked out.

Perfect timing. Kitan must have reached the muffin mages and convinced them of the danger. Rasher raised his hands and snapped again, timing the gesture for the exact moment when the next pastry winked out.

"You were saying?" he asked.

"How?" Leccino asked, clearly astonished.

"Charisma is a trait that evil traitors just never can seem to grasp. And wasting time telling me how clever you are kind of backfired."

Rasher lifted his battle staff with a grin. "So, do you want to do this the hard way, or the really hard way? Personally, I'm hoping you choose really hard because I'm really looking forward to cracking open your skull."

More and more of the pastries winked out in rapid succession. In seconds, the entire assembly hall would be cast into pitch darkness. People in the crowds started to notice, and even the Sous Chef paused his monotonous reading to glance up in annoyance.

At the same time, spectral blue light began to glow from the front of the assembly and spread into the hall. Several additional blue lights appeared, scattered around the hall.

Excellent choice. Kitan had also managed to find the seafood shamans. Their illumination would help avoid a panic.

"You haven't won yet," Leccino said with admirable optimism.

He flung open a hand, casting powder into the air between them. It ignited into a cloud of sugar glitter crystals that unleashed dazzling, multicolored light that seemed magnified in the otherwise dim assembly hall.

Blinded, Rasher lunged through the glitter sparkles anyway, staff lashing out toward where he'd last seen Leccino's head.

He hit nothing, but swiveled to follow the sound of rapid footsteps rushing toward the nearby rows of seats. Rasher gave chase, delayed by a fraction of a second because he'd expected Leccino to run for the exits, not flee deeper into the assembly hall. What was he thinking?

As he gave chase, he could only come up with one plausible idea, and it wasn't a good one.

His eyes recovered quickly and sure enough, he spotted his quarry standing in the open, gesturing up toward the closest illumination pastry, about a dozen feet directly overhead. He must be a muffin mage too, and even if he only managed to detonate one pastry, he could still wreak enough havoc that he might escape in the confusion.

Rasher didn't have time to think, but poured all of his remaining bacon stores into a single explosive rush. He crossed the remaining distance in a flash, cracking Leccino in the side of the head hard enough that the impact echoed across the assembly hall.

As Leccino staggered, Rasher jumped with bacon-enhanced agility, driving downward with the staff to give himself extra lift. Best jump of his life. His feet reached Leccino's shoulders in a single bound and he jumped again, pushing off with all of his remaining strength.

As his bacon stores ran dry, he rose high enough to snatch the illumination pastry lamp right off the wall. He planned to cast it out into the empty hallway where it couldn't hurt anyone.

It exploded against his chest.

He lacked bacon to call upon his higher bacon powers. Defenseless, the impact struck him like a kick from a mule, blasting all the breath from his lungs. Rasher fell to the ground, but twisted to land atop the pastry to reduce the spread of the explosion.

He hit the ground hard and rolled painfully over onto his back, staring at his singed jacket and the wide, golden stain covering every inch of his torso, neck, and face.

Crumpets. That could have gone better.

Leccino chuckled as he staggered past. "Know that your victory today is hollow. We will strike again, and you won't be here to stop us. Enjoy death."

As he walked away, Rasher muttered, "You would be a gallows humor kind of guy."

No response. He willed himself to leap back to his feet and give chase, but his body laughed at him and refused to respond.

All he managed to do was grimace in pain as his limbs shook under the poison onslaught. Poison cheese began to seep into every pore. The pain quickly intensified, and he writhed on the ground, trying to think of a solution, a way out. He reflexively tried to apply chewy bacon to his mind, but he was out, his reserves completely drained again.

Rasher fumbled at his belt for his personal protective cuisine, but he couldn't seem to think, couldn't remember what he had left, and couldn't seem to get his fingers to work. How could he block the poison?

"Oh, Rasher!" Cried Kitan as she rushed to him and dropped to her knees.

"Don't," Rasher croaked, terrified she would grab onto him and suffer his fate.

She had already been reaching toward him, but recognized the danger and recoiled in horror. Her voice broke as she cried, "Oh no! What can I do?"

He wasn't sure. She glanced back and shouted, "I need a milk mage! A milk mage, right now!"

Rasher wasn't even sure if a powerful milk mage could save him now. As soon as the curse reached his bloodstream, he'd be doomed in seconds.

That thought gave him an idea. It might not be a great idea, but at least it was an idea. He turned his head slightly toward Kitan and said, "Cut yourself."

"What?" She asked, her voice confused, her beautiful face blurry in his dimming vision.

"Blood," he rasped, the shakes intensifying as the cursed cheese sank in deeper. He was nearly out of time.

To her credit, Kitan did not hesitate. She drew her little belt knife, slashed her palm open, and held it out in front of his face.

His vision was failing. He couldn't see far.

He saw the blood.

The sight of it seemed to swallow his remaining vision. His world turned red, and he felt nausea churning in his stomach. As blackness consumed his mind, Rasher only had the strength for one final smile.

50

CHEESE CURDS AND COURT INTRIGUE

With a groan, Rasher blinked open his eyes. It took a moment for them to adjust to the bright lights.

He felt terrible. He always did after an episode, but this time it felt like while he was unconscious someone had dropped him on a table and spent an hour with a meat tenderizer, pounding every inch of him.

"Ow," he muttered, his voice hoarse and dry.

"You're awake!" Kitan exclaimed, coming into view as she hugged him tight.

He really was alive. Mostly.

"So it worked," he said, trying to smile.

Colly Wobbles shifted into view, kneeling on his other side. She was smiling brightly, as always, but her face looked drawn and tired. "Your blood phobia slowed your heartbeat, giving you critical seconds, otherwise we never could have stabilized you. But even then, we couldn't have saved you."

"It was Father," Kitan said, glancing over her shoulder. When Rasher followed her gaze, he was startled to see Lord Niffum standing nearby.

Rasher blinked at him, thunderstruck. Niffum took a step closer and said, "I just happened to have a bit of cheese curd antidote on hand."

"Lucky," Rasher said. It hurt to think, so he accepted the incredible coincidence at face value for now.

"Can't have the hero of the day dying in his moment of glory," Niffum said with a smile.

"No, don't want to be a tragic story cliche," Rasher agreed as Kitan helped him sit up.

He felt woozy, but stable as he looked around. They were in a spacious parlor. He'd been lying on a low divan, with several comfortable chairs and sofas arranged nearby. The walls were hung with rich tapestries, while a mirror stood above a small powder table.

"We're in one of the rooms used by speakers before they appear on the stage," Kitan explained.

Rasher wanted to think about his blood phobia. The sight of Kitan's blood had triggered it again. So why hadn't Otamot's blood affected him? It had to be the turkey bacon.

Hopefully there was more to it than that. He couldn't accept that the only way to heal the condition was to destroy his bacon powers, but his mind hurt too much to think.

So he asked, "My team?"

"They are well," Kitan told him. "Bibble took down the air shielding a moment after you blacked out. The Gleaners routed the traitors."

"The battle was terrible," Colly added. "Most of the traitors fought to the death, but a few were captured, and the inquisitors collected them."

They deserved whatever fate they suffered at the inquisitors' hands.

"The rest of the team are well," Kitan assured Rasher. "The plaza is still swarmed with soldiers and healers, but everyone is safe."

"Good," Rasher said, feeling relieved.

"I have more patients to attend," Colly said, standing. "Take your time moving, Captain. You very nearly died. I've ordered some bacon to replenish your stores."

"Thank you," he told her.

She left, and Lord Niffum said, "I too will withdraw. I will wish to speak with you soon, Rasher, but I can see you two need a moment."

"Thank you, Father," Kitan said. He'd won her adoring loyalty more with that bit of cheese curd antidote than he could have in almost any other way.

After Lord Niffum left, Kitan settled onto the divan next to Rasher and hugged him tight. They held each other in silence for a moment, just enjoying the fact that they were both alive and together.

"That was fun," Rasher said eventually. "We should do it again sometime."

"You're insane. You nearly died."

"I don't mean hugging cheese bombs," he clarified with a smile. "I mean hat flying and gelatin diving. You have to admit, that was fun."

She chuckled, placing one warm hand on the side of his face. "Oh, Rasher. I love you."

He was a mess, his skin raw from cheese burns, his uniform torn and in shambles, but she looked stunning. Sure, her hair was still a bit disheveled, she was wearing his hat, and she'd wiped off most of her makeup.

It didn't matter. Her big, beautiful eyes seemed to glow with joy, and he could stare at her face for days without tiring of it.

He leaned forward and kissed her lightly, trying to memorize everything about the moment. How she looked, the feel of her hands in his, the gentle scent of blueberries that somehow clung to her hair, and the joy he felt staring into her eyes and seeing the depth of her love.

"That will never do," she told Rasher with a mischievous glint in her eyes. "After pitched battle, death dives into gelatin, and nearly melting into the floor in a poisoned cheese puddle, you owe me a much better kiss."

"Happy to oblige," he told her with a grin, and set to kissing her so thoroughly she'd need a lot more than a bottle of milk to recover.

Some time later as they left the little parlor hand in hand, grinning like fools, his lips tingled from the workout she'd given them. Her father waited in the hallway.

Best way to crush a romantic moment.

"Father," Kitan said happily, rushing to hug him in an exceptional display of public affection. Rasher tried to hold onto the happy glow he'd been feeling with Kitan, but Lord Niffum's presence snuffed it out.

"I'm glad you're feeling better, Rasher," Lord Niffum said with no trace of hostility. "Kitan, will you excuse us? I have a couple of items of business to discuss with the captain before the legions march tomorrow."

Brilliant stroke. The reminder of his duty and the mountain of work to do to prepare for the looming mobilization sucked away the rest of Rasher's happiness, leaving him feeling very tired.

"Of course, Father," she told him. "I'll visit in the morning tomorrow to see you off," she promised Rasher before giving him a dazzling smile and leaving the two of them alone.

Rasher regarded Niffum and inclined his head politely. "Lord Niffum, thank you again for saving my life. It was an unusual stroke of good fortune that you happened to carry the perfect antidote for the unexpected cheese explosion."

"Indeed," Lord Niffum said, expression revealing nothing. "Lucky for you."

"You saved my life and smoothly avoided any suspicion of collusion with the enemy at the same time," Rasher said. "Your reputation is well earned."

Lord Niffum smiled. "Thank you, Rasher. You're right, saving you won me a lot of political points, which I will be happy to use."

"How deeply were you involved?" Rasher asked, still not quite believing that he'd misread the man so completely. Usually his instincts were so reliable.

"Involved? What an astonishing thing to suggest," Lord Niffum said, not sounding astonished at all. "I would never entertain thoughts of betraying the realm or supporting any such public atrocities as we've witnessed today."

"Of course," Rasher said dryly.

"I can't say I might not have benefited from the misfortune of the Les house, though," Lord Niffum continued. "If the vile traitors had succeeded in the attack, the entire First Course Assembly would have been thrown into shambles, the cheese guild would have been blamed and ruined, and the Les house might have been crippled as well."

"An absolute tragedy," Rasher agreed.

"For them," Lord Niffum said with a wolfish smile. "I might not have approved of the attack or known of it ahead of time, but I would not have hesitated to take advantage of the opening. I might very well have succeeded in supplanting the Les house, and my noodle goddess Makarna might have gained the opportunity to rise into the Pantryon."

His voice turned a shade harder and he added, "I guess we'll never know."

"I guess not," Rasher agreed, pondering the man's words. There were layers of meaning and warning embedded in there.

Lord Niffum added, "Unfortunately for you, none of that happened so my house fortunes have not changed." He paused before adding softly, "Instead, I saved your life, placing you deeper into my debt. Our deal has not changed."

Rasher suppressed a sigh. He'd saved the day, but hadn't broken free of Lord Niffum's clutches. He still might face the day when he'd have to choose to convince his family to betray the Takmor house to win permission to marry Kitan.

At that moment, the thought of willingly assisting in that intrigue made him as sick as if he'd chugged one of Lahanasi's forbidden recipes, but he kept his expression neutral. He would find a way to break free of Niffum's manipulations, somehow. He would marry Kitan, no matter what obstacles her father placed between them, but he wouldn't succeed by acting the fool.

So he inclined his head and said, "A conversation for when I return."

"Have a safe trip," Lord Niffum said sincerely. "I am looking forward to our next meeting."

After he left, Rasher took a deep breath. He felt exhausted, but content. He might not be the ideal Reaper, but he'd proven he could do the job. The weight of responsibility hung heavy on him, but he squared his shoulders and managed to hold it. As he headed toward the exit to find his team, he smiled. The challenges still loomed large ahead, but Reapers knew how to beat the odds.

"Bring on the Apocalypse."

51

NEXT BOOK AND FREE DOWNLOADS

Where's the next course?
And where can I find extra stuff like:
  1. A full listing of Rasher's Rules of Engagement

  2. A pronunciation guide

  3. A list of all the Guilds of Magic

  4. A list of all the gods of the Pantryon, along with concept
     images of the gods

I'm so glad you asked.

The best way to get book two of Bacon Master and support your favorite author is to order a signed copy directly from my website. Otherwise, you can pick up a copy from Amazon, Apple, or wherever you prefer. This link will take you to all the possible locations:
  https://smarturl.it/BMOASeries

Or use this QR code:

On to the next adventure!

52

BONUS CONTENT!

T his fun bonus chapter takes place immediately prior to the beginning of Bacon Master of the Apocalypse and introduces major characters in the Gloaming hordes. Since you don't actually see most of them until the second Bacon Master book, I decided to include it here as a fun final teaser.

Enjoy!

Geshwind had come to the Rubric Empire, and he carried the apocalypse with him.

As a fell lord of the glowan Bitter Court, he'd won the right to lead the assault that would usher in the end of the hated human empire.

He tried to savor the moment, but his new body fit so poorly, he couldn't quite manage to feel epic enough. Geshwind sighed and glanced down at his misshapen form.

"This is taking too long," he muttered, surprising the dozen glowan creatures attending him in the spacious farm kitchen he'd appropriated as his temporary command center.

"It's an excellent specimen," said Ostinato in her soft feline voice, rising from her haunches to pad around him.

The large, white cat glowed faintly in the light of the single, dim lantern, the only indication of her innate powers.

"It will be fine soon enough," he acknowledged. He hated waiting.

He towered over her, and at least his face already looked supernaturally handsome. The body of the deathmaster the hellhounds had captured for him hung far too loose, even though he wore the man's bones too.

A deathmaster, the human caretaker of the dead, was a perfect choice, but the fellow had been immensely fat. Rolls of loose, black cloth draped over Geshwind's sparse frame, concealing the many rolls of loose skin underneath, still not filled out to perfect form. The skin would shrink to fit, as would the clothing, but for the moment he looked like a child wearing his father's suit.

Not the image he hoped to project on the big night of their invasion.

The clothing would suffice, but he glared at the corpse's cursed hat, lying across the pile of flesh that marked what had once been a human. He shuddered to think of the lower changelings sometimes forced to endure the risk of putting on a human hat.

The one piece of clothing he'd brought to the new body was his cape. Tonight it chose to appear as midnight blue, and it billowed slowly around him, despite the lack of wind.

Geshwind tried to regain his feeling of destiny by considering the mighty horde of monstrous forces flowing with inhuman silence toward the city, without lamps or torches, moving like wraiths of living shadow. The unsuspecting humans patrolling the high city walls knew nothing of the doom creeping ever closer.

The metropolis of Ehverr was a key stronghold of the Rubric Empire, garrisoned by a mighty host, including full contingents of all of their battle wizards and mages. They were proud and confident.

The fools.

They'd assumed his horde would attack the fortresses situated closer to the border of his homeland, and indeed, many of the weaker glowan had protested his plan to circumvent them. It could be hard to resist such a tempting target, but this time they would prove themselves mightier and cleverer than the humans ever imagined.

The thought filled him with pride, triggering his bloodlust. They would savage the city of Ehverr, and that was just the beginning. His host would sweep across the land, laying waste—

The door banged open, interrupting his thoughts, and Nonet rushed inside in human form, looking like an eager young man.

Ostinato's mate lacked her decorum as he waved to the other creatures packing the room.

"It's a treasure trove," Nonet grinned, placing a short, covered bowl onto the floor with reverent care. He dropped a small sack, and foodstuffs spilled out, a ham, a small cheese, and several vegetables.

Other glowan recoiled from the dangerous fare, and Ostinato hissed, "What are you doing?"

"It's fresh," Nonet assured them. "You haven't seen such beauty in decades, my love."

With a flourish, he removed the cover over the bowl, revealing white, creamy milk filling it to the brim.

With a groan of pleasure, Nonet recklessly transformed into his sleek, black cat form and started lapping eagerly at the milk. Ostinato crept forward, tail lashing, ears perked before catching herself and restraining her curiosity.

Nonet glanced up long enough to say, "Do you have any idea how long it's been since I've enjoyed fresh milk, harvested by a pretty girl's supple young hands, still untainted by the powers of the milk mages?"

"You get carried away, love," Ostinato cautioned, glancing at Geshwind, who was watching the exchange with growing irritation. Nonet was brilliant in many ways, but he was ruining a moment weighted with purpose and glory.

Geshwind stepped closer, drawing Nonet's gaze, preparing to reprimand the foolish changeling for his levity and recklessness, but Nonet's eyes widened at the sight of him and he snorted.

When he did so, he managed to sniff a bunch of milk right up his nose. He staggered back, hissing and spitting milk everywhere.

Geshwind sighed. His moment was ruined. His cloak sensed his mood and tried billowing dramatically around him, but no one even seemed to notice the gesture.

"Are you quite finished?" Geshwind asked. He wanted to raise a hand, but the folds of flesh and cloth would just make him look ridiculous.

Nonet bowed his head and managed to speak between coughs. "I apologize, my lord. I've never seen you try to wear three sets of skin at once. Does that actually work?"

"It's one skin," Geshwind told him, casting another annoyed glance down at himself.

"Are you sure?" Nonet asked, padding closer, staring up at him.

"He was fat," Geshwind explained. The assault had better go better than his transformation.

As if reading his mind, Nonet said, "The horde's getting close to the wall. The stupid humans haven't noticed anyone yet. Was the plan to knock on the gate and ask them to rouse the guard? I thought we were going to make a big show but let them think they're holding us back."

"Maybe we should make a little noise," Ostinato agreed. "I feared we would find them already at full alert."

Ostinato was a gifted general, but like many of the troops, she feared the human guilds of food magic perhaps a little too much.

Still, they had a point. "It's no surprise they're unprepared. That was the point, after all. No one has ever moved such a horde so far through Ruzgar's Embrace. I doubt they've even considered the possibility."

"Their Reapers have interfered enough, is it not prudent to fear perhaps they will find a way to do so again?" she asked.

Mention of the vile Reapers triggered a flash of rage that he savored, using it to stoke the eternal embers of his long-festering hunger for vengeance. That helped restore his good humor a little.

In the past, the Reapers with their legions and guilds of magic had inflicted terrible destruction upon the glowan of Whisternfeet. Images of five-layer cakes exploding through ranks of goblins, clouds of confectioner sugar bombs tearing fairies from the sky, and rock trolls melting under the onslaught of cheese balls flicked through his mind, but he forced them aside. This time, things would be different.

One of the fairies flitting about the room, awaiting orders for auxiliary forces to move out, settled on the piece of cheese Nonet had dropped from his sack. She leaned down to take a piece, but screamed and launched off the cheese, trailing yellow haze.

"It's melting my feet!" she shrieked and buzzed angrily around Nonet's head.

"Sorry," he said with a shrug. "It looked fresh and untainted by a cheese wizard."

Geshwind tried to rescue the moment. "After tomorrow, the Reapers of the Apocalypse will no longer be a threat to us or our mission."

All eyes turned to stare, and Ostinato dared ask for the first time the question that he knew they'd wondered about during the entire clandestine trip up the Gewgaw River from their home, deep in the impenetrable forests of Whisternfeet.

"How is it possible?"

"Ruzgar has provided a way." The cryptic answer would not satisfy them, but it would keep them intrigued. Their curiosity was a trait he knew well how to exploit.

"Then should we not press the advantage and breach the wall?" Ostinato asked.

It was very tempting, but he shook his head. "Perhaps after we complete our other objectives. Maybe the night of the full moon."

Nonet cocked his head. "That barely gives us two weeks. You believe we can complete everything by then?"

Geshwind nodded, smiling, and his cape flared wide in dramatic slow motion in emphasis. In his human shape, his smile carried the full weight of Ruzgar's glamour, and not even other glowan could resist its power.

"We will accomplish all of my queen's wishes by that time," he promised them. And all of his objectives.

"And our queen's," Nonet added in a respectful tone, but with a flash to his eyes that hinted he had noted the lapse.

"Your queen will also be satisfied," Geshwind promised them. As the commander of the joint forces of both the Savory and Bitter courts, he had to at least appear to give both queens equal deference. His was an honor no other had received in more generations than any of the short-lived humans could imagine, and he would not squander it.

Finally the distant alarm bells of the city began to toll a panicked cadence.

Geshwind's smile widened. "About time."

Ostinato said, "I don't understand why we are playing with the prey. Why not crush them before they get organized?"

"They represent less of a threat than you fear. Within moments, they are going to realize most of their stockpiles of magical food stores are gone."

Nonet hissed in surprise. "How is it done?"

"We have allies inside the city."

It astounded him that through all the generations the glowan had warred with the humans, no one had realized the great weakness of the mighty food magics. Their mages, wizards, and shamans needed to prepare their battle foods well in advance, building up the power in them with time. Unleashing their devastating power then became a simple thing when battle was joined.

If they had no prepared battle foods, much of their power would be crippled. No burning muffins, no cheese poisons and acids, and not even the vital healing creams and yogurts from their vaunted milk mages. Ehverr was awaking for war only to find their most powerful weapons missing.

Geshwind chuckled to himself, imagining their horror. Too bad the loss of stockpiles would not affect the dreaded bacon masters or those enhanced by meat mages, but his forces could deal with those remnants easily enough.

"Will we see any of the spoils?" Nonet asked, his eyes glowing feline yellow with eagerness and unspoken longing.

"Not from Ehverr. Those supplies are tasked for another need."

"And from the capital? Will we get those?" Nonet pressed.

"Indeed, but they are purposed already," Geshwind said. Holding the changeling's gaze, he added, "The coffee not consumed by our mission will remain under strict guard until after we return to Whisternfeet."

Nonet sighed, licked his lips, then flashed pure white teeth. "But when we return, we will enjoy the spoils."

"Indeed," Geshwind agreed. All of his leaders would rejoice, and even the queens would join the revelry. He would celebrate his victories with the wondrous drug of coffee, but not before then. He could not risk coffee euphoria distractions.

For now, they had work to do.

This time, nothing would save the Rubric Empire from the long-delayed apocalypse. He would drive it right down their throats.

About the Author

Frank Morin loves great stories, great food, and great humor. He is an outdoor enthusiast, and loves to travel for inspiration.

Frank is the author of fast-paced adventures with quirky humor including:

- The Petralist – epic YA fantasy series

- The Facetakers – Urban fantasy thriller series

- *Bacon Master of the Apocalypse* – humorous epic fantasy

He and his wife are often found hiking, camping, Scuba diving, or traveling to research new books. Find out more about his novels and his shorter fiction, or join his readers group at: **https://bio.to/authorfrankmorin**.

AUTHOR'S NOTE

BACON!

How did I get so fixated on bacon?

It actually started with sweetbreads. In The Petralist series, a character named Hamish started as a goofy, clumsy side-kick character who absolutely loved food, especially sweetbread. As the story progressed, his love of food became the key to unlocking tremendous powers and helping him gain international fame as a food diplomat.

At the same time, my wife's love of great food has rubbed off on me. I love trying new food, traveling to new places and eating local foods and discovering new tastes.

All of that came together through the writing of the Petralist as I realized Hamish is so popular because lots of us love his quirky combination of humor and insane devotion to food.

So one day while talking with my kids, the idea of food as magic came up, and we started exploring it.

Of course, Bacon Masters instantly became the center of the discussion, because BACON!

And the rest is history. It came together as seamlessly a thirty-seven course meal, and I've had an absolute blast developing this world, the amazing characters who live in it, and the fantastic food magic they enjoy.

Thanks for sharing this journey with me. I hope you came away from it with a lot of laughs and a renewed love of great cuisine.

And now, on to the next course!

Frank

Also By Frank Morin

Find all books at https://www.frankmorin.org
The Petralist Series

- Set in Stone – Book One

- A Stone's Throw – Book Two

- No Stone Unturned – Book Three

- Affinity for War – Book Four

- The Queen's quarry – Book Five

- The King's Craft – Book Six

- Blood of the Tallan—Book Seven

Other Petralist Stories

- When Torcs Fly – Tomas and Cameron prequel

- Game of Garlands – Anika prequel

- Builder of Intrigue – Aunt Ailsa prequel

The Facetakers Series

- Saving Face – Book One

- Memory Hunter – Book Two

- Rune Warrior – Book Three

- Aeon Champion—Book Four

Short Stories

- Odin's Eye – Red Unicorn Anthology

- Only Logical – Unseen: United! Anthology

- The Essence – Dragon Writers Anthology

- "The Seventh Strike" – Cursed Collectibles Anthology